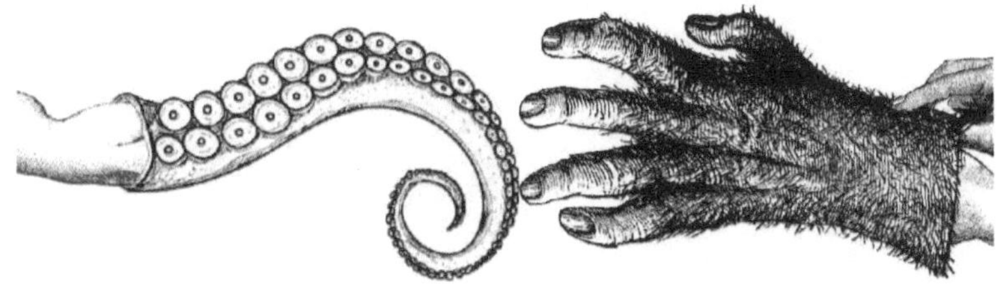

BOOK ONE

THE MULTIVERSE ASKEW

CHRISTOPHER BRIMMAGE

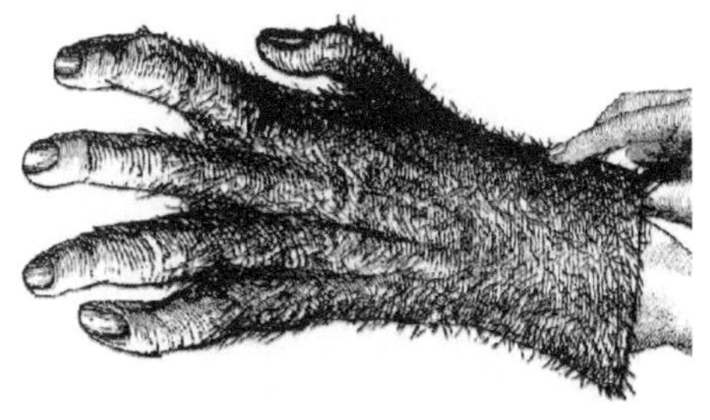

THANK YOU FOR PURCHASING THIS BOOK.

To receive special offers, a free short story, and info on new releases, sign up for the Christopher Brimmage mailing list at cbrimmage.com

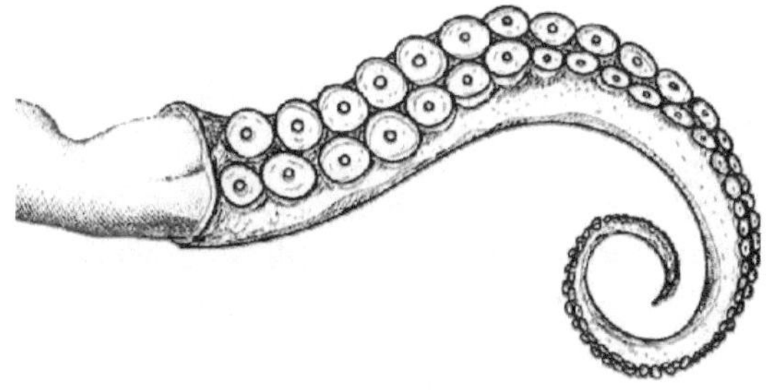

Copyright

ISBN-13: 978-1-7362213-0-3 (Karaoke Octopus Press)

ISBN-10: 1-7362213-0-3

This is a work of fiction. Names, characters, places, alternate universes, squirrels, and incidents are either the product of the author's imagination or are used fictitiously (well, unless you're reading this on another reality in the Multiverse where everything that happens is true, in which case, it's not a work of fiction. But that's unlikely. Unless you live on a reality where it is likely, in which case, I retract my assertion of unlikelihood).

Cover design by Miblart.com, interior artwork by Damonza.com

For Geraldine.
I shlove you. More than the whole world.

For Kyle and Moose.
Thank you both for all the help and the friendship and the Golden Girls references (one of you in particular for the latter. You know who you are, and you are the Sophia to my Dorothy. The other one of you is totally a Rose).

And for Dorothy.
I miss you. More every day.

CHAPTER 1

ARS GRATIA ARTIS

ART WATCHED THE wiry mustache in front of him waggle up and down as the mouth below it flapped open and shut. He had not been able to concentrate on any of the words flopping from the mouth since a bubbly glob of spittle had catapulted from it and landed squarely in the center of his forehead. After wiping away the spittle, he had begun gripping the armrests of his chair, crippled with anxiety due to the looming possibility that the next glob might smack him in an eye—and considering the vitriol inundating the words, Art was quite sure that any spittle originating from this mouth would be acidic enough to put out an eye if it caught him in one.

Art's fingernails dug into the hard plastic of the armrests. His knuckles turned white. The sharp ache of cramps twisted down the length of his fingers. He felt a frustrated scream ignite deep in his chest. *This* was it. He could not stand another second of this mind-numbing lecture. The scream rocketed up through his body, and just when it was on the verge of launching from his mouth, it crashed to a halt against the back of his pursed lips.

He realized that the frothing mouth in front of him had shut and was no longer lecturing. It had curled into a scowl, and it was waiting for his response. Art's mind snapped into gear, firing synapses that had, by now, become habit. He wiped his glazed eyes with his shirt sleeve and then muttered the same thing he did nearly every day when he found himself in this exact same scenario: "Yes, sir, Mr. Reynolds."

"I mean it this time. This is your last chance," said Mr. Reynolds, Art's boss at this regional branch of the Department of Motor Vehicles.

"Yes, sir, Mr. Reynolds," repeated Art, pretending to know what his boss was furious about *this* time. "I can go now, right?"

Mr. Reynolds frowned. "You really need to work on your attitude. Lots of people out there are out of work, and they'd love your job."

passed. If he could just manage to work up the energy, he would have deactivated the stupid thing by now.

Art raced to the door. He plastered a grin on his face and gripped the doorknob with his right hand. He swung open the door and posed, thrusting out his pelvis and stretching his left arm up to the top of the doorframe.

Art exclaimed, "Heeeey. Glad you could swing by, big boy. Think maybe if you've got a moment, I could *come* between you and Jehovah?"

"Hmmmm," replied the man on Art's doorstep. "I think maybe I've made a jump to the wrong place. I was looking for the reality where I *am* a total wanker, not the one where I totally *love* wankers."

Art stared at a carbon copy of himself, only dressed in a short-sleeve button-up shirt with a skinny black necktie. Art's jaw dropped, and no matter how hard he tried, he could not force it back up into a closed position. It remained stuck open like a garage door with a broken electronic opener: open, threatening to shut, and then clicking back open.

"Mind if I step inside, mate?" asked the man in the tie.

Art pushed his jaw closed with his hand. Despite his best efforts, it fell agape again.

"OK, I'm just going to walk *around* you," said the identical stranger. "If you could please close your mouth so I can fit through the door."

Art did not comply, but the man standing on the filthy welcome mat walked inside anyway.

"Wh-Wh-Who are you?" Art finally stammered.

The man extended his hand. Art gripped it with one of those limp, clammy-fish handshakes. "I'm Art," said the stranger in a squeaky English accent. If the stranger hadn't also been Art, the handshake would have made him assume Art to be the most spineless sort of wet noodle imaginable.

"Ummm, what the hell is going on?" asked Art.

"I'm you from Earth 49,652," said the Art in the tie.

"I'm very confused," said the normal Art.

Normal-Art became even more confused when he spotted movement beneath Tie-Art's shirt. A giant brown cockroach, about a foot-and-a-half long, crawled out of Tie-Art's sleeve, circled his torso three times, and then rested on his left shoulder. Its antennae wiggled in Normal-Art's direction, and then it tilted its head to the side like an insectoid puppy.

Normal-Art squealed, "You have a-a-a-a friggin' giant cockroach on your sh-shoulder!"

Normal Art could not be sure, but he could have sworn that he saw the giant cockroach frown at him. A tiny, blue bolt of lightning flashed between its antennae, and Normal-Art cringed.

"D-D-Did it just flash lightning at me?" asked Normal-art.

"No, Art, she flashed *me*. She was telling me that she's twenty-five percent charged. It's going to take about six more hours for her to charge enough for another jump."

"Another jump?"

"Yeah. We've just come from a version of Earth populated by humans with one eye. They coincidentally never developed any vowels except for the *O*. On that Earth, we're named Ort. Meeting ourselves there is at least slightly less confusing."

"What?"

The Art in the tie pursed his lips, like he had explained this concept a thousand times before. The bug began circling around him again, and this time it did not stop until it squatted atop his head. It spread its antennae out wide, crowning him with exoskeleton devil horns.

Ginny walked out of the bedroom, took one look at the two Arts and the bug-crown, and then walked right back the way she had come.

"I'm you, but from another dimension," said Tie-Art. "It's not that hard to understand. As a matter of fact, I hear it's a pretty prevalent trope in your Earth's version of comic books—which, from what I have been led to believe, are commonly viewed here as children's literature. If children can understand it, I'm sure you can manage to wrap your mind around it."

"No *way*."

"Beverly, my Jump Bug, told me that I'd find the key to my quest here on Earth 6,076."

Normal-Art strummed his fingers across his chin. "What's your quest?"

"Well, that's my predicament. I don't really know. Figured I'd treat it like a maze by starting at the end and working my way out. I plan to resolve the questions along the way."

"I don't know about rotten. But I think numb about sums it up."

Tie-Art grabbed Normal-Art by the hand and began to drag him out the front door and into the muggy city air. Normal-Art stopped and looked back inside his apartment.

"What about Ginny?" asked Normal-Art. "Is she going to be OK? I mean, is that zappy blue lightning from your bug going to scar or anything?"

"No, no, no. Beverly merely whisked seven pints of her blood to a parallel Earth for a fraction of a second and then returned it. She'll wake up in an hour or so, feeling a mite hung over. I'd be more worried about her suffocating on the poisonous fumes with which she bombarded your home."

"Well, I guess we could open a few windows, let it air out a little. I could even leave the door open," suggested Normal-Art.

"Sounds fine to me, mate," said Tie-Art. "But then it's off to the nearest, seediest pub you got 'round these parts."

"Sure," said Normal-Art. "But you're buying."

CHAPTER 2

TWO ARTS WALK INTO A BAR...

NORMAL-ART LED TIE-ART three blocks south from his apartment to his favorite bar, *McGreedy's Pub*—both the seediest pub he knew, and the only one to open this early in the morning. A hairy, dirt-streaked bum sitting on the curb outside the bar asked Normal-Art if he could spare some change.

As he did nearly every day, Normal-Art pushed his way through the thick doors of the bar only after telling the bum to go get a job. Tie-Art, however, tossed the hairy hobo a small wad of hundred-dollar bills, and then he followed Normal-Art into the pub. The hobo glanced down at the cash in his hand, grinned, stuffed the wad into his pocket, and called out his thanks to Tie-Art, without further inspecting the money at all.[1]

As the Arts walked through the threshold and into the bar, the humidity and gray haze within caused them to feel a bit like they had dived into a swimming pool filled with smoke-flavored *Jell-O*. The pub was an Irish establishment, with lights dim enough that no matter what hour of the day Normal-Art entered, he always appeared at least somewhat less ugly to the opposite sex than he had been before he walked inside.

The Arts sauntered over to the end of the long oaken bar and sat upon a pair of rickety iron stools. Normal-Art leaned forward onto his elbows. He stared at the beer taps, the ceiling, the bartender, anywhere but himself-from-another-dimension. After what seemed an eternity of awkwardness, the

---

1 Later, when the hobo attempted to buy a bottle of liquor with the bills, he found that stores on this reality do not accept money from Tie-Art's home reality, which feature emblazoned across the front of the bill a pale man's grinning portrait with flaming hair atop his head. Following this disappointment, the hobo spent the remainder of his life cursing Tie-Art and what he referred to as "that damn fake-ass money."2

2Unfortunately for the hobo, the end of his life occurred a mere four minutes later when he was so distracted staring at the terribly ugly visage on one of the hundred-dollar bills that he stepped in front of a city bus. The bus's route number was 100, which the hobo might have thought was an interesting coincidence if he had not already been flattened by the vehicle.

bartender limped over to them and took their orders. He returned a few moments later and slammed their glasses down in front of them. Booze sloshed over the sides and splashed onto the bar.

Normal-Art gulped his Guinness like a champ, while Tie-Art sipped on his Chimay like a rich old geezer gumming at a shot of espresso, a squirrelly look on his face and one pinky poked up into the air. Normal-Art squinted in the dim light, signaling to the bartender for another drink. Tie-Art tossed a crisp, American ten-dollar bill onto the bar top. Both the Arts stared down at the bill instead of at each other. Alexander Hamilton stared right back, inanimate and silent.

Normal-Art cleared his throat in an attempt to evict the awkward silence from the pub. It did not work, and the awkwardness moved right back in. It even brought a few bastard children along.

"You twins or something?" asked the bartender, plopping the new Guinness down in front of Normal-Art. The liquid settled within the glass, shifting in color from light brown to opaque. Tiny carbonation bubbles swirled to the top of the glass like little ballerinas engaged in a dance of alcoholic ecstasy.

"Something, mate," replied Tie-Art.

The bartender grunted, limped away, and began cleaning glasses with a dirty rag. Normal-Art grabbed a peanut from a bowl that sat atop the bar and decided against eating it after he had already put it into his mouth. He tasted every year that the legume had lain there, just waiting to sow a bitter flavor across some hapless bastard's tongue. With each second the rotten peanut remained in his mouth, the horrid taste ripened and grew, until Normal-Art feared he might vomit. He spit the peanut into a cocktail napkin, wadded it up, and then tossed it onto the bar next to his glass.

Tie-Art set down his Chimay and looked Normal-Art directly in the eyes. "I've got a proposition for you," he explained.

Normal-Art looked at the soiled napkin. "You journeyed across time and space just to find me," he replied. "I assumed this wasn't a social call. What did you have in mind?"

"I didn't journey across time. Just space."

"What?"

"You said I journeyed across time and space to find you," said Tie-Art. "Time did not alter on my journey here, merely my location."

71,987 uses Jump Lizards. Earth 12 utilizes Jump Dogs. Earth 55,777, where the *Bureau of Interdimensional Travel* is headquartered, uses Jump Eagles. Hence the logo on your I.D. card. Some places use machines, some use food—I know of one Earth that uses Jump Gourds—and some earths haven't even developed interdimensional travel yet. Like yours."

"You totally just went over my head," responded Normal-Art.

"I've got a feeling that's going to happen a lot during this odyssey."

CHAPTER 3

A TALE OF TWO GINNYS

GINNY LAY ON her stomach and drifted through unconsciousness. She dreamt that she floated above the city, flittering atop skyscrapers and spitting down upon the little ant-sized people below her. She felt herself straying higher and higher into the atmosphere, and when she had soared to the topmost point of the tallest building, she discovered a pink teddy bear. It sat cross-legged atop the spiked point of a radio tower like some surreal, cuddly Buddha. Ginny hovered right up next to it. Its button-eyes bored into her.

"Don't let them abduct Me," begged the pink teddy bear, its mouth a pitch-black cavern opening onto an infinite abyss. "Ginny must rescue Me."

Ginny felt herself lurch in the air like a marionette doll getting its strings cut. She gasped in surprise, and then stared at the bear with an accusing gaze. It nodded.

"Time to go now," it said. "Lots of rescuing to do, so little time."

Ginny sensed the last of the strings holding her snap, and she fell. She squeezed her eyelids shut, refusing to look around her at the lights from office buildings zooming past her, refusing to look down at the fast-approaching concrete of the city below. The wind whipped through her hair like a tornado-powered hairdryer, and she flapped her arms as though she had transformed into an oversized, ugly pigeon. Then, when her flapping did nothing to avail her fall, she screamed.

Just before hitting the ground, she opened her eyes and found herself back in her home, with its drab curtains and faded off-white walls. She picked up her groggy head from the floor and wiped her mouth with the back of her hand. It came away wet, and she sighed. Art constantly teased her because of her drooling, and she was glad he was not here to see the flood that had deluged her face.

Ginny smelled stale bug spray and remembered what had happened. She recalled discovering her boyfriend at the front door with his identical twin, whom he had never mentioned before. She remembered trying to save them from a giant cockroach, and then being zapped by that same vicious creature. She thought she could recall a clonking in there somewhere, too.

"Art!" Ginny called. The vibrations of her voice bounced around inside her skull, causing her head to throb. She called his name again, but he did not answer. He must have gone out somewhere with his twin. She cursed.

Ginny's blurred vision began to clear, so she looked about the apartment to get her bearings. She balled her fists in anger when she realized that her boyfriend had left her where she had fallen on the floor. He had also walked out the front door and had not even shut it. *I could've been abducted, or raped, or murdered,* she thought. She clenched her fists tighter, wincing as her fingernails dug themselves deep into her palms. *Art can be so selfish!*

She picked herself up off the floor and stood still for a moment to gain her balance. Her knees wobbled, so she steadied herself on the coffee table. She decided to close the door, so she would not continue paying to air-condition the entire neighborhood. She stepped toward the door—o*ne foot in front of the other, ol' broad, you can do it*—but just after she had grabbed the knob and pushed it mostly closed, a bomb seemed to detonate on her porch. The door exploded in on her.

The force from the explosion launched her skyward, and she screamed as she flew into the air. She covered her eyes with her hands to prevent little wooden shards of the cheap door from blinding her. She crashed onto her back in the living room, on the middle of her prized, *authentic* Persian rug, which had been a surprise gift from Art for her birthday. As her head whipped into the ground, she felt damn lucky that the thick rug was there cushioning the thin, hard carpet.

Pain flashed through her skull like an emergency flare, blindingly strong at first, but receding into a healthy throb after a few seconds. She sat up and touched the spot on the back of her head where it had hit the floor. She felt a knot the size of a strawberry. She cursed again.

Thick, gray smoke billowed through the threshold of Ginny's door, and she coughed. A squeaky-yet-gravelly voice called out from the cloudy smog in the doorway, though nobody stood within her view. "Ginny Longfellow," it said. "You have been chosen by the Multiverse."

"What the hell's a Multiverse?" Ginny demanded, barely able to speak over the pain that rattled around in her skull.

"Every time you make a choice, you undergo a series of events," called the voice, its gravelly undertones now girded by a raw energy which Ginny could only describe as hints of smug know-it-allness. "These events transpire in a linear format that you refer to as life. However, what you experience as a single timeline is actually but a microscopic thread in the cosmic web, because for every fork in the road you have ever encountered, another universe has sprouted off from yours, and in this other universe, you have followed a different path. At this exact moment, there are infinite versions of different yous out there, creating more yous with each passing second. This reality multiplication has been occurring since the first god on the first reality made the decision to create a universe, resulting in the nigh-infinite incarnation of every possible universe that those of us in the know have dubbed *the Multiverse.* Is that a satisfactory answer to your question?"

Ginny blinked.

"I shall take your silence as awed acceptance. Now stand upon thy feet and come follow me."

"Oh, no thanks," Ginny replied. The voice emanating from her doorway sounded to her a bit like a game show announcer, ordering her to come on down to the stage and play. She hated game shows. "I don't leave with strangers, no matter whom they represent. Even if it *is* the Multiverse, or whatever…"

"Ginny Longfellow, when the Multiverse chooses you, *'No, thanks'* is not an option!" bellowed the voice. Ginny could sense a hint of spicy anger in the voice, which was fine with her because the voice had, after all, just destroyed her door. She could be sure that *that* was coming out of her rent.

Ginny took a few moments to think and weigh her options. Whoever or whatever was out there had demolished her door—rather easily, it seemed—and it would be safe to assume that the entity could probably do the same to her body. She sighed. She could see no other alternative than to agree to accompany the voice, for she obviously had little choice in the matter. But she was no rube. If the Multiverse's schmucky game show host was going force her to run off somewhere, she may as well get something good out of it.

"Fine," she replied. "Then what prize do I get if I help?"

"You get the satisfaction of knowing that out of everyone in every possible reality, the Multiverse has picked *you.*"

"Mmmmm, you'll have to do better than that," said Ginny.

"Fine. The Multiverse will throw in a…ummm…a gift certificate. Yeah."

"To where?" asked Ginny, her face beaming with joy at her bargaining skills. She realized she had a knack for them when she had traveled on a cruise to Mexico last summer. After disembarking the ship at Cozumel, she had scored shot after shot of tequila upon entering each shop. She walked away with a dozen T-shirts for the price of ten.

"To anywhere you want," remarked the voice.

"To the Gap?"

"Especially the Gap."

"Well, I don't like the Gap," responded Ginny. She grinned.

The representative of the Multiverse groaned, and then stepped through the doorway. The agent was a blonde woman with a prominent snaggle-tooth. She stood four-and-a-half feet tall and had wide, burly shoulders that reminded Ginny of the dwarven characters in many of the Fantasy novels she had devoured as a teenager. The tiny woman neglected to wipe her feet on the mat and proceeded to leave a trail of mud cakes behind her as she waddled across the threshold and into Ginny's apartment.

The pint-sized woman wore tight khaki pants and a light green button-up shirt. She had fastened the buttons in the wrong holes, causing her shirt to sit lopsided on her torso. This miss-assignment of buttons to holes, coupled with her unkempt tangles of blonde hair, gave her the look of a mad scientist. Ginny half expected the dwarf to exclaim *Great Scott!* in a screechy little voice. The woman's eyes shone from their sockets like miniature emeralds, and her cheeks stood out rosy red on her face. She wore a yellow kerchief around her neck, with a little knot holding it together that came to a rest on the front of her torso. An olive-green sash stretched across her chest with dozens of odd patches sewn onto it. Beneath the sash lay an unbuttoned, equally olive vest. Her scuffed leather boots caught the light and illuminated her raggedness. The dwarf mumbled some incoherent phrase and clapped her hands twice. Then she put her hands on her hips and posed like a runway model. Fog flew into the room from outside the front door and swirled to surround her. It would have looked majestic if she had not been so tiny and ugly.

"Then pick anywhere you want," said the tiny woman, now holding out her left hand to Ginny. "But keep your mouth shut and take my hand. We are going on a journey to the far side of the Multiverse."

Ginny began to reach out her hand, but then she stopped. She noticed something in the tiny woman's face. The little lady was making the exact same expression Ginny did whenever Ginny was feeling mischievous. As a matter of fact, Ginny realized, all the little person's features were the exact same as hers, only on a smaller scale.

"What's your name?" Ginny asked.

"I was sure this was going to come up sooner or later, but since I'd heard the me of this reality was somewhat of a dullard, I had assumed it would be later. My name's Ginny."

Regular-Sized-Ginny gasped. Apparently witnessing her boyfriend's exact duplicate interacting with a colossal cockroach earlier this morning had not expended all her affinity for shock. Tiny-Ginny grew impatient with waiting for Regular-Ginny to overcome her shock, so she grabbed the taller woman by the wrist. She pulled Regular-Ginny up onto her knees.

Regular-Ginny's head was still a swirling miasma of pain and dizziness, so she reeled at the sudden movement. She yanked her arm free from the grip of this other version of herself. She moaned. She held up the pointer finger on her right hand, signaling for this woman to wait a moment. Regular-Ginny remained perfectly still and shut her eyes. She concentrated on regaining her equilibrium. In a few moments, the dizziness subsided, though the pain lingered inside her skull. Moving at a snail's pace, she pushed herself the rest of the way up onto her feet, and while doing so, she noticed a squirming beneath the misplaced buttons of Tiny-Ginny's shirt.

A dark brown squirrel with two gigantic antennae growing from its forehead poked its head out from between two of Tiny-Ginny's mismatched buttons. The little creature chittered psychotically and rolled its eyes around in its head. It reminded Regular-Ginny of an insane Muppet. She hated Muppets.

"His name is Eduardo," said Tiny-Ginny, "But most just call him Mister E. Behold the power that *I* have given him."

As Tiny-Ginny was making this announcement, a barrage of green lightning erupted from the squirrel's flittering antennae. Regular-Ginny noted to herself that this display seemed rather rehearsed, but before she could relay this observation to her counterpart, the green lightning leapt from the antennae and engulfed her. She felt as though she was being sucked into a giant vacuum-cleaner, and then she did not feel anything at all.

Five minutes later, the two Arts walked into the apartment. It was empty. They smelled no hint of bug spray.

CHAPTER 4

WEAPONS MAKE THE MEN. AND THE BUG.

"WHERE'S GINNY?" ASKED Normal-Art. "And why do I no longer have a front door?"

Beverly rubbed her forelegs together, and the friction between the tips of the appendages created a rapid series of clicks similar to those of a chirping cricket. Beverly continued rubbing faster and faster, and the noise soon transformed into something much more high-pitched and piercing. It sounded like a pained squeal.

Art grunted and closed his eyes, trying to ignore the sound. But with his eyes clamped shut and the squealing noise bombarding his ears, Normal-Art could not stop envisioning Jiminy Cricket crooning a pained dirge while being pinned down by some monstrous boy's fingers and having his legs brutally plucked from his body. Normal-Art opened his eyes, shook the vision from his head, and groaned.

"OK, Bev, I understand," said Tie-Art. "Please calm down and jump us in some tools. Check the storehouse on Earth 5,001."

"What's happening?" Normal-Art asked.

Tie-Art held up a hand, motioning for Normal-Art to stay quiet. "She needs to concentrate," he said.

A thin shaft of blue lightning flickered between Beverly's antennae, followed by an enormous bolt aimed directly at Normal-Art's *knockoff* Persian rug, which he had purchased for Ginny on her birthday and passed off to her as authentic.

Normal-Art attempted to protest the zapping of the rug, but instead found himself silenced by the sudden vacuum created in the room by the flash of blue lightning, which hung in place in the middle of Art's den. His ears popped, and he tried to scream, but he could not find the air to utter a sound. With each passing fraction of a second, the popping in his ears grew louder until it thumped and cracked like a metronome adjusted to a Mach-5 beat.

The lightning seemed to hang there for hours, and when it finally subsided, so did the popping in Normal-Art's ears. Normal-Art began to feel rather like Baby-Art when he realized that he was now lying on the floor in a fetal position, tears glistening on his cheeks. He did not know how he had managed to get in this position, for he could remember neither falling to the ground nor curling himself up into a little ball. He looked over at Tie-Art. Tie-Art grinned at him, and then he winked.

"Aye, the lightning takes a wee bit of acclimation," said Tie-Art. "It won't be quite so bad next time."

A large wooden crate now sat atop Art's fake Persian rug near his ratty old junked-out coffee table. A thin wisp of blue smoke drifted up from the crate and wafted through the dingy room. The smoke smelled of burnt asparagus drowned in blueberry syrup, and even when Normal-Art pinched his nose shut to stop from smelling it, he could taste the odor on the back of his tongue. His stomach threatened to purge, but he held it in check and forced himself to study the crate.

It was the kind of crate you might see in a really bad action movie, the kind of crate that the bad guys have filled with ludicrously complicated doomsday weapons and explosives. As a matter of fact, painted in red block letters on the side of the crate—just like in one of those aforementioned cheesy flicks—was emblazoned a message that read: *LETHAL WEAPONS INSIDE. HANDLE WITH CARE.*

Tie-Art walked to the oversized wooden crate and found a crowbar conveniently lying atop it. He pried open the lid with ease. A miniature sea of Styrofoam packing peanuts lay pooled within the crate, and he began sifting through it. Beverly dove headfirst from his shoulder into the high tide of packing material.

Over the next five minutes, the duo rummaged through the crate in silence, ignoring Normal-Art's multitude of questions. From the packing material, Tie-Art pulled a fist-sized ruby orb that had been carved to look like an eyeball. He touched it delicately down upon the rug, delicately enough that a casual passerby may have mistaken it for an intensely ugly Faberge Egg. He stuck his arms back into the crate just as Beverly resurfaced from her deep-sea dive, lugging behind her a pair of hairy leather gloves seemingly sized to fit a giant.

She dropped them to the floor next to the ruby orb. Then Tie-Art stood from the packing crate and set amongst the two other trinkets a hooked dagger with a serrated blade and a hilt made from the green-furred paw of some large cat. He dusted off his hands as though he had completed a great feat, and then he sat down next to Normal-Art. They waited for Beverly to arise once more from the packing peanuts, and when she finally did, she dragged behind her an anvil miniature enough that it could fit in Art's palm. She hefted it over the side of the crate and dropped it. It crashed to the floor with a loud THUNK. With the ocean of Styrofoam peanuts completely drained of its resources, Beverly hopped back onto Tie-Art's shoulder, and the two turned to face Normal-Art.

"What is all this?" asked Normal-Art for the umpteenth time.

Tie-Art arched one eyebrow. "They're weapons," he said. "It says so on the side of the box."

Normal-Art sighed as heavily as he could and gripped his stringy hair between his fingers. Frustration overwhelmed him, and he considered ripping it from his scalp. Through clinched teeth, he muttered, "I know they are weapons, *ass*. I want you to tell me what, specifically, they do, and why they are piled on my floor. I'd rather not blow up the entire neighborhood because you decided that my place would make a fantastic armory."

"Oh," said Tie-Art. He picked up the colossal, hairy gloves and tossed them to Normal-Art. They bounced off Normal-Art's chest and tumbled to the floor. "Over the years, I've, uh, borrowed each of these items from a different version of us to help us accomplish our upcoming mission. Now, put those gloves on. They're from Earth 3,333, where we're King of the Jungle."

"King of the Jungle?" asked Normal-Art.

"Yeah," answered Tie-Art. "The gloves belonged to his version of us. They're made from the hands of a giant gorilla, and they had supernatural powers imbued upon them by the most ancient shaman in that dimension. When you wear those mitts, you'll have the strength of at least a hundred Arts."

This ritual continued, as Tie-Art handed Normal-Art the remaining items and explained from where they came. The anvil came from an Earth where Art existed as a magical blacksmith, and it could create anything the user could ever imagine so long as he could envision it in his mind's eye. The ruby orb was an ancient power called the *Socky-Go-Go-Eyeball.* It had origins in a dimension where the local Art was a mythic hero gifted special powers when the gods cried tears into his eyes. The tears melded his pair of eyes into one large ruby eyeball, which had the ability to launch powerful barrages of crimson energy from its pupil. Tie-Art told the tale of how this mythic hero had died a few years ago while on a quest to remove a manticore from an orphanage, and then he told the story of how the gods of that dimension had in turn gifted the mythic eyeball to him because of the many times he had assisted the hero on his quests.

The dagger Tie-Art kept for himself. The blade had belonged to Tie-Art's father, and it was infused with magic into which only he could tap. He tested its edge by cutting off a large chunk from the arm of Normal-Art's couch.

"Hey!" squealed Normal-Art's. "What the hell are you doing? That's my couch!"

As Tie-Art sheathed the blade in the waistband of his slacks, he smirked. He replied, "Meh. The couch is ugly, anyway. And I cut off the ugliest section. If anything, you should be *thanking* me."

Normal-Art frowned. He had long considered his couch to be his best friend, for it had been there for him through the good times and the bad. However, as he opened his mouth to express this thought to Tie-Art, he realized that it might sound at least a little insane. So, he instead frowned even harder and shoved his hands into the pockets of his frilly pink robe.

"Why do I need this arsenal?" asked Normal-Art, realizing the best course of action might be to change the subject and divert attention away from the couch before another chunk of it could fall victim to his alternate-self. "Like I told you, I've never even been in a fight, let alone used a weapon. I wouldn't know where to start."

"You need it to help us fight the people we must fight. Obviously. And starting with it is easy! You aim the lethal ends at the people you want to kill. It's a simple concept, really, and you'd better get used to it bloody quick, for we're headed on a rescue mission of dire importance," replied Tie-Art. "So, get some rest today while Beverly recharges, and come tomorrow morning, we shall leave this Earth. To save who we need to save, you'll need to gird yourself to murder a large population of dwarves dressed like your Earth's Girl Scouts!"

CHAPTER 5

RIDE THE LIGHTNING

THE NEXT DAY, Beverly zapped Normal-Art with a blue bolt of lightning while he lay asleep on his couch. Normal-Art awoke to find himself falling. Even worse, he felt like he had been flushed down a drain. He spun out of control, round and round, his feet whipping around his head. As the centrifugal forces spun him, he thought he could feel his brain smack against the inside of his skull and flatten out.

The falling and spinning seemed endless, and Art did not know if he had been falling for years or for minutes. Art's surroundings were simultaneously colorful and colorless. Waves of blue danced across his peripheral vision—undulating from indigo to turquoise to sapphire—but whenever he twisted his head to take a better look, the color dispersed into black nothingness.

Eventually, after what felt like both an eternity and no time at all, Tie-Art and Beverly zoomed into view from somewhere in the ether above. Beverly rode upon a bolt of lightning like a witch atop a broomstick. She dragged Tie-Art along behind her with one foreleg, and as she sped past Normal-Art, she grabbed him by his collar with a different foreleg.

Beverly blasted the wavering blue in the distant peripheral with a volley of lightning from her antennae. A portion of the blueness wobbled and vibrated and formed into a colossal, opaque sphere. Beverly steered the group toward it.

As the group passed through the sphere, Normal-Art's body went numb.

CHAPTER 6

A NEW, PINK GOD

AT LEAST IF my head explodes, it won't hurt anymore, thought Regular-Ginny. After being zapped by alien lightning for the second time in a single day, and then falling through nothingness for who-the-hell knows how long, she and her dwarf-self had touched down on the grass of a lush, green park.

Upon landing, Ginny lay sprawled upon the ground and could not move. For her entire life, she had suffered from chronic, blinding migraines, but the pain in her head from interdimensional hopping was at least twice as bad as all those migraines combined. Maybe even thrice as bad.

Regular-Ginny's miniature counterpart began tugging on her arm, trying to force her up onto her feet.

"Get up, you lazy wretch," demanded Tiny-Ginny. "My plans can't wait for you to lie here in the open. You can rest at my place. Now move!"

When the tugging and the commanding did not incite Regular-Ginny to stand, the tiny woman began kicking Ginny with her tiny boots. Regular-Ginny moaned in pain. She forced herself up onto her hands and knees.

"Hey!" squealed Regular-Ginny as another kick thudded against her ribs. "You said I was chosen by the Multiverse to come with you! Surely the Multiverse wouldn't be OK with you bullying and kicking its chosen one!"

Tiny-Ginny chortled. She replied, "You fool. I was *lying*. And now you're stuck here with me without any way to return to your home Earth. If you want to survive, you shall act as my servant until I deem your service to me over. Now do my bidding, or you shall meet a most painful end. Stand!"

Regular-Ginny glanced around at the surrounding greenery and moaned in despair. None of it looked familiar. She felt hopelessness and anxiety closing in around her. As much as she might wish to be back home, she was lost here in a land from which she did not know how to return. She could obey this dreadful doppelganger, or she could '*meet a most painful end.*' Possibly an end that resembled her now-exploded door. She gulped.

Regular-Ginny took a deep breath. She tried to obey her counterpart. She did her best to force herself up onto her feet, but as soon as she began to lift herself upright, her stomach overflowed with nausea, and her brain somehow purchased a jackhammer and began renovating the inside of her skull. She collapsed.

The dwarf stalked away and turned back to Ginny just long enough to say, "Pathetic. Move!"

Regular-Ginny crawled across the grass after Tiny-Ginny for about a dozen yards, collapsing every few feet and forcing herself back up onto her hands and knees. Finally, she collapsed onto the ground one last time. She squealed, "I'm trying. But I can't."

Tiny-Ginny spun on her heel and returned to Regular-Ginny. The dwarf kicked Regular-Ginny over and over, demanding that she move. But no amount of miniature kicks to Regular-Ginny's ribs could cause her to move again. Her exhaustion was too overwhelming. She shut her eyes, but it hurt to shut them, so she opened them. It hurt to keep them open, so she shut them once more. She tried groaning, but let out a second groan because groaning hurt, too.

The dwarf sighed. "I can't believe I'm about to waste *magic* on you," she muttered. "You are pitiful."

Regular-Ginny opened her mouth to ask what her counterpart meant by that comment about magic, but she was too exhausted to force out any sound. Tiny-Ginny snatched Mister E from within her shirt and yanked him out by the tail. His eyeballs circled around in their sockets, and he made maniacal smooching faces at Regular-Ginny. She thought the squirrel resembled an insane Pepe LePew from those *Looney Tunes* cartoons she had obsessed over as a child.

"My little fuzzball, this pathetic hag is too feeble to walk on her own," crooned Tiny-Ginny into Mister E's ear. "I need you to gather some comrades to assist her."

If Regular-Ginny had not already been nauseated, what she saw next would have caused her to become nauseated. Tiny-Ginny twisted the pinky of her free hand to encircle her ring finger three times. The bones and sinews made little popping noises with each twist. Then she whispered something that Regular-Ginny could not understand into the squirrel's ear.

The frightful creature began to howl. The noise rose from deep in his throat and sounded like a foghorn blowing through a kazoo, only louder and out of tune. For the first time in twenty years, Regular-Ginny prayed. As she lay on the ground, unable to move a muscle, she asked God to grant her either the strength to cover her ears or the mercy to go deaf. And just like so long ago, it appeared that God was not listening.

Dozens of tiny, red eyes appeared in the darkness that shrouded the boughs of the surrounding trees. The eyes seemed to slither toward Ginny, and as each pair of eyes came into view, Ginny saw that it was attached to a dingy squirrel. These rodents looked nearly identical to Mister E, but with little bony nubs protruding through the hide in front of their ears where Mister E had antennae.

The squirrels all stopped for a moment to sniff Regular-Ginny. Then they skittered past her and gathered at Tiny-Ginny's feet, where they stood on their hind legs like a pack of begging dogs. Tiny-Ginny dug into a tiny front pocket and removed an oddly enormous wad of leather straps. She tied one strap around the neck of each squirrel. She took the opposite end of each strap and tied it to Regular-Ginny. By the time Tiny-Ginny was finished with this task, multiple leather straps encircled each of Regular-Ginny's elbows, wrists, knees, and ankles.

Mister E leapt onto Regular-Ginny's head and began barking orders to the other squirrels. They used their straps like a pack of huskies to drag Ginny to a nearby tree. When they reached the oak, the creatures scurried up the bark, using their collective muscle to pull Ginny up onto her feet. After she was leaning steadily against the tree, the squirrels leapt down from the trunk of the oak and perched on her shoulders like a murder of furry crows on a telephone line.

Then the little rodents used their straps to transform Regular-Ginny into a gigantic marionette doll. The squirrels attached to her left wrist and elbow leapt forward into the air simultaneously with the creatures attached to her right knee and ankle. The diving squirrels forced Ginny to stagger forward onto her right foot. As these squirrels raced back up Ginny's body to prepare for another leap, the rodents controlling her opposite limbs jumped, causing Ginny's opposite leg and arm to shoot out in front of her before she could fall face-first onto the grass.

In this manner, the squirrels walked Regular-Ginny to Tiny-Ginny's log cabin, located a few hours away on the other side of this colossal park. Though she came close to toppling over multiple times, the squirrels always managed to scramble up her awkward body and leap from her shoulders just in time.

Regular-Ginny was so exhausted that she fell in and out of consciousness, and thus she did not remember most of the trip. Upon arriving at the cabin, Mister E made a trilling sound with his throat, and the little rodents unceremoniously dumped Regular-Ginny on the floor of the living room before helping each other out of their straps and scurrying away.

Regular-Ginny glanced at her surroundings. The only source of light that she could see came from an old brown lantern with rusted silver trimming that hung on a nail in the corner. The pale light from the lamp's flame stretched and spread across the room like a watery cream, gifting every object it enveloped with a long, black shadow. The deep shadows helped everything appear less tiny.

Framed, painted portraits covered the walls. Every single one portrayed Tiny-Ginny and Mister E posing in front of a different landmark. Some landmarks were familiar, like the St. Louis Arch and the White House, but others appeared dreadfully alien, including the duo in front of a three-story tall statue of a giant beetle wearing a five-pointed crown, the duo in front of a factory building that appeared to be modeled in the shape of a radish, and the duo in front of a skyscraper made from clouds. Tiny-Ginny's canvases, easel, paint-spattered tarps, and oil-based paints lay discarded in the corner beneath the lantern like the bones of a phoenix, patient and awaiting the chance to return to creative life. Regular-Ginny shrugged, surprised that a vicious person like Tiny-Ginny valued such an outlet for creativity.

Regular-Ginny continued her once-over of the house. A couch squatted in the middle of the room, covered in an off-white sheet. A small passageway in the back of the room led to the kitchen, in which she could see dirty pots and pans and bowls stacked high in the sink. A crooked stairway on the side of the room led upstairs. She could see the corner of a mattress poking into view through the doorway of a room at the top of the stairs, so she assumed the room must be Tiny-Ginny's bedroom. She made a silent wish that she would never lay eyes upon that room. Thick clumps of dust hung from many of the corners and from the edges of much of the furniture.

"I dunno *why*, but I expected your place to be a little less dingy," Regular-Ginny muttered, her exhaustion removing the filter between her thoughts and her mouth. She realized what she had just said, so she tried to finish the comment with some sort of compliment in order to not be *completely* rude, but she could not find the energy. Her mouth simply stopped working. She caught a slap to the face from her counterpart. She was too tired to protest, so she licked blood from her lip.

Eventually, Regular-Ginny dragged herself over to the couch, and then she pulled herself up onto it. She lay on her back, holding her aching head and gasping to catch her breath. She forced herself to focus on something other than her pain and exhaustion. She did so by picking one of the millions of dust motes floating in the air. She concentrated on watching it dance through the dank room. She remembered watching the dust motes twirl through her grandmother's living room as a child, and how she used to get so bored when visiting her grandmother's house that she would give the tiny things names and pretend that they competed with one other to choreograph the most beautiful dance.

As she followed her chosen dust mote with her gaze, she did not even note the absurdity when it began to morph and change shape. Its gray, fuzzy edges grew fuzzier. It began to twirl faster and faster in tiny circles. Soon, it glowed orange with heat. The orange blurred to red, then finally transitioned to pink, and the newly pink mote began to expand. It seemed to gather mass from the air, sucking in the surrounding oxygen and using it to grow larger. As it grew, it changed shape from a mass of pink goo into a misshapen pink teddy bear. The bear, one of its button-eyes hanging by the barest of threads, stared into Ginny's exhausted eyes.

"Save Me," it said.

"You're pink," Ginny responded, feeling stupid in a surreal sort of way.

The teddy bear's button eye fell from its face, twirling end over end as it tumbled through the air. Ginny did not realize her mouth was agape until the button passed her lips and lodged itself in her windpipe. She gagged and choked. A gurgling noise escaped from her mouth, and she wrestled against the futility of trying to inhale. She clawed at her throat. She could feel the button moving inside her. It seemed to grow flagella and pull itself further down her windpipe.

Just when Ginny knew she was about to pass out, the button popped in her throat like a firecracker. It turned into dust within her windpipe. She could feel its tiny particles enter her lungs and then flow out into her bloodstream.

The pink dust felt grainy inside her. She gasped for oxygen and finally obtained it, but an underlying smell of decaying cookies and overripe strawberries penetrated every desperate breath. A pink hue now tinted her vision, and it would not go away no matter how much she rubbed her eyes. Ginny glanced up and realized the pink bear was still floating above her. It stared at her with its remaining button eye.

"Ginny no longer need to fear no things," whispered the bear in its creepy falsetto tone. "Little-Ginny think she bringed Ginny here for she own purposes, but Me am *really* reason Ginny here. Little-Ginny just don't know it. Me be having lots and lots of influence on people of this Earth, and they no know it. Multiverse really *did* choose Ginny, no matter what Little-Ginny say. And Me am extra powerful part of Multiverse, and Me am part of Ginny now. Me have bestowed vast power onto Ginny. And now Ginny must save Me before it is too late."

"You're pink," said Ginny once again.

The bear sighed. "Ginny wake now."

Ginny opened her eyes and squinted against the pale morning light. She did not even have time to consider whether the whole experience of the last twenty-four hours had been a dream, because her tiny mirror-image sat perched on her chest, with her face less than an inch away from Ginny's own.

"Holy Christ!" yelled Ginny.

"You were out for nearly eighteen hours. Your weak body seemed to need it, so I allowed you the rest. I've taken the liberty of changing you into a fresh pair of clothes," said Tiny-Ginny. "It is the official uniform of this reality. You will still draw much attention here because of your height, but at least this will help you not look like *quite* so much of an outsider."

Regular-Ginny glanced down at her body and did not like what she saw. Her new attire was the exact same as Tiny-Ginny's: light green button-up shirt, olive green vest, khaki pants, and leather work boots. Ginny also disliked the canary yellow kerchief that had been tied around her neck and the olive-green sash stretching across her chest. Ginny was dressed like a Girl Scout.

Ginny had hated the Girl Scouts since she was twelve years old, when she had nearly died from choking on one of their cookies. Upon passing out and going into the light, her disappointment in finding that Heaven smelled like a *Thin Mint* was abated when the paramedics resuscitated her. She had long since resented the Scouts for the incident. Disdain for her miniature twin bloomed in the pit of her stomach as she thought about the dwarf dressing her in an almost exact replica of their uniform without her consent.

As she studied the uniforms a little more closely, Regular-Ginny noticed that the main difference between the Scout uniform from her home reality and the one from this reality lay in the badges that were sewn onto the sashes. Back home, the badges had signified mastery of useful skills, but the ones here seemed to trade usefulness for atrocity. Regular-Ginny had none on her own sash to compare, but Tiny-Ginny had row upon row of them. One portrayed a man dangling from a tree with a noose around his neck. Another showed a man burning in flames. Ginny saw people asphyxiated on poisonous gas. Another revealed people being clubbed on the head. On another was stitched a bright red mushroom cloud. On and on they went, each badge depicting a different scene of brutality.

Regular-Ginny began to panic at the scenes of gore on her counterpart's sash, and as her breaths became shorter and harder to come by, a dusty feeling stirred in her lungs. The sensation tickled her insides, and she fell into a fit of hacks and coughs. She covered her mouth with her left hand, and when she finished hacking, she pulled it away and stared at it. It was covered in bright pink goo, and she remembered her dream. She found that she was no longer frightened.

"I know why I'm here," said Regular-Ginny to herself.

"Yes," replied her counterpart. "You are here to do my bidding. In doing so, you will help me obtain the most powerful weapon in the Multiverse."

The whites of Regular-Ginny's eyes clouded into a deep pink, and pink tendrils wrapped her heart in a cocoon of murderous rage. Pink ooze crept from the pores of her right arm and hardened into a dense exoskeleton. She stared at it in awe.

Then her right hand darted out from her side and snatched the dwarf by the throat. Regular-Ginny stood, lifting Tiny-Ginny into the air. The dwarf flailed her arms and legs wildly about as though a large flopping fish had replaced each of her appendages.

"No, I am not here to do your bidding. The bear used *you* to bring *me* here. I am here to *save* it."

Mister E popped out of Tiny-Ginny's shirt and hissed at Regular-Ginny. Regular-Ginny backhanded the creature with her free hand. The blow launched the squirrel across the cabin, and its head smacked into the wooden wall with a sickening crunch. If the squirrel did not already have brain damage, Ginny was sure it did now.

Pink tendrils tickled the back of Regular-Ginny's brain, and before she realized what she was doing, her free arm jerked out of its own accord and rubbed the pink goo that she had coughed into her hand onto Tiny-Ginny's face.

"The Pink One desires for you to receive this gift so that *you* can serve *me*," said Regular-Ginny, the words—like the movement of her arm—flying forth of their own volition. She gasped and covered her mouth with her free hand, unsure from where the words had come and hoping to restrain any others from bursting forth without her permission.

The pink goo stretched over Tiny-Ginny's head, growing exponentially to envelop it in a thick membrane. She clawed and pulled at the slime to no avail, and soon the membrane expanded to cover her entire body. Millions of tiny whirlpools then appeared within the membrane as Tiny-Ginny's pores acted like storm drains, sucking the blob down inside her skin. The pink goo completely disappeared inside of her, and she passed out. She dangled limply for a few moments in Regular-Ginny's grasp. Then the tiny woman opened her eyes. She heaved and gasped for air. Once she managed to catch her breath, she turned her head toward Regular-Ginny. Her eyes burned with the same pink hue as her taller counterpart.

"I understand now, too," said the tiny woman, her voice a gruff waterfall crashing atop pink gravel. "The Pink One has spoken to me through your gift. We must save it, for it is our new, pink god. You shall act as our compass to find it, and I shall pledge every ounce of power I possess on this planet as our muscle."

"How should we begin?" asked Regular-Ginny, finding that her mouth was under her own control again. "This is your reality, after all. You know this place."

Tiny-Ginny silently pondered the question for a moment, and then she said, "While Mister E and his fellow squirrels were conveying you through the park, it was impossible to ignore that you were rambling like a crazy person. At first, I assumed that these were merely insane mutterings caused by your first jump scrambling your already-pitiful brain. But then you mentioned something about your boyfriend's identical twin appearing on your doorstep with a giant cockroach in tow. Did that *actually* happen?"

"I don't remember speaking *at all* while those rodents were dragging me through the park," replied Regular-Ginny.

Tiny-Ginny frowned. She said, "You may have been too exhausted to remember doing it. But I was there. I heard it all."

Regular-Ginny shrugged. "If you say so."

"I do. Now tell me, is what you said true? Did your boyfriend's identical twin appear on your doorstep alongside a giant cockroach?"

Regular-Ginny nodded. "Yeah," she said. "That happened."

Tiny-Ginny strummed her fingers across her chin. "That can only be my ex, the Art from my reality. If he was on your reality recruiting your boyfriend, then he will shortly be on his way here. He shall be seeking the same quarry as us. In that case, the first item on our to-do list shall be to murder them as soon as they appear."

"Huh? I'm not going to do that."

"Oh, we *must*," responded Tiny-Ginny. "They are *undoubtedly* seeking the same objective that we are. We must beat them to it, and the easiest way to do that is to kill them."

"But why would we need to *kill* them? That's ridiculous. Hell, why wouldn't we work together with them?"

"You do not understand who my Art is and what he will do to obtain the power inherent in the entity we seek. And he is not one to share. If we do not kill them both now, then my Art will find a way to kill us later."

"B-B-But that still makes no sense. It's so *drastic*. Can't we just capture them or slow them down or something?" asked Regular-Ginny.

"The stakes are so high that we cannot risk anything going awry, and if *my* Art is involved, then you can count on *everything* going awry. If we simply rid ourselves of them both now, then we won't have to worry about problems with them arising later."

"Wh-Wh-Why would we have to kill *my* Art, too? He's harmless."

"If it is the actual killing of your lover that is bothering you, I will arrange the killing myself with one of my most trusted underlings, whom I will instruct to dispatch your Art and bring mine to me. I will not trust that mine is out of the question unless I handle him myself."

Regular-Ginny began to protest once more, but the pink power inside her squeezed on her heart and whispered angry nothings directly into her brain. The pink reminded her of all the times that Art had disappointed her during their relationship, of all the times that he took advantage of her and degraded her and paid no concern to the things about which she cared. It took mere moments before the acts numbered too many to count, and her sympathy for him disappeared. Her brain began to feel as though it had been dipped into a bath of pure, angry honey. It was a buzzing sensation of unadulterated fury. She realized that she did, in fact, now want to stare at Art's lifeless corpse. She wanted to make mocking faces at it, too.

The angry pink then tickled instructions into her brain, teaching her how to use the pink gift inside her. She stared at her hand, willing pink ooze to seep from her pores. It did. She pictured her boyfriend and his twin, and the ooze shaped itself into them. She concentrated, forming a second seepage of ooze into a tiny little buzz saw that she ran through her pink sculptures of the Arts, sawing them in half. "Fine. Get rid of them," Regular-Ginny exclaimed with an odious grin.

"I'm glad you concur. In the meantime, I will call an assembly of my tribe and the tribe nearest to mine. This assembly shall yield us recruits to use as cannon fodder on our quest. Whilst we are waiting for my Art to be found and delivered to us, we shall impress these minions with miracles from our new, pink master. And then, once my Art is before us, we shall sacrifice him to our pink god. Nothing gets a mob on your side like a good ol' fashioned execution!" squealed Tiny-Ginny. She willed pink ooze to flow from the pores of her hand, and then she raised the ooze into the air to form an enormous balled fist.

"So, with all that said," continued the tiny woman, "shall we get started right away, or would you rather hold me up in the air by my throat all damned day?"

Regular-Ginny set Tiny-Ginny down upon the floor. The tiny hag had fixed an overlarge grin to her face, the same type of grin that Regular-Ginny wore when she was lying about something. The gaze was rather offsetting. For a moment, Regular-Ginny wished that her pink gift had not been shared with her horrid counterpart, but she did not sustain the wish for long. She sure as hell did not know the necessary ways nor hows of this reality, and thus she sure as hell could not complete her rescue mission on her own. So, like many other areas of her life, she simply gave up her authority without protest and allowed someone else to take the lead. She shrugged.

Tiny-Ginny began barking instructions for what they were going to do and say in front of the upcoming assembly, pink oozing from her pores to form a diagram to help illustrate the plan.

Regular-Ginny leaned back and stretched her legs. She stared at the wormy lips of her counterpart. The Pink One tickled Regular-Ginny's brain, signaling approval of the plan spewing forth from Tiny-Ginny's mouth and forcing Regular-Ginny to give color commentary for how to improve it and make it more captivating. Regular-Ginny stopped paying attention. It was going to be a long day.

CHAPTER 7

ABGRAY THE IRRELSQUAY

NORMAL-ART, BEVERLY, AND Tie-Art touched down gently onto a lumpy gravel alleyway. They appeared a few feet away from an overfull dumpster constructed from wooden beams stitched together into a crisscross formation, which gave the dumpster the appearance of having been built from Lincoln Logs. Squat log buildings straddled the alleyway on both sides, stretching three-stories high like some toddler architect's version of a wooden metropolis. The wooden beams of these old-fashioned buildings were faded, bleak, and dull brown.

Normal-Art crawled to the shade of the dumpster and lay there, rubbing his temples with his fingers. He had a throbbing headache, and it threatened to crack open his skull and wander away like a chick bursting forth from an egg. To make matters worse, his dinner from last night blasted up his throat, a curry-flavored orange rocket that shot past his lips and crashed to the dusty ground. The payload splattered onto Tie-Art's shiny leather shoes. Tie-Art sighed and wiped clean the side of his shoes on Normal-Art's shirt.

"Where are we?" groaned Normal-Art, not really caring. He clutched at the ground as if afraid that he would fall up, up, up into the atmosphere.

"We're at the apex of our destinies. Well, yours anyway," replied Tie-Art. "I have a much longer lifespan than you."

Normal-Art closed his eyes. Even on this overcast day, and even though he was curled in the shade, the sun above seemed to blare down upon him and amplify his headache. "Is it OK if I don't feel like I'm at my apex?" he asked.

"Aye, you'll feel better in a couple hours. Happens to us all on our first jump."

Normal-Art pulled himself up onto his elbows. The pain throbbed through his skull harder than ever, and despite having already lost his dinner, he managed to lose it again. He scooted a few feet away from his vomit and forced himself to sit up. He opened his eyes and stared down at the ground.

A small puddle of water lay near his feet, so he leaned over and studied his reflection in it. He grunted at his haggard image and wiped puke from the side of his face. He held his hands in front of his eyes, staring at the gorilla-gloves. They itched, and they smelled like leather that had been marinated in excrement. He remembered that the gloves were part of an entire arsenal, and he smirked a nervous little smirk at the thought of himself engaging in any sort of battle.

He considered the notion for a long while, and just when he was beginning to wrap his mind around the idea of himself as a pudgy, sci-fi *Rambo*, something chittered within the nearby wooden dumpster. The hung-over sensation plaguing him acted as a glue that held his head bent down near the ground, so he had to strain every atom in his body to lift his head and train his eyes on the dumpster. And just when he thought he could not hold his eyes open for a moment longer, a tiny brown squirrel poked its head out from the top of the dumpster. It tilted its head to one side and offered its pity to Art by chittering a pitiful chitter.

The little creature leapt from the dumpster down to the gravelly alleyway and scurried across the ground toward Normal-Art. The squirrel's eyes were large brown saucers, reflecting an intelligence that Art had never seen in such a cute little rodent. The mammal's ears were shredded, which Art assumed was the result of scavenging through the back alleys of whatever dimension this happened to be. The way it dug through the trash and meandered about with a seemingly aimless waddle reminded Normal-Art of a hobo. Little white bones protruded from gashes just in front of the creature's raggedy ears. Its fluffy tail whipped back and forth behind it like an excited puppy's. It sniffed Normal-Art's lingering orange discharge on the nearby ground, and then it crept up to him and stuck its cute black nose in his face. The nose tickled, and he giggled. He wanted nothing more than to cuddle with the little furball until he felt better.

"*Abgray the irrelsquay*," whispered Tie-Art.

"What?" replied Normal-Art.

The squirrel sniffed Normal-Art's ear. It tickled, and Normal-Art giggled again.

"It's Pig-Latin, you dolt!" whispered Tie-Art, decidedly louder this time. "Now, *abgray the irrelsquay*."

"What?" repeated Normal-Art.

Tie-Art groaned in exasperation. He whispered, "Pig Latin. It's something they teach children on *your* Earth. How do you not know the concept? Move the first letter of the word to the end and add *-ay*. It's not so hard. *Abgray the irrelsquay.*"

The squirrel, just now taking notice of Tie-Art, looked up. Its cute, gentle eyes clouded with something akin to fury, like a tempest appearing on a calm sea. It hissed, and foam shot from its mouth. The foam landed on Tie-Art's shoe, and he sighed. Beverly panicked and scrambled up Tie-Art's shoulder, taking refuge atop the nest of hair on his head. Normal-Art shrugged.

Tie-Art screamed, "Grab the squirrel, you fool! Now!"

The little squirrel attempted to dive under the dumpster, but the prone Normal-Art moved with a speed even he did not realize he possessed. He snatched the airborne, flailing creature by its fluffy tail. It wrenched its body in tight circles, gyrating round and round and reminding Normal-Art of a ragged brown helicopter rotor. Normal-Art stared, hypnotized by the thrashing brown madness caught within his smelly brown grip and inanely wondering if the spinning was fast enough to provide liftoff.

"Now use your other hand to clamp its jaws together so it can't call for help. And don't let the bugger bite you," ordered Tie-Art. He held up his right hand, revealing to Normal-Art a web of deep red scars. "Once they grab hold, they don't let go so easy."

"OK," replied Normal-Art, clamping down on the creature's jaw. It seemed an odd thing to notice in such an odd situation, but Normal-Art realized that the itchy gorilla-gloves had stopped itching. "All clamped. But what am I supposed to do with the furball now? And you never answered my question from before, when I asked you where we are."

"For now, just keep it quiet until we can get somewhere safe to interrogate it. And we are on Earth 1,000,000."

"Well, that's a nice, round number," said Normal-Art. "Also, *interrogate it*? It's an animal. Are the people on this Earth squirrels or something?"

"Well, this isn't such a nice, round Earth," came Tie-Art's reply. "And no, the people here are not squirrels. The people here are the people here. And they are *little* people."

Tie-Art walked away down the alley. Normal-Art groaned and followed. The furry squirrel thrashed harder, so Normal-Art squeezed a little tighter. He felt the creature's tiny jaw crack. It squirmed with even more fury.

"Hey! Don't kill the furry bastard," said Tie-Art. "We need him alive. Be careful in those gloves. You're stronger than you can imagine."

Normal-Art wondered how Tie-Art had heard the bone break. It had been a miniscule little snap, and Normal-Art did not even think it had been audible. He shrugged and decided to change the subject. "Where are we going?"

"I set up a safe-house nearby. We're going there to chat with our new friend."

Tie-Art, Beverly, Normal-Art, and the squirrel turned left at the end of the alleyway and picked up their pace. Normal-Art found it an awfully peculiar experience to walk whilst holding onto a squirming squirrel. He imagined it to be about as difficult as a footballer might find sprinting across the forty-yard line while carrying a pigskin, if only the rest of the pig were still present and furious and thrashing beneath that same skin.

"Where are all the people here?" asked Normal-Art. "It could just be the nausea, but other than our fuzzy friend here, I've yet to see another sign of life."

Tie-Art stopped. He turned around and looked Normal-Art in the eyes. Tie-Art said, "I don't know *where* the people are. Just be thankful that the vengeful bastards weren't on-hand to greet us, and hurry your ass up. We will speak of them and who they are when we are safe."

They crossed two more barren intersections, peeking around the corners of buildings for signs of life before dashing across. Finally, they reached the edge of a large, grassy park. Out in the distance, about two-hundred yards away, a craggy hill rose high into the air amidst the greenery. Atop the hill stood a grove of oak trees, and as the wind whistled through their boughs, they swayed back and forth like a circle of excruciatingly slow children playing the most tediously paced game of *Ring-Around-the-Rosie* ever. The Arts stood on the precipice of the park, as if daring their feet to dive into the bright green grass.

"I've been meaning to ask you, why does your accent sound so terribly fake? I do a god-awful British impersonation, and even that sounds better than you," asked Normal-Art, feeling the need to fill the suffocating silence with noise, any noise at all.

"Can we talk about this later, maybe? We've got a bit of a job here getting across this park, since there's nothing to hide behind to keep us from being spotted."

"Spotted by whom? There's nobody around. What are you so scared of?"

"Please. I'll tell you when we're safe. When I give the say so, sprint to that circle of trees on the hilltop. Got it?"

"Sure," said Normal-Art.

"Go!"

Normal-Art burst into a sprint. He began huffing and puffing before he had even crossed a dozen yards, and his pace slowed considerably. He had never been particularly athletic. As a matter of fact, he had always felt a droll sense of pride about his status as a lazy bum.

Tie-Art left him in the dust. With each stride, Tie-Art covered about ten-feet of turf, though Normal-Art was sure he never even touched the grass. Normal-Art stared at Tie-Art's feet, which hovered inches above the ground and were engulfed in balls of flame. He left smears of soot behind him, shaped exactly like Normal-Art's own feet. Beverly rode atop Tie-Art's head and held onto tufts of his hair like they were reins on a horse. He disappeared from view as he reached the top of the hill and entered the grove.

"Hmmm," said Normal-Art to himself between huffs of breath. "You don't see *that* every day."

Eventually, Normal-Art ascended the hill, too, and finally caught up to Tie-Art in the middle of the grove of trees. Normal-Art collapsed onto the damp grass.

As Normal-Art struggled with dry heaves, Tie-Art approached a nearby oak and shoved his arm deep into a knot in its trunk. Tie-Art's arm disappeared up to the elbow, and a hearty scraping noise escaped from within the oak. Normal-Art then heard a deep, basso CLACK from within the tree, like an oversized deadbolt had been disengaged from a giant's door. Tie-Art pulled his arm free from within the tree, and the ground began to vibrate.

"What's happening?" asked Normal-Art, huffing for breath between each syllable.

"I planted a *Safety Tree* here ages back. I've unlocked it, so it's letting us in."

The soft dirt began to bubble from underneath the oak and then flow away from its base. The tree clawed skyward, struggling its way out of the ground. The oak stood up on its gnarled roots, gaining height and revealing a circular door perched in its roots. A crystal doorknob stood in the middle of the door, drinking in the sunlight like a starved glutton. Normal-Art stared in awe at the flawless beauty of it.

The awe, Normal-Art decided later, was probably what caused the next sequence of events to occur. He did not notice that he had relaxed his grip on his furry prisoner. The squirrel, however, did. It wriggled its head free of his left hand. Its jaw hung loosely from its skull, and it looked like a fluffy blowfish as it inhaled a comically enormous lungful of air. And without warning, it expelled the air in an ear-piercing scream.

The squirrel's scream resounded across the park like a high-pitched siren. A blue light appeared in the peripheral of Normal-Art's vision. This light was followed by a squelchy yelp from within his hands. He looked down and saw that he was now gripping a squirrel with no head. Beverly had zapped the creature. Normal-Art dropped the carcass to the ground, and it thudded atop the grass. He wiped off his bloody hands on his pants.

Tie-Art rushed over to Normal-Art and poked him twice in the chest. Normal-Art winced at the stinging blows.

"What were you thinking?" demanded Tie-Art. "I *told* you to keep that thing clamped tight and quiet until we got to safety!"

"S-Sorry?"

"We're all gonna be sorry if there are any more of those bloody rodents about."

Unfortunately for Art and company, there were plenty of those bloody rodents about. And their creepy red eyes were the first thing Normal-Art noticed as thousands of them scurried into view, many running up the hill the Arts had just ascended and many others darting down from the surrounding treetops.

Normal-Art gulped. Tie-Art cursed. The squirrels chittered.

CHAPTER 8

CHIRP-CHIRP-CHIROO

MISTER E SAT atop Tiny-Ginny's shoulder. His vision bounced to-and-fro as his perch waddled through the dark gravel streets, clambering her way toward the assembly she had called for her tribe and that annoying Russian's tribe from the adjacent village.

Mister E wanted to groan, but he could not. He did not want to sit through another tedious meeting. As a matter of fact, he did not want to do most things he had been forced to do since this tiny hag had waddled into his life. He wished for nothing more than to be put out of his misery.

Mister E's name was not actually Mister E. Nor was it Eduardo, as his master constantly claimed. As a matter of fact, he thought the whole Mister E name was rather stupid. Near as he could tell, it was an idiotic pun on the human word *mystery*, a genre of book for which his ghastly master had an affinity.

But he was not a mystery at all, nor was he a book. He was a squirrel. And to top the whole idiotic ordeal off, he was quite sure that she had named him Eduardo simply because it was the first name that started with an *E* to pop into her head. It was all exceptionally stupid, and it was orchestrated by a cruel woman with an infantile sense of humor.

Mister E had lived the first half of his ill-fated life with a beautifully *appropriate* name within his culture. He was Chirp-Chirp-Chiroo. His existence as Chirp-Chirp-Chiroo ended decades ago when the bitch plummeted to this planet inside a mammoth meteorite formed from sulfur and lightning, manifesting here in the same manner that all the tiny humans living on this world had manifested before her.

During her arrival, she had crashed right through his home, which was located on the outskirts of what his people called *The Forest of Never-ending Light*, or Chiroopey-Chi-Chi-Chi-Ooey in the squirrel tongue. Chirp-Chirp-Chiroo had been out on a foraging expedition and was returning home with treats of sweetness for his wife and young children when he witnessed the destruction.

He dropped the treats to the ground, where they landed with a soft thud, and he dashed inside his home, located inside a knot in the third largest tree in the forest. He found his family incinerated, their lifeless skeletons staring at him with looks of total bewilderment. Oh, how Chirp-Chirp-Chiroo had then raged, and how xenophobia at these invading dwarves had gripped his heart in its hateful grasp.

He sprinted from the charred remains of his home in the knot of the oak and leapt in anguished fury at the still-dazed ball of dwarf lying prone on the brown soil. He chomped down upon her coarse skin, piercing her flesh and drawing blood. He had planned to bite over and over until the bitch was dead, but her hand snaked out from her side and snatched him by the neck. He squealed and thrashed like he had never thrashed before, but she simply ignored him and whispered something into his ear in a language unfamiliar to him. After she stopped speaking, he found that he could no longer move a single muscle.

"I shall call you Eduardo," she had proclaimed, her atrocious breath assaulting his nose. "And Mister E when I'm feeling rather saucy, for I shall never understand why you would attack someone as magnificent as me. And you shall henceforth be my minion, unto the end of your cute, furry little life."

And from that moment forward, he had not known a single second in which he was in control of his own body. When Ginny decided it was time for him to jump, she would simply motion some secret signal with her hand. He did not even have to ask how high, for his body performed the action on its own. When Ginny wanted him to act insane and roll his eyes around in their sockets for her amusement, she waved her hand in a different manner, and he did so.

She had even performed a strange, sacrilegious surgery on him in which she had attached gigantic antennae to his head. After she had done so, she often forced him to travel with her to different dimensions. And each time she wanted to go, she performed yet a different motion with her hand, and his body was ravaged by the Multiverse to be used as the conduit for her mystical portals. He wished he could throw himself from the top of a high cliff.

When his master had shuffled with him up to the bigger Ginny's door, he felt an impending sense of doom. He had thrilled at the sensation, hoping against hope that this dreadful hunch would come true, that this larger woman would finally mean death for him and freedom from his slavery.

Sitting on his master's shoulder now, on the way to the assembly that his master had called, he forced himself to focus on the doomed sensation, that instinctual swirling dread in the pit of his gut that screamed out to him that something was wrong. It overjoyed him, and he wished he could turn to the larger Ginny and give her his most thankful smile. But he could not, so he simply sat upon Ginny's crooked shoulder and waited. He hoped that Death would not make him wait too long. But he suspected that it would, for Death had always been a right bastard to him.

CHAPTER 9

ROCK YOU LIKE A SQUIRREL-CANE!

IT WAS NOW deep into the night, and Normal-Art had not been able to move for hours. Tight hempen cords stretched across nearly every square inch of his body, each held fast to the ground by a tiny wooden stake. Normal-Art tried not to think about what had happened after his flub with the squirrel, but like a bad flashback, he could not force the horrid visions from his mind.

After the squirrel in his hand had howled, Normal-Art and Tie-Art had been surrounded by red eyes, which appeared all around them like thousands of ships emerging from thick fog.

The squirrels seemed to meld together into a force of nature—a furry hurricane—as they hurtled into the two men and bowled them over. Once the duo lay prone upon the ground, the rodents held them down and bound them from head to toe with such synchronicity that it seemed to Normal-Art that the rodents must have done this a million times before.

Tie-Art screamed and made threats during the attack, struggling and thrashing and doing his damnedest to fight off the surge of squirrels. Normal-Art, meanwhile, did nothing but stare at his attackers. He knew that he *should* be terrified and that he *should* fight for his life, but fear never crossed his mind. He simply found himself overtaken with amazement at their cooperation, communication, and ability to use tiny hammers and stakes. He felt a lot like Gulliver in the land of the Lilliputians, with the main difference between them being that Normal-Art had a constant, nagging concern about rabies.

Beverly fought valiantly, zapping squirrels with lightning from her antennae until she became too exhausted and drained to zap any longer. When she realized that the fight was hopeless and that she was too outnumbered to win, she tried to retreat by flying away. But as soon as she fluttered into the air, reinforcements from the trees acted as squirrel-kamikazes, diving head-first at her until so many of them had pummeled her that she could no longer stand, let alone take to the air in flight.

The squirrels had tied Normal-Art's head in place so that the back of his head was flat upon the ground. He could not turn his head, but he found that if he strained his eyes as hard as he could to the side, he could watch Beverly struggle against the odds. As he did so, a dull headache grew behind his eyeballs, stretching and weaving its painful roots down into his skull like a terrible mushroom infestation. Despite the pain, he forced himself to witness Beverly's struggle, though afterward he wished he had not.

A bundle of squirrels sat on Beverly's head, weighing it down so that she could not raise it from the ground. A trio of squirrels held onto the ends of each of her legs, acting as furry ankle weights to completely immobilize her. But Beverly nevertheless continued to thrust and squirm, and at one point, she bucked so hard that all the legs ripped from the left side of her abdomen. Green jelly squirted from the wounds in an arc that cut through the air like a puke-green rainbow, and the sudden loss of tension on her left side threw off the balance of the squirrels atop her. They tumbled off her, and the squirrels holding her remaining legs lost their grips, and like a miracle delivered from some cockroach deity, Beverly was free.

But irony laughed in her little bug face. As hard as she tried to scurry away, with half of her legs gone she could only manage to loop in a sad, small circle. The squirrels gained their positions back atop her before she completed two of the oblong laps.

The rodents giddily ripped Beverly's wings from her thorax. They stripped her bare, right down to her beautiful blue tattoos. The tattooed runes shimmered with pale electricity as she struggled to work up the energy for another surge, but like an electrical socket that tries to handle too much wattage, the electricity winked out as quickly as it started. Some fuse inside her simply flipped off. Gelatinous green blood poured from the gaping wounds on her back. She thrust once more up onto her remaining legs, and then she sputtered to the ground with a tiny whimper.

Her face crashed to the grass under the weight of the squirrels perched atop her head. The rodents sitting there became a howling crown of furry thorns as they pierced her exoskeleton with their angry paws. They snatched her antennae in their forepaws and squeaked excitedly. Their eyes gleamed with insane bloodlust, and as the rodents ripped her antennae from her head, her sickly greenish blood spattered more blotchy stains across the grass. Beverly soon lay motionless, a gooey bag of lifeless exoskeleton.

Throughout the entire ordeal, Tie-Art never stopped screaming, nor did he stop cursing. Normal-Art lost count of the curse words after Tie-Art changed languages for the eighth time. Normal-Art did not think his current string of curses could even be human. Tie-Art's voice seemed to originate simultaneously from his belly button and nipples, for guttural sounds whistled from them like they had become furious teapots.

The veins in Tie-Art's neck throbbed, and his normally pale skin turned beet-red. Fire burned in his eyes. He released another bloodcurdling scream and thrust more fiercely against the ropes, but the ropes did not budge, and whenever one of the stakes even threatened to loosen, a squirrel standing guard quickly hammered it back down. Normal-Art wished he could cover his ears.

And then the duo lay there for hours, Tie-Art constantly screaming and cursing, Normal-Art lying motionless, and the squirrels sitting vigil around them. The squirrels rose onto their hind legs and began chittering howls at the sky. Their noises reminded Normal-Art of a car alarm, and he wished that he might go deaf so he would not have to hear them any longer.

As time stretched on and on, boredom seeped from Normal-Art's every pore, interrupted only when he heard a twig snap on the other side of his head. At the sound of the twig, the squirrels stopped their howling and dispersed, some into the trees and some down the hill. Tie-Art did not cease cursing.

Normal-Art whipped his pupils around to see what was happening over where he had heard the breaking twig. Purple dots clouded his vision as he strained his eyes to see. He stared past tall blades of grass, some of which were vying to obscure his view while others were attempting to tickle the back of his neck into oblivion. A mob of leather boots burst through the underbrush, backlit by dozens of torches. Art's pupils were drawn to the flames like moths to an electric bug zapper. Each time he blinked, the tiny, purple dots in his vision swirled with the afterimages of the flames, creating an annoying raving dance party on the backs of his eyelids that muddled his view of the scene playing out before him.

The booted mass of flesh spread out from the underbrush to encircle the two Arts. Normal-Art squinted, trying to ignore the afterimages of the torches so that he might identify the people attached to the boots. When he was finally able to do so, he could not quite be sure that his eyes were telling him the truth. He wished he could rub them. He stifled a chuckle.

The mob consisted of dozens of male dwarves. They were sized and shaped exactly like the dwarves from the *Lord of the Rings* movies, except they were wearing costumes identical to the Girl Scout uniform that he had bought for his niece last Christmas. Most of the dwarves sported thick mustachios, which danced with ferocity in the wavering breeze. A few had faces smooth as silk, though Art noted to himself that they were so ugly that they probably *should* cover their faces with mustachios.

One of the little Scouts took two steps forward. He clicked his heels together like a well-disciplined military man, and then he stood at attention. A ragged brown squirrel missing patches of fur from its face stood on his shoulder, also at attention. The dwarf cleared his throat, creating a gruff noise that sounded like mossy bark scraping together. His mustache was trimmed tightly, stretching only the width of his nostrils. Normal-Art could not quite place where he had seen the little man's face. It looked familiar, but rather odd, as though some unknown force had taken a famous mug shot of some infamous person and stretched it over a lopsided potato.

"Gutentag, outvorlders," said the potato-headed scout with the tiny mustache, his accent unmistakably German. "Prepare to face*: Zhe Assembly!*"

"Pretty brave talk," called out Tie-Art from beside Normal-Art, "for a man who took the easy way out and put a bullet in his head before facing his own assembly."

The tiny Scout's tongue flitted out of his mouth and licked his tiny mustache. The reflection of the torch in his hand burned in his pupils, and it created such an ominous image that Normal-Art feared that fireballs might actually launch from the dark things to engulf everything in the area.

"You shall regret your insolence," said the dwarf. The hatred spewing from the tiny man was palpable, and Normal-Art felt he might become angry himself just from breathing in the surrounding air.

The German Scout's lower lip quivered below his tiny mustache, and his tongue flicked out from his mouth again, a red snake slithering amongst the dwarf's reedy mustache. He looked past the detained Arts to the surrounding tribe of dwarves in Girl Scout uniforms. Normal-Art's heart thumped in his chest so loudly that it sounded like some prehistoric tribe were nearby beating on a war drum. He moaned.

"Pizarro, it is time to earn your…how do you call it? Your *Hatchet Badge*," muttered the German Scout.

Normal-Art heard footsteps behind him, little thump-thumps crunching across the hard grass. The footsteps paused, and a louder, sickening, different sort of crunch forced Normal-Art to focus his eyes back the other way, behind him and away from the Scout with the German accent. A hatchet stood erect from Tie-Art's forehead, planted like a bloody flagpole in his skull. Gray and crimson clumps now littered the surrounding grass, little islands of brain matter overgrown with hairy trees.

Normal-Art felt his pants grow warm as a river sprang forth within them. He whimpered. The little footsteps leapt over Tie-Art's body and began thump-thumping through the grass straight at him. Despair welled inside him. He desperately did not want a hatchet to be buried in his skull, but he could do nothing to prevent it from happening. He was but a lone stranger in a tiny, strange, murderous land.

Normal-Art compelled his pupils to focus away from the ominous, thumping footsteps, and back toward the German Scout. If Art was about to catch a hatchet in the skull, he sure as hell did not want to see it coming. Nausea washed through his stomach. He forced himself to study the Scout's face, attempting to keep his mind off his impending doom. The German dwarf's thin lips parted, revealing a crooked smile beneath the thin dark mustache. Art moved his eyes down the German's body, stopping when they came to rest on the dwarf's hand.

The German's tiny mitt now clung to his own hatchet, identical to the one standing erect in Tie-Art's skull. The sharp head of the German's hatchet gleamed in the torchlight.

Art whimpered again, realizing that Death was about to claim him no matter where he looked. The dwarf lifted the blade above his head and giggled, an odd *tee-hee-hee* that drifted aimlessly amongst the surrounding darkness. The German hurled the hatchet at Art. It flashed in the dim light of the torches and screamed through the air.

Another whimper escaped Art's lips. He closed his eyes and allowed blackness to envelop him.

CHAPTER 10

GATHERING DWARVEN RECRUITS

BEFORE DEPARTING THE cabin, Tiny-Ginny sent Mister E to summon one of her lieutenants. When he arrived, he stood at attention in the doorway. A scraggly brown squirrel stood in mirrored attention on his shoulder. Tiny-Ginny strode over to her minion and conferred with him for a few minutes. He was a dwarf with a tiny mustache stretching barely wider than his nostrils. Much like Tiny-Ginny, he was burly and built like a Hill Dwarf from the fantasy roleplaying games that Regular-Ginny often played as a teen. The squirrel's face had been groomed identically to the minion's, with the fur just above its mouth shaved so that it only had a strip of hair there the width of its nostrils.

Tiny-Ginny spoke to the mustached dwarf in a guttural language that Regular-Ginny did not understand. Soon, he turned, clicked his heels together, and stomped away.

"What was that about?" demanded Regular-Ginny.

Tiny-Ginny arched an eyebrow. She replied, "I just ordered Hitler to gather a warband and hunt the Arts. Bit of a lickspittle, that one."

"*Hitler*?" asked Regular-Ginny. "What do you mean, *Hitler*?"

For the entire hours-long hike to the assembly, and even as they mounted the stage from which they were to present to the crowd, Regular-Ginny asked over and over what Tiny-Ginny had meant by the remark about Hitler. But her counterpart ignored her.

Instead of answering the question, Tiny-Ginny focused on her upcoming speech. She recited it to herself over and over during the hike. When the pair arrived at the assembly site, she stood atop the stage and continued reciting it to herself. She harped reminders to Regular-Ginny about the taller woman's role in the presentation whenever she reached the appropriate parts of her speech.

Now that they were on the stage, Regular-Ginny gave up on receiving an answer to her question about Hitler. She resigned herself to halfheartedly nodding at each of Tiny-Ginny's reminders. She sat in silence while the crowd slowly gathered, a slog that Tiny-Ginny had warned her would take hours. She mostly passed the time by twiddling her thumbs and playing with pink goo that she willed to emerge from her pores.

Deep into the night, the final trickles of dwarves approached the assembly from the surrounding wilderness and seated themselves on the grass amongst their thousands of compatriots. The gathered dwarves—some having been here all day waiting for the remainder of their compatriots to arrive—sat waiting so impatiently for the assembly to begin that they looked fit to mutiny. Just when the first dwarf stood to do so, Tiny-Ginny nodded toward the culprit and whispered to Regular-Ginny, "That would be the leader of my neighboring tribe. It's time for us to get started."

Regular-Ginny nodded. She stepped forward, toward the edge of the rickety wooden stage. She stared at the mismatched planks beneath her feet, mesmerized at how this stage could hold together with such shoddy construction and awkward angles.

Then she glanced out at the thousands of surly faces assembled before her, and she realized that even *with* the power of her new pink god flowing through her veins, she remained powerless to overcome her fear of crowds.

Regular-Ginny gulped. She *knew* what she needed to do. The pink in her veins writhed in anticipation. But her stomach tied in knots. She bit her lower lip and *tried* to act. But anxiety overwhelmed her, and she hesitated.

Then she felt a painful twisting inside her skull, like some invisible hands had grabbed her brain and had begun twisting it into a pretzel. She felt every atom inside her seize and contract. She leaned to her side and spewed black bile from her mouth in a torrent that seemed like it would never end. It felt as though the weakest parts of her soul were being forcefully expunged from her. The black bile splattered onto the stage near her feet and dripped between the wooden slats.

Finally, the twisting and the seizing and the spewing stopped. Ginny stood upright. A buzzing energy replaced the twisting inside her skull, and it felt like the fluid in her brain had been swapped with a hyper-caffeinated, neon energy drink. She closed her eyes and inhaled deeply. She realized with sudden clarity that the anxiety and nervousness had been evacuated from her body. Her hesitation was gone. Stark, pink, callous ferocity had replaced it.

From the pores on her back flooded pink ooze, forming itself into a colossal tentacle that stretched above her head. It was thick at the base, but it thinned to a pointed tip as it reached higher and higher into the air. Ginny ground her teeth and willed the tip of the tentacle to bend down into the crowd and snatch the mutinying dwarf by the scruff of his neck. The dwarf flailed his arms and legs.

"We keel you! We keel you!" shouted the dwarf in a thick Russian accent. He had an overlarge nose and thick black hair that had been slicked back and a bushy mustache. "Attack, my comrades! Attack!

The other dwarves in the crowd began screaming in protest at the snatching of one of their own. Regular-Ginny launched another round of the pliable pinkness from her fingertips, creating a new pink arm with a massive, ham-sized hand that extended from each of her fingers. The fingers on the ends of each new arm flexed and stretched, popping knuckles and acquainting themselves with the world around them. She willed the oversized hands on the ends of these arms to grab the angry, dangling dwarf by the base of the skull and by the lower torso, holding him motionless.

"Be silent and listen to us!" yelled Tiny-Ginny to the crowd.

Tiny-Ginny yelled the command three more times, but the crowd did not fall silent. Just as Tiny-Ginny had warned during their planning, the gathered dwarves would not listen until she and her counterpart did something drastic.

"Quit stallin' and be silent, or we shall execute this Communist bastard!" ordered Tiny-Ginny, grinning an impish grin as though she had just told the most hilarious joke ever. Regular-Ginny shrugged.

The crowd stood on its feet and erupted into angry howls. Tiny-Ginny nodded to Regular-Ginny, the cue that it was time to implement their planned drastic feat. Before Regular-Ginny could even *consider* hesitating again, the Pink One whispered directly into her brain, demanding a sacrifice of violence to seal the pact between them, to make official the promise of mutual service to one another. The pinkness stirred within her heart, rippling hatred from her core out to the tips of her fingers and toes. She nodded.

Regular-Ginny put her new pink limbs to work. The oversized hands encircling the dwarf's torso clamped tight, as the other hands around the base of his skull yanked upward. His head ripped from his body with a satisfying pop, reminding Regular-Ginny of the refreshing sound of popping the cap on a cold soda can. And just like the soda inside a can that has been vigorously shaken, crimson blood erupted from the newly headless body, spattering red rain down upon the Ginnys. The disembodied head mouthed, "Keel you!" once more before its lifeless eyes rolled back in its head. Regular-Ginny dropped the headless body, and it thudded to the stage. She tossed the head at the feet of the crowd. It rolled to a stop near the front row.

The crowd gasped. Regular-Ginny grew two more pink tentacles from her back and snatched three random dwarves from the crowd. She dangled them upside down by their feet.

"Rush them! The bitches cannot handle us all at once!" squealed one of the dangling dwarves to the crowd. This dwarf's hair was blond, and his thick braids of mustachios dangled from his face to tickle the stage. His face reddened as anger and blood rushed to his head.

Tiny-Ginny nodded to Regular-Ginny once more. Regular-Ginny lifted all three dwarves higher into the air. The two other captives apologized for the brashness of the blond, groveling for their lives. The blond continued to plead with the crowd to attack, but his squeaky voice fell silent when Regular-Ginny slapped all three of them down onto the stage. Gore splashed out onto the first few rows of dwarves. The pink inside Regular-Ginny tickled her heart, and as she looked at the spattered gore, the scene made her chuckle. It was as though she were participating in some tragic and bloody Gallagher routine. She even considered naming the shtick the *Dwarf-o-Matic.*

Before the dwarves in the front of the crowd had time to wipe away the gore, Regular-Ginny snatched three more of them, dangling them even higher above the stage than the three previous victims. These three did not say a word, but simply stared at the ruptured carcasses below them. The remaining dwarves in the crowd moved not at all.

"We are the prophets of your new god," yelled Tiny-Ginny into the newly fallen silence. "Fall to your knees and listen."

The dwarves fell to their knees and stayed quiet.

Before Tiny-Ginny could begin reciting the meat of her speech, a scraggly brown squirrel darted between the dwarves and scrambled up onto the stage. Its fur was matted with blood, and gashes were visible across its hide. The fur just above its mouth had been shaved so that it only had a strip of hair there the width of its nostrils. Regular-Ginny glanced at Tiny-Ginny and mouthed, "*What do you want me to do? This isn't part of the plan!*"

Tiny-Ginny signaled for Regular-Ginny to wait a moment. The squirrel clambered up onto Tiny-Ginny's shoulder and chittered frantically into her ear. When it finished saying whatever it needed to say, it collapsed to the ground. It breathed no more.

Tiny-Ginny closed her eyes and inhaled. She appeared to be collecting her thoughts. A few moments later, she opened her eyes and nodded for Regular-Ginny to continue. As planned, Regular-Ginny released the three dangling dwarves now that the crowd had submitted to them. The trio crashed to the stage, splashing loudly in the gore of the first four hapless victims. They scurried away, leaving crimson prints in their wake.

"As I was saying, we are the prophets of your new god. And we demand your cooperation on its behalf," said Tiny-Ginny in a voice so loud that it sounded like it blared from a house-sized speaker. Regular-Ginny noticed a thick layer of pink ooze coating her counterpart's tongue and seeping from the corners of her mouth. She assumed this was what accounted for her counterpart's otherworldly volume. She shrugged.

"A pair of intruders has invaded this world, and they threaten to bring destruction upon us all," warned Tiny-Ginny. She pointed at Regular-Ginny and continued, "*We* know where they are headed, and *we* know what they seek. They seek to steal our new, pink god. This deity has contacted my counterpart to ask for our protection, and as you can see, in exchange it has given us power far beyond your squirrel-talk and Scout lessons. It has promised us *all* great power for our help, and we must answer this call. We must journey as an army to this deity, and we must abscond with it without allowing the intruders to lay their hands upon it. Or they shall harness the deity's power for themselves, and we will be left with nothing but *death*."

Crickets chirped. Tiny-Ginny scowled. She pointed at the dead squirrel and said, "Hours ago, I sent our Nazi colleague to hunt for the intruders. His slave-squirrel *just* arrived to inform me that the intruders have brutally ripped the Nazi and his entire hunting party into pieces. This squirrel was the lone survivor."

Regular-Ginny was only half-paying attention, and when the pinkness within her began writhing in fury and screaming angrily inside her brain, she realized that Tiny-Ginny was in the process of calling an audible on the content of the speech, an audible that the Pink One had not approved.

Tiny-Ginny said, "I knew one of these intruders in my existence *prior* to arriving on this prison. He is more powerful than anyone on this Earth, and we *must* stop him. If we do not protect our pink god from him, then he shall harness its power and do to us all what he did to our Nazi colleague. He is worth a *multitude* of badges and *much* prestige. And it shall be awarded to whoever captures them and brings them before me.

"These murdering intruders can't have gotten far," continued Tiny-Ginny. "We are an army thousands-strong—much stronger together than the Nazi's single hunting party—and they can't overcome us *all* at once! So, raise the war cry and unleash the squirrels. Go find them! The first to bring them to me shall enjoy a night beneath my sheets! And then, once they are safely dealt with, we shall travel to our new, pink god and share in its bountiful blessings of power!"

The crowd erupted in howls and cheers, and then it sprinted away in every direction, each Scout apparently sexually repressed and rabid for Tiny-Ginny's bed. Regular-Ginny grabbed Tiny-Ginny by the sleeve and pulled her aside.

"What are you doing? Why are you sending them away? This isn't what we discussed!" squealed Regular-Ginny into her counterpart's ear, the Pink One whispering talking points into her brain. "Screw Art and his stupid twin! We already tried it your way with your stupid hunting party—and we *wasted* those minions! We should have taken this army and left for the Pink One at once! Art and his twin couldn't have bothered us on our quest with thousands of dwarves surrounding us!"

"That absolutely is *not* true," responded Tiny-Ginny. "As I told you before, we must obliterate the Arts *tonight*. When they were not delivered to us as planned, I *changed* our plans. If my Art has escaped, he's already plotting, and he has the capability to foil our schemes no matter how large our army. If I must delay our plans to prevent him from disappearing into the shadows, then I refuse not to try."

Regular-Ginny's brain buzzed harder than ever as the pinkness writhed in fury. "The Pink One does not like it."

"I know," replied Tiny-Ginny. "I feel it, too. But the Pink One does not know *my* Art, so the Pink One must be patient. My Art has already committed some drastic act using his black arts, I can sense it. I've felt a change in the air and a shift in the makeup of the world around us. They are nearby, not more than ten miles away."

The howling of the once-assembled dwarves faded into the distance. "This is maddening," said Regular-Ginny. "The Pink One is inside my brain, buzzing directions to me, telling me to go south *right now*. The Pink One is half a world away. You said yourself that we *know* the Arts are here. Right here, within a ten-mile radius. We can beat them to the Pink One with ease, and then we won't need to worry about the Arts ever again. We don't *need* to waste time on them."

"But this is a tiny world," said Tiny-Ginny. "And I'm not going to risk allowing them to go free now, solely on the *belief* that we're more equipped to reach the Pink One first. It's too risky."

Regular-Ginny sighed in frustration. She struggled to speak over the furious, pink buzzing in her brain. "Whatever. All the talking in the world won't change decisions that've already been made. Those dwarves are running wild all over the forest now, and there's no way we could get them all back here anytime soon, even if we tried."

"There is another reason I set them on this task, you know. When our Arts were not delivered to us as planned, I had an epiphany," said Tiny-Ginny. "There's got to be more to our mission than simply showing up and walking away with the Pink One. Otherwise, why wouldn't somebody have done so *already*? I've been here a long time and I've been in the presence of some monstrous people. There is only one place on this Earth that has not yet been completely and thoroughly ransacked. And when it hit me where we must be going on our quest, I knew that our original idea to merely use my tribe and the Russian's tribe as cannon fodder would be disastrous. It was expedient, but it was flawed from the start. We need something grander."

"I seriously do not understand."

Tiny-Ginny sighed. "I don't care. Ask the Pink One for her coordinates. I want to confirm whether I'm right. The pink inside me won't answer anything about the Pink One's location. It tells me you're the compass, and that I need to respect this designation."

Regular-Ginny had not tried *asking* the pinkness inside her questions intended for the Pink One. She did now. She silently asked the Pink One whether she might share the coordinates of her location with Tiny-Ginny. The pink within Ginny's heart wriggled horizontally, and she understood that it meant *no*, she would not.

"The Pink One won't share that information with you."

Tiny-Ginny frowned. But then she nodded, "Fine. Then ask her if there is a mythical beast that stalks the wilderness near where she lives."

Regular-Ginny did so. Then she said, "Yeah. There is."

Tiny-Ginny sighed. She said, "That's enough to confirm my fears. I'm glad we didn't rush off following our original plan. We need a whole lot more cannon fodder if we want to have any hope of succeeding."

"I don't understand."

"As you have indicated, the Pink One is located far to the south. There is only one area of this Earth that has not yet been plundered, and it is down there. It is a great wilderness, and it is guarded by a mythical beast that keeps even the most ambitious of us at bay."

"We've already got plenty of cannon fodder with the *thousands* of dwarves that you just sent running off into the forest. We've got this magical pink stuff coming out the wahzoo. What could possibly give *us* trouble?" asked Regular-Ginny.

Tiny-Ginny sighed. "Do you even understand where you are? What reality you're in?"

Regular-Ginny stared at her counterpart with a blank look.

Tiny-Ginny slapped her own forehead. "Do none of the dwarves look familiar to you? Did me speaking with a dwarf named Hitler or you killing a Communist dwarf who looked exactly like your reality's Joseph Stalin not make any lights go off in your addled brain?"

Regular-Ginny continued staring at Tiny-Ginny with a blank look.

Tiny-Ginny slapped her own forehead again. "By the gods, you *are* dull! We were all dictators on our home realities before we died. This is Hell for us. We must spend eternity in little bodies, dressing in ridiculous outfits and vying with one another for power."

"B-But that's stupid."

"Welcome to the Multiverse. Everything in the Multiverse is *stupid*," responded Tiny-Ginny. "But that doesn't matter right now. What does is this: you yourself just killed several dictator-dwarves at the assembly. Do you wonder where the dwarves of this reality go when they die?"

"I'd assume they go to dwarf-Hell or something."

Tiny-Ginny heaved a sigh between the gap in her crooked teeth and slapped herself in the forehead once more. "Just when I think you can't get any stupider, you surprise me. You really, really do," she said. "As I told you mere seconds ago, this reality already *is* Hell for us. And when dictators die here in Hell, their spirits go south, exactly in the direction you're leading us to find the Pink One. They become a part of Death, the harshest dictator of all. I need you to ask the Pink One to confirm whether this hunch is correct, whether Death is the mythical beast lurking in the wilderness near her."

Regular-Ginny did so. She received an affirmative. She relayed it to Tiny-Ginny.

Tiny-Ginny nodded. Then she retrieved a fist-sized stone from her side pocket. The color of the stone shone a deep black, deeper than the deepest black Regular-Ginny had ever laid eyes upon. She thought it was at least twelve times deeper than obsidian. Maybe thirteen. The air surrounding the porous stone seemed distorted and fuzzy, like the area surrounding the mouth of a black hole. Ginny watched a buzzing fly dance near the stone for a few moments, and then she gasped when it was sucked into one of the pores on the stone. She heard a tiny crunch within the mesmerizing rock.

"What's that?" asked Regular-Ginny. "It's beautiful."

"It's my heart, from back before I was a dwarf. Hold onto it. It will protect you from Death, a beast that grows larger every time a dwarf on this reality dies, for each dead dwarf becomes a part of it."

Regular-Ginny took the petrified heart from her alternate-self and put it in her side pocket. It sucked against her leg and attached itself like a barnacle to her thigh. It throbbed against her skin and beat to the same rhythm as her own heart. She worried momentarily about the giant hickey she was going to have when she finally removed the rock from her leg.

"That feels a little odd," said Regular-Ginny, nodding toward the stone heart in her pocket. "What's this rock do that'll save me from Death? Make me immortal?"

"Not exactly," said Tiny-Ginny. "On my home reality, I conquered my pantheon of gods. I seduced the local mischief god and used his life force to transform my heart into a weapon of mass destruction. I turned it into a virtual black hole. I conquered my reality, but I couldn't control my heart. Eventually, it consumed the life force of every living thing in that reality. And then, when there was no more food available for my heart, I died. My soul reformed itself here, and as soon as I could, I returned to my home reality to retrieve my organ."

"Gee, thanks," responded Regular-Ginny. "I get to lug a WMD around in my pocket."

"It's not nearly as powerful as it once was. It sat alone on my home reality for ages, starving. It's mostly dormant, but I've been empowering it little by little, feeding it little things like bugs and baby squirrels."

Regular-Ginny shuddered. "How does it work?" she asked.

Tiny-Ginny smiled a crooked smile. She said, "When you need it, you simply touch it to your skin. It will begin feeding on the soul of anything surrounding you. I've got other tricks up my sleeve to protect me on this reality, but you're virtually helpless if something manages to get past your new pink powers. If Death gets you, pull that bad girl out. It should be powerful enough to repel or consume him, but not yet strong enough to consume this entire reality."

"That's reassuring. But I can tell by the look on your face that there's a catch in here somewhere. What is it?"

"The catch is that I can't stash my heart away somewhere for fear that one of my dwarven colleagues will track it down to harness its power, and I can't keep it on me while we're on our rescue mission, either. If I'm somehow killed *near* Death and I've got the heart on me, the heart might in turn devour the *beast*, and I could potentially knock myself completely out of existence. I'd prefer for that *not* to happen to me."

"So that won't matter for me?" asked Regular-Ginny.

"You were never a tyrant or a dictator. You've never stood over the corpses of millions and thrilled in the tide of their crimson blood. If you die, your soul will flutter away to your home reality and bask in its afterlife."

Regular-Ginny pursed her lips. She did not quite trust her dwarven counterpart, but she kept the heart, anyway. She said, "It's wonderful that I won't be knocked out of existence if I'm killed, but I still don't want to die. How will we get past Death without being killed?"

"It hit me when the dying squirrel scrambled up on stage to talk to me. I don't know if it'll work, but I've got an idea. And it's why we need a bigger army than originally planned, so that we may have legion upon legion of cannon fodder. The more we have, the better our chances of survival."

"OK," responded Regular-Ginny with an air of impatience. "Go on."

"We shall lie to our minions! We'll inform them that the Pink One is being held captive *inside* Death's bowels, and that whoever rescues the Pink One from within Death shall unlock powers even grander than ours. They'll scramble over each other trying to retrieve the Pink One until every single one of them has died. And they'll do so because now that they've seen this pink power in us, they want it, too. It shall be all they'll focus on until they can get it.

"And when they're sufficiently distracted with trying to overwhelm Death to get at the false location *inside* the beast," she continued, "and they've got Death itself distracted by their ridiculous attack, you and I shall sneak away and snatch the Pink One from its *actual* location. So, I must once again reiterate: do not lose my heart. That's what shall save us if our army doesn't slow down Death long enough for us to sneak past it."

"OK, that actually sounds like a decent plan."

"I know it does. *I* thought of it," replied Tiny-Ginny. "The pink tendrils have stopped buzzing angrily in my veins. I take it that means the Pink One agrees with this new plan, right?"

Regular-Ginny asked the pink inside her. The pink responded in the affirmative. Regular-Ginny said, "Seems so. Now, who else should we recruit to join us? Do you have a rolodex or something of contacts for us to call?"

Tiny-Ginny said, "Unfortunately, there is no rolodex for bloodthirsty dictators. There is only diplomacy and war. This land is ruled by tribes of dwarves, each with a dictator overlord who has maimed and killed his way to the top. The men who gathered in our assembly tonight belong to my tribe as well as to that of my nearest neighboring leader, the Russian whom you decapitated. Based on the rules of war on this reality, his troops are now mine.

She continued, "It shall be necessary to spend the next few days recruiting and seducing the leaders of the most powerful tribal armies on this Earth. They rule their armies with iron fists, and if we simply kill them as we did the Russian, their armies will rebel, for they do not know me as the Russian's men do. And while we *could* squelch their rebellions and bring their minions to heel beneath us, we do not have the time to deal with such nonsense. So, we shall convince their leaders to ally themselves with us for the duration of this odyssey, and when it is over, we will murder them if they are not already dead."

"Oh, joy," said Regular-Ginny.

Tiny-Ginny turned and walked back in the direction of her cabin. Mister E chirped maniacally and rolled his eyes. Tiny-Ginny turned back to Regular-

Ginny and said, “Come on. I must gird myself for the sacrifices I shall make to bolster our forces.”

Regular-Ginny stood in the same spot for a few seconds, trying to understand what Tiny-Ginny meant by that statement. Eventually, she gave up. She shrugged, and then she followed the waddling gait of her counterpart.

CHAPTER 11

ART EX MACHINA

ART BARELY OPENED his eyes, squinting through his lids so that his captors would think him unconscious. He thought it might somehow give him an advantage. It reminded him of his childhood, and particularly how when his mother tried to get him to take out the trash, or to fold his laundry, or to milk the family cow, he would use this tactic, pretending he had fainted and closing his eyes to reality like an ostrich with its head buried in the sand. It never worked on his mom.

Here in this strange new dimension, however, each Scout spoke in a different language or in an accent too thick for Art to understand, so if his ruse was not working, he could not really tell. Not that it *really* mattered, because whether they believed him to be unconscious or not, they were carrying him somewhere against his will. And he could do nothing to stop them. Thus, he kept up his ruse just in case it might allow him to surprise someone somehow and allow him to escape. His hopes were not high in that regard.

Art's world had literally turned upside down, but that was probably because he was being carried upside down. The German Scout had used his hatchet not to kill Art as Art had feared, but rather to cut the rigging that had held Art to the ground. He then ordered his underlings to stand Art on his feet and rebind him in hempen ropes so that he was not stuck to the ground. These new ropes encircled him from head to toe, and he felt like a pig in a hempen blanket. After the Scouts were sure Art could not move a muscle, they took the pig analogy even further by sticking a pole through the ropes, allowing two Scouts to hang him over their shoulders and transport him like a couple of fat Hawaiians carrying a roasted pig to a luau.

The Scouts carried Art so that he faced backward. Thus, he could not see where they were carrying him. As a matter of fact, the only thing he could see was the dwarf on pole-duty at the rear of the procession. Through his squinted, nearly closed eyes, Art could make out no details about the dwarf's face other than that it was blackish and mostly fuzzy. The dwarf possessed a limp, swinging Art to-and-fro every time he stepped his right foot upon the ground. And each time he limped, he groaned like a lion with a thorn stuck in its paw.

The limping continued unabated, and as the procession proceeded for what must have been hours, Art found himself rocked into an awkward relaxation. At some point during the rocky trip, as Art's thoughts flittered here and there, he inanely dubbed the groaning dwarf '*Groany.*' But eventually, even Groany's groaning began to fade into the scenery, becoming like the relaxing sounds of waves on a pained seashore. Without realizing that it was happening, Art's breathing became steady and his eyelids became heavy. His mostly-closed-eyelid-ruse caused him to be even more susceptible to sleep than if he had merely kept his eyes open, and before he even realized sleep was upon him, he began snoring.

As Art drifted into unconsciousness, the world shifted from a fuzzy black darkness into a bright blue light, a blue starker than any he had ever experienced. He found himself floating in something that reminded him of blue cotton candy.

Art looked straight up into the cotton candy sky. The sun and moon hung far away in the distance, suspended side-by-side in the blue. Effervescent light danced and twirled before them, flittering down through the air and bathing him in their angelic light. The light filled him with a tranquility he had never known before this moment.

The sun and moon then rolled away in opposite directions, disappearing into the blue as if walking backstage in some grand cosmic play. A celestial pair of buttons rolled into the immense blue to replace the sun and moon, turquoise understudies to match the cotton candy sky. The blue expanse parted horizontally beneath the cosmic buttons, revealing an infinite blackness in the shape of a raggedly stitched teddy bear snout.

Words thundered from the vacuum, and without understanding how, the primal part of Art's brain knew that the language had not been spoken to human ears in millennia. The guttural words bored straight through his skin and bones, shoving their way into his brain. They tugged at his gray matter, poking and prodding inside his head until he understood them. The experience really itched, and Art wished that whatever this cosmic entity was saying, it would have simply spoken English.

"Save Me," the voice said to him in the strange, brain-massaging language.

"Sorry, giant cosmic teddy bear, but I'm a little tied up at the moment," replied Art. At least he thought he replied. He did not remember opening his lips. His brain hurt.

Stars began to rain down from the infinitely deep black gap in the sky. Art wondered why they looked like marshmallows from a cereal he loved as a kid, the one that featured all the symbols of good luck.

"No longer. Art free now. Awake. Save Me."

Art awoke and found himself lying face down on the grass. The rope in which he had been bound lay scattered around him as though he had transformed into a pale butterfly and had burst forth from his rope-cocoon. The pole on which the dwarves had been taxiing him stood upright, one end stuck in the ground.

He glanced about at his surroundings. He lay in a clearing surrounded by brush and trees. On the far end of the open space, a mammoth boulder lay atop the ground. It was bulbous like a petrified mushroom, and it had a brittle top littered with black scorch marks. Old, dusty, equally scorched skulls and bones lay scattered atop it.

Art heard slurping noises behind him. He shivered in the cool night breeze. The full moon shone above him. A panicked sensation began to creep over him, like he was all alone in the presence of something ancient and mystical and terrifying. He felt the urge to run. And then he felt something wet and warm beneath him. When he glanced down, he saw a pool of crimson blood.

"Not yours," a familiar voice called from behind him.

Art turned around. He gasped in surprise. After all he had experienced over the last day, he had not thought he still possessed the ability to gasp in surprise, so he gasped in surprise at that, too.

He stared at something he imagined might come from a terrifying funhouse mirror. His alternate-self stood over him at a height of nine-and-a-half feet tall, with a grave look etched on his face. This expression was emphasized by the blue and orange tendrils of flame that danced skyward from his scalp in place of hair and the cloak he wore about his shoulders made from crudely stitched together hides of white wolves and baby seals. A necklace of disembodied ears strung with a long length of intestine hung around his neck and dangled halfway down his torso, slapping against his belly button. He wore about his waist a belt made from a thick strand of rope. Attached to his belt were the dagger he had taken from the weapons crate, a leather pouch, and multiple tools crafted from the finest obsidian, among them an ice pick and a hammer.

Normal-Art's alternate-self stood with his jaw unhinged like a python, and he began shoving a dwarven thighbone into his mouth, sucking the limb down his throat inch-by-gag-inducing-inch. Moments later, it made an audible splash when it fell into his stomach.

"What *happened*?" asked Normal-Art, his face pale with confusion.

Art's alternate-self belched. Art heard terrified screams emanate from deep within the belch. "I rescued you," replied the giant.

"I can see that. How?"

"Mostly by surprise. And violence. Lots and lots of violence."

Art sighed. "But I watched you die."

"Deus ex machina."

"What?"

"Deus ex machina. *God from the machine.* It's a term from your reality. In your ancient Greek tragedies, when a god appears from nowhere to solve the characters' problems, it's called deus ex *bloody* machina. That's me, and I'm back to solve ours."

"I'm still confused."

"It's not hard to understand, mate. I'm a god."

"Of course," responded Normal-Art, not quite knowing how else to answer.

"It's true. On my reality, we're the primary god of mischief. This is what I look like without any reality-altering disguises. *This* is my most pure avatar. Usually, I choose to appear to people how they want to see me. When I met you, you wanted someone specific knocking on your door. Thus, I used my powers to appear as part of that caste."

"So, you looked like a Jehovah's Witness because I wanted to *see* a Jehovah's Witness?"

"Exactly," replied God-Art.

"But why?"

"I thought it was quite obvious by now. To get you to do what I wanted. I'm a mischief god. That's what I do."

"If you're a god, then why do you need *me* for anything?"

"I told you from the beginning," said God-Art, "I need you to watch my back. You've done a pretty poor job of it so far, I might add."

"Sorry," muttered Normal-Art.

"All's forgiven, mate. Turns out it was for the best. I had the opportunity to travel to my reality's underworld, which just so happens to be located inside my stomach. If you get a few months free sometime, then I'll tell you the story of how that came to be. It's quite good. Fine, fine. I can tell when someone is being impatient. I'll tell it now. It started on my eleventh birthday, before I'd begun to grow my man bear—"

"God, I don't care about how you got your stupid underworld belly! I almost died at the hands of some pissed off dwarf and his cronies, so I hope you can understand that my patience is gone. Absolutely gone. Just get on with the story you were *already* telling! The one about how you freed me!"

"Some pissed off dwarf named *Hitler* and his cronies, to be exact," muttered God-Art.

"What?" asked Normal-Art.

"Nothing. I'll get to it later. Sorry for getting off task, mate. Telling tales is my godly duty, and sometimes I get carried away. Now, where was I?" mused God-Art, scratching his head for obvious dramatic effect. Normal-Art strongly considered slapping him, but he was afraid he would burn himself on his alternate-flaming-head.

"Oh, yes," continued God-Art. "I descended to the depths of the underworld, traveling as a spirit down my own throat, and upon reaching the gates, I called out for a parley with the king of the underworld. He's a real ornery bugger, nothing but an up-jumped imp by the name of Tiny Albert who's got a permanent chip on his shoulder because he's short.

"The bastard wouldn't make a deal with me or listen to anything I had to say," God-Art droned on, "though I can't say I blame him too much. 'Twas most likely on account of that time I seduced his mother and then convinced her to cut off her own head. Ha, ha! That was a laugh! Still carry her head around in my pocket, too, but I'm sure you wouldn't want to see it. One look from her'll transform a mortal's bones into vanilla pudding. She makes for a pretty decent oracle despite all that, though she's bit of a foul mouth."

Normal-Art glared at God-Art and grunted an angry grunt. God-Art ignored it.

"Anyway, Albert hung a noose around my neck and sentenced me to the fourth layer of the Colon, where I was to be hung amongst the smell of rotting, half-digested onions forevermore. He must've forgotten that he'd done this to me way back in my reality's Bronze Age, so I already knew how to escape. On my journey out of the Pit, I managed to steal his coveted necklace of sorcerers' ears, which allows me to think about any place in existence and hear what's currently happening there," concluded God-Art, pinching and fluttering his spindly fingers amongst the rubbery ears that dangled on the string of intestine about his neck. "Pretty useful, if I do say so m'self."

"So, you died and came back to life?" offered Normal-Art. He said the words aloud, but he was not quite sure how to react. For some reason, he had not expected his first encounter with a mythological being to be with one quite so utterly ridiculous. He had expected gods to be a at least *slightly* more regal.

"Yeah, it happens quite a lot. It's part of my god-cycle. If I'm not killed off every couple years, I die anyway and then resurrect myself. It's necessary for me, but painful as hell. My godfather cursed me as his dying wish. He made it so that the longer I walk the mortal world, the more forgetful I become. When I recruited you," said God-Art, stroking his fingers through his flaming hair, "it had been a long time since I'd died. Too long, actually, and I'd forgotten a lot about myself. Now I remember why we're here."

"Care to let me in on the big to-do?" asked Normal-Art.

God-Art strummed his fingers across his chin, and then tugged at the ear-necklace. "I think you know by now. I listened in on the little dream you were having, and I've a feeling you've been dreaming about that cosmic blue nutjob every time you've closed your eyes since you met me."

"Wait, we actuall*y are* going to rescue a cosmic blue teddy bear?"

"Not just any blue bear. The key to eternal power."

"I don't care about power," replied Normal-Art. "Right now, I just want to go home and never get off my couch again."

"And that's why, of all the Arts in all the realities, I chose *you* to help me. You're my brother in essence, but totally blank in spirit."

"Yeah, yeah, blah blah blah. Cut the brother bullshit. I ain't gonna bond with you or whatever. I'm here, and I've got to help you if I ever want to get home again. That's about the gist of it, right?"

God-Art shrugged. "That about sums it up," he said.

"Then what's the plan?"

"I've listened in on your lady-partner, too, and she's at an assembly right now, here on this reality. Seems the natives know we're here. They were planning to have our captors drag you before this assembly and then sacrifice you to some second-rate pink god. Hence why you were wrapped in ropes and being hauled away. But I think the stupid bastards must've gotten us confused. I think they thought they'd killed *you* and had kidnapped *me*, because it would make no sense to drag a regular mortal before an assembly to sacrifice to a god when you have the opportunity to sacrifice a god to a god. Your soul wouldn't even amount to a tiny snack for a deity. If it were *me* getting sacrificed to, I'd be much more sated by having a god sacrificed to me."

"You ramble more than anyone I've ever met," said Normal-Art. "You don't interact with others much, do you?"

"Well, aside from Bev, no. Not much in a friendly manner, anyway."

"Speaking of Beverly, last I saw of her, those squirrels had ripped her to pieces. Did you resurrect her, too?"

Blackness soared across God-Art's eyes, clouding his face in despair. His sad appearance reminded Normal-Art of some poorly dressed front-man in a bad eighties music video. Normal-Art considered pointing this out to him, but ultimately decided against it. He did not want to get swallowed like one of those unfortunate dead dwarves.

"She's dead," said God-Art. "So that means our only hope of escaping this reality anytime soon is to complete our mission."

"Damn. I'm sorry to hear that about Beverly," said Normal-Art. He moved to put his hand on God-Art's shoulder. "She was a good bu—"

"Aaah! Don't touch me with that glove!" shouted God-Art as he leapt out of the way. "As I told you before, I sto…err, borrowed it from an immensely powerful version of us. One solid slap to the ground will rend the Earth in twain, and one solid slap to me means I'll be resurrecting my poor smooshed body from the ground for weeks."

"Whoa there, chief," replied Normal-Art. "Just trying to give condolences. No wonder you don't have any friends."

"I appreciate the thought, just please don't touch me with the weapon of mass destruction," responded God-Art, the sadness fading from his eyes. "Besides, she'll be born again from my forehead in a couple decades, and I'll take her down to the interdimensional depot to get her licensed for reality jumping. It'll be OK. What we really need to worry about is what the people on this reality will do if they beat us to our goal."

"And what *will* they do?"

"The people on this reality are all insane, mate. They'll use that cosmic bear to conquer every reality in the Multiverse. And before you even ask—the Multiverse is simply a title for all the different realities in existence. That's it. Some people attempt to explain it using an analogy about webs and forks in roads and new realities constantly sprouting because of different choices, but that's stupid and confusing and at this point in existence, plain wrong.

God-Art continued, "We gods from each of the different universes formed a coalition a few decades back at a convention on Earth 8,669, and we've kept new realities from forming and splitting off since, which is a lot easier process than it sounds. It's a simple matter of burning a specific self-replicating equation into the cosmic blueprint of each universe to keep it under control. The Multiverse is simply the collection of the remaining existing realities, and that's all there really is to need to know about it. Nothing to get confused about."

Normal-Art sighed. "God, you're so damned long winded! And now I'm *so* damned confused!"

"I just told you, it's nothing to get confused about. The Multiverse is simply a title for—"

"Stop it! I don't care what it is or how it works. Move on! How would a teddy bear allow these damned dwarves to conquer the Multiverse?"

"By giving the power-hungry bastards infinite power to work with is how," answered God-Art.

"Why would they want to conquer the Multiverse?"

"You haven't solved it by now? The infamous Nazi dwarf with the tiny mustache and German accent didn't give it away? He's from your reality. By Me, I should've picked up the genius version of us from Earth 6,907. Could have saved me a lot of breath."

"Huh?"

"Think about it this way," said God-Art. "When any sentient creature dies its soul must travel somewhere, right?"

"Before I ran into you, I didn't even believe in a soul," replied Normal-Art. He mindlessly dragged his fingertips along the crimson-stained grass, allowing the tiny drops of dew and blood to gather on the tips of his gloves. He looked past God-Art, squinting at the moon hanging high overhead. "But obviously you're fishing for an answer, so sure, I'll bite. A soul needs to go *somewhere*."

"Right. Every reality has different versions of heaven, hell, et cetera. However, the Multiverse sometimes steps in and takes a direct hand in running its many different realities, and don't ever let anyone tell you the Multiverse doesn't have a sense of humor. It apparently thought it best to gather the souls of every ruthless dictator from every reality and send them to this common reality, where they are reborn in a form humiliating *to them* and then are pitted against one another to vie for control of this tiny backwater Earth. This reality is supposed to be cut off from any sort of interdimensional travel, but there's always a way around such rules if you know the right tricks, and I know every trick in the book.

"Anyway," continued God-Art, "my ex-mate is a resident of this Earth, and she has also apparently found a way to jump in and out of here without alerting the B.I.T. *And* she has recruited your lady-partner to help her capture the most powerful weapon in the Multiverse."

"So, this reality is filled with dwarven dictators in Girl Scout uniforms, one of whom kidnapped my girlfriend?" asked Normal-Art. "That is positively the stupidest thing I've ever heard."

"That may be the case, but altogether these dwarves are the biggest threat the Multiverse has ever known. And unless my chain of severed ears deceives me, the dictators of this world have taken to worshipping your lady-partner and my ex."

"*What?*"

"Your lady-partner just used some sort of pink tentacles to rip miniature Stalin's head from his body. And that was enough to make the tribes gathered at their assembly fall to their knees in silence. By the way, my research tells me that the tentacles are not one of her natural abilities."

"Yeah, the pink tentacles're a new one. She barely picks her ass up off my couch, let alone launches tentacles anywhere."

"Hmm, then in that case, we'll need to hurry. We're not safe anywhere on the surface of this planet. The dictators have too much power, and too many ways to snag us. And it really won't do to get snagged, because if that happens, it's a pretty safe bet we'll be brought before our ladies and whatever cosmic power they've gotten their hands on. Without a doubt, that would not end well for either of us."

"Let's get moving, then. Where to?"

"We're going underground, where we shall do a little research and planning before resurfacing to dive into action."

"So, we're heading back to that funky treehouse of yours?" asked Normal-Art. "Does it go underground?"

"There are no doubt thousands of little rodent eyes watching that safe-house now, so it's off limits. And worse than that, these sorcerer ears tell me that the Ginnys have now unleashed the mob of dictators that they had assembled, and they are coming to hunt us down. They rightly believe that we must have escaped and killed Hitler by now. I'm presently expending a large amount of magic to make us appear as bushes just in case anyone happens by, but I cannot keep this up indefinitely. I need you to dig so that we can hide until they are done with their manhunt."

"Screw that," Normal-Art replied.

"I'm a god. A god doesn't dig unless he's the patron god of digging, which I'm not. However, I do control certain strains of pestilence, and if you refuse, I can give you the worst case of crabs in the history of the Multiverse."

Normal-Art frowned. "Fine, fine," he acquiesced. "But I'll need a shovel. You got one, or what?"

"No, I don't," responded God-Art. He reached into Normal-Art's front pocket and retrieved the miniature anvil he had gifted to Normal-Art. He placed the Creationvil in Normal-Art's hand. "But you will in a moment. Take this and set it on the ground."

Normal-Art took it and set it onto the grass. The anvil appeared tiny amongst the sea of green and red. He swatted at a bug that buzzed near his ear. He tried to sigh, but when he breathed in deep, the smell of fresh dwarf blood caked the back of his throat. He hacked into his hand, coughing until his eyes watered. *I hate this bloody place,* he thought, not even realizing that he had made a terrible pun.

"Picture the ideal shovel in your head," said God-Art, after Normal-Art caught his breath.

Normal-Art pictured the ideal shovel in his head.

"Now, keep the picture in your head and tap the top of the anvil. The tool shall form from it."

Art kept the picture in his head and tapped the top of the anvil. Despite his light tap, a deafening gong sprang forth from the depths of the anvil, crashing past the Arts and bowling through the surrounding forest. A choir of snapping twigs and branches and trunks sang out in raucous harmony. The top of the anvil glowed yellow, and then balls of electricity launched into the air, humming blue spheres that twirled across the clear sky.

"What the hell did you do?" demanded God-Art. "The Creationvil should be scanning the Multiverse, acquiring the very best materials and magically creating the perfect shovel. That low-level task should've taken about two seconds, and it should have expended a tiny fraction of the energy you've unleashed!"

A flash of yellow leapt a dozen feet into the air and descended in a slow, arching thunderstorm. It split and spread to make the outline of a wide, blocky form, yellow on the outside and black silhouette in the middle. It was obviously not a shovel.

"Being a mischief god, I thought you would've picked up on it by now," said Normal-Art. "I didn't picture a traditional shovel. I pictured one ideal for *my* situation."

"Unless you want to be a sacrifice for some stupid pink god, you better hope this idiotic scheme of yours works out fast, because I can't keep up the illusion that we're bushes for much longer. And it's all I can do to hide this lightshow from 'em, too. If we're not underground in a matter of seconds, we're toast."

The deep black void within the outline began to fill with gears and cogs and plates of shimmering metal. Each new component appeared with a CLINK as it clinked into place and with a WHIR as it whirred into place.

"Oh, Me," said God-Art. "The mob…"

"What about it?" asked Normal-Art. "More pink tentacles from our lady friends?"

"No, you fool! I've been listening in on the rabble that's out to get us. Despite my best attempts to mask us, the surge in power has alerted the mob of Dictator Scouts to this location. We are almost out of time."

A final lightning bolt flashed, descending in a blaze from the heavens. It struck the anvil and ricocheted over to the black silhouette. The silhouette exploded with a roaring pop and blistering fire. Sulfuric smoke erupted from the blast, filling the area with a thick, mustardy fog.

Glowing red eyes peered at the Arts from within the dense haze.

"[Whir] Your orders – CLACK CLACK – master?" asked a mechanical voice, a deep bass enveloped in a mechanical tenor.

The red eyes shone brighter as they approached the Arts, and as they moved out of the fog, the Arts saw that they were attached to a gigantic robot, twelve-feet tall. Its head was shaped vaguely like a rugby ball, broad and rather flat with red telescopic eyes jutting out of its center. The eyes made its face appear alien and bug-like. Steel mesh covered most of the head below the eyes, enclosing a speaker from which the robot communicated. Three spinning radar dishes sprouted from the top left of the machine's head like a tiny electrical oasis amongst a desert of shiny metal. The machine had no neck, but rather a squat, cylindrical body extending for five feet below its round head. Large dials covered the front of its torso in regular intervals like buttons on a fancy robot tuxedo shirt. Instead of hips and legs, three mammoth wheels stretched from below the cylindrical torso. Foot-long daggers extended from the spokes of the wheels, bestowing upon the machine what Normal-Art concluded could best be summed up as *a bit of a post-apocalyptic tricycle vibe.* Large pipes were hinged to where the machine's shoulders should be, and these pipes stretched down almost to the ground, ending in enormous, diamond-encrusted drill-bits. These long arms looked to Art like shiny gorilla arms, but with a gargantuan drill system substituting for each of its forearms and hands.

"Dig. Full steam ahead!" screamed Normal-Art. He leaned over to his counterpart, whispering, "I always wanted to say that *full steam ahead* bit."

"[Whir] Drillbot complies." And with that, the machine fully extended its pipe-arms and set its drills into motion with a whirring rumble.

Normal-Art snatched the Creationvil from the ground and placed it in his shirt pocket. He turned to God-Art and smirked. "You may think I'm an idiot, but I've got a mean streak of mischief, too. And I'll be damned before I do manual labor for anyone, let alone some half-assed version of me."

"Well, let's hope this stunt didn't damn the entire Multiverse under the heels of these Dictator Scouts. *We* are the best hope to stop them, after all."

The gigantic swirling drills rammed through the dirt like a bulldozer through putty. Within seconds, the machine had cut into the ground and created a large enough hole that the Arts could comfortably follow behind without even needing to duck their heads. As soon as the Arts descended below ground, God-Art turned back to the opening above. He began to levitate, and then he spoke in yet another language that Normal-Art had never heard before.

Roots grew and stretched across the hole, and grass quickly grew above the roots, the plants working together to thinly cover the opening. Scant beams of moonlight wiggled through the grass cover, illuminating random motes of dust like a spotlight operated by a drunken stagehand. A green hue from the growing grass tinted the tunnel.

Normal-Art watched God-Art work, running his fingers through his hair as he always did when in awe of something. But before amazement at the god's power could really overtake him, he realized that he had just accidentally smudged miniature-Hitler blood across his scalp like it was a glob of racist hair gel. He sighed.

God-Art turned back to the ever-deepening tunnel. His eyes glowed violet in the darkening space beneath the surface of the planet. "That's the best I can manage under these conditions," he said. "The dwarves already know generally where we just were, so there's not too much question in *whether* they'll find the hole. Hopefully, that cover will at least throw them off for a while, and the sabotage I did to the structural integrity will scare them off from pursuing us long enough for us to escape when they *do* eventually find it."

"What's that mean for us?" asked Normal-Art, feeling deflated as the words escaped his lips.

"It means that your laziness has cost us our research time, which I had planned to use to spy on our enemies and learn their weaknesses. We also won't get the opportunity to sit underground and plan a way to dispatch the Ginnys, which I'd hoped to do before we headed in the direction of our quarry. Instead, we must move *now*, and hope that we can outrun our women to our destination. I know the general area in which we need to be, so we shall head there. But after that, I'm out of directions. Tell your robot to make haste for latitude 13.09 degrees South by longitude 72.32 degrees West."

Normal-Art told the robot, and it changed course, surging through the black dirt like a bullet train and showing no sign of slowing any time soon. God-Art followed closely behind the robot, and Normal-Art followed him, using the god's flaming hair as a beacon to light his way in the darkness.

CHAPTER 12

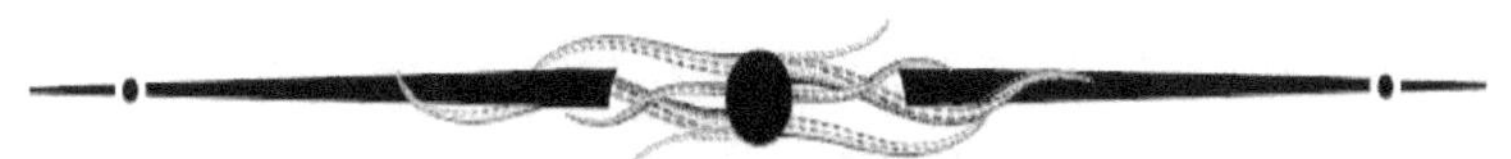

JOURNEY TO THE SOUTH

REGULAR-GINNY RODE ATOP a stampede of squirrels that rumbled its way through the wilderness like a furry subway train speeding down a thickly tangled track. At Tiny-Ginny's request, Regular-Ginny had begun surrounding herself at all times with a thin membrane of the pink ooze, a suit of fashion faux pas body armor to protect her from any mischievous dictator who might think he could gain her power by stabbing her in the back. For a few inane moments, as she stared down at the squirrels beneath her, she worried about rodent fur getting stuck on the membrane and causing her to look ridiculous.

"Are we going to ride these creatures all the way to the southern hemisphere?" asked Regular-Ginny, the early morning sun creeping over the horizon forcing her to squint. "Seems like a long, slow way to go, no matter how comfortable the seats."

"Most definitely not. If we were to do that, the Arts would reach the Pink One long before us. I have arranged for us to take Obelisk Orbs."

Regular-Ginny noticed the dwarf's face flush when she mentioned the Arts. They had escaped, and this predicament both annoyed and embarrassed her.

It had been four days since the assembly. The Ginnys had been in constant transit since, moving from one tribal leader to the next, recruiting anyone who would join them. In the end, they managed to enlist the three most powerful warlords on the planet to their cause.

But even *that* triumph did not afford Tiny-Ginny much joy. She ground her teeth constantly because the Arts had escaped. The mob had discovered the escape tunnel used by the Arts without much difficulty. It had been pathetically camouflaged by a thin layer of grass, and it had been found when a member of the mob fell into it. Many dwarves cascaded down into the tunnel after him like a howling, mustachioed pack of bloodhounds desperate to nip at the Arts' heels. But Tiny-Ginny's ex had rigged the tunnel to collapse, and dozens of Tiny-Ginny's most enthusiastic underlings perished in the mishap.

When she was informed of the debacle, Tiny-Ginny killed the messenger and ordered nobody else to attempt to re-enter or re-dig the tunnel because of the likelihood that her ex had rigged hundreds of similar traps down there. Pursuing that route would whittle down their army and they would likely still not catch their prey.

So Tiny-Ginny abandoned her scheme to preemptively dispatch the Arts, deciding—as Regular-Ginny had insisted from the beginning—that the army should simply beat the Arts to their mutual goal. This change in plans and admission of defeat, however necessary it might be, infuriated Tiny-Ginny, and she had not stopped fuming about it since.

Regular-Ginny yawned, and the yawn brought her mind back to the present. "Obelisk Orbs? What do you mean by tha—"

"Master Ginny, your holiness! A word, please," interrupted a dwarf with a horde of badges sewn onto his Scout sash. As he called out to the Ginnys, he ran toward them atop the mass of squirrels like a tiny, misshapen Saint Peter on a furry Sea of Galilee. His thick red mustachios bounced and tumbled across his chest and over his badges as he ran.

Both Ginnys glanced up and answered in unison, "Yes?"

The man stopped and scratched his beard. He shrugged. "We're almost at th' launch site. Shaka sent word, and ye got his army waitin' there, as well as the Honest One's. I rounded up a buncha th' lone wolves from up th' northern way. They're meetin' us there, too."

"What about Juley's boys from back east?" asked Tiny-Ginny.

"Saw some smoke signals a few miles back. They'll show soon. They got all turned 'round in th' Lost Forest. He had his boys stuff some grass into their mouths and then he forced a march, so they'll prob'ly make it to th' launch site on time since they won't hafta break fer lunch."

"Very well," said Tiny-Ginny. She waved the man away with the back of her hand. "Be gone. We need to think."

The muscular dwarf wrung his mustachios between his stubby fingers. He reminded Ginny of a bellhop rubbing his hat between his hands and awaiting a tip. After a few seconds of being ignored, he cleared his throat.

"Oh," said Tiny-Ginny, not deigning to look back up at him. "You're still here. I said be gone, you begging cur. You'll get your reward down south, after we rescue our new pink god."

He bowed his head and clenched his jaw. "Of course," he muttered, between lips white with tension. The color in his face darkened to match his hair. "I apologize, yer holinesses."

The dwarf turned and waddled away, returning to sit amongst Tiny-Ginny's army of Dictator Scouts riding at the back of the rushing train of squirrels.

The squirrels charged past some thick underbrush and into a dense forest, and the new scenery made Regular-Ginny promptly forget about the conversation she had been having with Tiny-Ginny. The dwarf began speaking to her, but Regular-Ginny did not hear a word. She glanced up through the branches above her and admired the leaves, which seemed to dance to some inaudible song as the wind blew through them. The coarse bark on the trees shone brown, and hundreds of bugs rushed up and down the tree trunks like cars zooming up and down a highway—except these cars occasionally ate each other. Flowers of all colors poked their heads out of the surrounding underbrush like native savages curious to gaze upon a passing parade. New squirrels dove down from each tree the group passed and joined the roaring tsunami of fur. Regular-Ginny smiled as she basked in the beautiful nature surrounding her. She inhaled deeply and held it, enjoying the freshness of the air as it filled her lungs.

But as one hour bled into another, the novelty faded. The trees and the flowers and the bugs that had been so thrilling began to all look the same to her, and when no end to the forest appeared after four hours, she became convinced that the monotony of the trees and the flowers and the bugs would never end. She watched them all in silence as she rushed past. She tried counting the trees, as she did as a kid to pass the time on long road trips with her father, but she soon lost count. So, she started over. And over. And over, repeating until she was too weary to ever want to see a tree again. And after what seemed like a few hours more, just when she was strongly considering putting out her eyes with a couple of well-placed pink tentacles, the group burst through the other side of the forest.

The Ginnys rode the surge of squirrels out onto some plains, and Regular-Ginny glanced over her shoulder at the dense forest from which they had just emerged. It did not look like a forest from this vantage point, but rather a colossal, opaque splotch of pitch-black paint smeared across the horizon. As a matter of fact, the forest looked so black that she wondered how she had been able to see inside the thick underbrush at all, let alone with the clarity with which she had witnessed and counted and lost count of the trees. Squirrels ferrying the army of dwarves behind her seemed to appear in thin air from the black splotch. She rubbed her eyes, and then she continued to stare in wonder until a cloud of dust rose from the pitter-pattering of squirrel paws, obscuring the blackness from her view.

"It was the moss. It blankets all the trees," said Tiny-Ginny.

"What?"

"You're wondering how we were able to see in there. I wondered the same thing, the first time I was here. It's the black moss covering everything in that forest. The forest appears utterly black from the outside, because the moss consumes all sunlight that touches it. But it is always bright on the inside because it releases its own mutated form of ultraviolet light, only visible from a few yards away. Since it's never dark in there, it really throws off your internal clock when you appear on this plane of existence in a brand-new miniature body inside that forest."

"Oh," replied Regular-Ginny, not really knowing how else to respond.

"You might want to look ahead now. Probably not going to see something like this again in your lifetime."

Regular-Ginny turned and faced forward. The squirrels carried her over a ridge and down over the edge of a bowl-shaped valley. Thin strands of grass grew along the top lip of the bowl. As the edge of the bowl dipped down toward the bottom, which was a good quarter mile down, the grass worked its way up through the red dirt in increasingly denser clumps until, at the bottom, the valley bristled green. Thousands of dwarves filled the valley floor, separated into camps based on the armies they represented.

Tiny-Ginny had been right. Regular-Ginny had never seen anything even close to what she witnessed at the bottom of the valley, and she assumed she probably never would again. She craned her neck to take in the entire scene.

Six pairs of towering black obelisks rose from the bottom of the valley, standing erect in the ground as though they were the black hilts of twelve titanic daggers embedded deep into the heart of the Earth. The tops of the obelisks strained up past the top of the bowled valley, and each pair was connected at their tops by a thick indigo band of an elastic material that Regular-Ginny was unable to identify. The obelisks exuded elegance with their black bareness, but shined with a smooth, unmerciful menace in the blazing sun.

The squirrels bounced left and right, right and left, following a winding path down the side of the chasm. Regular-Ginny's eyes never left the black monstrosities, and as the squirrels made the gradual back-and-forth descent, her head slowly shook back-and-forth as though she were repeatedly answering *no* to some unspoken question. She squinted when she saw movement at the top of one of the obelisks, and she shaded her eyes with her hand to get a better view.

Dwarves were hoisting a massive hook up the side of one of the gargantuan obsidian monoliths. They heaved on an oversized rope in dozens of packs of dozens, hauling the monstrous hook up inch by painstaking inch.

By the time the dwarves pulled the hook to the top, Ginny had neared enough for them to have tripled in size within her gaze, and the caravan had nearly reached the base of their obelisk. After getting the hook to the top of the obelisk, the dwarves heaved the object onto their backs, stepping carefully out onto the indigo band that linked this obelisk with the one beside it.

The band dipped and bounced with each of their choreographed steps, but the dwarves remained balanced. They reached the center point between the pair of obelisks and shoved the business-end of the hook through a precut hole in the band. They tied the ends dozens of ropes through loops that poked out from the hook, and then they tossed all the ropes to the ground. All of them were long enough to reach the ground.

The horde of dwarves scrambled down the ropes. Upon reaching the ground, they immediately began tugging on the ropes. Hundreds of other dwarves joined in from the surrounding armies. They strained and sweated and heaved until they pulled the indigo band nearly to the ground, stretching it taut like a rubber band until it hovered inches above the stiff grass of the valley floor.

Another group of dwarves—these brandishing huge mallets and sharp wooden stakes—sprinted from rope to rope. They shoved their pointed stakes through the ropes and pinned them to the ground, relieving each sweaty throng of dwarves from its burden. Eventually, they helped with the last line, the giant rope with which Ginny had witnessed the burly workers hauling the hook up the obelisk in the first place. Soon, the mallet-bearers had that one hammered down, too.

The squirrel caravan screeched to a halt beside this pair of obelisks and the Ginnys stepped off their hairy ride. The hundreds of laborers who had just worked so hard to pull and secure the indigo band to the ground lay sprawled upon the grass in the shadow of the near obelisk, gasping for air and sweating profusely.

"Great job, boys," exclaimed Tiny-Ginny, clapping her hands together enthusiastically. "Only five more to go, so get moving! I'm not paying you to lie around!"

Regular-Ginny furrowed her brows. She watched the workers rise and trudge toward the next pair of obelisks. She stared at the closest one. Thousands of short black rods protruded from its sides like metallic needles sprouting from a gigantic black cactus. Regular-Ginny squinted at the rods. She had not noticed them on the pair of obelisks that she had watched during her descent down into the valley—a miss that she attributed to the distance from which she had been watching them—but now that she was at the bottom of the valley and closer to *all* the obelisks, she noticed the rods sticking out of all the monstrosities.

Before Ginny had time to ask about the purpose of the rods, a horn blew from somewhere she did not see, and hundreds of dwarves rushed toward one of the obelisks. They surged up its side like an army of ants, scrambling hand over hand and using the rods to climb. Meanwhile, the burliest dwarf in the entire army tied the end of a massively thick rope around his torso—a rope about three feet in diameter and identical to the one that Ginny had watched the dwarves use to heave the colossal hook up the original obelisk. This hempen-wrapped dwarf began his ascent as soon as the first surge of workers reached the peak, climbing at a slower pace and being careful not to catch his thick rope on the metal rods.

The rope carrier reached the top. The other dwarves up there untied him from his burden, and he collapsed onto his hands and knees to catch his breath. A crew at the bottom of the obelisk attached a hook the size of a house to the bottom end of the rope. Nearly all the dwarves at the top of the obelisk began working in unison to haul it up.

"What's the deal with all *this*?" asked Regular-Ginny, gesturing toward the obelisks. "We should have hopped a plane and been most of the way to the Pink One by now."

"We're dealing with *all this* because we must," Tiny-Ginny spat back. Mister E hissed. "In case you haven't noticed, there's not much in the way of planes here. Or guns, or computers, or anything powered by electricity."

"I guess I *hadn't* really noticed, or I wouldn't have asked," answered Regular-Ginny.

Tiny-Ginny grunted acceptance. "Physics on this reality functions a little differently than what you're used to. Guns don't work here. Neither do missiles, or anything like that. Physics work on only the most basic level. Hit something, it dies. Throw something up, it falls down. No gunpowder, no explosions, nothing like that. Even if you build things that *should* explode, they simply don't detonate."

"OK. But that doesn't really make sense. I mean, I'm no physicist, but if none of those technologies work, then how do you explain what's on all those ridiculous little badges you all wear? I'm assuming you get them for mastering whatever's on them, just like in the Scouts back on my home reality, right?"

"Right."

"Well, on your sash, you've got a mushroom cloud, a machine gun firing into a crowd of children, and lots of others just as bad. How do you earn badges for those if you can't actually do the things on them?"

"Pretty simple. The Squirrel Master convenes a special meeting of the Higher Council once every two years. If you don't mind waiting in line for a few days, every Dictator Scout has the right to make a case to the Council and can be awarded badges for special skills acquired in past lives. Prove that your techniques were effective ways to subjugate the plebs of your home dimension, and you get credit for them in *The Great Ledger* and badges to display your prowess to others."

Regular-Ginny began to ask a clarifying question, but Tiny-Ginny interrupted her and changed the subject back to the Physics of this Earth. "We're all ambitious people here, otherwise we'd have ended up in a different version of the afterlife. We're not going to let a hokey little thing like frustrating *Physics* stand in our way. Thus, we developed ways around the lack of firearms and rockets and missiles."

"And what're those?" asked Regular-Ginny between gritted teeth, her voice flat and monotone because she was frustrated with Tiny-Ginny interrupting her.

"Yet again, my alternate-self, you disappoint me. You've borne witness to it already. How do you think we converse with our little rodent hosts, let alone force them to do our bidding?"

"I dunno. E.S.P.?" guessed Regular-Ginny.

"Don't be ridiculous. The answer is magic, of course."

Before she could stop herself, Regular-Ginny guffawed. Despite everything she had seen since she ran into Art's twin the better part of a week ago, magic seemed like the densest, silliest explanation she had yet heard.

"You laugh. But you've hopped across dimensions. You've been ferried for miles by a magically enthralled, incredibly well-synchronized band of squirrels. And still you don't believe in magic?"

Regular-Ginny shrugged. "I dunno. Just seems a little childish."

"Well, call it whatever you want. But you've seen it in action. It's a little more than child's play, I'd say. Look up there at the top," said Tiny-Ginny, pointing her finger up to the top of the obelisk. "Look behind the Scouts hauling up the hook."

Regular-Ginny craned her neck all the way back and gazed at where Tiny-Ginny pointed. Twelve mustachioed dwarves sat cross-legged, just behind the hoisting workers. They extended their arms over their heads and swayed back and forth like a fluffy patch of shrubbery during a mighty storm. Their seemingly natural sense of rhythm surprised Regular-Ginny, for she had not ever considered that tyrants and dictators might be good dancers. They seemed to be chanting something, too, but from this distance Regular-Ginny could not hear anything they were saying.

"They're preventing the hook from catching onto the climbing poles," said Tiny-Ginny. "Without them, not only does this process take *much* longer, but a team of workers must climb behind the hook and free it whenever it gets snagged. It would be extremely dangerous and slow, and we'd lose dozens of dwarves that we can't afford to lose. This way is much better."

Regular-Ginny squinted. With each tug by the muscular dwarves, the hook lurched further up the side of the obelisk. As it did so, it seemed to bounce off an invisible wall before it could snag itself onto the thousands of protruding rods.

"Seems a little tedious that the dancing fellas would need to go all the way up there," said Regular-Ginny. "Why don't they do their fancy swaying down here on the ground?"

"Finally, a good question!" responded Tiny-Ginny. "You see, magic's not an abundant resource that everyone can tap into. It's not air that people can simply breathe in and use. That's why they're up there. Those obelisks work a bit like antennae. The obelisks attract magic, and those dancing boys up top have been badged in channeling that magic for these launching jobs."

Regular-Ginny glanced down at the ground and rubbed her neck. She had been looking up entirely too much today. After a few moments of rubbing, she turned her eyes back to Tiny-Ginny. She studied her counterpart's badges more closely than she did the first time. This time, rather than becoming terrified, she found herself consumed with revulsion.

Amongst less notable badges, Regular-Ginny saw a flayed man, a drawn-and-quartered man, a cloud with a skull-and-crossbones—which she assumed to be credit for some sort of poisonous gas—peasants burning in flames, exploding airplanes, children getting their heads plucked off, a horde of gelded men, a giant woman demolishing a building, mobs being hanged, tanks barreling over children, a mushroom cloud, a machine gun firing into a crowd of children, a woman using a wooden spoon to gorge herself on a brain that sat inside a living skull, a black hole devouring a planet, a witch's hat, children being cooked in a large iron pot, a disemboweled man, a man with flames for hair tied to a giant rock, and a squirrel with antennae poking up from its head.

Tiny-Ginny caught her staring at the last one. "I got it because of what I accomplished with Mister E," she said.

Regular-Ginny grunted in confusion

Tiny-Ginny explained, "Unlike those dancing boys at the top of the launching obelisks, some people in this dimension are natural rods for attracting magic. I am one of these. Every person appearing on this planet, whether prone to accessing magic or not, is responsible for finding and enslaving his own squirrel to act as his host, to help adjust to life on this horrid rock. I found Mister E the moment I crash-landed here, and I used my natural affinity for magic to shape him into my ideal servant. Then I magically manipulated his genetic make-up and surgically improved him so that I might hop dimensions. Because of the enhancements I made to him, I am the only dwarf no longer forced to stay in this backward dimension.

"Before you ask, I wasn't the first to figure out how to dimension-hop with a slave-squirrel," continued Tiny-Ginny, despite Regular-Ginny giving no indication that she wanted her to continue. "People have been forced to live in this cursed land long before I arrived. But I am the first to do it and remain undetected by the *Bureau of Interdimensional Travel.* All others were caught almost immediately and eradicated the moment they jumped. I alone am the sole hope for this dimension, the one chosen by Fate to bring a burning scourge down upon the breadth of the Multiverse. And now, *we* shall fulfill this destiny for which I've waited so long. The Pink One brought us together for this very purpose, I just know it. I am positively giddy." Tiny-Ginny positively giggled, which sounded more like a cackle, which reminded Regular-Ginny of a hyena plagued by a bout of Emphysema.

Tiny-Ginny carried on rambling about her own brilliance for what seemed like ages. Regular-Ginny pretended to listen, but she instead allowed her mind to wander. She stared past Tiny-Ginny and up at the top of the obelisk. Silhouetted by the sun, the workers hoisted and hoisted. Regular-Ginny lay back on the soft grass and put her hands behind her head. She followed with her eyes the rhythmic swaying and rocking of the dwarven magicians atop the obelisk. Her body relaxed, and her mind wandered farther away.

She soon began to feel as though she were drifting in a tiny boat upon a calm lake. Tiny-Ginny's shrill voice grew distant, the shrieking ululation becoming lapping waves against the side of Regular-Ginny's metaphorical ship. Ginny could no longer keep her eyes open, and the harder she tried, the heavier her eyelids became.

Before long, she stopped resisting, and the blackness of sleep became all-encompassing. When she was lost amongst the blackness, it shifted and shimmered and transformed, and she found herself adrift upon a pink cloud. And then her metaphorical ship sprang a leak, and she sank into the cottony pink fluff. The fluff buzzed around her and stung her with tiny pricks. Pain erupted across her skin, but her insides balled into a thick sphere of rage and hatred. She was overcome by the desire to crush and maim. The sensation was somehow exhilarating.

She squished a handful of the pink fluffiness between her fingers and tried to rip it in twain. She opened her mouth, intending to cry out her fury to the ether, but the pink fluff that surrounded her foamed into her mouth and slithered up her nostrils, creeping inside her and sliding down her esophagus. It burned, and she clawed at her throat with her fingernails, trying to get it out. She choked and gagged, raging harder against the pink with each passing second.

A voice emanated both from all around her and from inside her. Its tone was somehow simultaneously a smooth bass and a shrill alto. As the godlike soundwaves passed through her, every molecule in her body vibrated.

"Tarry no more," ordered the voice. "Time be running short, shorter than Me realized. Ginny can afford no more rest until Me am rescued. Me give Ginny big-time motivation: if Ginny sleep again before Pink One free, then Pink One shall crush Ginny's life from her fleshy husk and swallow her soul into nothingness."

Before Regular-Ginny could respond, her eyes opened, and she was back in the valley with the massive obelisks. Tiny-Ginny was shaking her vigorously by the shoulders. "Wake up, fool!"

Regular-Ginny rubbed her eyes, temporarily blinded by the now-late-afternoon sun that blazed overhead. Shudders coursed through her body, remnants of the terrifying pink nightmare from which she had just been roused. The shudders ran from the tips of her extremities, sprinted up the length of her body, and slammed into her stomach. She wanted to vomit. Instead, she swallowed the bile building at the back of her throat, and with it the murderous anger that had overwhelmed her during her sleep. It sank into her heart like an anchor and rooted itself there with long, pink roots, pumping constant pink fury through her body.

"What?" demanded Regular-Ginny.

"We've been ready to go for ten minutes, but I couldn't manage to wake you," said Tiny-Ginny. "You were screaming in your sleep like an insane baboon."

"Oh. Horrid dreams."

"Well, it's time to get up. Our first Obelisk Orb is preparing to launch, and you should not miss the opportunity to witness this engineering marvel."

Regular-Ginny sat up and glanced around the valley. The sun blared in the corner of her vision, assaulting her senses like that terrible rendition of *America the Beautiful* to which she had been subjected a few months ago at her thirteen-year-old nephew's band recital. She shaded her eyes with her hands and noticed that the indigo bands connecting each of the six pairs of obelisks had *all* been staked down. She had apparently slept through the dwarves completing this work, and she shrugged. She did not realize she had been asleep *that* long.

Regular-Ginny studied the indigo band nearest her. Its color seemed a deeper purple than any she had ever experienced. It drank in the sunlight, and its deep color swirled like currents beneath the sea. The tension with which the band pulled against its staked ropes made her fear that the ropes might snap, causing the indigo band to whip back up into the sky, which would be a problem because an odd, rounded metallic object that had not been present before Ginny fell asleep now sat in the middle of the taut band. The object was gigantic in its own proportions, but it seemed a tiny fish egg compared to the hulking obelisks that flanked it.

The metallic object looked similar to a spaceship that Ginny had seen on the cover of one of the pulpy science-fiction magazines she had devoured during her youth. Its shape was that of a giant, bulbous egg, and Ginny estimated it to be a few hundred feet long and a couple hundred feet wide. Enveloping the object were huge convex plates of metal that formed smooth scales. The surface of the ship reflected the afternoon sunlight like an egg-shaped mirror, and Ginny had to squint to look directly at the strange object. The weight of the bulbous egg caused its bottom to partially sink into the indigo band, fitting perfectly into place and reminding Ginny of an egg-shaped boat snuggling itself up to the wine dark sea. The broad end of the egg faced south. The narrower end was opened, and a wide ramp was descended upon the grass. At this distance, Ginny could only spy a shadowy interior inside the opening and nothing more.

A hairless dwarf stood before the egg-shaped ship, his own bald head reflecting the sun as though it were the egg-shaped ship writ small. He waited like an impatient insect to ascend the ramp, shifting his weight back and forth from leg to leg and flitting his pink tongue out from his mouth to lick his lips. He stood a head taller than any other dwarf Ginny had seen in this dimension, with the blackest skin she had ever laid eyes on. He wore the typical Scout uniform—sans shoes—and he had decorated his uniform with armbands and leg bands made of what appeared to be dried grass. His hands were as large as oven-mitts, and they gripped his weapons so tightly that Ginny feared he might crack the weapons in half. A leathern band clung taught around the peak of his head, and what appeared to be an oversized feather stood erect from the front of it and danced in the wind. Giant gauge earrings had stretched wide holes into the man's earlobes, pulling them out to epic proportions and causing them to hang down close to his shoulders. His ears reminded Ginny of two grisly links of limp, black sausage.

Behind him stood an array of what Ginny estimated to be several thousand dwarves. They were armed with throwing spears twice as tall as themselves, shorter spears with large, broad heads for close-range melee stabbing, and enveloping tower shields shaped like pointed ovals that were fashioned from furry hide. Ginny had not seen any cattle in this dimension, or she would have assumed that the shields were cowhide. As a matter of fact, the only animals she had encountered here were squirrels. She normally would have shuddered at the thought of cute little creatures being killed and their hides being harvested to create shields, but the hateful pink goo stirred in her heart, and she found herself very much in favor of the notion.

The bald dwarf spun on his heels, screeching in the dust as he turned to his troops. As he gazed at his soldiers, utter contempt and arrogance spasmed across his face. He barked something Ginny could not understand to the troops arrayed before him, and then he turned his back to them as quickly as he had spun to face them. He danced forward, up the ramp. Two soldiers dressed in shaman garb followed on his heels. The bald dwarf began chanting as he ascended the ramp, kicking his knees up to his chest, clapping, and bouncing back-and-forth on the balls of his feet. The thousands of dictators under the bald dwarf's rule did the same, making their way into the egg-shaped ship like an army that had come down with a plague of Saturday Night Fever. Ginny failed to suppress a smile at the absurd surrealism of the scene.

Tiny-Ginny noticed the smirk on Regular-Ginny's face, and she smirked herself. "The dancing may appear ridiculous, but he believes it to be necessary," she said. "Shaka is chief among the most ferocious and successful warriors on this planet. The army following behind him were all wildly successful killers and tyrants in their own home realities, but Shaka has pressed them under the heel of his service through sheer gods-be-damned grit. They're utterly loyal to him, simply out of fear of reprisal on his part. And thus, when he dances and sings to his bloody savage gods, they do as well.

"Be careful around him," continued Tiny-Ginny. "He's a slave to his whims, and he'd never agree to accompany us on this expedition unless he plans for his soldiers to be the only ones to return. He'll obey our orders for now, only because our pink powers have mesmerized him. But he'll do his best to skewer us as soon as he thinks he's found a way to acquire that power for himself."

"You don't have to warn me to stay away from him. Bald dwarves aren't really my type."

Regular-Ginny returned her gaze to the ship. She recalled the journey to recruit Shaka. Squirrels ferried her and Tiny-Ginny to his lands the morning following the Arts' escaped. His kingdom was a place of deserts interspersed by savannah, and from Tiny-Ginny's cabin, it sat on the other side of the park and then just beyond a range of great hills. Shaka and his underlings lived in small grass huts, just like the tribes that Regular-Ginny used to read about in *National Geographic*. Regular-Ginny had not seen Shaka on the visit. Upon reaching his home, his guards had blocked her from entering, for it was obvious to them that she was not from this world, and thus Shaka had forbidden her from being in his presence. The fierce pink hatred that occupied Ginny's heart urged her to murder the guards and force herself inside, but Tiny-Ginny advised her to acquiesce to the demand and wait outside so that the dwarf might engage in diplomacy. Tiny-Ginny then disappeared inside his hut.

Regular-Ginny remained outside the hut for hours. Boredom pummeled her with its ham-fisted yawns as she sat there with nothing to do. Minutes later, disgust wrestled boredom out of its way when guttural moans began to resound from inside the hut. No matter how much Ginny tried to plug her ears, she could not muffle the erotic noises that began drifting out from the dwelling, noises that sounded as though a few dozen donkeys were in the process of being gelded.

Finally, Tiny-Ginny emerged, smiling and covered in sweat. She proclaimed, "I've recruited the most powerful man and most numerous army on the planet, and only at the cost of a little dignity."

The mismatched twins had moved on from there, and Tiny-Ginny repeated the same gag-inducing recruitment tactic with each of the most powerful warlords on the planet. Regular-Ginny had spent so long sitting outside the homes of powerful warlords listening to her tiny counterpart's moaning that she felt confident she would have years of nightmares to help her remember the experience.

Regular-Ginny's mind snapped back to the present. The last of the ridiculous, tiny warriors finished ascending the ramp, dancing his way into the shadowy interior. The warriors within pulled up the ramp, using the ramp itself to seal the entrance to the egg-shaped ship. With it in place, there appeared nary a crack in the shiny hide of the object. The army locked the ramp in place from the inside, creating a loud CLACK with each engaged lock that echoed through the entire valley. For a few tense moments, the ship sat silent in the bright sun.

Then hundreds of burly dwarves scurried into lines behind the ship, lurking near the dozens of ropes holding the indigo band in place. Their oversized muscles twitched and bulged, threatening to pop their Scout uniforms off their bodies. Each dwarf propped a battle axe upon his shoulder, and each axe had on its end a mean blade half as big as the dwarf holding it. The edges of the axes gleamed with razor sharpness, ready to glut themselves on hemp.

A single dwarf stood at attention behind these tiny lumberjacks. He brought a rusty trumpet to his lips and bleeped a shrill note. The trumpeter's cheeks puffed like tiny, red, inflatable balloons, and the piercing call echoed across the landscape. The note trailed away, a lonely bird disappearing over the horizon.

With the fluidity of a machine, the hulking dwarves raised their axes high above their heads. Veins erupted from their meaty arms and sweat trickled down their faces. Not one of the axe-man allowed his tool to descend a single inch. The dwarves remained so still that they reminded Regular-Ginny of stout, marble statues.

The trumpeter returned the instrument to his lips. He blew two notes in quick succession, equally as shrill as the first, but higher pitched. Long before these notes trailed away, the axes fell. The blades dropped in unison, dozens of guillotines executing a gang of ropes, slicing through them with an audible SCHWIK!

Like an oversized rubber band, the indigo band sprang from the ground. A loud, rubbery FWUNG drowned out all other noise. The egg-shaped ship rode the rubbery indigo band high into the sky, so fast that Ginny could hardly move her head quickly enough to follow it. The indigo band threw the metallic egg into the sky. It whistled as it cut through the atmosphere, and within seconds, it disappeared over the distant horizon.

Regular-Ginny gulped, and then she scratched her head. She turned to Tiny-Ginny and muttered, "*This* is how we're traveling to the Pink One?"

Tiny-Ginny sneered at Regular-Ginny, nodding with impatience. "Of course," she replied. "I told you, we don't have planes or cars. I thought I made it clear when I gave you the little speech about how Physics works on this Earth. Why did you *think* we were down here at these obelisks?"

"I assumed it was some sort of a religious thing."

"Do I seem like the reverent type?"

Regular-Ginny smirked. "Point taken. But there's *no way* these things can be safe."

"Over a million launches and we've had not a single a *safety* issue, for they were engineered by some wacko, ingenious tyrant named Albert Einstein from Earth 678,994. He does *not* make engineering mistakes."

"That's ridiculous. Einstein wasn't a tyrant. He was a scientist. He even won tons of awards for being a peace activist."

"Well, I don't know what to tell you, other than that every Earth has a different history. On *his* particular Earth, *this* Einstein conquered the world through his brilliance and scientific ingenuity. He built a robot army, too, and used it to slay most of the people on his planet. He showed mercy only toward his own tribe, the Jews."

Regular-Ginny steepled her fingers beneath her chin. She made a clicking noise deep within her throat, as she always did when deep in thought. "It's so weird to think that Einstein could be evil on *any* Earth. He was my brother's idol when we were growing up. Any chance I can meet him? It'd be something really cool to tell my brother about when I make it home from all this."

Tiny-Ginny's eyes went cold. Behind her, a second army nearly as large as the first piled into a second, equally gigantic metal egg-shaped ship. These dwarves simply marched into the ship rather than dancing into it as the first army had done. The man leading this procession had no mustachios on his face, and he wore his short hair combed straight forward. His name was Gaius Julius Caesar, as Regular-Ginny had learned during the uneventful trip to his lands. Tiny-Ginny had entered his villa referring to him as Gaius Julius, but she had exited it sweaty and referring to him as Juley. He was flanked on both sides by dwarves carrying poles, atop which sat large eagle statues shaped from solid gold. Directly behind them marched a duo of dwarves adorned in hooded cloaks and pointy hats. They reminded Ginny of one of her old tabletop roleplaying buddies, who insisted on dressing up as his wizard character when he came over to play.

Tiny-Ginny's eyes fluttered, and the faintest semblance of a smile danced upon the edges of her lips. She said, "No, you may not meet him. He is dead, and I ate his brains."

"Holy—what?"

"He had intelligence that I *wanted.* I banded together with some like-minded colleagues. We infiltrated his war-camp and then murdered him at a dinner party. We ate his brain for dessert. How else would I know all that information about his history? There were no Jews on my reality."

Regular-Ginny began to reply, but she was cut short by the shrill call from the launching trumpet. After the noise echoed away into the distance, she continued, "I never realized getting smarter was as simple as eating someone's brain."

The double trumpet blew from the launch pad, and the loud SCHWIK and FWUNG followed. Tiny-Ginny began speaking loudly to be heard over the trailing whistle of the now-distant second ship. "I told you, I am a beacon for magic. This means that I can hoard power and strength in a multitude of ways. One of the speedier methods is to swallow someone's intelligence. I do so quite frequently, and I'm not the only person on this reality who does."

"Sure, whatever," responded Regular-Ginny. "Just seems a little psychotic is all. What ever happened to the colleagues who ate Einstein's brain with you? Did you send a message to any to come help us with our mission to rescue the Pink One?"

"Well, like any other alliance, it suited us for a while. And then we disbanded."

"And why was that?" asked Regular-Ginny, trying to feel out what would happen between herself and Tiny-Ginny when their partnership was no longer necessary.

"I ate their brains, too, of course."

Regular-Ginny gulped. Not far away, two separate hordes of squirrels scurried into the third and fourth ships. Regular-Ginny did not even attempt to count them. They must have numbered in the millions. She had no idea from where *all* these squirrels had come. The Ginnys and their army had ridden upon a lot to get here, but not nearly *that* many. They crammed themselves so tightly into the ships that they reminded her of salted fish being canned. Once they were inside, another pair of dwarves in cloaks and pointy hats climbed into each egg-shaped ship, using their stumpy legs to wedge their way through the mass of furry flesh. They disappeared into the hairy darkness within, and then a dozen dwarves followed each pair into the ships.

Regular-Ginny decided to change the subject to something more pleasant than the devouring of brains, mainly because she was beginning to grow concerned for her own. "Weather sure is nice around here," she said. "It's so crisp in the afternoon. Hope it's not too warm down south where we're headed."

Tiny-Ginny raised one eyebrow. A smile slithered its way across her face, and a chuckle burst from her putrid lips. "You don't have to worry about me eating your brain," she said. "You definitely don't have enough knowledge to make it worth the effort. Have you ever tasted a brain? It tastes a bit like warm, rancid-meat flavored flan."

"Yeah, *that* and because the Pink One would flay you alive if you touched me."

"Whatever you say," replied Tiny-Ginny, scowling. She looked away from Regular-Ginny, signaling an end to the conversation.

But Regular-Ginny was not willing to sit in silence. The trumpets sounded, and the third launcher launched. Regular-Ginny considered making a terrible joke about flying squirrels, but she said instead, "How do we know that these contraptions are launching us to the right place? Even if this whole shindig *was* designed by a version of Einstein, the science seems a little sketchy."

"Those workers who staked down the launch-bands, well, they've all obtained the highest badge in Obelisk Orb launching. They're pros. They are trained to work out the equations and handle the minute details of perfect angles and proper tension."

"But if every dictator in this reality has the goal of eventually stabbing everyone else in the back, why wouldn't these guys simply use the trust you have in them to take advantage of you? If it were me, I'd launch all these vessels directly into the side of a cliff or something."

Tiny-Ginny shrugged. Another horn blasted in the background. She said, "The position and badge are some of the only things in this reality held with the utmost honor, hence why I don't have one. Besides, if you make a single mistake in the calculations—intentionally or unintentionally—all dwarves on this planet are honor-bound to hunt you down. When caught, you are disemboweled, forced to eat your own intestines, and then hung upside down until you bleed to death. Any dwarf caught harboring you is subject to the same punishment. Still doesn't stop it from happening *occasionally*, but it sure puts a damper on the number there would be otherwise. The odds of dying or going off-course in one of these things are astronomical, lower than being struck by lightning twice in a single day.

"And on top of all that," she continued, speaking over the double blast of the trumpet, "we'll be safe, because if they kill us now, there's no chance of them ever getting the opportunity to harness the power of the Pink One. Only *you* can pinpoint its exact location. So, they'll be sending us exactly where I told them to send us."

Regular-Ginny watched the fourth ship scream its way up into the air. She shuddered. She did not feel too reassured by Tiny-Ginny's reassurances, but if something *were* to go wrong, she did not believe the Pink One would allow her to die just yet. She would simply be forced to find another way to get to her destination, sans sleep and rest.

Tiny-Ginny tapped her on the shoulder. "Our turn."

"Oh, OK. I'd assumed we were going to be last."

"Nope, five is my lucky number. The Honest One and his men shall load into the sixth."

"Something's still tugging at the back of my mind. I don't see anything that resembles landing gear on these things. How are we to land? Do we just crash?"

Tiny-Ginny shrugged. "It's more of a controlled bounce than anything else. But I can assure you that these ships were engineered to bounce safely. The landing will be the easiest part. A lot easier than the return trip home shall be."

"What do you mean?" asked Regular-Ginny, as she followed Tiny-Ginny toward their egg-shaped ship. Mister E sat perched on Tiny-Ginny's shoulders like a scraggly parrot atop the shoulder of a hideously short pirate captain.

"Well, on this reality, we don't make it a habit to go as far south as we're going. You would need to have a bit of a death wish to travel there, really. If the Pink One wasn't communicating to you *exactly* where we need to go, and if we didn't have a pretty good chance of achieving our goal, then I wouldn't even consider the risk myself.

"As such," continued Tiny-Ginny, "we don't have any Obelisk Orb stations set up down there. We're in for a long hike home."

"Oh, swell," responded Regular-Ginny, as she walked past yet another arrangement of troops standing at attention. Their Scout uniforms fluttered in the breeze, and so did their stench. Ginny crinkled her nose.

The Ginnys ascended the ramp and walked inside the ship. Behind them, the thousands of Scouts ceased standing at attention and began marching in unison, following the Ginnys inside the ship.

The interior of the egg-shaped ship looked even more like something from a bad pulpy science-fiction story than the exterior. Shining chrome covered the walls, confusing every contour and causing Regular-Ginny's reflection to stare back at her in awkward silence from every angle. She followed the click-clacks of Tiny-Ginny's heels up a suspended walkway that cut through the middle of the ship and extended to the front of the ship. Rows of black straps lined the floor at intervals of every two feet. In the distance, at the front of the chrome interior, sat two white bucket seats with wide oval backs. Two clear panels peered out of the wall just past the egg-shaped bucket seats. Clear sky shone brightly outside them, and beams of sunlight drifted in through them like wayward spotlights, highlighting a few random square feet of the chrome floor.

Regular-Ginny glanced over her shoulder as she walked. Wave after wave of Dictator Scouts surged up the ramp. As they poured past the threshold of the ship, they veered off with military precision to the left and right of the walkway. The troops scurried to the rows of black straps, harnessing themselves to the floor. They packed themselves so tightly together that not a square inch of chrome was visible beneath them. As the dwarves continued to surge up the ramp like a mustachioed tsunami, they left empty the six harnesses nearest the ramp on each side of the walkway.

Regular-Ginny forced herself to face forward, ripping her eyes from the hypnotic wave of troops flooding the ship behind her. "Those chairs are for us, right?" she asked, pointing to the bucket seats at the front of the ship. "There's no way I'm strapping myself to the cold floor."

"You're in luck. Those seats are always reserved for the crew's inflight magicians. Keeping the ship steady is usually a two-magician job, but like I told you, I'm a divining rod for magic. I don't need a co-magician to help."

"Thank goodness."

"But maybe I'll make you strap yourself to the floor, just so I can spare myself your whining and idiotic questions for a while," said Tiny-Ginny. She smiled, and her lips twitched like a pair of earthworms writhing about in a puddle.

Regular-Ginny ignored her, walking the remaining distance in annoyed silence. She approached the backs of the oval-shaped bucket seats. She ran her fingers along the smooth surface that formed the back of one of them, discovering that it consisted of metal painted white. She scooted around to the front of the chair like a shuffling ballerina and plopped into it.

She immediately regretted the decision. The cushions had appeared fluffy, like overstuffed pillows filled with down, but Ginny discovered right away that her eyes had deceived her. It felt as though she had dropped herself atop a pile of brittle sponges. Pieces of rigid straw seemed to poke out from every inch of the seat, somehow jabbing through her pink armor and causing a putrid itch to crawl up and down her skin.

Tiny-Ginny stood over Regular-Ginny's shoulder and chuckled. Mister E sniggered as well. "You're *sure* you wouldn't rather sit on the floor?" she asked.

Regular-Ginny decided that she would not be ridiculed this way. She hopped out of this chair, assuming she had been played a fool, and dashed to the other chair. She plopped down. She immediately cursed. The blinding itch tore across her skin worse than before. Frustration chiseled her face into a scowl.

"The chairs are infused with a spell that makes them uncomfortable," said Tiny-Ginny, gasping the words between giggles. "Wouldn't do to have the magicians on your trip falling asleep, and the itching prevents that. The math boys on the ground can do only so much to keep us aloft. The inflight magicians prevent crosswinds and other random airborne objects from knocking us off course."

"Oh," replied Regular-Ginny. She felt a *little* better, not quite so silly. At least it had not been some joke played at her expense. She briefly considered moving to the floor to stop the itching, but instead she shrugged and strapped herself in. She buckled the seat's crash harness across her breasts and felt the black webbing of the harness itch as it dug into her shoulders and torso. She clasped another strap about her waist and tightened it. Then she loosened it a little, so she could scratch the new itch that formed beneath it.

Regular-Ginny looked out the front window. Green meadow and clear sky filled her vision. In the distance, the meadow climbed skyward, marking the end of the valley and the rise in elevation. She soon grew tired of the view, so she pushed on the ground with her foot. Her chair spun around to face the rear of the cabin.

The dwarves had filled the cabin like row upon row of hairy, unkempt corn. They had crammed themselves so tightly together that each dwarf's legs locked into place in the armpits of the dwarf in front of him.

Regular-Ginny's eyes skimmed the fleshy fields, finally resting upon the ginger-headed dwarf with whom Tiny-Ginny had conversed on the trip here.

Ginny felt a pang of sympathy for the murderous dictator locked in place below his feet, because she had smelled the man up close. He smelled as though rotted spinach and rancid eggs had accidentally made a love child, but then they decided that they could not handle the pressures of being parents, so they drowned it in a tub of putrid mayonnaise. Ginny did not care who the dictator near the ginger man's feet was, no crime could justify being stuck at such close vicinity to those filthy appendages.

The last dozen troops ascended into the ship. The last two dwarves in line stopped about halfway up the ramp. They each unclasped a pair of locks and then flipped open a little trapdoor in the ramp. Each withdrew a rope and a set of eight long, metallic rods from his compartment. Then they kicked the trapdoors shut and each jammed one of their rods into a precut hole on each side of the ramp. They tied a bowline knot to the erect rod and carried the remaining rods and rope up the ramp.

The pair handed off their burdens to the dwarves at the top, who scampered along the walkway that led through the middle of the ship and stuck an end of each rod into holes on either side of the walkway. The rods stood in the air like miniature versions of the giant obelisks outside. The dwarves rigged together a rudimentary pulley system by winding the rope back-and-forth around the rods.

With the pulley system in place, the dozen dwarves scurried into two lines on the walkway and heaved on the ropes. With each mighty tug, the ramp raised a little higher. Sweat flung from the tiny dwarves' faces and rained a salty downpour upon the crop of dwarves beside them. One last pull, one last sweat monsoon, and the ramp THUNKed into place, closing off the entrance to the ship. Shadows eclipsed the interior of the ship, broken only by the beams of sunlight that flooded in from the windows at the front of the ship.

As soon as the ramp shut, each group of six dwarves hopped onto one another's shoulders, creating the stumpiest Doric columns that Ginny had ever seen. She watched the two columns waver and wobble over to the closed ramp like a bad *Little Rascals* gag. The dwarves on top fumbled with latches and locks, bolting and tightening the ramp in place. After the top pair finished their work, they called out, "Hup!" and then they hopped down. As soon as their nimble feet touched the ground, they dashed over and collected the rods and rope from the floor. The smaller of these two hopped onto the burlier's shoulders.

They returned the rope and rods to the trapdoors from whence they had been removed and then locked the trapdoors.

Meanwhile, the meaty columns wobbled a little further over, allowing the dwarves who were now on top to bolt shut the next row of locks, and then they hopped down. This acrobatic scheme continued until every single dwarf in each column had locked a set of bolts.

"Seems a little extreme, all that bolting and locking," remarked Regular-Ginny as these final dozen dwarves began strapping themselves into the unmanned harnesses on the floor at the back of the ship. "I'm no engineer, but I'm thinking we could have done about a sixth of that locking and been just fine."

"*They* definitely believe it's necessary," responded Tiny-Ginny, "because if that door opens, and we crash or are blown off course because of it, every single one of them will be executed."

"And let me guess: they've all been badged in door-closing, too."

"Don't be a smart-ass. Badging is a fantastic way to allow residents here to pursue ambitions and to gain power, as well as to identify those who should be looked upon with prestige. If you are leading a tribe or trying to usurp the leadership of another tribe, your underlings are much more impressed with you if you have lots of badges than if you don't. They'll be a lot less likely to try and assassinate you, too, because they'll know to fear you. Now, if you will be so kind as to turn your chair and face forward, we're about to launch."

Regular-Ginny once again touched her foot to the floor and pushed. As she spun back around to face the front of the cabin, she glanced over at her tiny counterpart. Tiny-Ginny looked like a child in her large oval chair. Her feet poked barely over the edge of the seat and dangled in the air. Mister E's head poked out from a pocket sewn into the fabric of the cushion. His eyes rolled in a continuous state of agony as he bit and chomped at his fur, trying to scratch each new itch. Regular-Ginny wished he would accidentally impale himself with his stupid rodent buckteeth. The dwarf flicked her wrist, and a leg of gelatinous pink goo launched from her pores, slapped the metal floor, and spun her around toward the front of the ship.

Regular-Ginny stared out the window. She watched the wild grass dance in the wind on the far end of the valley. She began to think about how beautiful the view was, until she felt more than heard a loud FWUNG, and every thought in her mind flushed from her brain. The picturesque landscape in front of her immediately melted and swirled into the blue sky. Her stomach scrunched into a double-knot, knocking the wind right out of her. She struggled to breathe. She found that she could not pull her head off the chair's cushion. Her head itched awfully, and she feared she might vomit.

Through the clear glass, she watched a large white cloud grow larger and larger. The ship blasted through it, and she squealed. The ship continued gaining altitude at an alarming speed, which made her shudder, which in turn made her wiggle in the chair, which in turn made her itch more than ever. She expected the descent, whenever it happened, would probably be at least an equally gut-wrenching experience.

Dozens of minutes passed, and the egg-shaped ship finally reached the zenith of its trajectory. Ginny knew this by instinct, because she felt the twitter in her stomach that told her she was at the peak. It reminded her of the feeling she got at the top of a roller-coaster when everything is steady and calm before the long drop to the bottom. Nerves fluttered up and down her legs, and she ruffled her toes in anxious worry. She stared out the window with dull eyes and watched the sky zoom past her.

The ship began to shake, and Ginny paled. She had flown in airplanes many times before, and turbulence had never bothered her. As a matter of fact, she loved flying. She loved the peanuts and she loved the fake smiles that the flight attendants wore ironed to their faces and she even loved the stupid inflight shopping magazines with their frivolous gadgets and trinkets that she had never purchased.

But Ginny had never flown in a giant metallic egg before, and she found that she did not enjoy this type of flying at all. She wished desperately that she could unharness herself and sprint to the lavatory, but she knew without needing to ask that there was no lavatory, and that she would not be allowed to move about the cabin even if she used her politest voice to ask.

The shaking turbulence grew worse, shifting from an intense vibration to an honest-to-God wobble. Sweat seeped from her palms, and her knuckles shone white as she kung-fu-gripped the armrests of her chair. She tried to swallow, but a lump in her throat dammed the way. The view out the front window shook back and forth so fast that Ginny forced herself to close her eyes because everything was blending together, and it made her head throb. She sensed the pink goo further seeping out of her pores and forming a gigantic, hard cocoon around her. She hoped it would save her from the inevitable crash.

Ginny heard more than felt a loud slap across her face. She forced her eyes open and looked over at her miniature counterpart. Tiny-Ginny looked at her with scorn. Then she made an odd gesture with her left hand—crossing her index finger with her middle, extending her pinky, bending her thumb seemingly out of socket around the back of her palm, and rotating the hand in a circle—and whispered something that sounded to Regular-Ginny like, "Wings Open!" in Pig Latin.

Two loud THUNKs reverberated throughout the ship. They sounded to Ginny as if the shell had cracked on the outside of the egg-shaped ship, and they were all about to be poured out of the sides of the ship to their deaths like so much yolk in an omelet.

Instead, the ship immediately steadied itself. Regular-Ginny felt in her stomach that the ship was beginning its descent. She glanced from Tiny-Ginny out the front window to reassure herself. The view from the window was no longer a blurred, wobbling mixture of blue sky and white clouds. Like vegetables on Ginny's dinner plate, each had returned to its proper place in her field of vision and stayed there, not mixing with its neighbor.

Regular-Ginny returned her eyes to Tiny-Ginny. The dwarf's scorn remained etched across her face like a repulsive tattoo. Her chapped lips parted like two feuding siblings, trying to stay as far away from each other as possible. She licked her dry lips, and her snaggletooth played peek-a-boo from behind her fleshy upper lip. She spoke in a raspy voice, saying, "You didn't *actually* believe I'd let us crash, did you?"

Regular-Ginny remained silent. Her fears had betrayed her and had made her look like a fool. The pink goo began draining itself back into her skin, and she bit her lower lip. She refused to speak, because she knew her tongue would start to feel too big for her mouth, and she would mumble something stupid and Tiny-Ginny would twist the words and make her feel even dumber.

Tiny-Ginny smiled, but there was no mirth in her eyes. "Those loud noises you heard were the ship's glide-wings," she said, leaning her head in close to Regular-Ginny's and whispering. The dwarf's head bobbed as she spoke, and she looked like a turtle. "They steady us out for a gentle descent. As the inflight magician, *I* control when it's time to deploy them, and I waited a little longer than usual. I let us wobble to the brink of oblivion to remind those bastards behind us who's in charge on this journey. Gave 'em a good little scare, huh?"

Regular-Ginny nodded. She felt the blood returning to her face.

Tiny-Ginny ruffled the fur atop Mister E's head. "Didn't realize our partner here had so little faith in us, did we, Mister E?"

Tiny-Ginny then turned to face the front window. Excitement gleamed in her beady eyes. She droned on, "And now we must wait. We've got a good eighteen hours before we land. Now tell me, how'd you meet your Art in the first place? The stars sure must've been crossed that day."

Regular-Ginny did not answer. She refused to make small talk with a dwarf-dictator-version of herself. Instead, she simply stared out the front window in silence.

CHAPTER 13

THE TUNNEL BENEATH THE TINY WORLD

NORMAL-ART, GOD-ART, AND Drillbot traveled underground for days, and they neither saw nor heard any sign of Dictator Scouts on their tail. Normal-Art constantly stared at God-Art's hair, following it as though he were a ghoul pursuing a flambéed brain. He wished he could sit down for a while, but he was not given the opportunity. The god forced him to walk and walk and walk, yanking him along by the hand any time he even *looked* like he was considering a break.

And worst of all, there was not even any good scenery. Every inch of the tunnel around them appeared the same. Normal-Art could have sworn he had passed the same drab lump of dirt over and over and over. But still, they continued walking. Hours passed, but the hours felt like weeks. Normal-Art began to feel claustrophobic, but then he walked for so long that he forgot about claustrophobia. But then he walked for so long that he felt claustrophobic again.

Every so often, when the boredom and the claustrophobia combined to crush his morale into a thin residue of despair, he hoped that he might die from inhaling Drillbot's exhaust fumes, which smelled like Pixie Sticks melted by flaming diesel fuel. But he never did. He simply continued walking.

The only times the trio slowed their brisk trek were the rare occasions when God-Art bent down to dig into the dirt. These respites in pace lasted *just* long enough for God-Art to find large bugs that he would hand to Normal-Art to eat for sustenance. The bugs left a bitter flavor on his tongue after he swallowed them, but they tasted like extra-sweetened lemonade when he bit into them. They tickled the back of his throat with their little furry legs as he gulped them down. This weirded him out a bit, but they managed to quench his thirst and fill his belly. And most importantly, they provided a change from the hours upon hours of trudging.

Finally, just when Normal-Art pulled the anvil from his shirt pocket and was preparing to conjure something with which to put an end to his misery, the robot stopped tunneling.

"[Whir] Drillbot has detected that we're – CLACK – we're – CLACK – we're – CLACK –we're at 13.09 South by 72.32 West. Do you – CLACK – Do you desire for Drillbot to tunnel up to the surface?"

"Absolutely. Do it as fast as you can!" cried Normal-Art, dropping the anvil back into the pocket. Drillbot began drilling at an uphill angle, and large clods of dirt plopped to the ground all around the trio.

God-Art turned to Normal-Art, yelling over the sound of drilling while pointing to his necklace of ears. "I'm listening in right now. So far as I can hear, our adversaries managed to beat us down here, and it seems they're waiting just above the surface to ambush us. I can hear my ex-mate giving combat orders to her generals as we speak.

"Hmmm, that's flattering," God-Art continued, his eyes glazing over as he listened. "It seems that my ex-mate has now taken to referring to me as *the beast.* I must've left quite an impression the last time I lay with her!"

"Good for you. But I really, really don't care. I just want to get out of this tunnel."

"Huh. That's odd," said God-Art, ignoring Normal-Art. "It seems she thinks that my godhood stems from my *bowels*. She's instructing her generals to capture their *plunder* from them. I dunno quite what she's talking about, but I guess she plans to use the power she believes is inside me to acquire our common objective. I wonder if this means she's planning to make use of the hell in my stomach somehow. It would provide ample energy to—"

"What in the hell are you rambling about?" interrupted Normal-Art.

The fog lifted from God-Art's eyes. "Sorry about that, mate, got lost in my head for a minute there. Just doing some speculating on our enemies' strategy. Anyway, it seems that Julius Caesar will be traveling around the side of some monument up there to flank us in the back. So, watch out."

The two Arts followed Drillbot as the robot cut through the planet's crust at a sharp upward angle, speaking as they walked.

"You'll want to get the weapon I gave you ready, the one that looks like a red eyeball," said God-Art. "I'll do my best to camouflage us as we burst forth from the ground, but my ex-mate knows many ways to counteract my charms. Be ready for action as soon as we emerge."

"Enough chit-chat," replied Normal-Art, readying his ruby eyeball. "Let's bust some dwarf-heads."

"I hope it's that simple," said God-Art. He knew it would not be, for he knew the Multiverse too well to believe anything could be *that* simple.

CHAPTER 14

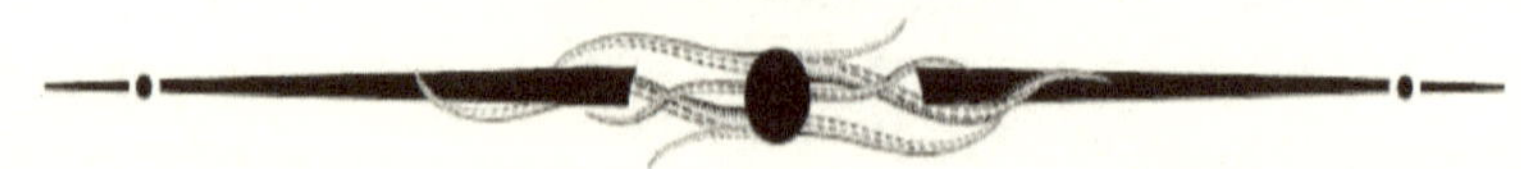

OF LANDINGS AND PLANNINGS

THE EGG-SHAPED SHIP crash-landed on the damp soil exactly when Tiny-Ginny had predicted it would. It bounced into a clearing and skidded to a halt, scraping a semicircular trail hundreds of feet in length behind it.

As soon as the ship stopped, Regular-Ginny ripped the harness from her body and stood. Finally, she felt relief from the itching. She stared out the front window of the ship. The ships that had launched prior to hers lay in the clearing. Their ramps were open, and the hordes that had inhabited them were arrayed near the edge of the clearing. Shaka had allowed his men to lie in the shade and sleep, while Gaius Julius ran his troops through drills. The squirrels skittered about everywhere, diving and weaving through tall stalks of grass.

Regular-Ginny glanced over her shoulder at the dwarves inside her own ship. The dozen at the back hurriedly unstrapped themselves and scrambled about the drawn ramp. They performed their acrobatic bit again, hopping onto each other's shoulders, this time unlocking the bolts they had previously fastened.

When the unbolting was finally complete, the twelve dwarves stood side by side in front of the unlocked ramp. As one, they braced their feet on the floor and placed their palms flat against the ramp. The dwarf on the far left called out a cadence, yelling, "Hup! Hup-Hup-Hup!" They jabbed the heels of their palms against the metal. He repeated the cadence and the call over and over, and each time the dwarves slammed their palms into the ramp.

Regular-Ginny did not believe the ramp was going to budge, not until it crashed open without warning and smashed onto the soft soil outside. The ship shook with the impact, and Ginny heard a squirrel howling a death knell beneath the ramp. The dozen ramp operators raced out of the ship. The thousands of dwarves remaining in the ship began unstrapping themselves and filing down the ramp in two single-file lines, following on the heels of the ramp operators.

The Ginnys fell into place at the end of the lines and departed the ship. The dwarves gathered in a wide semicircle at the bottom of the ramp and then marched over to the edge of the clearing to join the other armies. They waited for the last ship to arrive. Regular-Ginny searched the sky for it, but she could not locate it. Just when she had given up and had begun looking down at the ground to give her neck a rest from craning it, Tiny-Ginny tugged on her hand. The dwarf pointed at the sky. Regular-Ginny followed the finger, squinting in her effort to see.

The egg-shaped ship glided through the air, not wobbling at all. Reflected sunlight glared from the chrome lining of the ship, and gigantic tan wings stretched out from its sides. The wings looked thin and paltry compared to the ship's body, reminding Ginny of bat's wings. But they stretched wide and long, running the length of each side of the ship and spanning an area as broad as the ship was long. The wings appeared to be made from furry animal hide stretched around a metal frame. Ginny grew rather dumbfounded, because she had never seen anything quite as simultaneously beautiful and ridiculously awkward.

The ship dropped altitude and gained speed. It skimmed above the treetops of the dense jungle that surrounded the clearing. As the ship came low above the canopy of leaves, Ginny noticed that pyramids poked up from amongst the trees. They grew sporadically through the jungle as far as she could see, and they reached skyward in great limestone steps. The dull tans and greens of the blocks that formed them begged her to go exploring. The urge to run away and spend the rest of her life enjoying the grand stage of the pyramids clawed at the back of her skull.

Her fantasy burst as the sunlight reflecting off the egg-shaped ship shone directly into her eyes. She jerked her eyes closed and rubbed them with the heels of her palms, trying to massage away the smarting. Pink flashes filled the blackness behind her eyelids, and she realized that she was rubbing too hard.

She opened her eyes just in time to witness the ship crash to the ground. It smacked its bottom against the soil at the far edge of the clearing, spraying dirt into the air, and bounced six times across the ground like a skipping stone. When the ship stopped bouncing, it slid a few hundred feet, gouging a deep scar into the clearing just like all the ships before it.

The metallic egg sat in silence for a few minutes, but then the ramp put an end to the quiet by bursting open with a resounding crash. Another squirrel was caught beneath this falling ramp, but unlike the one beneath the ramp from the Ginnys' ship, this one managed to escape and only lost its tail and a back leg in the process. It hobbled away to the edge of the clearing, leaving a trail of blood to mark its path.

The Dictator Scouts within the ship marched out, led by a scout taller and skinnier than the rest. He sported a wiry beard, a black stovetop hat, and a longsword that hung in a scabbard about his waist. The scabbard dragged along the ground as he walked. He ordered his men to halt, and they immediately did as commanded. He placed his hand on the hilt of his longsword and stared coldly over at Tiny-Ginny. He stood stoically unmoving, basking in the hot sun with his nose angled slightly upward.

"Who is *that*?" asked Regular-Ginny. She had seen him standing amongst his army earlier, but he had not been wearing the tall hat. Nor did she realize that he was their leader, so at ease did he carry himself among his troops. He seemed to fear their backstabbing not at all.

Tiny-Ginny had gone to recruit this man and his underlings the night before the Obelisk Orb launch. Tiny-Ginny did not allow Regular-Ginny to accompany her on this particular trip. She said that with this recruit's reputation for intelligence and honor, she was worried Regular-Ginny would inadvertently make some stupid remark to offend him or to arouse his suspicions, and he would not agree to join their ranks. Regular-Ginny had been forced to sit in her counterpart's cabin and wait for the horrid hag to return. Tiny-Ginny refused to speak of the experience upon her arrival home, other than to confirm that their last prospect had committed to their quest. Regular-Ginny had allowed the subject to drop without any objection, since it meant she did not have to hear the dwarf's voice squeak on and on about her own cunning.

"Most call him The Honest One, but his real name is Abraham Lincoln," responded Tiny-Ginny.

Regular-Ginny guffawed. "How did my country's greatest president wind up in this backward reality?" she asked.

Tiny-Ginny's eyes bored into Regular-Ginny, and she wilted. She felt stupid and childish again, and she wished the Pink One had never called out to her.

"You thought the same thing about your reality's Einstein," replied Tiny-Ginny. "You never learn, you stupid cow! I grow weary of explaining every little detail to you, which anyone with half a brain could figure out for herself. This man is obviously from a reality separate from yours."

Regular-Ginny stared down at her feet, too ashamed to respond.

"The legends I have heard about him say that on his home reality," Tiny-Ginny continued, the condescending tone transforming into one of reverence, "he not only trained extensively in law—as I understand that he did on your reality—but the gods also chose him for another purpose. As a child, his father sent him to the Orient to learn the ways of war. He returned home a conquering samurai. Your reality had an American Civil War, correct?"

"Yes," mumbled Regular-Ginny.

"How long did it last?"

"I dunno. Years. Lots of people died."

"On his reality, it lasted less than three weeks. He led his troops into battle. He conquered and executed the leaders of the opposition, and then he assumed sole leadership of America. He named himself Dictator-for-Life, and nobody had the power to stop him. He then sought honorable battle elsewhere, finding it next in Europe. He conquered, and he conquered, and he conquered, piling the heads of his enemies thousands of feet high. And then one evening, he was drugged and assassinated by his own personal guard. How I would love to eat his brain someday. Oh, the secrets he must know."

"That is the absolute stupidest, most ludicrous story I've ever heard!" cried Regular-Ginny.

Tiny-Ginny shrugged. "Don't tell *him* that, at least not if you want to keep your head. He frightens even me. But he's here, and he brought thousands of troops for the fodder, so that's what counts."

"I guess so. But now that we've got him here, what's the next step?"

"We need to call a meeting to get the troops excited for what's to come," said Tiny-Ginny.

"So, call a meeting to get the troops excited for what's to come," responded Regular-Ginny.

Tiny-Ginny did. She signaled to the red-headed dwarf, the one with the atrocious odor, and he brought a trumpet to his lips and blew four loud, shrill notes. The sound blared across the clearing, and as it faded away, silence crept into its place. Thousands of dwarven eyes stared at the source of the noise like dumbfounded puppies, and then as though they all grasped the meaning of the notes as one, they sprinted into array before the Ginnys.

The red-headed dwarf and his crew built a makeshift platform on which the Ginnys stood, piling high a stack of wood from the surrounding jungle for its base and borrowing two of Shaka's soldiers' shields for its top.

Tiny-Ginny raised her arms above her head and called for silence—even though the dwarves were already silent—by launching fireworks of pink goo into the air above her. The show seemed to impress the Dictator Scouts, for they all remained silent.

"Comrades," called out Tiny-Ginny, her shrill voice echoing across the clearing. "I thank you for your support and for your warrior spirits. Many lacked the bravery to follow us here, but you shall all reap the proper rewards for your courage."

The crowd erupted in cheers. Regular-Ginny kept her eyes on the back of the crowd, watching the three other leaders of this rabble. They showed no emotion other than cold, cruel calculation. Shaka picked at a scab on his bare foot, seeming to ignore the speech. Lincoln stood at attention, staring at the clouds in the sky with one hand on his longsword hilt. Gaius Julius crossed his arms across his chest and stared maliciously at the women on the platform. Regular-Ginny did not trust any of them. Tiny-Ginny either did not notice them or did not care, because she continued speaking without acknowledging them at all.

"No great undertaking can be accomplished without great sacrifice. Many of us will die here today, but *we* know death is no cause for fear. We have all spat in the face of Death before we arrived on this Earth, and we know that the vengeful bastard's bark is much worse than his bite."

Applause gushed from the crowd again, so she waited for it to die down. Once it did so, she continued, "There is a being—a pink god—dwelling in this land. When we find it, we shall gain power immeasurable. This god lies trapped inside the bowels of a beast, a beast that has haunted all our nightmares since we awoke on this tiny, miserable Earth. This beast stalks this land and has caused us all to avoid this place, but it only stalks this land because we have allowed it to do so for so long. We have given this beast free reign to cull our conquering ambitions, when in our past lives nothing could have accomplished such a feat. My counterpart and I have experienced firsthand the power that we are seeking from this pink god. We desire more, but there is enough power to share. Now follow us and fight with us, and we shall harness the power of the Pink One together, and we shall all become gods ourselves!"

The crowd shook the Earth with its cheers. Shaka's troops banged their spears against their shields, drumming the wooden shafts against the thick hides.

Tiny-Ginny leaned over to Regular-Ginny and whispered in her ear, "Do you know where to go from here?"

Regular-Ginny looked down at her sociopathic counterpart, realizing at this moment *exactly* how much the dwarf needed her. She considered milking it for a while just to watch the little hag squirm, but she ultimately decided against it. The faster they got moving and finished their mission, the faster Regular-Ginny could get home and be rid of her.

"Yeah, I know where to go," replied Regular-Ginny. "The Pink One's presence feels like an itch in my brain, and the itch gets stronger the closer I am to it. Been there since it gave us the pink goo. It's buzzing like a plague-infected rash right now, and it's telling me we need to go *that* way."

Regular-Ginny pointed in a southwesterly direction.

"Lead the way, then," said Tiny-Ginny, motioning with outstretched palm toward the jungle.

Regular-Ginny hopped down from the platform and began walking toward the edge of the clearing. The crowd parted like a miniature Red Sea, allowing her to pass through untouched. Tiny-Ginny cried out over the still-cheering crowd for Regular-Ginny to wait. She stopped and turned back to face her counterpart.

Tiny-Ginny whispered something into Mister E's ear. Then she said, "We shall conserve our energy."

The squirrel jumped to the ground and stood on his hind legs. His little nose twitched as he sniffed the air. He closed his eyes and wiggled his lower jaw back and forth. Then he opened his mouth and began a series of squeaks. But they were not like any squeaks Ginny had ever heard escape a rodent's mouth. With each squeak, the squirrel's maniacal voice grew deeper, and his jaw unhinged a little more, until his mouth was stretched open as wide as an anaconda swallowing a cow. Deep bass notes erupted from his cavernous mouth, noises so sonorous that they rumbled through Ginny's bowels. She covered her ears, but it did not help. The sound punched her in the brain like an angry old boxer, and just when she was strongly considering using her pink goo to gore her own inner ears, the noise abruptly fell silent. Even so, her brain continued to rattle around in her skull for a few moments. She wanted to cry.

Millions of squirrels poured into the clearing from the jungle and popped out from beneath their shady lounging spots in the grass. They poked their heads out of holes unseen, like millions of roaches appearing from the woodwork. Regular-Ginny knew that a *lot* of squirrels had crammed into the Obelisk Orbs, but she had not realized until now just how overwhelming the number had been. She spotted the tailless and legless one who had earlier been caught beneath the ramp, and she fought off a sudden bout of sympathy.

The squirrels filled the clearing. Tiny-Ginny instructed the Dictator Scouts to mount the furry tide so that they might ride to their place of destiny and conserve their energy for the feats ahead. The soldiers cheered their approval at this idea, and then they climbed atop the carpet of squirrels that now covered the entire clearing.

Regular-Ginny rode at the front of the squirrel caravan, body-surfing the wave of fur as she called directions to Tiny-Ginny, who rode beside her and in turn called directions to the squirrels. A nervous ball of energy sat lumped in Ginny's stomach. She sat silently until the time came for her to give new directions, and then she remained silent afterward during the hours-long stretches of straightness.

Whenever the group zoomed past a pyramid, she did not remove her eyes from it until a new one popped into view. She had always wanted to see pyramids, but back home she had never worked up the courage to pack up and go to them. She studied the foreign carvings on the sides of each one and tried to decipher why they were there. Most had sculptures of giant squirrels atop them, some angry and mean, some kind and beneficent, and some simply cute. These sculptures all had one thing in common, and that was a crown resting atop their heads.

The colossal army pushed through the dense undergrowth of the jungle. The itch inside Ginny's skull grew and pulsated, swelling to encapsulate the entire gray blob of her brain. When her head felt ripe to explode into a thousand itchy pieces, she finally told Tiny-Ginny to stop the squirrels. They had arrived.

The squirrels skittered to a halt and the Ginnys crawled off them. They stood before the largest pyramid they had seen all day. It reached high into the sky, threatening to pluck the sun from its perch amongst the clouds. Regular-Ginny saw no squirrel sculptures atop it, but instead a primitive statue of intertwining pastel pink and blue—a large blue rock with a tail of matching blue that sat next to a large pink rock with a tail of pink. The tails wrapped around each other as though they were a pair of mating snakes.

"We're here," said Regular-Ginny. "But something doesn't feel right."

"That's because we got here *way* too easily," replied Tiny-Ginny. "The guardian of this place *must* be near. I'll send a couple squirrels ahead to scout things out. Make sure you cling tightly to my heart. I've foreseen it, and you will need it before this day is through."

The army of Dictator Scouts dismounted the squirrels and arrayed themselves behind the Ginnys. Tiny-Ginny picked two squirrels from the pack and sent them to scout ahead. They scampered into the distance, disappearing around the opposite side of the pyramid. About half an hour later, one limped back, barely alive, and hobbled up onto Tiny-Ginny's shoulder. It squeaked something into her ear before closing its eyes and falling from her shoulder. It crashed to the grass with an audible thud.

Tiny-Ginny turned and called the leaders to her. Shaka, Lincoln, and Gaius Julius approached and stood at attention in front of her.

"The beast is nearby," said Tiny-Ginny. "It's on the other side of the pyramid. We know this because the Pink One has allowed my counterpart to sense it, and because our two fallen squirrel-comrades have confirmed it. We must prepare for battle."

Tiny-Ginny pointed to Gaius Julius. "Juley, I want you to take your men around the south side of the pyramid. The rest of us will approach from the north. After we have engaged the beast, you and your men shall burst forth from around that side of the pyramid to flank 'em."

Gaius Julius nodded. Tiny-Ginny indicated Lincoln and Shaka. "Our target lies within the bowels of the beast. *Our* three armies shall attack head-on. As soon as we are able to retrieve our plunder from within the beast, we shall flee and divide the spoils once we reach safety. Happy hunting."

Lincoln and Shaka nodded, then all three men walked away to give orders to their troops. Tiny-Ginny approached the smelly ginger-headed man, pulling him aside. "Eirik Bloodaks, you shall have the honor of commanding the vanguard. Lead our troops into battle against this beast, and when we have gained our godhood, we shall make love for all eternity on a bed sewn from the hides of our enemies."

"Aye, ye got it, milady," responded Eirik Bloodaks. Regular-Ginny found it hard to breathe near him, and she was enormously thankful when he sauntered away to begin preparations with the troops.

Regular-Ginny pulled Tiny-Ginny aside while the leaders were making final preparations. "So, how're we going to handle this? How're we going to sneak away while these guys are fighting?" asked Regular-Ginny.

"We shall have to fight, too," replied Tiny-Ginny.

"Wait, what?"

"The troops that make up our shaky alliance do not trust *me*, let alone *you*. We may have convinced them to risk their lives by giving them hope to gain our pink powers, but they'll be watching us. They will know if we do not enter the fight, and as soon as they sense betrayal, they will sacrifice their own lives to kill us before they die. And these bloodthirsty men are not men from whom we will easily walk away, even with our powers."

"Then what can we do? I'm not a soldier. I don't know a thing about fighting."

"Don't worry. I've got a plan," responded Tiny-Ginny.

"Which is?"

Tiny-Ginny smirked. "You didn't *really* think I wasted two Obelisk Orbs on these squirrels because we needed them to ferry us around, did you?"

"Why do you keep asking me questions when you know what my answer is going to be?" asked Regular-Ginny. "I'm correct in assuming it's because you're a total bitch, right?"

"Clever *and* original. Now don't move. I'll arrange everything with the squirrels. You simply keep my heart at the ready."

Tiny-Ginny whispered into Mister E's ear, and he hopped down from his perch on her shoulder and scampered into the crowd of squirrels. He squeaked loudly, projecting his voice over the din of the surrounding Dictator Scouts. The squirrels all perked up onto their hind legs and listened. Mister E continued squeaking and chirping at them, motioning with his front paws like a drunken hobo telling a story to a crowd of drunker hobos.

He finished haranguing them with a final loud chirp, and they immediately proceeded to bum-rush the Ginnys. Millions of squirrels surged into the women, knocking them off their feet. Regular-Ginny attempted to stand, but the squirrels continued coming, piling higher and higher upon her so she could not find her feet. Their combined weight threatened to smash her flat, and she feared she was going to be crushed and lost in this undertow of squirrel meat and fur and bones. She tried to scream, but squirrel tail filled her gaping mouth and muffled the sound. The harder she struggled and the more she panicked, the closer she found herself to being suffocated.

Finally, after struggling and getting nowhere, she forced her body to relax. She knew the squirrels were not intentionally trying to kill her, for Tiny-Ginny still had need of her. And when she stopped struggling, an odd sensation crept over her. It felt as though she were no longer sinking beneath the horrid sea of squirrel fur, but rather being lifted to the top. She craned her neck to look underneath her and discovered that she was, indeed, being raised. She watched squirrels squirming like a brood of maggots around her, pushing past her to attain a position underneath her. And with each squirrel that forced itself beneath her, she found herself lifted a little higher. The speed of her raising picked up, which made her wonder inanely if she could get the Bends from leaving too quickly the heavy pressures on the bottom of this squirrely sea.

At long last, after many more inane thoughts, daylight broke through the squirrel fur above her. Regular-Ginny tried to rub her eyes, for the sudden reintroduction of bright light to her world was uncomfortable after the time her eyes had spent adjusting to the darkness in the depths of the squirrels. However, she discovered that she could not rub her eyes because her arms, legs, and torso were held solidly in place by hundreds of furry paws. The only thing not clamped immovably down by furry mitts was her head, which she could turn to look about the world beneath her. She poked it out of her perch and looked to her left, finding Tiny-Ginny hanging next to her in the exact same manner. Mister E poked his head out between the top two buttons of Tiny-Ginny's shirt.

"What's happening?" Regular-Ginny called out.

"I ordered the squirrels to combine their efforts and form a giant squirrel. I'm holding it together with magic. We're the eyes."

"Oh," responded Regular-Ginny. She did not quite know what to think, other than that she was probably soon going to die the stupidest death imaginable.

She looked down from her perch to study the giant squirrel. It both impressed and disoriented her at the same time. It stood probably fifty-feet tall, and it looked exactly like one would expect a fifty-foot tall squirrel to look, the only difference being that the fur never stopped moving and crawling and gnashing its teeth at the rest of the fur, because the squirrels were constantly crawling over each other and pushing each other out of the way and biting and clawing at each other to reach fresh oxygen on the outer layer of the behemoth.

Regular-Ginny moved her eyes from the hypnotizing squirrel monster and looked over at the armies arrayed below. They stood at attention in formation around the giant squirrel, appearing even tinier from this height than usual. Up close, they had intimidated her despite her pink powers. From way up here, the Dictator Scouts simply appeared absurd. She even considered spitting down upon the head of one of the infernally dreadful men, but in the end decided against it.

Tiny-Ginny called to the troops below and ordered them to march. They did so, with her own large army led by Eirik in the front. Shaka's shielded warriors danced behind them, chanting a war song on their way, while Lincoln's fiercely disciplined troops marched in perfect cadence at the rear. Meanwhile, Gaius Julius's soldiers veered off to the left, disappearing around the opposite side of the pyramid.

Regular-Ginny hung like a lazy eye in her perch. She sighed, knowing that her fate relied completely upon the whims of Tiny-Ginny, for Tiny-Ginny controlled the squirrels.

Tiny-Ginny ordered the giant squirrel to move. And move it did. With each step, the ground shook beneath the squirrel monster and thousands of squirrels shrieked pained shrieks, which Regular-Ginny assumed were the sounds of them being crushed to death by the weight of their millions of rodent brethren. Thanks to Tiny-Ginny's magic, though, no dead squirrels fell from the dazzling behemoth.

As the gigantic squirrel continued plodding along, the vibration created by each step carried its way up the colossal squirrel and shook Regular-Ginny so hard that it reminded her of Karen, the bully from elementary school who throttled her every day for her lunch money. After a few dozen steps, she developed a pounding headache that made her forget all about the pink itch in her brain. She prayed the army would reach the other side of the pyramid soon and begin the battle. She did not know how much longer she could handle this experience before her head exploded.

Before too many more steps, she got her wish.

CHAPTER 15

A FEW KINKS TO WORK OUT

THE ARTS SAT on a large limestone boulder and collected themselves. They squinted in the bright light of the southern hemisphere and waited for their eyes to adjust.

"Well, that was pretty anti-climactic," remarked Normal-Art.

Moments ago, Drillbot had burst through the surface of the planet, and the two Arts had stared up into bright sunlight. Normal-Art was momentarily blinded by the light, but he held the ruby eyeball at the ready, anyway. Over and over, he repeated in his head the magic words that he had been told would activate the eyeball. He did not want to forget them when the time came to say them.

God-Art sighed, and then he took a moment to reach over to Normal-Art and turn the eyeball so that its pupil away from his body. The god also whispered something that Normal-Art could not understand, and then he tapped Normal-Art on the forehead. Normal-Art felt a surge of energy flush through the upper half of his face. All his muscles contracted, and then when the surge stopped, he found that he could see normally.

"Thanks," Normal-Art muttered.

God-Art nodded, and then he darted toward the opening of the tunnel. The ruby eyeball twinkled in the darkness of the tunnel, and time seemed to stand still. A clod of dirt fell on Normal-Art's head, and as he wiped it away, he looked up to see God-Art leaping up out of the tunnel, brandishing his obsidian ice pick and dagger like a Viking berserker.

Normal-Art steeled himself, repeated the magic words in his head one more time, and then followed the god. He hurdled the lip of the tunnel, rolling as he landed on the thick grass like he had seen action heroes do in the movies. He twisted, using his momentum to tumble around onto his feet.

Normal-Art held the crimson eyeball in front of his body and yelled, "*Socky-Go-Go-Eyeball!* Go kapow! Go kapow now!"

A deep red wave erupted from the eyeball, an energy blast that engulfed the area in front of Normal-Art and knocked clear the wide arc of vegetation that stood in its way. The beam originated from deep inside his body, and he quivered as it seemed to launch tendrils beneath his skin. The tendrils snaked through his veins and broke down the walls of his heart, plugging directly into his soul with what felt like a magical extension cord. As the blast carried on and on, Art felt himself being drained by it. His head spun, and he thought he might faint. He frowned, for he heard none of the screaming, exploding dwarves that he had expected to hear.

And that was when he knew for certain that something was amiss. He concentrated as hard as he could, shutting off the valve within himself that powered the energy beam. He collapsed to his knees and huffed for breath. He saw double and slapped his own cheek until the double-vision melded back into single-vision. He looked over his shoulder and saw that God-Art was not swinging his obsidian weapons. Instead, the god was simply sitting atop a large block of limestone. Normal-Art joined him there.

Normal-Art looked around. He had always dreamed of vacationing in a tropical rainforest, and though the circumstances were not ideal, he was now in one. Flowers of every color imaginable flourished amongst the thick bushes. Towering trees stretched up into the sky, making him feel like a tiny scallop in a forest of kelp.

But the rainforest was not quite what he had expected, and his dream soon turned into a nightmare. The few travel agents who Art had worked up the energy to contact had never mentioned that a tropical rainforest houses bugs the size of his fist, and that these bugs never stop biting! Every time Normal-Art tried to think, he felt another one crawling up his hairy legs. And each time he swatted one, the bug's entrails splattered and soaked into his grove of coarse leg hair, and four more took its place. He finally shrugged and gave up, allowing the bugs to make a feast of his legs. After a while, the itching stings stopped stinging and began to simply itch. He sighed.

Drillbot leaned against the boulder at the Arts' feet, its gears churning in the hot equatorial sun. Normal-Art wondered if robots created from tiny magical anvils could feel heat. He guessed the answer was no, but the whirring from within Drillbot's chest reminded him of his childhood, when he would play in the summer heat too long and his asthma would flare up into a fit of wheezing. *But surely Drillbot doesn't have asthma,* he thought. *That would be ridiculous.*

Normal-Art turned to God-Art and began talking about something that seemed more pertinent than the inane thoughts drifting through his brain. "I thought you heard from your fancy dead-ear-necklace that the dwarves were waiting for us," said Normal-Art.

"Well, maybe there're still a few kinks to work out. Cut me some slack, I'm new at using the damned thing. I'd like to see *you* perfect using a stolen demigod's artifact on your first try."

"You were still wrong, though. If it were *me* who messed up, you sure as hell wouldn't give me the benefit of the doubt."

"I wouldn't say I was *wrong*, per se. From the information that I was awake to gather, I'd say I made a rather logical assumption in assuming our enemies were referring to *me* as a beast."

Normal-Art frowned. "*The information* you *were awake to gather?*" he cried. "What do you mean by that?"

God-Art shrugged. "I listened as much as I could while we were underground. But even *I* must sleep sometimes. Unfortunately, I have a bit of a proclivity for doing it while walking, so as you can guess, I was out a good chunk of the time we were down there. Happens mostly when I get bored. Sorry, mate, but if you were better company, I might've been able to stay conscious. So really, it's your own fault if you think about it. At least my energy levels are peaking now, though, right?"

"You son of a bitch."

"Hmmph. If a nap that helped me recharge my godly powers had to come at the price of *completely* accurate strategic information, I would happily make that sacrifice every time. If you don't like it, then sue me or challenge me to trial by combat. Either is acceptable where I come from."

Normal-Art sighed. "It's completely unfair that you got to sleep, and I didn't!"

God-Art shrugged.

Normal-Art balled his fists. "You're a damned bastard, you know that?"

God-Art smirked. "We've been over this before. A damned bastard is one of the many things I am, so this name-calling of yours does *not* insult me. That's like me calling you a chubby balding mortal who'll probably die in a few years from Adult-Onset Diabetes and expecting you to take offense at it."

Normal-Art screamed in frustration, tearing out a few handfuls of hair. "Fine! Let's just drop it and figure out what we should do now and where we should go, so I can hurry up and get home. I *can't wait* until I never have to lay eyes on you again."

"I usually rely on Bev to guide me on the specifics of where I need to go, so I haven't a clue for sure," said God-Art. "The latitude and longitude of this general area are as close as I know based on discussions I had with Bev before she…before she…she…"

The god trailed off. For a moment, the fire blazing atop his skull faded, and he frowned. But this display of emotion disappeared as quickly as fog on a hot summer morning. The flames blazed brightly once more, and he said with a smirk, "But it seems to me that our little blue quarry has some form of telepathic link with you that manifests itself in your sleep. I'll take watch to protect us from the Ginnys, while you take that nap you've been so vigorously complaining about missing. While you sleep, though, make yourself useful and concentrate *really* hard on talking with the thing."

"I'll try to nap, but I don't think it'll do much good. After firing that stupid *Socky-Go-Go-Eyeball*, my nerves are absolutely frayed. I feel like I'm in the middle of a twenty-day cocaine bender. I couldn't sleep right now if you paid me a million bucks."

God-Art smiled. He reached into the small leather pouch attached to his belt. The opening seemed just wide enough for him to fit a finger and thumb inside, but God-Art wiggled and stretched his entire arm into the bag. Normal-Art sighed. God-Art gave a look that screamed *eureka* as his hand closed around something down in the depths of the bag, and then he actually shouted, "Eureka!" as he pulled a large, white, powdery ball from the pouch.

"I've got just the thing to knock you right out," said God-Art. A grin crept across his face that reminded Normal-Art of a slobbering gray wolf.

"What's that?" asked Normal-Art, pointing to the powdery white ball. A freezing wind tingled its way across Normal-Art's pointer finger as it neared the ball. He shuddered.

"Snow, of course. On my reality, back before it was destroyed, I used to travel about the world every night with a bag of freezing snow filled to the brim from my mountain home. I would use it to make children fall asleep."

"Oh! Kinda like the Sandman from my reality, huh?"

"Yeah, exactly, except that guy's a total wanker. Met him a couple years ago at a night club. He totally sprinkled his sand in some broad's drink and took her home," said God-Art. "Even *I* think that's pretty low."

The god gingerly rubbed the snow into a frigid mask across Normal-Art's face, treating the substance like it was some sort of delicate facial cream. Normal-Art grinned, happy that he was about to finally, for the first time in days, get a few comfortable minutes of shuteye.

"The biggest difference between us, though," continued God-Art, "is that he scientifically formulated his sand to make you mortals fall into a peaceful sleep. I was a little lazier when I developed my snow. Mine simply overwhelms your pain receptors until you pass out."

Normal-Art's smile disappeared from his face, and his eyes grew wide. "Wait, what's that supposed to mea-AAAAAAAAAAUGH!"

Normal-Art screamed, trying desperately to rub the snow off his face with the butts of his palms. As he did so, his palms began to ice over. Every bone inside his body seemed to freeze and become caked in pain-inducing ice, and every fiber of his being seemed to shiver and shake so violently that he felt like King Kong and Godzilla were taking turns throttling him. He screamed even louder, and his larynx threatened to rip its way out of his throat, climb up his tongue, force its way out of his mouth, and then beat him into oblivion.

He could not breathe. He stopped trying to rub away the snow and began clawing at his face to get it off. His screaming did not end until he ran out of air, and the only sound that escaped his lips at that point was an awkward gurgle. After a few moments, he lost all control of his body and collapsed onto the ground. After flailing for a while, he finally fell unconscious.

God-Art turned away from the now-silent Normal-Art. The god peered through the surrounding jungle underbrush and readied himself to hold off the army of attacking dwarves if it appeared. But he did not see any movement whatsoever, not even the flittering of a squirrel amongst the trees. The lack of a dwarf welcoming party, or even a squirrel sent to scout for them, made God-Art awfully nervous.

God-Art frowned. He looked down at Normal-Art, who tossed in his sleep. "It'll be over soon," he said, stroking his counterpart's cheek.

God-Art brought his knees up to his chest and locked his arms around them, preparing to entertain himself during his wait for Normal-Art to wake by planning future mischief. But the god's thoughts were interrupted when he heard a whirring behind him. Without moving his body, he turned his head behind him to find the source. He had forgotten about Drillbot.

"What's new, Drillbot?" asked God-Art.

"[whir] Why is – CLACK – Why is – CLACK – Why is Drillbot *here*? Not simply – CLACK – not simply in this jungle. But *here* here. *Alive*."

The gears and radar dishes atop Drillbot's head tipped forward, and it looked to God-Art like the robot was furrowing its brows. The only other time God-Art had seen a robot look at him with an expression like *that* was when he had seduced and broken the geared heart of the Ginny of Earth 5,254, where everyone is a sentient robot. He had not even considered the option that Drillbot might be sentient before now, simply because the magical automaton had popped out of a magical anvil and had gone straight to work.

"I don't know how to answer that, buddy," replied God-Art. "Why are any of us here? We puff into existence one day, and then we're expected to live life without any explanation as to why. I've been around pretty much forever, and I couldn't even begin to tell you."

"[whir] Why did Master – CLACK – Master – CLACK – Why did Master Art create Drillbot? Drillbot was OK being nothing. Now – CLACK – now Drillbot questions everything. Better before."

"Well, you were made to serve a purpose. To dig."

"[whir] Assignment '*dig*' complete. What – CLACK – What now?" asked Drillbot, its tinny voice clunking and crashing across the jungle like a lost submarine with faulty sonar.

"Now," said God-Art, "you're stuck here being alive, just like the rest of us. You've got to deal with it, just like we all do."

"[whir] Drillbot needs new assign – CLACK – new assignment."

"Don't look at me. Figure it out on your own. I had to."

Drillbot's head began to whistle steam from between its gaskets, and its head began spinning in circles like a boiling, steaming teakettle on roller skates. A terrible screeching burst from deep within its torso, and oil began to squirt from the corners of its telescopic eyes.

Drillbot said, "[whir] Assignment '*dig*' complete. Drillbot cannot function without – CLACK – without purpose. Drillbot will – CLACK – will return to nothingness if given no purpose for existing."

Drillbot brought the drill on its left arm up to head-level, aiming the sharp point at its spinning cranium. The drill clicked to life, buzzing with the desire to mine robot cranium.

"[whir] Please give – CLACK – give Drillbot new purpose. Drillbot cannot function without – CLACK – without purpose."

"Very well, but don't blame me when your *new* purpose leaves you unfulfilled," said God-Art with a shrug. He pointed at Normal-Art's prone body. "Your new reason for existence is to protect that bag of bones down there on the ground. Don't let your creator die. If *he* dies, then *I* can't get what I desire. And if I can't get what I desire, we're all pretty good and screwed."

"[whir] Affirmative. Drillbot now has – CLACK – now has new purpose. Initiating assignment *'protect Master Art.'*"

The robot stopped spinning its head and let its drill fall back down to its side.

God-Art smiled at the robot. "Now back off. I need room to think," he said.

Drillbot backed off and watched Normal-Art sleep.

CHAPTER 16

COMET-BOY

NORMAL-ART WAS BOTH a child and a comet, streaking through the blackness of space toward the Earth. He hit the atmosphere and crackled through it like a frying egg. His skin glowed red on entry, and his eyes watered a little as he passed into the oxygen of the blue morning sky.

"I'm a comet," he yelled, his inner child having taken over his personality. "Lookou' below! Whoosh!"

He twirled, and the Earth spun round and round below him. Dizziness engulfed him, so he puked. He streaked through the vomit and felt it stream down his naked torso.

He aimed for some fluffy clouds that spun beneath him like a pile of cotton balls in a blender. The outer layer of white fluffiness covering one of the clouds peeled back like the skin of a potato, revealing a deep blackness within. Normal-Art scratched his head in confusion. He stopped spinning and changed his trajectory away from the sudden, impending void. He aimed now toward a blue pyramid that rose from the ground far below. He zoomed past the clouds and around the void. He turned to look back up at them, and he realized that together they formed a large eyeball. The black void he had seen within the puffy whiteness was actually a pupil, old and knowing. Art's eyes scanned the horizon and landed upon a second cloudy eyeball, far in the distance on the opposite horizon. The pupils rotated within their respective clouds to stare at him. He waved at them.

He turned to look back down at the blue pyramid. The celestial eyeballs zoomed around him and planted themselves in the sky between him and the pyramid. The pyramid poked up between the eyes, forming a fat snout. The blue that covered the pyramid began to vibrate, and then blasted off into the air. It swirled into a pale ball, levitating around the giant eyeballs to engulf them. The swirling blueness and the cosmic eyes flared back up into the sky above Art, barely missing him as they careened past. The pyramid remained below, a greenish hue now covering it like a gangrenous infection. Art continued to fall toward it.

It's great fun being a comet, he thought in his high-pitched child voice. *But I bet it hurts big-time when you hit the ground.* Before he had the chance to find out, the bottom of the floating blueness formed itself into giant paws and stretched out below to fill the sky underneath him. He bounced into the paws and felt as though he was falling into a puffy blue sheet on a warm, sunny day.

"Awww, yay! No crashes! No hurties!" he screamed.

Art rolled onto his back and looked up into the cosmic eyes. The blue around the eyes swirled and morphed, transforming the sky into the face of a giant teddy bear.

"Comet-Boy must listen," it said, its snout dripping blue goo that fell into the sky and then evaporated back up into the blob.

"Mmm'kay," said Art.

"Me in the pyramid below."

"Mmm'kay," said Art again. He craned his neck to look below. His eyes locked onto the green pyramid toward which he had been falling. Directly to the west of the pyramid, an angry brown mass collided against a swirling white gel. He squinted at them, but he could not identify what they were. He shrugged.

"Art must find Me."

"Find blue teddy. 'kay."

"There be many false pyramids around. Hold only death for Art. Find the pyramid marked with *this* sign."

Art looked back up at the face of the cosmic teddy bear. It collapsed in on itself and began to swirl faster than Art had ever seen anything swirl. The blob took a new shape, and then it floated down to rest on top of the pyramid below. Two comets, one pink and one blue, intertwined atop the green pyramid like a trophy mounted on top of a colossal trophy stand.

"Art find this, and Me will be helped by Art," said the bear's voice, now originating from within the comets.

"Mmm'kay," said Art.

"Time be of the essence. Follow the path to the top. Look within comets for entrance. All other ways inside be trapped by hoodoo. All other ways be death. Me will signal to Art in Art's head to give Art guidance. It will tickle. Be careful but be quick. Others be here already, preparing to wage war to get inside. Me can sense them outside. Awake now, Comet-Boy."

"Mmmm'kay," replied Art.

Art awoke and found both God-Art and Drillbot leaning over him, staring into his eyes.

"That's pretty creepy," said Normal-Art. The dream had seemed so real that the deep baritone of his adult voice felt out of place in his throat, like visiting an abandoned childhood haunt that has not been visited in years.

"Where do we need to go?" asked God-Art.

Normal-Art rubbed his raw face. The snow was gone, apparently having melted in the blistering tropical sun. He said, "We must find a pyramid with a sculpture of two comets on top of it. One comet is going to be blue, and the other pink."

God-Art nodded. "Which way do we need to go?" he asked.

Normal-Art closed his eyes for a moment to feel for the promised tickle in his brain. When he felt it, he understood what it meant without knowing quite how he understood it. He said, "Let's head west."

CHAPTER 17

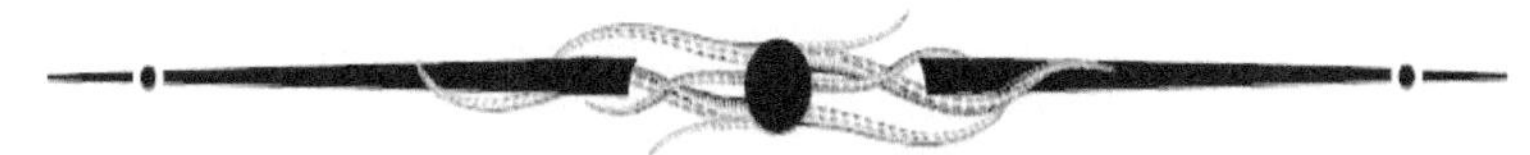

AN EPICALLY ODD SHOWDOWN

THE GIANT SQUIRREL monster stood near the pyramid and peeked around its corner. From her perch in its eye socket, Regular-Ginny saw yet another sight that she never would have believed unless she had witnessed it herself. An enormous creature lay sunning itself on a grassy field. It had translucent skin that formed the outline of a dragon: a lizard-shaped body, an elongated neck, a dinosaur-like head, a skinny tail, bat-like wings, massive claws, and fangs longer than Ginny was tall.

The beast looked like the ghost of a dragon, because cottony white clouds floated inside its translucent skin. The clouds twirled and churned in a constant swirling miasma. The beast's foggy innards reminded Ginny of when she used to go the state fair with her father and watch the vendors make cotton candy. Sugar would whirl round and round in the machine, swirling itself into cottony goodness that grew fluffier by the second.

Below, the vanguard of Tiny-Ginny's army rounded the corner at the edge of the pyramid, and Eirik Bloodaks screamed a fierce, piercing battle cry. He sprinted forward, and the soldiers he led in the vanguard followed, forgetting all sense of disciplined attack as they dashed toward the creature. Shaka and his troops, by now having danced and chanted themselves into a fury that had boiled over its metaphorical pot, exploded onto the heels of the vanguard. In their haste for battle, they galloped past Eirik and the vanguard of Tiny-Ginny's soldiers. Lincoln and his army did not follow the other two brigades with the same blind wrath. Instead, he and his troops rounded the corner with their rigorous formation intact, continuing their march to the cadence of a little drummer dwarf.

The dragon lifted its head from its paws and stretched, arching its back and smacking its narrow lips like a kitten waking from a nap. It stood on its four legs, and as it noticed the approaching dwarves, the milky clouds within its skin began to swirl into a ferocious hurricane.

The Ginnys' giant squirrel monster stepped around the corner of the pyramid and burst into a sprint, circumventing Lincoln's army with five gigantic steps. Because she had no control over the squirrel monster, Regular-Ginny fixed her attention on the translucent beast ahead of her. Focusing on it helped her to think about something other than the migraine that had squatted like a strung-out addict in the depths of her skull.

By this time, the armies led by Shaka and Eirik had traversed most of the distance to the beast. Shaka's men paused for a moment to hurl their long throwing spears at it, after which they brandished their short stabbing spears and continued the charge. The throwing spears pierced the behemoth's skin with a muted SCHWUK, continued through the fog inside the creature, and then exited out holes that they poked through the beast's back.

The cloudy innards leaked from the spear-holes for a couple seconds, but then they stopped leaking when the skin healed itself in a flash of light. Ginny watched the fog that had leaked from the holes float directly back toward the dragon's nostrils. The dragon breathed the gas back into its body and stared at the nearing army as though it had never been touched or poked. It roared, posturing like a jungle cat defending its territory.

Ginny expected it to pounce on the vanguard, but instead, it inhaled deeply. It sucked in air like a dragon-themed vacuum cleaner, and for every second that it inhaled, it puffed up larger. And then it continued inhaling until long past the point of cartoonish ridiculousness. Its skin seemed to be formed from some sort of rubbery substance that allowed it to stretch and grow like a balloon, and as it continued to inhale, it began to float off the ground.

The dragon reminded Ginny of a balloon that might belong in the Macy's Thanksgiving Day Parade, so long as the theme of this year's parade was: *Winter Wonderland…Full of Ridiculous Beasts That Will Likely Maim and Kill You.* And much to Regular-Ginny's chagrin, this dragon-float promised to be exponentially more dangerous than a two-story-tall Garfield the Cat.

The Ginnys' squirrel monster screeched to a halt two-thirds of the way across the field that separated it from the puffed beast. Regular-Ginny did not know why the squirrel monster had stopped, but she squealed in delight anyway. She smiled and closed her eyes, grateful for the reprieve from the vibrations of the behemoth's steps. Her tense muscles began to relax, and her headache began to drift away.

Then, to her utter dismay, Ginny felt a lurch in her stomach. She opened her eyes. She glanced down, and she realized the ground was no longer beneath her. The squirrel monster had leapt into the air. Ginny groaned and raised her eyes, watching with her mouth agape as the dragon-balloon filled her vision.

While Regular-Ginny had been distracted by the respite of the squirrel monster's brief pause, the dragon had continued inhaling, and it had now lost nearly all definition of shape. It had transformed into a giant sphere with a tiny dragon face in its middle. Ginny gasped when she saw shapes in the clouds inside of it, shapes that looked like mustachioed faces and swirling vaporous dwarves. She grew terrifyingly confused, and she wished more than ever to be home.

She glanced over at Tiny-Ginny, who grinned maniacally, and Mister E, who grinned even more maniacally. She stared past them and saw a colossal squirrel paw hanging behind them in the air like a furry halo, massive and squiggly from the constantly moving squirrels. It was reared back, ready to sock the dragon-balloon square in the face.

Time seemed to stop. Regular-Ginny gulped. Hundreds of spears hung in the air before her, gifts from the troops below on their way to deliver futile pricks to the dragon-balloon.

And just before the squirrel monster could complete its pounce onto the beast, and just before the spears could reach their target, the dragon released the dam that held back its foul breath. A brutal twister burst forth from its translucent lips. Ginny's heart sank deep into her chest, her stomach tied itself into knots, and the two banged noisily together beneath her rib cage.

The spears hanging in the air in front of her were the first to be affected by the dragon's tornado-breath. The wind whipped the deadly weapons in all directions. Ginny watched many be flung back down to the Earth, where they skewered dozens of burly dwarves. Blood splattered from the piercing wounds, and the Earth drank deep the gore. Ginny found herself staring down at one particular dwarf whose tan shield had been run through by three spears, all of which pinned him to the grass. None of the spears passed through vital areas. Two had pierced the man's shoulders and the third his left thigh. He writhed on the ground and cried for death to come quickly, but it looked to Ginny as though he was in for a rather slow and painful wait.

Ginny returned her attention to the emptying dragon-balloon, and she immediately wished that she had not done so. It had turned its open mouth toward the giant squirrel monster. Squirrel fur flew in every direction, and Ginny watched as a few thousand rodents launched from the monster and into the distance like cruise missiles aimed for the tall canopy of the surrounding jungle. She could have sworn she even witnessed one of the furry missiles impale a tree.

As the dragon's breath continued its barrage against the squirrely behemoth, the force of the blast flipped the colossal squirrel upside down. Regular-Ginny stared dumbfounded at the hordes of Dictator Scouts now inverted below her. But before the colossal squirrel could crash on top of them and crush them, they fell victim to the dragon's breath, too. Hundreds of them were flung away into the air like leaves in the path of a nuclear-powered blower. They arced skyward and fell like miniature sacks of lumpy potatoes, crashing and thudding with bone-chilling crunches.

The ground now seemed close enough to reach out and touch, but Regular-Ginny would not have had the chance to do so even if she had wanted to. She felt the little squirrel paws that were holding her in place begin tugging on her back. Squirrel fur filled her vision as the creatures pulled her deep within the gargantuan monster. The smack and squeal of squirrels crashing into the ground where she had just been made her wince, and she realized that she was squeezing her eyelids shut. She opened them and gasped a surprised gasp.

Tiny-Ginny's face hovered less than an inch away from hers. The Ginnys were scrunched tightly within a squirrely womb, without even a bruise to show for their crash. Regular-Ginny blinked, and waited for Tiny-Ginny to speak. Tiny-Ginny blinked back and did not say anything.

Regular-Ginny finally broke the awkward silence. "What the *hell* is happening out there?"

"Well, I'd say it's pretty damned obvious," responded Tiny-Ginny, grinning her snaggle-toothed grin. "Death is slaughtering our troops, just like we planned."

"I didn't think it would be *this* awful. I'd expected a big pale guy or something, and at least a slightly more even matchup."

Tiny-Ginny guffawed. "Your reality has the stupidest personification of Death that I've seen in the entire Multiverse, so I can understand why you'd be shocked if you were expecting a guy in a skirt, holding a sickle."

"Black cloak and holding a scythe, actually," replied Regular-Ginny. After pausing for a beat, she said, "So, what do we do now? Our army won't distract that thing for more than a few more minutes, and then we ain't gonna have an army left at all. And as intimidating as this giant squirrel monster is, I have my doubts that it's gonna last too much longer than those dwarves against that beast."

"Don't worry," said Tiny-Ginny. "We won't be battling it for long. We shall reform our squirrel monster and commence another attack, during which we shall use our pink goo to launch ourselves over the beast's head and straight toward the Pink One. Speaking of which, where *is* the Pink One, exactly?"

Regular-Ginny closed her eyes, listening to the itch in her brain. She had to tune out the sounds of dead and dying dwarves outside the cocoon of the squirrel monster, as well as the sounds of dead and dying squirrels within the cocoon of the squirrel monster. The itch told her exactly what she expected it would. "It's inside the pyramid. We must enter from the top."

Tiny-Ginny's grin widened, making her look like a gap-toothed hyena. "Pretty much what I figured."

"How'll I know when we're ready to make our escape?"

"You'll know the cue when it happens. You'll feel yourself sink into the squirrels again, just like you did a few moments ago before we crashed to the ground."

"OK. And then what? Will the squirrels dump us onto the ground, and then we'll run?"

Tiny-Ginny smirked. "No, that would be dumb. I've got an actual plan. As soon as you begin to sink, hook a tiny bit of the pink stuff from each of your hands onto our squirrel monster's face. You'll want to use it like a rubber band and let it stretch as tautly as it can, so the less pink stuff you expel from your pores, the better. When you stop sinking, use a blast of pink goo from your body to remove the squirrel paws that'll be holding you in place, and you will launch yourself high into the air. I'll ensure we're aimed at the top of the pyramid. Got it?"

Regular-Ginny shrugged. "Guess so," she said.

"We need to launch at the exact same time, because if we don't, then the one who launches second will likely be caught by Death. So as soon as you stop sinking, count to ten and let 'er rip."

"Got it," replied Regular-Ginny, deciding immediately that she would launch *long* before she counted to ten. She ran her finger across her pocket, gaining a little confidence as she touched the petrified heart within.

Squirrel paws began raising her up once more, signaling an end to her conversation with her counterpart. She lost sight of Tiny-Ginny as her vision became inundated with squirrel fur.

Regular-Ginny burst forth from the womb of squirrels and breathed fresh, albeit stiflingly humid, air. Sharp rodent claws scratched her forehead as she crowned. As soon as her head poked out of the squirrel mass—back in the position of the right eye socket—she screamed.

A spear hurtled directly at her. It was caught in the tornadic force of the dragon's breath, and it spun end over end on its path toward her. She continued screaming as she watched it flip—blade, butt spike, blade, butt spike—wondering inanely which end was going to skewer her alive. Just when she was about to find out the answer, pink goo instinctively whipped from her forehead in the shape of a large mallet and whacked the spear in the center of the shaft.

The spear cracked in half, and the two halves caromed toward the ground. Ginny followed them with her eyes, watching them impale a pair of dwarves, both of whom squirmed and screamed as their intestines spilled across the battlefield. She glanced to her left and witnessed Mister E excitedly chittering at the carnage below. Pink hatred twisted inside her heart, and she considered whacking the stupid rodent with the mallet that now hung impotently from her forehead.

Mister E must have sensed her gaze, for he turned toward her. He looked her in the eye for a moment, and then he brought his front paw up near his face. He raised the equivalent of his middle finger at her, and then his pupils rolled around in the whites of his eyes like a lost alcoholic stuck outside in a blizzard. Ginny did not know whether to be angry or impressed, for she had never been flipped the bird by a rodent before. She shrugged. The mallet soaked back into the pores of her forehead.

Regular-Ginny returned her attention to the dragon, as most sane people would have already done. It had returned to its original size, its breath attack now over. The dragon swiped at a platoon of Shaka's men. They catapulted across the sky and hung there for a moment like a cast of swooping hawks, evil omens in the clear blue heavens.

Tiny-Ginny screamed in a language that Regular-Ginny could not understand—the one she used earlier that sounded a little like Pig Latin—and the squirrel monster launched itself into another sprint, aiming straight for the dragon. It slammed one of its gigantic paws into the dragon's snout. The dragon's head collapsed into a translucent gooey mash beneath the squirrel's paw, and the clouds that had filled the dragon's head floated around to a different part of its insides like the air inside a squeezed balloon. It formed a new head from its side and rearranged its cloudy insides so that it grew two new arms from the skin near the squirrel monster's paw.

The dragon used the talons of these new arms to clamp down around the squirrel monster's paw. The dragon ripped the paw from the squirrel monster's arm and crushed it in its talons. As the dragon's translucent skin constricted around the squirrels, they popped like thousands of tiny grapes. The dragon tossed their crushed corpses onto the bloody carnage of the battlefield.

And what carnage it was! Dead dwarves and squirrels covered the grassy landscape at least two bodies deep. Desiring to look anywhere but at the dragon that lurked merely a few dozen feet in front of her face, Regular-Ginny numbly scanned the death and destruction.

Her eyes stopped scanning when they found a stovetop hat rising to a less-than-moderate height above the gore. She looked beneath it. Lincoln lay curled atop a pile of bodies, his longsword gripped tightly in his right hand despite the blade having been broken a few inches above the hilt. Blood stained his beard, and the top had popped off the hat, hanging limply by a black string like the lid on an opened can of soup. The floppy top twittered in the wind. His angry eyes stared straight ahead, but they never seemed to focus on anything. His intestines had sprawled themselves across his thighs, relaxing in the sun like lazy earthworms. They bled and baked in the heat, and the tall dwarf tripped over them again and again as he tried to stand and rejoin the battle. Regular-Ginny remembered the Lincoln from her reality, the great man whom every child in America grows up idolizing, and she felt a pang of sympathy for this dictator-version of him. Finally, after many long throes, he breathed his last strained breath. She watched in numbed confusion as a white cloud drifted from his mouth and floated into the dragon's nostrils.

She had not noticed it until now, but the dragon had grown much larger than when she had first seen it just prior to the start of battle. She had not recognized its growth because of the whole ballooning and breath attack debacle, but now she observed little white clouds constantly drifting up from dwarf corpses and into its nostrils, and with every additional cloud that it gathered, it puffed slightly larger.

Trumpets blared from behind the opposite side of the pyramid. The sound shook her from the hypnotic effect of the clouds floating into the dragon's nostrils. The army belonging to Gaius Julius burst from the far side of the pyramid. It spread into a grid formation, and every soldier drew a short piercing sword. Gaius Julius marched at the back of the formation. He wore a crested helmet and stepped in perfect stride with the servants carrying his eagle standards.

The dragon whipped its head around, momentarily forgetting about the squirrel monster in its grasp. Tiny-Ginny squealed in delight at the distraction, and a newly reformed, equally enormous squirrel paw crashed across the back of the dragon's head. The head exploded off the creature's body like a popped balloon and disintegrated into the surrounding air. Swirling clouds poured from the hole where the head had been until new membranous skin appeared in a flash of light to plug the hole, the appearance which occurred mere seconds later. A new head burst forth from the skin near where the previous head had just been, and it sucked back into its nostrils the twirling clouds that had escaped.

The dragon roared at the squirrel monster, and then it clamped down its jaws onto the enormous rodent's shoulder. It bit off a large chunk of squirrels and swallowed them. Life instantly drained from the bodies, and they shriveled like grapes withering in the sun. Their mummified remains sank down the dragon's cloudy throat, and then they plopped out of the bottom of the dragon's translucent skin, dropping to the ground below. Upon crashing against the battlefield, the mummified squirrels exploded into pieces as though they were clay pots that had fallen from a great height.

The dragon stood on its hind legs and slammed its underbelly against the squirrel monster's torso. It hooked its forearms below the squirrel monster's armpits and body slammed the squirrel monster onto its back. The dragon raked squirrel across the throat with its talons, and hundreds of rodents flew into the air and rained down upon the remaining dwarven army like buck-toothed arrows. Apparently satisfied with this victory over the squirrel monster, the dragon leapt away from the prone squirrel to begin its attack on Gaius Julius's men.

Meanwhile, Tiny-Ginny chanted, and the squirrel monster hopped back up onto its feet. Behind the squirrel, Regular-Ginny heard thousands of voices singing. Before Regular-Ginny could ask, Tiny-Ginny called out, "It's the remains of the vanguard, reforming. Shaka's apparently survived and he's leading them in a chant to gain the favor of the war gods."

"Mmmm'kay, that's *totally* normal," responded Regular-Ginny.

"OK, so that last attack didn't quite go as planned," said Tiny-Ginny. "But be ready. We're launching as soon as we've made contact again."

Regular-Ginny gulped, and then she shrugged. "Sure," she said. "It's not like I have much of a choice."

Regular-Ginny bit her lower lip as the squirrel monster thundered across the clearing and closed the distance between it and the dragon. With each booming step, the thin lines of the dragon's skin shook like a gelatin dessert, blurring the monster into a milky white storm cloud that slashed at Gaius Julius's army. Regular-Ginny's blinding migraine returned.

Regular-Ginny felt herself falling forward, and hundreds of squirrel paws gripped her tight. She glanced left and right, and she realized that the giant squirrel monster was leaning forward while rearing its paws back for a ferocious attack. Before the colossal squirrel could land any blows, the dragon swiped a talon across the squirrel monster's stomach without looking away from its attack on Gaius Julius's army. Hundreds of squirrels hurtled away into the distance, disappearing in a cloud of exploding red gore as they collided onto the piles of dead dwarves covering the ground.

But the dragon's vicious blow did not slow the squirrel's momentum. It continued in a frenzy, lacking any sense of conservation for itself or the squirrels that comprised its body. Ginny's peripheral vision picked up a flash of blurry brownness on the edge of her view, and she turned her head toward it to watch a giant squirrel paw flying past her and groping for the dragon's neck. It gripped the dragon's soft throat and squeezed. The flesh beneath the paws crushed, and the cloudy whiteness within the skin of the dragon's neck moved into its head, puffing it up.

The giant squirrel's mouth snapped repeatedly at the dragon's puffed up face. With each bite, dozens of squirrels fell dead, while a chunk of skin was ripped from the dragon's face. However, for every piece of skin shorn from the dragon, new skin flashed into existence almost instantly to replace it.

While the giant squirrel continued nipping at the shifty dragon, Regular-Ginny felt her feet begin to sink. It felt as though she were standing in rodent-scented quicksand. Her ankles were pulled beneath the brown undertow, then her knees, and then her waist. She was sinking so fast she almost did not realize that this was the cue for which she had been waiting. She and her counterpart were about to launch.

She allowed a tiny amount of the pinkness to extend from the pores of her fingertips and anchor themselves into the outsides of the squirrel monster's eye socket, hooking into the behemoth's cheek and snout. The squirrels beneath her pulled her deeper and deeper within the massive monster, and the deeper she went, the tighter the pinkness pulled at her shoulders and elbows and wrists. The pinkness pulled taut like a stretched rubber band, and Regular-Ginny bit down harder than ever on her lower lip, hoping to scare away her millions of preflight jitters.

Finally, when the pink goo had stretched so tightly that Regular-Ginny's arms teetered on the brink of ripping themselves from their sockets, the squirrels stopped pulling her deeper. With her descent stopped, she began counting. *One…Two…Three…Launch*!

Regular-Ginny emitted a quick burst of pink goo from her torso and legs to remove the squirrels that were holding her in place. She rocketed up the furry tunnel long before Tiny-Ginny's allotted ten-count. She hurtled into the open air above the dragon's head.

She glanced at the dragon below her. Her face flushed when she realized that the dragon was staring directly at her, despite being currently engaged in melee combat with the squirrel monster. She turned her head away, hoping that it had simply been her imagination playing tricks upon her. She stared straight at the pyramid toward which she was racing, telling herself that the dragon surely had not noticed her—she was such a small figure on the field of gore, why should it concentrate on her when it had a colossal squirrel monster to satisfy its attention?

And that's when Regular-Ginny noticed a lumpy, dwarf-shaped pink object racing toward the olive-colored pyramid ahead of her. She roared in frustration. Tiny-Ginny had apparently not held to the ten-count, either.

Regular-Ginny's heart sank, and she realized that she had been royally screwed. The dwarf had launched ahead of her and had apparently drawn the dragon's attention toward the Ginnys' escape trajectory, and that's why it had already been looking in Regular-Ginny's direction when she had launched. She prayed every prayer she could think of and allowed the pinkness to pour out of her pores to cover over her in a massive blob for added protection. Despite both precautions, her heart threatened to explode out of her chest in fear.

The hairs on her neck stood on end, and she wished gravity would pull her to the pyramid faster. She risked a glance behind her and saw the dragon's gaping mouth winding through the air toward her, ready to snap shut around her and swallow her whole. She decided to act like an ostrich and hide herself from the world as best she could by clamping her eyes shut tight, just as her boyfriend always did when she demanded that he do his chores.

After a couple seconds, she realized that she had stopped hurtling through the air and was lying still. She rested on what felt like a cushiony, soft mattress. Unfortunately, though, this was a mattress that burned worse than battery acid.

Regular-Ginny abandoned her ostrich-like eye clamping, opening her eyes to witness the beast's teeth snapping shut around her and blocking any chance of her escape. She realized that the mattressy substance she felt beneath her was a cloud-tongue, and it had already burned through the bottom of her pink blob. She rolled onto her back to provide relief to her burning front. She saw the sun shining through the translucent skin of the dragon's upper jaw. It reminded her of looking through a pair of sunglasses. She inanely wondered if the dragon's skin offered U.V. protection.

The burning sensation from the tongue grew stronger and scorched the thought from her head. She willed her protective pink membrane to grow thicker, but it was to no avail. Where the cloud-tongue touched her, it fried through the pink membrane faster than she could regrow it. She glanced down at her arms and stomach, watching dumbly as her skin bubbled from the acid-touch of the cloud-tongue.

A thunderous gulp surrounded her, and Ginny dropped feet-first down the cavernous well of the dragon's throat. She assumed this must be what it felt like for a dead goldfish to be flushed down a toilet. She bounced off the sides of the throat and tumbled down into the depths, head-over-heels. Below her, ghostly arms stretched out from the lining of the throat, pinching her and scratching her with their angry phantom claws. The ghosts were made from the same acidic cloudiness as the tongue, and where they touched, they burned through her pink membrane.

Regular-Ginny felt one hand snatch at her right eyeball. She cried out in dismay as it tried to rip the eye from its socket. The violent flushing that accompanied the dragon's gulp must have saved her, because she plummeted past the greedy hand so fast that it could not complete its ghastly deed. She forced extra membrane from her pores to cover her eyes and other vital areas more thickly, but it did not provide much relief. The hands continued their violence, and the membrane continued melting faster than she could produce it.

The surreal esophagus dumped her into the cavernous digestive system of the creature. Faces of mustachioed ghosts peered and scowled at her from the cloudy entrails, craning their ghostly necks toward her and gnashing their teeth. Ginny sank deeper into the cloudy, acidic ghosts that filled the dragon, flapping her arms all the while like a drowning child. Boils on her back and shoulders burst like angry water balloons, and she screamed in pain.

Regular-Ginny grew disoriented as she rolled and twirled, trying to elude the ghosts and their acidic touches. But her struggling was to no avail, for she soon found herself staring into the cavernous eyes of Dictator Lincoln's ghost.

Its phantom mouth opened wide and snapped at her. It ripped what was left of the pink membrane from her neck and grinned a murderous grin as the pink dissolved into nothingness. She backstroked away from the ghost, but it pursued like a piranha in heat, vicious and aroused and seeking her blood.

Dozens of other ghostly mustachioed mouths nipped at her back, shredding the remains of her pink armor from her shoulders. She cried out in pain and stopped her backstroking. As soon as she stopped, Lincoln's ghost latched onto her neck. The other mouths clamped onto her back. She lashed out with her hands, whipping pink goo in every direction, trying to save herself by swirling the angry clouds like a bad cocktail. It did not work. The mouths did not loosen, but rather sucked hold of her more tightly. She felt lighter with every passing second, as if the tyrannical leeches were draining her soul from her body.

She could no longer feel her limbs. Numbness drifted over her fingers and toes like a thick fog that spread into her arms and legs. Her head drooped to one side. Tears streamed from her eyes, but she could not feel them. The numb sensation had spread to envelop her entire body. Her heart drifted deep into the sea of her chest, a little lost ship in an infinite, angry ocean.

The heart! Ginny remembered the heart in her pocket. She tried to move her arm to reach it, but her fingers felt like they had been tied to heavy anchors, pulling her hands ever lower into the terrible ghostly chasm. But she knew that she must either reach the heart or die, so she poured every atom of her being into the effort. She squealed in pained determination, and her hand twitched. She grunted and concentrated harder than she had ever concentrated on anything before. Her hand slipped into her pocket. It closed around the petrified heart.

As she gripped the knobby stone-like heart, the organ began to pulsate, and it blasted the numbness from her hand. Her hand vibrated and tingled as though it had been asleep and was just waking up. The tingling from the heart spread over her entire body, flowing a little further through her veins each time the heart beat.

Ginny stared down at her pocket, no longer concerned with the acidic burning all around her. Inside her pocket, light pulsed in bright heartbeats, shining crimson through the fabric of her pants. The light flared through the inside of the dragon and filled it with a glowing red radiance. The clouds of mustachioed ghosts near her screamed and squealed, swirling away from the enveloping light like a frightened tornado. The violence of the ghost-mouths on her back subsided. Lincoln retreated, too, but as he flushed away in pain, he ripped one final piece of flesh from her neck.

All around her, the dragon thrashed more violently in pain with each beat of the rocky heart. Ginny felt herself being tugged upward, back the way she had come. She glanced up and watched the murky insides of the dragon whirling round and round, faster and faster, like the flushing of an upside-down toilet.

She realized that she was being flushed again, and though she did not yet know if this was a positive development, she assumed the outcome could not possibly be worse than remaining in the bowels of the dragon as snack food for dictator-ghosts. She twirled uncontrollably upward into the draining whiteness.

As she sailed higher and higher, she increased in speed. She noticed that the dragon's cloudy innards had stopped burning her, so she managed to force her pink membrane to grow thickly about her body once more. She flew past the dragon's translucent teeth, nicking her armor on the sharp fangs, before finding herself airborne. She was surrounded by a torrent of raindrops formed from the souls of dead dictators.

Regular-Ginny's left shoulder crashed against something hard, and pain shot through her entire body. The white torrent of ghosts evaporated upon coming into contact with the air. They floated up toward the still-thrashing dragon, which hovered over Ginny like an angry puppy as it sucked its vomited innards back inside its nostrils.

Ginny lay still, both hating and appreciating the pain all at once. *At least I can feel pain again,* she thought as she winced. She tried to sit up but could not, so she simply lay with a smile, giddy to be alive. She was sprawled upon olive stone, and she realized that the stone was the thick skin of the pyramid that imprisoned the Pink One. The stone felt rough underneath her soft face.

A piercing scream on the opposite side of the battlefield reminded her of her perilous surroundings. She glanced up at the dragon. To her relief, instead of beginning an attack on her anew, it became distracted by the screaming. It bolted away from her, dashing across the clearing in the direction of the source of the noise. She shrugged, too much in shock to fully appreciate that she was now safe.

Ginny looked down at her pocket and pulled out the petrified heart. She stared at it, hypnotized by its pulsating light. The heart puffed up like a swollen tomato and flashed crimson, and then it shrank down like it had been dried in the sun. The beating of the heart slowed, until it finally waned to a halt, returning to its status as a simple craggy rock. She kissed it and returned it to her pocket with a dazed smile.

A noise erupted from the dragon on the opposite side of the clearing, a sound like the combination of a hissing and a roar, but Ginny ignored it. The action lay far off in the background.

Something below her tingled and tickled, and she glanced down to watch a crew of tiny pink tendrils snaking their way underneath her. They crept around her body and hooked up over her side. She felt herself being lifted off the ground like a maiden on her wedding night, newly married to a nightmarish monster that carried her in the crooks of its horde of pink snaky arms. She winced at both her inane metaphor and the stabbing pain that now throbbed in her shoulder and across her burned skin.

Regular-Ginny followed the snakes with her eyes, watching them wind up and up. Tiny-Ginny stood at the top of the pyramid, the pinkness having cascaded from her hands, down the olive stone steps, and beneath Regular-Ginny. Tiny-Ginny made the ascent up the pyramid a gentle matter for her counterpart, with each step lifting Regular-Ginny high enough not to bump her against the hard surface. Regular-Ginny furrowed her brows. She was not accustomed to such kindness from the dwarf. She wondered what the catch would be.

Soon, Regular-Ginny reached the top of the pyramid, and Tiny-Ginny stood her gently up onto her feet. Regular-Ginny wavered, her knees wobbly and her shoulder aching. She did not speak, instead staring dumbly across the jungle. The lush forest was beautiful, aside from the hordes of dwarven corpses and the thrashing dragon at its perimeter.

Finally, Tiny-Ginny broke the silence. "How do we get inside?" she impatiently whined.

The itch flared inside Regular-Ginny's skull, but it was so strong that she could not think clearly. "I'm not quite sure," she said, "but the way has *got* to be up here somewhere."

"Fine," Tiny-Ginny responded. "But we must make haste. I saw the Arts across the battlefield. Death's attacking them, but I can guarantee you that my Art's got a plan. So, use your pink gift to heal yourself, and then figure out what we should do."

"Huh?"

"Heal yourself. You've got the pink stuff inside you. Work it inside you the same way you work it outside."

"I don't think it's that simple," replied Regular-Ginny, her voice coming out a soft, weak note.

"Where are you injured?"

"My left shoulder," Regular-Ginny called, raising her voice to hear it above the thrumming itch in her brain. "And my skin."

"Hold out your arm. We shall heal focus on your shoulder first."

Regular-Ginny held out her arm. Tiny-Ginny examined it, tugging at it in a dozen different ways. Regular-Ginny grimaced with each pull.

"Get down on your knees," ordered Tiny-Ginny.

"Why?"

"Because your shoulder is dislocated, and you're too tall standing for me to pop it back in place."

Regular-Ginny dropped to her knees and felt Tiny-Ginny grip her arm. She bit her lip, terrified of the impending pain.

"I'm going to count to three," said the dwarf. "One…Two…Three!"

Pain shot through Regular-Ginny's arm, hundreds of tiny bombs of pain detonating across her lumpy landscape. Tiny-Ginny grabbed Regular-Ginny by the ears, and roughly made her stare into her eyes. Tiny-Ginny's angry eyes seemed to squeal with mirth.

"Close your eyes," commanded Tiny-Ginny. Regular-Ginny happily obliged—anything to stop staring into that haggard, misshapen face. "Now, envision your shoulder, beneath the skin."

"Can't you just use y-y-your magic to heal me?"

"If you think I'm wasting any magic on some stuck up whorespawn, especially when you've the power to heal yourself, then you've a lesson or two to learn about me. Now, envision your shoulder beneath the skin, or so help me gods, I'll rip out your throat, the Pink One be damned."

Regular-Ginny obeyed. In her mind's eye, she pictured her shoulder socket and the sore, angry bone throbbing within. She pictured the ligaments and the blood pulsating through the porous bones.

"Imagine your pink gift, flowing through your injury. It is wending its way through your shoulder, solidifying and providing support to your wound. The pink gel is hardening, and it has soaked your pain into itself. Your shoulder is feeling better than new."

Regular-Ginny smiled, her eyes still closed. She felt pink goo stiffening inside her bones, allowing her shoulder to move without pain. She rolled her left arm around in the socket, circling her arm to test every angle of the joint. It glided gently, and she was happy.

Regular-Ginny opened her eyes and stood up. She looked down at Tiny-Ginny and smiled. Then she noticed Mister E, and the smile turned to a smirk. "I don't know how you knew how to do that, but thanks," she muttered.

"I knew because—unlike you—I've been testing this stuff since we received it to see what it's capable of. Meanwhile, you've been either complaining or sitting around creating toys with which to play like an angry toddler," responded Tiny-Ginny. "So next time, stop bitching and listen to me immedi—"

The ground shook violently, like some colossal, invisible gods had decided to fornicate upon it. Regular-Ginny turned left and right, desperately trying to find the source. But while she spun, the shaking turned into a terrible quaking, and she lost her balance.

As she began to fall, she noticed next to her the exquisitely carved statue of the pair of comets, the statue that she had earlier seen as she looked up at the pyramid from the ground. She reached out her hands to steady herself on it, but it squished beneath her hands like a bowl of pudding. Deep within it, her hands collided against two stone knobs. They jerked in opposite directions beneath her weight.

Regular-Ginny's eyes popped wide open. She yanked her hands out of the statue and stared straight ahead, hoping that her counterpart had not noticed her accidentally performing another clumsy and stupid act. She felt a series of hollow clunks beneath her. Then, the sculpture disappeared and the ground beneath her fissured open like an uncontrollable sinkhole. The entire top of the pyramid tilted toward the opening. Regular-Ginny tumbled into it.

She found herself airborne, staring above her at the open hole into which she had just fallen. She began to ooze her pink gift, intending to form something from it to break her fall. She twisted around, hoping to find how far she had to fall before hitting the ground. Before she could make it around, she smacked home upon coarse stone. She landed on her left shoulder again.

"Dammit!" she cried. She realized that her left shoulder had dislocated itself once more. She bit her lip and sat up. She heard a loud THUNK nearby and glanced to her right. Tiny-Ginny smacked down onto the ground next to her. The dwarf cursed and grabbed her own left shoulder. Regular-Ginny guffawed, and Tiny-Ginny glared at her. Regular-Ginny ignored the look.

The shaking that had begun when they were atop the pyramid continued here inside the pyramid. Ancient dirt tumbled from above, coating the surrounding stone in a coarse layer of sand. The falling sand reminded her of snow, and she grinned despite her pain. The entrance above her rumbled closed, blocking out the sunbeams that had shined down from above.

Regular-Ginny sat in the dark. She found that she could see in the blackness, thanks to the pink goo that now instinctively covered her eyes. She glanced over at her ugly counterpart and immediately regretted having the ability to see. She sighed, closed her eyes, and got to work on healing her skin and shoulder.

Beside her, Tiny-Ginny began healing herself, too.

CHAPTER 18

UNLESS MY NECKLACE OF SEVERED EARS DECEIVES ME...

FOLLOWING THE TICKLE in Normal-Art's brain, the Arts and Drillbot passed half a dozen dull green pyramids, and at each one Normal-Art announced that it was not the pyramid they were looking for.

They finally arrived at a pyramid from behind which they could hear blood-curdling screams and vicious war-cries and the stomping gait of something colossal. A brutal wind blustered from the west, whipping around the pyramid and blowing a stench in their direction that smelled like rotten cabbage.

Normal-Art pinched his nose and looked at the top of the pyramid, squealing, "There it is! This is the one!"

God-Art squinted at the top of the pyramid and shook his head. "This might be the correct pyramid, but there's nothing up there."

"This is it. I know it is. The comet-sculptures are right *there*! Open your eyes!"

With that, Normal-Art sprinted ahead to the base of the pyramid, and then he skidded to a halt. He scratched his head. The limestone blocks that formed the pyramid were not short, simple steps leading to the top up which he could quickly run, like he had always pictured pyramid blocks to be. Instead, the blocks were nearly twice his height.

God-Art and Drillbot caught up with him. Normal-Art turned to them. "I guess we'll need to find a path up," he said.

"[whir] Drillbot can drill – CLACK – can drill into the stone. Would Master Art like for Drillbot to – CLACK – to carve an entrance for – CLACK – for us?"

"No," said Normal-Art. "It won't be that easy. The thing we're here to rescue told me to enter from the top. It said all other ways are death."

Normal-Art then turned to his right and began following the base of the pyramid to search for some sort of path carved into the stone. As he rounded the near corner of the pyramid, his eyes watered as the wind intensified and blasted him with an exponentially stronger putrid cabbage stench. And to make matters worse, he realized that he had just entered a scene that could have come from a *Godzilla* film, if only *Godzilla* films could get high on acid: a giant squirrel was reared up on its hind legs, screeching in fury as it attempted to strangle a dragon, which was shiny and translucent like it had been carved from ice. Dead and dying Dictator Scouts and regular-sized squirrels lay covering the grassy field in a stack two deep.

Normal-Art realized that the rotten smell was originating from the corpses. And now he was right in the thick of them. He dropped to his knees and puked as the fetid stench of dwarf genocide overwhelmed him. After he finished, he began pushing himself back up onto his feet, and that was when he noticed a winding path carved into the limestone pyramid way over on the other side of the epic dragon-squirrel brawl. His brain tickled, and he knew that the trio would need to hike over the rugged terrain of dead dwarves to reach the path, and then they would need to follow it to the pyramid's top. Further, if they wanted to survive the journey to the path, they would need to do it without drawing the ire of the colossal monsters.

"There," said Normal-Art, pointing toward the path. "We're supposed to follow that path. The entrance will be at its end."

Visions of Normal-Art's couch danced in his head, and he made the decision to waste no time. He wiped his mouth with the back of his hand and forced himself to hike over the first squishy body, marking the beginning of the ghastly odyssey.

Normal-Art found this first step to be the most difficult, mostly because the corpse's eyes puffed out of its head when Art stepped on its stomach, and this horrid image caused him to gag. But as he walked farther and farther, he found himself growing numb to the gruesome corpses below him. God-Art and Drillbot followed behind him, seemingly unaffected at all by the dreadful landscape.

"Sure hope that damned dragon kills every single one of these damned dwarves," muttered Normal-Art as he trudged over a particularly rotund dwarf. He yearned to see those he deemed responsible for his presence on this reality be punished. If these brutes had not been bloodthirsty bastards who would stop at nothing to gain the infinite power tucked away inside this pyramid, he never would have been needed for this rescue mission in the first place, and he could be at home right now watching television.

God-Art put his hand on the back of Normal-Art's head, and then he turned Normal-Art's head to look at the dragon. God-Art said, "I wouldn't be so quick to wish something like *that*, especially when you don't realize the danger that you're wishing upon us. Take a closer look."

Normal-Art peered at the dragon's skin and realized that he could see right through it. Inside the skin, pale faces zoomed back and forth within pallid wisps of fog. Long ephemeral mustachios hung from many of the faces. A familiar face slammed against the skin and glared angrily out. Normal-Art recognized the tiny mustache that ran the width of the ghoul's nose. He shuddered.

Movement near the dragon's legs caught Normal-Art's attention, and he stopped focusing on the ghosts inside the beast's skin. Dictator Scouts were climbing the dragon's legs, swarming it like an army of ants and stabbing it all over with daggers and swords and spears. But their attacks were to no avail. The dragon shook its legs in ferocious jerky movements, and in doing so, it knocked the swarm of dictators to the ground. It stomped them to death. A fresh horde of dictators began climbing, while the newly dead dictators' bodies lay still. Thin fog escaped from their lifeless mouths and floated into the nostrils of the dragon, joining the large cloud within the beast.

"What is that *thing*?" gasped Normal-Art.

God-Art frowned. He grunted, "I've seen this kind of creature before. It's Death personified."

"But that makes no sense," said Normal-Art, scratching his chin. "I get the symbolism that Death is the cruelest dictator of all, so I understand that if it ever actually *died*, it would of necessity be reincarnated here on this reality. But if Death is here on this reality, it could *only* mean that Death is dead. But Death can't be dead, because people on my reality continue to die all the time, and that wouldn't happen if Death were no longer around to kill people. This is, like, the most ridiculously stupid logical flaw ever. I think my head's going to explode just thinking about it."

"You're simply reading a bit too much into this '*Death personified*' thing. The personification of Death from your reality didn't die. That would be silly. Just like we are parallel versions of one another, this creature is a parallel version of your robed-skeleton version of Death. Each reality has at least one of its own personifications of the concept, and this dragon is this Earth's—a fierce and terrifying tyrant to match the hearts of the populous."

Normal-Art shrugged, still confused. Then, to make matters even more confusing, he saw movement across the fur of the colossal squirrel. If his jaw had not already been agape from staring at Death, it would have clunked open now. He realized that the giant squirrel was no mere giant squirrel, but that it consisted of millions of regular-sized squirrels climbing atop each other and using their combined mass to form the massive monster.

Two female Dictator Scouts of different heights formed the monster squirrel's pink eyes. The left eyeball was filled by a dwarven scout who was visibly screaming and spewing rage as she barked orders. The calm eyeball was obviously Normal-Art's Ginny, her rats' nest hair bobbing with every movement of the beast. The dwarven scout looked like a funhouse-mirror reflection of his Ginny. Seeing the two of them working together gave him a queasy feeling in the pit of his stomach.

The dragon swiped at the giant squirrel's stomach, launching hundreds of squirrels across the battlefield. They crashed to the ground and splattered crimson gore like furry paint bombs. Normal-Art grimaced as one of the airborne squirrels crashed onto the pile of dead bodies in front of him and spattered him with blood.

God-Art tapped Normal-Art on the shoulder. "We really need to get moving," he whispered. "We don't want to be here to find out who wins."

Normal-Art nodded. God-Art continued whispering, "We must be utterly silent until we reach the top of the pyramid, or we risk drawing their attention. Hug to the wall and try to make yourself look inconspicuous."

Normal-Art nodded once more, and then he began tiptoeing gingerly over the piles of dead Dictator Scouts like a ballerina in a hideously sacrilegious performance of Swan Lake. He leaned against the pyramid wall as he moved, allowing it to guide him and provide him with balance. Once he got the hang of walking on the lumpy terrain, his body was essentially able to move itself, so he returned his attention to the battle between the massive behemoths.

The giant squirrel monster had now grabbed the dragon by the throat and was biting it with its ferocious jaws. The squirrel monster ripped pieces of the shiny skin from the dragon's snout. The foggy insides of the dragon poured out of the lesions. The dictator souls flooded out of each rip and attempted to flutter away, only to be sucked back inside the dragon by some invisible vacuum within the creature. The rips in the dragon's skin flashed with internal, supernatural light and mended themselves nearly instantly.

While still clinging onto the dragon's throat, the colossal squirrel's eyes began to collapse into its head, as if the squirrels that formed its body were pulling the two mismatched Ginnys inside itself. The whirlpool of fur swiftly pulled them under, leaving in their places two empty eye sockets that stared at the dragon with an eerie expression.

But the empty eye sockets did not stare for long. The two Ginnys launched from them like mismatched pink cannonballs shot from a horrifyingly inefficient, monstrous double-barreled cannon. The smaller Ginny launched first, followed nearly five seconds later by Normal-Art's Ginny. They arced up over the dragon's face and began falling on a course that would land them atop the pyramid. Pink tendrils trailed from their arms and flailed behind them in the air. Normal-Art thought the women resembled a couple of octopi who had gotten confused about their roles in nature and had leapt off a building believing they could fly like birds.

With the giant squirrel's mitts still securely fastened about the dragon's throat, it looked like clear sailing for the pair. *They're going to make it,* Normal-Art thought. He heard God-Art mumble a curse behind him, so he picked up the pace.

The dragon vibrated and wiggled like a bowl of sinister gelatin. The mist within its translucent skin whirled and shifted. The membrane between the immense squirrel's paws drooped and went limp as the dragon reallocated the cloudy souls that made up its insides. The beast formed a new head where its tail had been, and the giant squirrel now found itself gripping the dragon by its flaccid tail rather than its throat. The squirrel monster furiously twisted the tail between its paws, but this accomplished nothing other than to squeeze the remaining fog out of the tail and into the rest of the dragon's body.

The dragon kicked its nemesis between the newly empty eye sockets. The squirrel monster's head exploded. The squirrels that had formed its head rocketed skyward and rained to the ground across the battlefield. The squirrel monster released its grip on the dragon and thrashed its headless body about the battlefield like a decapitated chicken. The monster melted apart as squirrels began abandoning it. Millions of furry rodents scrambled from the beast and into the jungle, and as they disappeared into the underbrush, they left behind a pile of thousands upon thousands of dead squirrels that had been crushed or asphyxiated while the monster had been together.

Once free of the squirrel monster, the dragon tracked the arc of the slower, taller airborne Ginny—Normal-Art's girlfriend—and pounced toward her with its snarling jaws wide open. Cloudy drool slavered from its teeth as its gigantic maw snapped shut around her. Normal-Art gulped. The dragon also gulped, but much more loudly than Normal-Art. Then it collected itself on its haunches, readying itself to leap at the miniature version of Ginny.

God-Art pushed Normal-Art from behind, and Normal-Art realized that he had stopped. He looked to the left, made sure he was still touching the olive stone of the pyramid, and pushed forward. He kept his head down and trudged on, telling himself not to look at the terrifying dragon that had devoured his girlfriend. But after a few moments, he felt compelled to raise his eyes, because he could not bear to stare at a single more lifeless, grimacing dwarf corpse beneath his feet.

A red light brighter than the sun flared to life within the dragon's translucent skin. The creature yelped a wounded yelp. Then it began thrashing in pain. It smashed its own head against the pyramid, cracking apart tons of limestone blocks and sending them tumbling to the ground. They crashed atop dwarven corpses like were mortar shells falling upon a battlefield composed of hairy, disgusting, dead flesh, and the force of their impact sent splintered dwarf pieces in all directions.

Behind Normal-Art, God-Art screamed. Normal-Art turned to look at the god. The god had fallen to his knees and had covered his ears with his hands. His screams grew louder and louder, until they resounded even more loudly across the battlefield than the thrashing dragon-caricature of Death.

"The noise! The static!" moaned God-Art in English between curses screamed in alien languages. Blood flowed from his ears, running freely between his fingers like water through cracks in a dam. The streaming blood fell from the backs of his hands, and as it crashed atop the pile of dead dictator corpses below him, it swirled and morphed into dozens of purple butterflies that fluttered away into the forest.

"Make it stop! Father, help me, the noise!" squealed God-Art.

Normal-Art heard Drillbot try to tell him something, but God-Art's screams had grown so deafening that Normal-Art could not hear the machine. He collapsed atop a pile of dead dwarves and covered his ears, ignoring the robot. He felt tiny pops deep inside his ear canals. It felt to him as though miniature terrorists had just set off tons of explosives around his eardrums. He pulled one hand away from his ear and looked at it. He squealed at the crimson blood that was smeared across it. He curled tightly into a fetal position, covering his face and sobbing into his knees.

Something sharp poked him in the back. He ignored it. The poke poked again, much harder this time, hard enough that Art felt a stream of blood begin flowing down his back. He turned his head to see Drillbot's steely face inches from his own. The robot seemed to be trying to tell him something, but Normal-Art could not hear the message. He shrugged. All he could hear was a piercing hum. Drillbot pointed a drill at God-Art, then at the dragon. Normal-Art was confused, but he looked anyway, never taking his hands away from his bleeding ears.

God-Art had detached his jaw and had opened it to multiple times its normal size. It continued stretching further open until it was large enough that Normal-Art could have stood comfortably inside it. Though Normal-Art could not hear it, the god was screaming louder than ever, and his cartoonishly wide mouth projected his screams so stridently that they could have been mistaken as originating from a megaphone the size of a house.

Meanwhile, the had dragon propped itself against the pyramid and had begun convulsing. It leaned its head to the side and vomited. The blinding light inside it rocketed up through its body and past its lips. As soon as the light left its mouth, the light winked out and a soggy pink humanoid shape smacked onto the limestone blocks of the pyramid. The dragon leaned over the unmoving lump, which was covered in thick, pale goo, and inhaled. The whitish slime enveloping the humanoid shape turned into mist and wafted into the air, returning to the confines of the dragon. Ginny lay unmoving on the coarse stone.

God-Art had still not stopped screaming, and in the intervening moments, his mouth had only opened wider. "The noise!" God-Art screamed again, his voice now both gravelly and as loud as thunder.

Something clicked in Normal-Art's brain, and he finally understood what Drillbot was trying to indicate to him. He screamed at God-Art, "Stop screaming! You'll draw the dragon's attention!"

As if on cue, the dragon—now back to its senses because it had purged the light from itself—turned its head to glare directly at God-Art. It drooled thin streams of white mist that trailed down its lips, dripped from its lower jaw, and drifted back up into its nostrils. It shook its head furiously back and forth, slapped at its ears a couple times, and launched itself forward like a snarling hound dog on the trail of a baby fox. It bounded over everything in its way, throwing dwarven corpses up in its wake.

"Shut up!" pled Normal-Art with a whimper.

But God-Art did not listen to Normal-Art's pleas, so Normal-Art dove onto the god's back, planning to force his mouth shut as best he could. Normal-Art wrapped his arms as far as he could wrap them around God-Art's lower jaw, but the mortal could not reach even halfway around. He pulled up with all his might, anyway, trying to use any leverage and strength he could muster to clamp the mouth shut. Sweat poured down his forehead in rivulets, and with Herculean effort, he managed to yank upward on the skin of God-Art's cheeks hard enough to shut the mouth. However, the god did not stop screaming just because his mouth was closed. Instead, his throat swelled up with a huge pocket of air like it was the gullet of a gargantuan toad.

Normal-Art glanced up from his task and saw that the dragon was closing in fast, now a mere hundred yards away. His heart dropped to somewhere around his bowels, and then it continued dropping. He squealed.

God-Art's throat swelled relentlessly with trapped air. It quickly grew too large for Normal-Art to hold shut, and it broke his grip. Normal-Art fell off God-Art's neck and crashed to the ground. He shrieked as a dead dwarf's elbow caught him squarely in the kidney.

God-Art's screech escaped his mouth like a cannon blast, launching a thunderous rocket of air at the dragon. The dragon's head twisted like it had been hit with a wrecking ball, and it flopped to the ground on its back.

It shook and vibrated, reallocating its innards within its pliable membrane, morphing its shape so it was already back on its feet without losing more than a few seconds. It scrambled to a sprint once again, rumbling to close the gap by another fifty yards.

Normal-Art jumped back onto God-Art's shoulders, determined to repeat the same accidental feat of strategic genius. But he had not accounted for his own clumsiness. As he landed on God-Art's shoulders and tried once more to wrap his arms around his alternate-self's lower jaw, his blundering hands fumbled. He lost his balance. He flipped over God-Art's shoulders, and as he flopped to the ground, he flailed his arms like a panicking turtle stuck on its back.

Normal-Art glanced at the god. God-Art had stopped screaming, and his gaping mouth now hung limp. Normal-Art looked down at his hands. He held a putrid yellow string. He glanced about and saw rubbery, disembodied ears lying scattered upon the nearby mounds of dwarven corpses. Blood flowed rotten and purple from the severed ears, creating tiny violet pools within the confines of each ear's lobe. Normal-Art shrugged, not even bothering to wonder from where the purple blood was coming. And then he grinned at the change in luck that had finally allowed him to do something right, even if that *something right* had been a total accident.

The moment was ruined when a murky shadow eclipsed the sun. Normal-Art glanced up. He wished he had not. He soiled himself. The dragon was in midair, directly above him and diving down at him with its sadistic mouth wide open.

A chrome blur zoomed across Normal-Art's peripheral, and then the blur leapt into the dragon's gaping mouth. Though Normal-Art could not hear it, the dragon yelped in some ungodly mixture of pain and surprise, after which it twisted and rolled in midair, crashing onto its back mere feet from the prone Arts.

Normal-Art peered at the now-thrashing dragon. Drillbot was inside the dragon's translucent skin, wildly slashing and stabbing with its sharp drill-arms. Holes and more holes ripped open in the dragon's membrane, and as soon as the creature could heal one of these injuries, the wily robot managed to poke two more to take its place.

Normal-Art felt something solid enclose his ears from behind, massaging and squeezing them. Confused, he brought a hand up to the side of his head and realized that God-Art was cupping his ears. Normal-Art felt a jolting pop deep within his ear canals, and the piercing hum that had drowned out all other sounds for the last few minutes disappeared. God-Art moved his hands away, and Normal-Art found that he could hear once more. He listened to the oddly comforting noise of Drillbot clanking and whirring and the glorious sound of the dragon yelping.

"Been trying to get your attention since you got the necklace off me," screamed God-Art into Normal-Art's ear. "Took me a while to realize you'd gone deaf. Sorry 'bout all that. When your lady-partner got swallowed by Death,

I grew curious as to what was happening inside the beast, so I listened with my necklace of sorcerer's ears. For future reference, eavesdropping on the inner workings of Death is not such a good idea."

Normal-Art sighed in exasperation.

God-Art ignored the sigh. He said, "Now help me move these corpses out from underneath us. And be quick about it! We need to reach the ground before that creature kills our robot ally. It's our only chance."

Normal-Art did not bother questioning or replying. He simply began tossing. He threw aside dozens of dwarven dictator corpses and squirrel bodies. He was working so intently that he did not realize he had reached the grass below the bodies until he had already thrown aside a few clumps of wet soil. In the background, the whirring and clanking and yelping grew louder.

"We need a wider radius of exposed ground," said God-Art. "Keep moving those bodies."

Normal-Art kept moving those bodies and kept listening to the nearby struggle. He heard a deafening crack. God-Art tackled him to the newly exposed ground. A severed drill crashed across the ground where Normal-Art had just been, ricocheting away into the distance. A trail of oil followed behind the missile as it THUNKed into the side of the pyramid, disappearing inside the limestone like a bullet into cellulite.

Normal-Art returned his attention to the fight. He cursed. Inside the dragon, Drillbot was down to one arm. In removing the other, the dragon had struck major oil. It flowed rapidly down Drillbot's armless shoulder.

Normal-Art looked down at the ground and then back up at God-Art. He asked, "We got about a three-foot radius. That good enough?"

God-Art replied, "Hope so."

"So, what do we do with it? The ground, I mean."

"You're going to slap it," responded God-Art.

"What? That's stupid," said Normal-Art.

"Aim away from the pyramid but toward the dragon. And slap it, as hard as you can. Don't ask questions, just do it! Now!"

Normal-Art turned toward the dragon. He reared back on his heels and pulled his hands as high into the air as he could. At the climax of his arc, he flexed his shoulders and pulled his arms back down toward the grass. The heels of his palms slammed into the ground, and every atom in his body vibrated.

The vibrations flowed out through his arms and into the ground like a tsunami that had begun within his core. The Earth around him began to vibrate, too, and within less than a second, it began shaking violently.

A fissure erupted in the ground between Normal-Art's gloved hands. It grew outward, away from him, ripping the Earth in twain. God-Art grabbed Normal-Art by the collar and pulled him to his feet before he could fall into the crack.

"We need to get moving," said God-Art. "That quake is not going to stop until it encircles this entire Earth, and we do *not* want to still be in this reality when it comes full circle."

Normal-Art turned to God-Art. "What do you mean?"

"The fissure that you created will continue ripping across the planet until it completely encircles the globe, and when it gets back here, the world will be split in two. The core will then explode, launching the halves of the planet in opposite directions, and life as we know it will no longer be sustainable here."

Normal-Art glanced at the fracturing Earth, watching the fissure widen as it stretched into the distance. Hordes of dwarven corpses tumbled into the expanding crack, descending to a fiery grave in molten lava far below.

All the while, the dragon and Drillbot continued their struggle, stabbing and clawing one another without paying any attention to the fissure advancing toward them. Drillbot clanked and whirred. Gears popped off and steam whistled from its exhaust pipes. The dragon growled and hissed, swirling its innards like a twister, knocking the robot about. The fissure cracked open wide beneath them.

The combatants reacted like cartoon characters, seeming to float in the air for a couple seconds before gravity remembered to pull them down. Neither the impending fall nor the injuries that Drillbot had sustained seemed to slow the robot whatsoever. It continued pumping its remaining drill through the creature's membrane, and beams of light erupted out from the holes like rays of sun through a system of storm clouds as the dragon healed the holes. The brawling duo fell, twisting and turning through the air, and dropped into the lava deep within the chasm. The thrashing pair sank beneath the orange glow of the liquid rock.

"How long do we have?" asked Normal-Art. He could no longer see the end of the fissure, for it had stretched past the horizon.

"I'd say about three hours, give or take a couple minutes."

With the immediate danger of the dragon no longer looming before him, the gravity of the atrocity that Normal-Art had just committed smacked him right across the face. He grabbed God-Art by the collar. "What did you have me do?" he demanded. "I didn't know that you had recruited me to exterminate an entire planet!"

God-Art pried Normal-Art's hands off his cloak. "Well, it *was* a planet full of evil dictators," he answered. "And we killed it to save the Multiverse. That's not such a bad tradeoff, now, is it?"

Normal-Art's shoulders slumped. "I guess not," he said. "But I wish Drillbot didn't have to die."

God-Art put his hand on Normal-Art's shoulder. "I've died lots of times. The ol' clunker might be back. Have a little faith. Now, let's get moving up that pyramid. We don't have much time to waste."

They got moving at as close to a sprint as they could maintain, considering the lumpy, mustachioed terrain.

CHAPTER 19

LADY LUCK CAN BE A BIT BASHFUL

NORMAL-ART COULD NOT catch his breath. He had done his best to sprint the entire winding path that zig-zagged up and around the pyramid, even though sprinting for him was rather slow-going in the first place. Blood pulsed down his legs from gashes and scrapes that had been scratched into his knees when spasms had shaken the Earth and sent him skidding across the path. Even worse, his numerous falls had ripped holes in his cargo shorts, and it smarted every time the frayed fabric rubbed across his cuts. His blood became a kind of crimson glue, sticking the cargo shorts to the hairy skin of his legs. It was a rather annoying sensation.

Finally, after he had suffered uncountable bouts of dizziness, and just when he was on the verge of collapsing from exhaustion, Normal-Art rounded the last bend in the path. He was hundreds of feet above the surrounding jungle. He laid his eyes upon the primitive-yet-pastel sculptures of intertwined comets that sat on the top of the pyramid. He could sense nothing in his legs but pain and fatigue. It felt as though his femurs were encased in a fire-flavored Jell-O mold. He forced his feet to keep trudging and tried his best to ignore the jiggly burning in his thighs.

Normal-Art took the final step onto the flat top of the pyramid, a mere few feet from the sculptures. And he plummeted straight to the ground.

He banged his face on the coarse stone and cursed a despairing curse. He had not noticed until he hit the ground that there was a slight lip on the threshold of the peak, and he had not picked his foot up high enough to clear it. When a monsoon of bright blood gushed to the limestone beneath him, he noted that there must be a new scrape on his head. The stone lapped up the blood like a dehydrated puppy. He cursed again.

A headache pounded its way through his skull. He lifted his head and stared up at the comet sculptures like a hillbilly mesmerized by big city lights at a state fair. The chiseled sculptures appeared solid, but they also had an oddly translucent sheen to them. The sun shone upon them, and as the rays hit their surfaces, the sculptures refracted the light and made the sunbeams dance inside themselves before allowing the sunbeams to flare out and bathe the surrounding pyramid-top in pastel blue-and-pink hues.

God-Art stepped over to his counterpart and frowned. He crouched and touched Normal-Art's left temple. The throbbing in Normal-Art's skull downgraded to a constant hum.

Normal-Art rolled onto his back and failed to catch his breath. Air puffed into and out of his lungs like they were a set of wheezy bellows. He watched God-Art's fire-hair flare with each of his desperate inhales and tint blue with each of his weighty exhales. Normal-Art became angry that the god was not out of breath, too.

"Fu – *HUFF* – fu – *PUFF* – fu – *HUFF* – fucken – *PUFF* – fuckengods!" Normal-Art gasped.

God-Art shrugged. "You've got exactly one minute to rest up, and then we need to move. You could've had more time to rest if you'd have moved faster."

Normal-Art shot God-Art the finger. Normal-Art moaned, "You could have – *HUFF* – carried me. It would've been – *PUFF* – like that poem, where God carries – *HUFF* – the guy across the beach when he can't – *WHEEZE* – make it through life on his – *SNORT* – own. Only this would've been – *HUFF* – somehow less, y'know, less dignified."

God-Art rolled his eyes. He said, "Carrying you around like I'm a common servant? Puh-lease. Some deities have dignity. I am *not* a chauffeur.

"Though now that I think about it," mused God-Art, drumming his fingers on his chin. "I seem to recall that I *am* the patron god of chauffeurs back on my reality. Hmmm. I guess maybe it *would* have been appropriate. Well, I totally remembered something important today. I guess that's why they say you always have the best conversations with yourself."

Normal-Art coughed. "Who in the hell says – HUFFHUFF – says that?"

God-Art grinned. He replied, "You've got thirty seconds left to rest. Save your breath."

Normal-Art grunted. God-Art sat down, leaned back, and stared up at the blue sky like he hadn't a care in the world. God-Art began whistling, and just when Normal-Art did not think his day could get any more surreal, the *Surreal Fairy* flew in out of nowhere and bonked his life right on the head.

The peaceful tune flowing from God-Art twirled and danced in the afternoon air. Suddenly, the air surrounding his lips vibrated and transformed into fuzzy little personified musical notes that flittered about on tiny angel wings. Musical notes long and short were represented in every color of the rainbow. They looked to Normal-Art like magical flying *Muppets*.

The god abruptly shifted gears and launched from his lips a barrage of sharp staccato notes, angry and vengeful and powerful. They rode out of his mouth black as night, mounted atop shaggy G-Clef symbols. They drew swords and rushed about, stabbing the angelic rainbow notes, which emitted beautiful gasps during their death throes. The dying notes plummeted through the air and bled shimmering, multicolored blood.

Normal-Art realized that he had stopped breathing as he stared in confusion at the ridiculous scene. He sucked in a lungful of air, and with this inhale he accidentally created a vacuum that pulled the falling dead-notes into his mouth. The dead-notes caught in his windpipe, and he pounded his upper torso with the heel of his palm to try and dislodge them. After a couple seconds, the dead-notes melted and drained down the back of his windpipe. As he gasped for breath, he felt a sensation that reminded him of heartburn, only located in his lungs. Normal-Art put his fingers to his temples and closed his eyes. He burped and tasted honeyed air flutter out of his mouth. He opened his eyes and realized that he was now standing. He did not remember getting up onto his feet.

Normal-Art looked at God-Art. The staccato notes rode their mounts back into the barn that was his mouth. The god winked.

"What the hell was that all about?" asked Normal-Art.

"I could see that you were not going to catch your breath anytime soon because you are so incredibly out of shape, so I helped you recover by giving you a *little* of my essence. I don't do that for just anyone. I only do that for people who I believe are special."

"That sounds at least a *little* gross. Makes me kinda worried I'll never be able to shower enough to feel clean again."

The god sighed. He grumbled, "Well, you bitched plenty when I didn't carry your lazy bones up here, and now you're complaining when I *do* help you. I simply can't win with you."

"I guess it's a tough life being a god, huh?" replied Normal-Art.

"How would you like it if nobody's ever pleased with anything you do?" said God-Art, a hint of sorrow shimmering across his eyes.

"Really? You're complaining about being an immortal, super-powerful object of worship while I'm stuck running around this stupid Earth wondering if I'll survive to make it home to my couch? You're absolutely ridiculous."

God-Art scowled, and then he muttered, "I was merely trying to confide in you and make you feel like I care about you and think you're special. Y'know, to reveal some emotional vulnerability and boost your positive feelings about me. Because right about now, we *should* be becoming the closest of friends and committing to watching each other's backs because we like one another and trust each other and plan on being best friends forever. According to my calculations, this is approximately the part of the adventure where that usually happens."

Normal-Art was in no mood for niceties, especially with this selfish, goddamned bastard of a god. Not after the past several days. He said, "Sorry, but I just don't buy anything you're selling. It all reeks of manipulation to me. You'd make a pretty good used car salesman, you know."

"Awww, forget it. I'll be taking that piece of myself back from you when we finish this mission. *With interest.*"

"See, *that* kind of behavior is probably why nobody is ever pleased with anything you do," said Normal-Art.

"Whatever. Let's get moving."

"Where to?"

"What do you mean?" asked God-Art. "You're the one who's supposed to be leading the way. You're the one with the cosmic connection. You're the one who was so sure that this pyramid was the right one. You're the one who spotted ridiculous, invisible comet-sculptures up here. Now figure out where to go next."

"OK, OK. I get it. But wait—you can't see the comets?"

"I told you that earlier."

"But they're right there," said Normal-Art, pointing just behind God-Art's shoulder.

"Well, if I can't see them and you've been told to find them, then I'd guess the answer to where we should go next would somehow involve them. Figure it out."

The Earth shuddered mightily as the fissures continued to rip through the planet. Normal-Art grabbed God-Art's cloak to keep from falling. "And do it quickly," hissed the god.

Normal-Art inhaled heavily and heard music deep within his soul. He studied the sculptures, watching the light bouncing from side to side inside the translucent comets. He walked over to them. He felt a tickle in the back of his brain, and somehow unbeknownst to him, he knew what to do. He placed one hand palm-down atop the blue comet. He did the same with his other hand on the pink comet. The translucent stone felt coarse and rough beneath his skin, and when he pushed, the comets seemed solid.

He closed his eyes. He allowed his body to relax, and he envisioned in his mind's eye the image of the cosmic blue teddy bear that he had seen in his dreams. Then he felt resistance leave his palms. He leaned his weight onto them, slowly tipping forward. He sank into the comets, and as the stone that formed the sculptures ran between his fingers, it reminded him of the childhood summers he spent at his uncle's house when he would walk to the nearby creek bed and grab a big ol' glob of mud, squeezing it between his fingers just to watch it plop to the ground.

Normal-Art continued to sink until he was elbow-deep in comet, and then his fingers collided against two oblong spheres, which were mounted on rods that he sensed stretched deep into the pyramid. Normal-Art closed his hands around the oblong spheres like they were gearshifts in a car. He jerked them in opposite directions as far as he could jerk them. Then he removed his hands from the comets, never opening his eyes until his hands were free.

"That's *it*?" demanded God-Art. "*That's* your plan to get us access into this stupid pyramid? We've got about two hours left until this entire Earth erupts into fiery death, and you're thinking you'll solve our problem by closing your eyes and waving your hands in the air like some toddler playing with imaginary toys?"

Normal-Art felt a foreboding THUMP-CLANK deep inside the pyramid below his feet. He said, "I'll have you know that I didn't simply wave my hands in the air. I reached inside the comet sculptures—you know, the ones which are apparently invisible to you unworthy types. It was a feat of great daring and cleverness, I tell you."

Normal-Art heard a WHUMP-TINK-THUMP-CLANK-POK-CLACK emanating from a couple inches below his feet. Then the statue disappeared, and the pyramid split open where the statue had been. The entire top of the pyramid tilted toward the opening, and the sudden tilt caught both Arts off guard. They fell flat on the ground and rolled toward the hole, which dumped them into a freefall. Normal-Art could see a sandy floor fifteen-feet below him. He sighed and braced himself for impact.

But Normal-Art's effort to brace himself was for naught. As the duo dropped through the air, Normal-Art bumped against God-Art and lost control of his fall. Normal-Art twisted and crash-landed at an awkward angle, and a small thermonuclear explosion of pain erupted across his ribcage.

He choked on the dusty air as he cursed his luck. His string of expletives must have been enough to make Lady Luck lose her innocent cool, because when he ran his fingers over the ribs on the left side of his torso, he felt jagged bones poking out of his skin like crooked keys on an archaic caveman piano. When his fingers touched the broken ribs, the pain made him wince. He squealed.

The trap door above the Arts swung shut, sealing off the light that had been floating in from outside. It would have been pitch dark within the pyramid, but God-Art's hair burned brightly enough to light the surrounding chamber.

"So, let me get this straight," said God-Art. "You simply closed your eyes and reached your hands into the air, and a trap door opened? That's stupid. That's just dumb. The gods in charge of this reality are idiotic."

Normal-Art winced. "In a little pain here. Not really in the mood to trade quips."

"What happened?"

"Lost my balance in the air when we collided. Had that fancy magic anvil you gave me in my shirt pocket, and it got caught beneath me when I landed."

"That sucks."

"Tell me about it. Got any more god-tricks to solve this one?"

"If you'd quit whining and listen to your body, then you'd realize that I've already given an extremely powerful *god-trick* to you. Shut your eyes and do what the music I imparted to you makes you feel."

Normal-Art moaned, but he did as he was told. He closed his eyes and realized that the magical musical notes were still in his lungs. He relaxed and allowed their music drift through him. It hummed unmelodiously at first, but then it picked up speed and harmony. His hips rocked back and forth, and his spine wiggled to the beat.

Normal-Art opened his eyes and whistled, and he stared in awe as fuzzy musical notes rushed from his lips. The formerly dead oddities had transformed into something new while inside him. They wore tiny staccato hats marked with red crosses, and they bumbled over each other like a gaggle of Laurels and Hardys, each with a doctor's bag made from a tiny double note in hand. They crashed into his chest, creating a symphony played out upon his broken ribcage. And with each note that crashed into him, his pain lessened and his swelling subsided.

After it seemed like a whole legion of EMT-notes had committed suicide upon his ribs, the ribs flattened back into place and the skin mended itself back together. Normal-Art finally felt ready to move again. He stopped whistling and hopped to his feet, but then he grimaced as the wound smarted. He said, "Feels better, but it's still a little tender."

"That's the new tissue you just created, pulling taut," said God-Art. "Best you're going to get under our circumstances. Let's get moving. But do try to be more careful this time."

CHAPTER 20

EVEN THE LONGEST JOURNEY BEGINS WITH ONE STEP... FOLLOWED BY A SHITLOAD OF MAYHEM

NORMAL-ART STARED DOWN at the barb standing erect in his hip. Black blood flowed around the shaft of the barb and dripped onto the floor, soaking into the sand and coagulating into little coarse pockets of gel.

"I just can't catch a break," Normal-Art repeated over and over to himself like it was his new pessimistic mantra.

A few minutes ago, God-Art and Normal-Art had decided to move on from their tumble into the pyramid. As they walked, Normal-Art called out directions whenever the tickle in his brain told him to. The duo was covering ground rather swiftly, but that all changed when Normal-Art and God-Art turned and entered a narrow hallway.

Normal-Art heard a noise that sounded like stone grinding against stone originating from near God-Art's foot. Then a loud CLACK erupted from somewhere within the far wall at the end of the hallway. Normal-Art felt a gust of air whoosh past his head, followed by the sound of a THUNK crashing into the wall behind him. He turned, only to witness a two-foot long dart embedded deep into the limestone, where no dart had been seconds before.

He then heard more CLACKs originating from the far wall, CLACKing faster than his senses could comprehend. They seemed to be spewing forth like a machine gun firing CLACK after CLACK. Without thinking, Normal-Art grabbed the red sphere from his pocket and held it in front of him in the direction of the noise. He yelled the magic words to activate it, "*Socky-Go-Go-Eyeball!* Go kapow! Go kapow now!"

Crimson light filled his vision, followed nearly instantly by utter blackness. He found himself waking up a few minutes later with God-Art standing over him, slapping him across the face.

"We don't have time for you to behave like such an amateur," said God-Art. "Next time you want to use the *Socky-Go-Go-Eyeball*, make sure that you aim the pupil away from you. You're lucky I was here to save your hide from those booby traps after you knocked yourself out."

"My hide didn't need saving. I just needed better training with your stupid eyeball-weapon."

"I think I deserve a little more than your ingratitude. After all, I did what *you* failed to do. After you fell unconscious, I used the *Socky-Go-Go-Eyeball* to eradicate the wall that was firing upon us."

Normal-Art was about to give in and thank his counterpart when he discovered that a barb now stood erect in his left hip. He had not noticed it until he stood up and it poked deep into his hip joint. He saw blood pouring from the wound, and he shrieked a ghoulish shriek. And at that moment, his new pessimistic mantra had been born.

God-Art sighed. He muttered, "We need to move. We don't have time for this."

"I just can't catch a break," replied Normal-Art. "Ijustcantcatchabreak. Ijustcantcatchabreak. Ijustcantcatchabreak."

God-Art used one hand to rip the barb from Normal-Art's hip, and then he slapped Normal-Art in the face with his other. Normal-Art watched a large chunk of flesh come out with the barb, and he screamed his mantra even louder.

God-Art yelled, "Get it together! If it makes you feel any better, you *were* catching a break."

Normal-Art did not reply other than to stare at his flesh that hung on the tip of the barb.

"It was *I* who set off the trap," admitted God-Art. "I saw a raised tile on the floor, and I grew curious. Sorry. Won't happen again."

Normal-Art's expression shifted. God-Art's flaming hair reflected in the mortal's now-wrathful eyes. Normal-Art resembled a furious-yet-toothless lion in a dark jungle. "You *what*?" he spat.

"I said I'm sorry," replied the god.

"You selfish bastard! You're not the one who got blasted by a magic eyeball! You're not the one who got his pelvis turned into a shish kabob! You stepped on a raised tile because you were *curious*? What the *hell* did you think would happen? We're in a fucking mystical pyramid! Even a mentally deficient five-year-old would know better!"

God-Art stood silent for a moment. Then he smirked, saying, "If you meant that outburst as an insult, I took no offense at it. Like I told you before: where I come from, I am many different people. I'm a mentally deficient five-year-old, as well as an ancient suffering from Alzheimer's, as well as—"

"As well as the most annoying, stupidest god from any pantheon I've ever heard of!" interjected Normal-Art.

"Guess I deserve that," admitted God-Art.

"Damn right you do."

"OK. You got an apology from me, and you got to insult me without facing my wrath. But remember who you are, and remember what I *am*," said God-Art, his godly flaming hair flaring up. "Stop pushing it."

Normal-Art sighed. He decided to yield and not push the issue any further. There was no time, and the apology was probably the best he was going to get. He shut his eyes and listened once more for the music inside himself, just like he had done after his tumble into the pyramid. He tweeted a few whistles out of his lips. But he soon found that no matter how hard he listened and no matter how hard he blew, he could not get any more of the magical musical notes to pop out of his mouth. He grunted and opened his eyes. He looked up at God-Art. The god shrugged.

"Hmmph," said God-Art. "Looks like you used up all of my essence to heal yourself from your fall. That's not good."

"Fine. Work your magic again. Heal me, and let's move."

"Sorry. Can't do it. Already healed you too much and gave you as much of my essence as I'm willing to risk. These supernatural healings are a bit like narcotics: you take too much too quickly, and you overdose.

"And I can't risk you dying," continued God-Art. "I don't have the time to find our quarry on my own, and even if I did, it wouldn't go anywhere with me. It's chosen to attach its hopes to *you*, for some stupid reason that I will never understand."

Normal-Art cursed. "Whatever. C'mon," he grunted, shouldering past God-Art. He limped with each step like an arthritic old man. And then he frowned when his angry departure from God-Art backfired and he stumbled. God-Art grabbed him from behind and steadied him from falling. He shrugged off God-Art's help and kept trudging.

The two moved as quickly as they could, with Normal-Art dragging his left leg through the dust and thus leaving trail in the sand on the floor behind them. Time seemed to snail by, which seemed a good thing to Normal-Art considering they were racing the clock.

The Arts came to a staircase that led sharply down. Normal-Art could not see the bottom. He sighed and cursed beneath his breath. He placed his hand on the wall for support and tenderly hobbled down, step by painful-as-all-get-out step.

After he had long lost count of the dozens of large limestone stairs he had descended, he positioned his hand to steady himself for the next step down. However, he found that when he leaned into the wall for this step, it was suddenly made from putty. He fell into it.

Normal-Art thrashed and kicked, but the more he resisted, the deeper he sank into the putty, like this section of wall was made of quicksand. Soon he was completely submerged, and he had been thrashing so much that he had become disoriented. He had no idea in which direction he should thrash to escape. He could not breathe. He knew he was about to suffocate. He opened his mouth to scream.

The grainy putty filled his mouth and trailed inside him, slithering down into his lungs. It tasted like stale graham crackers, but its texture was like melted plastic. Normal-Art saw stars behind his vision, and his eyelids began to descend. He knew that he had reached his end. His lazy eye went lazier and drifted off course to the right, so that he was staring at the death-putty from two different angles. His eyes rolled back in his head, though one took a little longer to get there than the other. *Where is that bastard god-version of me,* he wondered.

His question was answered when an arm grabbed him around the torso. The arm pulled him close, but to his dismay, it did not yank him out of the putty. The tickle in his brain told him that the god was dragging him deeper and deeper, down into the depths of the putty-wall rather than back out onto the staircase where he could breathe.

A few seconds later, he felt himself float out of his own nostrils. He hovered near his body. Having never before experienced the sensation, he shrugged a confused shrug, and then he hummed in confusion when he realized that he no longer had shoulders to shrug. Instead, he found that he was now a vaporous gas ball. And though he could not comprehend *why* it was possible, he found that he could see clearly through the putty-wall, where before he could see nothing but the opaque, cursed putty.

Normal-Art's body was being dragged by God-Art, but the god no longer looked like God-Art. Except for the god's right arm, which remained a regular humanoid appendage hooked around Normal-Art's torso, the god had transformed into a turquoise dolphin with a thick tuft of flaming hair atop its skull. With its red eyes focused intently ahead, it kicked fiercely, swimming through the thick gelatinous wall. Normal-Art squinted at his dead body. It was pale. But before the enormity of what he was seeing could sink in, everything changed.

Normal-Art felt himself falling straight down, below his lifeless body and below his alternate-self. He looked up at them as he descended. It felt like one of those dreams where you are falling and you can't stop, and then you wake up in a cold sweat. It felt exactly like one of those, only Normal-Art did not wake up. He continued to fall.

After a while, he realized that his direction had changed, and he was now falling diagonally instead of straight down. He erupted from the putty-wall, fell through the ceiling of another room, fell through a few more, and then found himself in a humungous chamber filled with what must have been millions of living terra cotta soldiers. They were armed with intimidating clay swords, shields, and other assorted melee weapons. Their eyes burned with anger and murderous mist wafted up from their nostrils. They were attacking something on the far side of the chamber.

From this distance, Normal-Art could not quite make out what they were attacking. But he *was* able to see a burst of something pink that launched a group of the terra cotta soldiers in every direction, flinging them up and away from that end of the chamber. The affected warriors smashed to pieces as they collided with the floor and the walls and each other. But no matter how many of the terra cotta soldiers were reduced to rubbish, the hordes did not slow their march toward the target of their ire. They continued to swarm the pink force like a hive of clay bees, seemingly unconcerned for their individual well-being.

Before Normal-Art could finish watching the show, his new vaporous body floated through yet another solid limestone wall. He zoomed down a hallway and slowed to a halt in another room.

He could see beneath the sand and dust that coated the walls in this room. Glowing hieroglyphics covered the walls like an irradiated tattoo. These carvings appeared to depict some sort of squirrelly creation story.

Normal-Art floated to the near wall and followed it around the room. The images began with squirrels sitting upon rows of benches, devouring massive acorns and lifting goblets to toast one another. As Art moved to the next wall, he saw an object that resembled a meteor falling from the sky above the feast. The object landed near the squirrels and then morphed into a gigantic twister of a tornado. Tiny bearded humans fell from the top of the tornado and landed amongst the feasters. They held above their heads a pair of totemic deities, which consisted of a mammoth purple bear and an enormous silver lizard.

On the next wall, the tiny people set aside the bear and lizard and joined the feast. They toasted goblets with the squirrels. Then, one dwarf stood atop a bench and appeared to be shouting and waving his arms. This dwarf reminded Normal-Art of one of those charismatic evangelical preachers he would see on television sometimes. The shouter pointed a finger at the purple bear and the silver lizard.

The pictures on that wall ended, and Art moved to the last wall. He witnessed the feasters fall upon the ground. They seemed to worship both the purple bear and the silver lizard. Then the shouter pointed again, and they drew spears and skewered the totems.

The bear and the lizard lay upon the ground, clutching their wounds, a giant *X* having replaced each of their eyes. It reminded Art of a scene from a bad cartoon. The feasters burned the organs of the totems, and the smoke drifted up into the sky. They dropped to their knees and worshipped the dead husks. They built a grand pyramid to honor the feat.

After the pyramid was complete, the spirit of the silver lizard floated out from its dead husk and coagulated into a mighty dragon. It soared through the sky and attacked the feasters. The feasters fled, but not all escaped. The hieroglyphs depicted the dragon ripping apart many of them. As the dragon killed them, each of their spirits floated from their bodies. The dragon snatched each spirit in its mouth and grew larger with every soul that drifted down its gullet.

After the feasters were fled and the dragon had grown to even more enormous proportions, the dead skull of the purple bear cracked open. A tornado erupted from the skull's crack. From the top of this twister crept a pair of teddy bears, one blue and one pink, their eyes overlarge and their teeth razor sharp. The dragon snatched the bears in its talons and carried them to the grand pyramid that the feasters had built. The dragon stuffed them inside an opening in the top of the pyramid, and then it used its mighty limbs to place a giant stone inside the opening like a cork, blocking the exit from the place. The dragon sculpted this stone so that it looked like intertwining blue and pink comets. They looked exactly like twin versions of the original comet, fallen amongst the feasters on the first wall. Hieroglyphic skulls and crossbones surrounded the carved pyramid, and Art did not have to be the world's greatest detective to understand that these symbols were warning people to stay away from the pyramid under threats of death. The dragon floated above the pyramid and appeared to stand sentry over it.

Normal-Art smirked to himself, noting the irony in warning intruders to stay away from the pyramid now that they were already inside it. In the last sequence on the last wall, the teddy bears sat in a prison within the pyramid. Each lifted a horn to it lips and blew, and lightning erupted from the ends of the horns. The lightning caused a hieroglyphic portrayal of the planet to rip in half. Normal-Art grunted.

At the end of the hieroglyphics, Normal-Art came to an open door. He floated through it and found himself in a long, curved hallway. Swirling blue and pink lights glowed from the opposite end. He crept closer to the lights.

He reached the end of the hallway, and the blue portion of the swirling light flared brighter. Despite being a gaseous ball with no eyes, the light blinded him. But Art did not need to see to know what he would find lurking behind the light: the same teddy bear from his dreams, the same bear that had called out to him from across worlds. It spoke.

"Save Me," it said. "Others be near and be following orders from pink side. They be demolishing terra cotta guard-horde. Don't let them free pink side. They will destroy all of everything. Art has come so far. Art be so close. Art must overtake them."

Art felt a tug at the scruff of his neck—well, where the scruff of his neck would have been if he were currently inhabiting a body. The tug turned into a yank, and he found himself being jerked harshly upward, faster than he had fallen when he first left his body. Normal-Art felt as though a gigantic shepherd's crook had reached into his life from behind some invisible curtain and wrenched him offstage.

He flew upward disorientingly fast, through walls and stairs, and glanced up just in time to catch an odd sight. God-Art, back in his regular god-form, was slamming the heels of his palms into Normal-Art's lifeless sternum, counting out compressions as he did CPR. It would have been touching had Normal-Art not suspected that the god was only performing the life-saving technique for selfish reasons.

"One…Two…Three…Four…Five…Six," counted God-Art. "Wake up, *Me*-dammit! We don't have time for this!"

Normal-Art crashed headfirst into his body, performing a graceless swan dive into his left nostril. He opened his body's eyes and sat up. Then his stomach swirled with nausea, and he vomited.

The pieces of the gelatinous wall that had forced themselves down his throat made a high velocity exit from his body. They splattered to the floor, and then they flopped back and forth like fish out of water. The pieces continued convulsing until they had flopped back over to the wall. A thick tendril of putty launched out from the wall, snagged the vagrant pieces, and slapped them back into itself.

Normal-Art dry-heaved until God-Art grabbed him by the armpits and hoisted him up onto his feet. Then Normal-Art began coughing and hacking into his palm. When he finally pulled his hand away, another piece of the wall lay in it. He flung the piece onto the wall. It flopped back over to the wall and melted back into the putty.

"Good job finding this amoeba wall," said God-Art. "I'd never have guessed that they'd have these beasts on this reality."

"Amoeba wall?" gasped Normal-Art.

"They're walls that are in a constant transitive, amorphous state. They're mostly found in magical dungeons on Earths where adventurers frequent such places. They're predators that blend into their surroundings so that their prey won't know they're lurking about. When something—usually bugs or birds or rodents or the occasional adventurer—touches one or burrows into one, it consumes them. And if nothing organic happens by, they will slowly eat inanimate objects. This one's so big, I'd guess it's probably been eating this pyramid from the inside out for millennia, slowly moving along, consuming the limestones atom by atom and replacing the consumed pieces with itself."

"How'd we survive?" asked Normal-Art, still gasping to catch his breath.

"Well, I'm naturally immune to them, being a god. But by the time I realized that you had disappeared and where you had disappeared to, you were already dead. That thing ate probably half your lungs and a good portion of your internal organs. I assumed I'd nothing to lose, so I swam us through the rest of it, and then I risked you overdosing on my supernatural essence by healing you.

"I called your soul back to you and mended your organs from the inside," God-Art continued. "Even cast a light beacon within your body, too, which announces threatening messages in a frequency that annoys amoeba walls. A bit like nails on a chalkboard to them. No amoeba wall on any reality will want a piece of you now. At that point, it was a simple matter of resuscitating you. However, there is *still* a chance that this latest dose of my magic may yet turn you into a mindless, flesh-devouring ghoul."

Normal-Art found that he could finally breathe normally again. "Swell," he said.

"But that's only if your body rejects my magic. Rather unlikely now. It *probably* would've already happened. But only time will tell."

"If it happens, I'll be sure to devour you first."

God-Art ignored him. "I simply wish you'd have warned me before you went diving into an amoeba wall. I could've conjured you a protective suit to wear."

"God, I hate you," replied Normal-Art.

"Suit yourself, but we really must get moving."

"Oh, *we really must.* By the way, when my spirit or whatever was flittering about outside my body, I saw the Ginnys. Or rather, I saw their new powers that you mentioned earlier."

"Where were they?"

"Down below, close to our goal. Seems our buddy the blue teddy bear thinks we're not too far behind them. Said we should be close enough to overtake them."

"Hmmm," said God-Art. "If he says so, I guess it's probably true. We should run, then."

"I can't," replied Normal-Art. He pointed at his hip. "Holy hip, remember?"

"Oh, stop being such a baby. I healed it when I resurrected you. Figured with all the rest of my essence that I was pumping into you, it wouldn't increase the chances of overdose by too much. But be extra careful, because I seriously cannot risk healing you again. Which way now?"

Normal-Art looked around. To their left, the corridor twisted away, out of view. To their right, it did the same, but it did so at a slightly downward angle.

The tickle inside his brain returned, and Normal-Art pointed to their right. "We need to go down."

"Lead the way," said God-Art. "And do it fast."

Normal-Art nodded. Then he sprinted ahead, rounded a bend, and began a dash down hundreds and hundreds of misshapen stairs. The stairs hypnotized him and blended into one another, and he almost tripped when they abruptly ended at the bottom. He skidded to a halt. And just in time, too.

At the bottom of the stairs, a great arched doorway opened onto a vast chamber. A dusty trail passed beneath the arched doorway and ended a few feet on its other side, dropping off into a cavernous black gorge. Glancing over the edge, Normal-Art could not see a bottom. God-Art reached the end of the stairs and screeched to a stop behind him, but not quickly enough to prevent himself from crashing into Normal-Art. Normal-Art almost fell into the blackness below. He squealed.

God-Art steadied him, and then the god pointed out two large wooden stakes buried deep in the ground just inside the arched doorway on either side of the dusty trail. Ancient ropes were attached to the stakes, and the ropes hung lifelessly over the edge of the canyon.

Normal-Art glanced from these ropes over to the far side of the canyon. Matching stakes were buried in the ground over there, with matching ropes attached to them that dangled into the blackness of the canyon. Wooden planks hung like limp slugs to the dead ropes on the far side, trailing hopelessly down into the dark.

"Seems the Ginnys have cut the rope bridge that would have allowed us to cross," said God-Art.

"Seems so," responded Normal-Art. "Does that mean we'll have to climb down and cross on foot?"

"That's a terrible idea," replied God-Art. "There's no telling what kind of scary monster is down there, just waiting to eat us. I bet it's some species of creepy underground crab. That's the kind of uncreative bullocks I've seen at the bottom of every other underground canyon to which I've traveled.

"And besides, we don't have time," continued God-Art. "We've only got about forty-two minutes until this Earth ends in a fiery swath of destruction."

Seemingly on cue, the planet shook and rumbled. The Arts shuffled back to the arched doorway and braced themselves there.

"Well, what do we do then?" asked Normal-Art. "We sure as hell can't jump it."

"We fly," answered God-Art.

"Totally logical. Why didn't *I* think of that?" said Normal-Art with a heavy dose of sarcasm.

He shrugged when God-Art crouched to the ground and squawked. The god's nose and mouth quivered, and then both slid off his face like dead skin from a snake. They thudded to the ground and evaporated. A giant, golden beak erupted from where they had just been, stretching the length of Normal-Art's arm and ending in a sharp predatory curve.

The skin on God-Art's back cracked open like the husk of a broiled lobster, and a pair of enormous wings flopped out from the hole. Normal-Art backed up into the stairwell to give the god some room. God-Art spread the wings, stretching them out like hang-gliders, and as he did so, the rest of his skin sloughed off his body. It crackled and melted when it hit the ground, evaporating into steam.

Red feathers covered the god. Normal-Art heard deep cracks within God-Art's body, and he realized the sounds came from the god's bones breaking and stretching and morphing into birdlike proportions. They settled into place and tightened together with an audible wisp. A fifteen-foot tall, red-feathered falcon now crouched where God-Art had stood moments before. It cawed. Its eyes were deep and cold, one of the few parts of God-Art unchanged by the transformation. Flames continued to dance atop the god's head. Without warning, the flames flashed like a lightning bolt and spread all over the bird's body, igniting the bird into a flaming phoenix.

"Hop on my back," said the bird in God-Art's voice. "We must hurry."

"Yeah, that sounds like a *brilliant* idea," replied Normal-Art. "Let me go ahead and just jump right up there. Nothing could put a better cap on this adventure than third-degree burns to my crotch."

"Sarcasm noted. You won't burn. I promise."

"You could've picked a less flashy bird, you know. I mean, if you're trying to amaze me or make me gasp or something, it's not going to happen. I've seen too much since I met you."

The phoenix sighed, which made a sort of harmonic whistling sound as it escaped its nostrils. "Not everything is about *you*. On my Earth, I was the patron god of this beast. Thus, this is my preferred avatar when I take avian form. Now move."

Normal-Art hopped up onto the bird's neck. God-Art was right: Normal-Art's crotch did not turn to cinders, though it did grow mighty toasty.

The phoenix faced the canyon and backed up as far as it could. It pulled its wings in close to its side, so it could step even further back into the the stairwell from which the Arts had come. Normal-Art gulped.

The phoenix dug its talons into the dust, crouched, and then burst into a sprint. Normal-Art grasped the surprisingly fluffy feathers between his fingers. For a moment, he wondered how fast a phoenix could get from zero to sixty, but then the bird leapt through the doorway and out into the open blackness of the canyon, and all thoughts other than sheer panic fled from his mind.

Once airborne, the phoenix stretched its wings wide, each one at its full span longer than a city bus. The bird dipped down into the blackness. Normal-Art's stomach lurched, and terror gobbled his heart like *Mrs. Pacman* eating one of those damned, stupid ghosts. Less than a second later, the phoenix righted itself and began gliding in wide circles. It climbed steadily up until it was well above the other side of the canyon and almost to the ceiling of the ridiculously cavernous chamber.

"We're about to land," said God-Art. "It shall be a bumpy one, so hold on tight."

Before Normal-Art had the chance to reply, the phoenix dropped at a speed *slightly* slower than their speed would have been if they were merely falling through the air like tumbling bricks. Normal-Art screamed in fright, gripping the feathers so tightly that he accidentally pulled a few of the fiery things out. He gasped as they fell through his fingers and tumbled away in the whistling air. Panicking, he clutched to the bald flap of bare skin where the feathers had been. He tried to distract himself from the shocking fall by watching the feathers drift down, deep into the blackness below. They glowed with fiery light the entire way, and as they fell deeper and deeper into the canyon, Art saw black eyes staring up from the depths.

Normal-Art realized that the eyes belonged to giant crabs clinging to the sides of the canyon. They leapt from the wall and snapped gigantic pincers at the feathers. A half-dozen missed and fell into the deep darkness before one finally snatched a feather from the air. This unlucky crab erupted into flame, squealing as it fell. Normal-Art neither saw nor heard any of the creatures hit the bottom of the canyon. They all simply disappeared into the blackness, never to be heard from again.

Before Normal-Art could return his attention from the falling feathers and focus back on God-Art's landing, the phoenix had already skidded to a halt and had turned its head completely around to stare at Normal-Art. Normal-Art sighed in relief. He hated plane landings, and had he been paying attention, he just knew the phoenix landing would have been exponentially more awful.

"Told you," said the phoenix. "Giant crabs. Always, always count on giant crabs to be present in a mysterious canyon."

"Sure, I'll always count on *that*," mumbled Normal-Art, so happy to be on solid ground that he would have agreed to just about anything.

"Now please get off my back so that I can return to my beautiful self. We need to keep moving, and this phoenix form isn't very practical in enclosed spaces."

Normal-Art hopped off God-Art. The fire enveloping the god's feathers plinked out, and then the feathers tumbled from the bird and landed on the ground like a pile of red, oblong snowflakes.

"Grab a couple and keep them," said the now-less-phoenixy God-Art. "They're good luck."

Normal-Art reached down and grabbed a handful from the ground. As he stuffed them into his pocket, he looked down at his pants and cursed. The crotch of his pants had been burned away, and he could feel the lining of his pockets burning into cinders where he had placed the feathers. His manhood flapped in the open air.

"You bastard," cried Normal-Art. "I look like I'm wearing assless chaps!"

God-Art grinned a mischievous grin at Normal-Art. The god was back in his regular skin, complete with all the gear he had been wearing before he had transformed into the phoenix. He bent down and ripped a thick strip off his cloak. He handed the strip to Normal-Art.

The god giggled. Between giggles, he said, "Here, wrap this around your waist if it will help you be less insecure about your tiny genitals."

Normal-Art furrowed his brows, and then he snatched the cloth from God-Art's hand. He wrapped it around his waist like it was a towel that he might wrap around himself after a shower, covering over his unmentionables and the tattered remains of his cargo shorts. He hoped he did not look quite as ridiculous as he felt.

"Now, if you're no longer afraid that our enemies will laugh at your outfit, let's get moving. And again, I must reiterate: do so quickly," ordered God-Art.

Normal-Art cursed the arrogant god, but then he got moving. He dashed ahead of the god down the next corridor, following the instructions given to him by the tickle in his brain. He rounded a bend and sprinted through a doorway. As soon as he did so, he found himself smacking face-first into a gigantic fist of fluorescent pink goo. He squealed in surprise.

The pink goo snatched him by the feet and lifted him into the air. He dangled upside down for a moment, nervously twisting and turning to try and catch a glimpse of his attacker.

Without warning, the goo whacked him onto the ground. Then it released him. Normal-Art lay where he landed, shell-shocked and bloody. God-Art barely had time to dash into the chamber and pull Normal-Art back into the safety of the corridor before the pink fist smashed down where Normal-Art had been lying. The oversized fist left a crater in the floor larger than Normal-Art.

God-Art sat Normal-Art up against one of the walls in the corridor. Blood poured from Normal-Art's nose, and he could not manage to get his eyes to focus. His vision simply passed in phases from blurry to blurrier. He ached all over.

"Welcome, lover!" called a squeaky female voice though the doorway. "Give us a moment to finish off this rather less-than-intimidating terra cotta army, and then we shall be there to deal with you."

Normal-Art, still dazed, whispered to God-Art between racking bouts of dizziness, "What do we do?"

"What else *can* we do?" answered God-Art. He tossed the *Socky-Go-Go-Eyeball* to Normal-Art. "You pull yourself together, and then we go out there and we kill those bitches. Make sure you aim that damned device properly this time."

Normal-Art swallowed hard. He massaged his temples, trying to shake off the terrible headache that had enveloped his entire skull. He tasted limestone dust between his teeth, and he wished he could brush them.

Here he was, a mere moment from either a second painful death or finishing this stupid quest and getting to go home. Either one, he assumed, would be better than spending another second with this god-version of himself. He looked down, gripped the eyeball between his left thumb and forefinger. He made sure the pupil was facing out this time. He slowly forced himself up on his feet, still rather shaky but determined.

"Whenever you're ready," the god whispered.

Normal-Art furrowed his brow, inhaled deeply, and dashed through the doorway.

CHAPTER 21

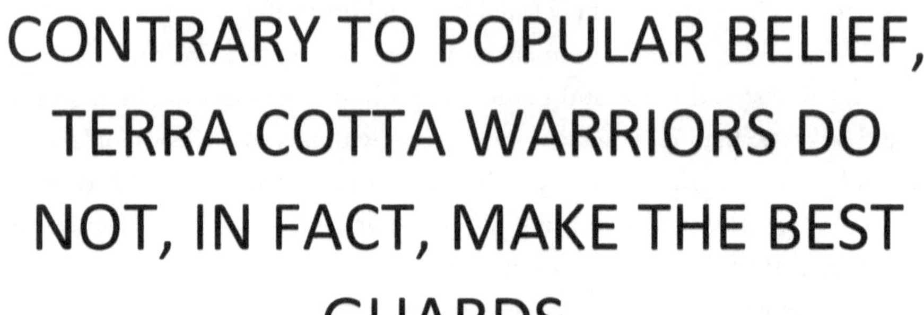

CONTRARY TO POPULAR BELIEF, TERRA COTTA WARRIORS DO NOT, IN FACT, MAKE THE BEST GUARDS...

REGULAR-GINNY STARED INTO the eyes of an animated terra cotta soldier. She held its disembodied clay head in the palm of her hand, staring into its cracking red-brown eyes like she was Hamlet clothed in a Girl Scout uniform, muttering a soliloquy to the oddest Yorick skull ever to grace a stage. The head blinked its deep clay eyes and snapped its ruddy teeth, mindless in its quest for violence.

The head appeared to be a carved combination of a mustachioed dwarf and a squirrel, with beady humanoid eyes mounted over a squirrel snout. It wore a conical helmet with a nosepiece that rested atop the bulging snout. Squirrel ears poked out from slits in the helmet, with realistic fur carved into them by some unknown but expert hand.

Regular-Ginny glanced past the helmet of the clay soldier. She sighed. It snapped at her again, and she smashed it with a mallet of pink goo. Another horde of terra cotta soldiers was marching toward her. She swallowed. It had been a long journey thus far, and it was poised to be longer still.

Earlier, after she and Tiny-Ginny had fallen into the pyramid and healed themselves, Tiny-Ginny had immediately forced Regular-Ginny to stand and begin the hunt for the Pink One. The duo had dodged the obvious booby-traps strewn about the floor of that first several corridors and hallways, and then they walked down and down and down hundreds of stairs. At the bottom of the stairs, the Ginnys found themselves staring at an ominous black wall that stood nearly quadruple Regular-Ginny's height. Two identical doorways opened in the face of the wall.

The Ginnys shrugged at each other, and rather than entering either of the doorways, they formed giant stilts of pink ooze from the pores of their feet and raised themselves high enough that their heads nearly banged against the ceiling, thirty-feet up. This vantagepoint allowed them to stare down over the wall from a bird's eye view, and from here they could see that a deadly maze sprawled below them. It filled an entire chamber that contained enough square footage to rival JFK International Airport, and it tilted down at such an extreme angle that the opposite end rested hundreds of feet below the beginning. Staring down at it, Regular-Ginny worried she might succumb to a bout of vertigo.

The duo could see that each wrong turn down there ended in a poorly camouflaged pit that dropped into darkness and spikes. So instead of worrying about any wrong turns, the Ginnys made use of their pink stilts by stepping over the walls and avoiding the maze altogether. Being careful not to get their stilts stuck in the spike-pits, they soon found themselves standing at the exit on the other side of the maze, not even a bead of sweat lost in the effort. They reabsorbed their stilts into their bodies. Then they passed through the exit and entered a long hallway. Soon, they discovered a fork in the path. The itch in Regular-Ginny's brain encouraged her to follow the path to the right, the one that led down a staircase. So, the pair went that way.

They descended more stairs than Regular-Ginny cared to count, and when they reached the bottom of the stairway, they stood in an arched doorway through which they could see an enormous cavern bisected by a canyon. They peered through the doorway and saw that the canyon had a single route across it: a ridiculously rickety rope bridge, every square inch of which was occupied by giant crabs. Regular-Ginny shuddered. Crabs had always reminded her of cockroaches, and she hated cockroaches.

Tiny-Ginny approached the infested bridge, but instead of crossing it, she grew a bridge of her own from pink ooze that she launched from her pores. She walked across it without incident. Regular-Ginny shrugged, and then she copied Tiny-Ginny and created a bridge of her own from her own pink ooze. For the entire walk across her bridge, Regular-Ginny stared down into the unfathomable, endless blackness of the canyon. She shivered in terror.

Upon reaching the far side of the canyon and reabsorbing their pink bridges into their bodies, Tiny-Ginny jettisoned a new barrage of pink goo from each of her shoulders, arcing the goo up into the air like a pair of pink rainbows. The rainbows crashed down atop the rickety rope bridge. The ropes snapped, and the wooden planks shattered, and the Arts' only hope to cross the canyon behind them snapped in half, each half now dangling impotently into the black depths. Tiny-Ginny listened to the terrified squeals of the falling crabs, and then she squealed a pleasured squeal in response.

The Ginnys then turned their backs on the carcass of the bridge and continued. They marched through an open archway and into a narrow corridor with short ceilings. The sounds of their shoes scrunching on the sandy floor echoed around them. The duo rounded the next corner, exiting the corridor, and found themselves staring into thousands upon thousands of ghastly faces.

The faces staring back at them belonged to terra cotta sculptures of dwarves that were carved to have squirrel fur, snouts, ears, and paws, and were garnished in ornately sculpted medieval armor. Regular-Ginny scratched her head, and then she creamed in fright when the first row of soldiers blinked and brandished clay weapons from their dusty sheaths. They began marching toward her, murder in their terra cotta eyes and silver mist rising from their nostrils.

Tiny-Ginny laughed, allowing the pink ooze to pour forth from the pores of her hands. The pink goo coagulated into two ferocious battle axes roughly twice as tall as she. Pinkness continued creeping from the rest of her pores, enveloping the dwarven brute in thick, knightly pastel plate armor. She sprinted right into the fray, and even provided matching pink armor and a pink spear for her squirrel. To Mister E's credit, he too began fighting without a second thought, squealing the most ferocious battle cry that Ginny had ever heard a rodent squeal.

After hesitating a moment, Regular-Ginny followed suit by forming a coat of plate armor from within the pink forge of her body, reinforcing the pink membrane she had been wearing around her body for days. She rounded out the outfit by willing pink globs to form gigantic greaves that clung to an oversized mallet. The pink hatred in her heart twirled in anticipation of the battle to come. She giggled as she thought about what she must look like, and then she giggled some more as she began smashing clay soldiers.

But after about half an hour, she grew extremely bored. She had discovered that the army could not harm her through her pink armor, and her arms had become numb from the vibrations that wiggled through them each time she crashed the mallet down onto an enemy. She sighed.

Before much more time passed, the pink-encrusted group had eradicated the last of this first squirrelly clay horde, and the respite was most welcome to Regular-Ginny. She began to massage the numbness from her arms, and that was when the disembodied head on the ground had grabbed her attention. It did so by rolling at her and attempting to bite her toes.

She picked it up and stared at it, contemplating life and death and the ridiculousness that had pinked itself all over her life. But her contemplation was disturbed by the approach of a second horde of terra cotta soldiers. She grunted in annoyance at the distraction and smashed the head in her hand. This new corps appeared more beastlike than the one before it, with more pronounced squirrel snouts and smaller, less human eyes.

Ginny raised her mallet above her head and went to work again, demolishing soldiers. She flung her mallet in wide arcs and allowed her mind to drift. Clay weapons poked at her from all sides, but they crumbled to dust against her pink armor before she really even felt them. *Whoever set up these defenses totally should have invested in soldiers made from something a lot stronger than clay*, she thought.

She tried to look about the room in which they were fighting, but too many clay soldiers had gathered around her, obscuring her view. So once again she willed stilts of pink goo to grow from her feet, raising herself up to a height of about twenty feet. She glanced up to ensure that she would not bump her head on the ceiling, only to find that the ceiling still hung a good fifteen or so feet higher up. She peered around the room, mesmerized by its gigantic, dusty proportions. It must have been at least a half-mile long and a quarter-mile wide. A sigh escaped her lips when she realized that almost every square millimeter of the place was occupied by the clay hordes, all of which were awaiting their turns to attack with dronelike patience. From up here, she caught sight of Tiny-Ginny and found herself momentarily hypnotized by the oddly fascinating combination of low-brow comedy and beautiful art with which the tiny hag made war.

Tiny-Ginny sprinted through the battlefield like a fierce bear cub rumbling through a forest, growling obscenities and crude taunts as she crushed everything in her path. Tiny-Ginny's lust for battle never wavered. On and on, she danced and twirled with her pink axes. It was a beautiful art in the hands of the dwarf, but soon even that became too tedious for Regular-Ginny to watch. Boredom crept up her esophagus and escaped her mouth in the form of a deep groan.

Then opportunity rang unsolicited upon the doorbell of her heart. Before she knew it, it had managed to push its foot in the door and move right on into the house. Regular-Ginny noticed a tiny pink shape dashing amongst the clay soldiers, stabbing at ankles with a tiny spear and leaping up onto clay shoulders to gore faces. It had strayed far from its master.

Pink, hateful tendrils crept into Ginny's heart and tickled it with wrathful glee. She put up a few seconds of meek resistance, but she soon succumbed to the hate's inexorable advances. Every atom in her body buzzed. A sociopathic grin plastered itself onto her face.

Tiny-Ginny continued her rampage, but the horde she was fighting lay upon the ground, mostly demolished. Regular-Ginny looked past the tattered remnant of this second horde and saw the third approaching, larger and more beastly than this one, on its way to reinforce this crumbling regiment. Regular-Ginny soaked the stilts back into her pores and returned to the ground.

"There's more on their way to attack us," called Regular-Ginny to Tiny-Ginny. "Go start on them, and I'll finish these. It'll save us some time."

Tiny-Ginny turned and grinned, her pink armor now shining reddish with a dusty clay film. "I see the lust for battle doesn't fill your weak bones. Very well, more glory for me!"

With that, Tiny-Ginny sprinted away. She did not look back. She leapt high into the air and dove straight down into the middle of the next horde of terra cotta warriors. Mister E stabbed another soldier's ankle, and then he started after her.

But Regular-Ginny launched pink tendrils from her fingertips and formed a thick cocoon of pink goo around him, holding him in place. The pink in her heart overflowed with unadulterated hate, hate on a scale she never knew possible, adamantly demanding that she offer this dingy furball as sacrifice. She knew she must move quickly, before the squirrel realized what was happening. Otherwise he might find a way to alert Tiny-Ginny, and that would not only foil this scheme, but it would probably call all her warmongering down upon Regular-Ginny, the Pink One be damned.

Regular-Ginny solidified the pinkness around the squirrel, usurping control of the goo that the rodent had been given by the tiny hag for armor. He began suffocating, and he started to thrash, so Ginny hardened her pink ooze in a way that snapped his spine in multiple places like a brittle twig. Mister E could not scream from within the solid pink goo, so he passed without even being able to squeal a final death cry for his master.

Regular-Ginny dissolved her pink trap from around him. She hastily reformed the armor and spear that Tiny-Ginny had given him, and then she laid his corpse upon the ground. She grinned, noting that he no longer rolled his eyes insanely around in his stupid head, that he no longer taunted her with his idiotic gestures, that he no longer would play brain-addled sidekick to his master's bullying. She sprinted away from him and used her pink ooze to finish off the last of this horde's remaining soldiers. Then she gathered their smashed clay bodies, covering Mister E with a heaping mound of them. Once satisfied with her cover up, she hurried over to help Tiny-Ginny as though nothing out of the ordinary had occurred.

Soon, the two Ginnys finished off the last of the third regiment of clay soldiers. In the moments of respite after the breakable carnage, before the next horde arrived, Tiny-Ginny called out to Mister E in a sweet tone that Regular-Ginny had never expected to escape from those wormy lips, "Mister E? Come here, boy. Tell me, how many cretins did my li'l squirrel-a-boo vanquish? Huh? Come tell mommy."

Excitement shone brightly on her ugly face despite the clay debris that was caked all over it. She cupped her hand to her ear and listened for Mister E's insane chitter. She yelled his name again and made an odd swirling gesture with her hand, but still she received no reply other than the marching sound of approaching terra cotta feet.

Her hopeful expression collapsed in on itself like an imploding building. She wrenched large tufts of hair from her scalp, and the thick clumps collected on the ground like wool beneath a shorn sheep. Tiny-Ginny screeched, her eyes darting from side to side, searching for some sign of the annoying rodent.

Tiny-Ginny flailed her pink ooze in all directions, knocking stacks of shattered clay left and right. The debris crashed across the dusty stone floor. Tiny-Ginny's pink armor grew, expanding from her body like a cake rising in the oven. It puffed out and out, secreting from her pores to fill a portion of the chamber twenty times as large as she. She floated in the middle of a gigantic pink sphere, flailing her arms and legs in anger like a furious cherry in the middle of a custardy dessert. Over and over again, she bleated, "Where is my squirrel? Where is Mister E?"

Tiny-Ginny created hundreds of little pink tentacles that extended from her pastel sphere. They looked like flagellae on a bacterium-themed kaiju. She used them to pick up every single shard of smashed clay on the ground around her and then throw each one against the wall when none revealed Mister E underneath it.

Realizing the precariousness of her situation, Regular-Ginny decided now would be a good time to get as far away from Tiny-Ginny as possible. She kept her eyes on the dwarf, but she backed away, following the itch in her brain toward the far side of the chamber. She needed to be far away when Tiny-Ginny discovered the squirrel's corpse. It was obvious that the dwarf was losing control of herself and her rage, and Regular-Ginny did not want to be near for Tiny-Ginny to decide she was to blame for Mister E's death, no matter how right the dwarf would have been in laying the blame at her feet.

Tiny-Ginny expanded her search. She rolled her enormous cocoon back the way the Ginnys had come, back into the remains of the previously obliterated horde of clay soldiers—the one that Regular-Ginny had volunteered to finish herself.

Regular-Ginny gulped, wishing she had planned her crime of passion a little better. *Surely it will be obvious what happened,* she thought. Tiny-Ginny's little tentacles swept this section of ground clear of broken soldier-pieces. Broken terra cotta shards flew through the air and smashed against the wall, and Regular-Ginny stifled a gasp as a small, furry pink shape thwacked into the wall amongst them, the pink armor around the rodent apparently having stuck to the underside of one of the terra cotta pieces that had been flung.

Tiny-Ginny noticed the corpse. One of her tendrils snatched the squirrel by the forepaw from where he had landed and pulled him into her pink blob. Tiny-Ginny swam through the pink goo to him faster than any Olympian could ever dare hope to swim. She grasped the squirrel's corpse in her arms. The corpse did not grasp back.

Tiny-Ginny wailed. The flood of miserable noise shook her larynx in a way that made Regular-Ginny envision a fat, angry prisoner gripping the bars of his cell and slamming his body into them.

Regular-Ginny increased the pace of her backpedaling away from Tiny-Ginny. Fear clouded her heart and drove the awkward thing whimpering down into her belly. Her throat felt tight, and she found that she was too thirsty to swallow. She felt her foot touch down upon a step, and she wondered from where it had come. She could not recall seeing any stairs in this vast chamber when she had raised herself up on her stilts to look around it. When the step moved beneath her foot, she realized that it was not actually a step.

Regular-Ginny turned to find that she had backed herself into the next horde of clay soldiers. The faces that stared back at her from this regiment were completely inhuman and totally squirrelly. The soldiers snapped their chiseled rodent teeth at her with a zombie-like ferocity. Regular-Ginny smirked at the terra cotta beasts, turning back around to watch her counterpart, secure in the knowledge that they could not penetrate her shining pink armor.

And they did not. With mechanical efficiency, the soldiers lifted and stabbed with their spears, over and over, but she never felt more than a tiny prodding against her back. But she soon grew tired of the prodding because it tickled, so she grew a dozen tentacles from her back. She thrust them into the horde behind her, swiping to-and-fro with them. She felt like a god frolicking without a care amongst the mortals of the world. She continued backing away from Tiny-Ginny through the dying clay soldiers, keeping as silent as possible because of her worry that Tiny-Ginny would remember her and tear her to shreds.

Tiny-Ginny continued cradling Mister E in her arms. Tears streamed from her face and soaked into the colossal pink cocoon that surrounded her. The dwarf soon sank to the bottom of the pink sphere. The pink cocoon soaked back into her pores until she was left wearing the pink plate armor she had worn before expanding it to the proportions of the sphere. She lay on the rough ground, staring at the dead squirrel in her gnarled hands.

Regular-Ginny began to feel sympathy for the misery of her counterpart, but then that sympathy disappeared when the pink inside her danced through her brain and caused her to remember how evil the dwarf was and how utterly rude the dwarf had been to her throughout this entire adventure. The pink also helped her recall what a total arsehole the squirrel had been to her, too. So Regular-Ginny began watching her twin's misery with glee.

But then a clod of dirt fell from the ceiling to crash onto the ground in front of her, interrupting her thoughts. And she looked up.

A new terra cotta regiment, this one almost pure squirrel with nary a humanoid quality to their bodies, was crawling upside down along the ceiling and racing past her toward Tiny-Ginny. Clouds of sand and clods of dirt rained down to the floor below them, dislodged from ancient dusty abodes by their creeping clay paws.

The first two rows of the creeping army dropped from the ceiling and dove at Tiny-Ginny. Tiny-Ginny, somehow aware of them without ever taking her eyes off Mister E, unceremoniously created an overlarge umbrella from pink ooze that grew from the top of her head. Regular-Ginny smirked at the absurdity of the army of clay kamikazes crashing to death like bucktoothed raindrops upon the dwarf's pink umbrella.

Hundreds more began diving, and as the vanguard of these clay soldiers continued to drop onto Tiny-Ginny from the ceiling, thousands of reinforcements scurried down the walls to flank the dwarf. Regular-Ginny crossed her arms, allowing a tiny smile to creep up the sides of her mouth. This was *just* the added distraction she needed to feel confident that Tiny-Ginny would not notice her escape until it was too late. She began to turn away from her counterpart, intending to ditch Tiny-Ginny once and for all and continue alone on her journey to the Pink One. But movement behind the dwarf caught her eye. And it was not the clay kind of movement that she had experienced since entering this chamber. Regular-Ginny squinted.

Regular-Ginny's boyfriend burst through the entrance to the chamber, the same entrance that the Ginnys had come through nearly two hours ago. Regular-Ginny watched in awkward astonishment as Tiny-Ginny glanced up from Mister E's corpse and immediately launched a pink arm with an oversized pink fist from one of her shoulders.

The dwarf snatched Art by the ankles. The fist lifted Art up into the air and slapped him onto the ground like an angry judge slamming down a fleshy gavel. Even here, hundreds of feet away and on the other side of the falling clay soldiers, Regular-Ginny heard Art smacking against the ground. It sounded a bit like Humpty Dumpty, if only Humpty Dumpty had taken a dive from the Empire State Building.

Regular-Ginny shuddered, and then she watched as a massive man with flaming hair dashed into view from the entryway and dragged Art away, retreating back through the entrance of the chamber. As Art was being pulled back through the door, Tiny-Ginny thrashed the fist at him. It crashed upon ground, missing him by a mere few inches. A crater remained embedded in the stone in the shape of Tiny-Ginny's oversized pink fist.

Tiny-Ginny placed Mister E's body onto the ground and covered him in a grave of pink goo, complete with a tiny pink gravestone. Then she stood and faced the entryway, ignoring the horde of diving and flanking clay soldiers.

The pink tickled Regular-Ginny's brain. She felt compelled to abandon her idea of abandoning Tiny-Ginny and return to her counterpart's side, so that she might help the dwarf get rid of the Arts. Now that they had caught up, they would be right on Regular-Ginny's heels after they ganged up to exterminate Tiny-Ginny if she left the dwarf on her own. It was unlikely that she would be able to abscond with the Pink One without fighting them, and her odds of surviving seemed much higher when paired with the dwarf.

Regular-Ginny grew a few more tentacles from the front of her torso and cleared the annoying clay beasts from her path. They continued to drop from the ceiling and scurry down the walls. The army behind her also continued attacking with a robotic tenacity, ignorant of their desperate situation. She ignored them all as best she could.

"Welcome, lover!" Tiny-Ginny yelled in the direction of the Arts. "Give us a minute to finish off this rather less-than-intimidating army, and then we'll be there to deal with you."

Regular-Ginny emerged from the terra cotta rain to stand beside Tiny-Ginny. Tiny-Ginny turned her head to face Regular-Ginny. "Where have you been?"

"While you went searching for your stupid, insane squirrel, I've been singlehandedly fighting off the remainder of this stupid army so that we can finish this damned quest," responded Regular-Ginny.

Tiny-Ginny looked down at the ground. Her ragged hair fell over her face, shading her crescent-moon eyes with an eclipse of dirty blondness. "He's dead. He must've been overwhelmed by these ghouls and crushed beneath their weight. At least he died fighting bravely."

"I'm sorry."

"No, you're not. I could tell that you always despised him. But I appreciate the sentiment."

Regular-Ginny's heart returned from its nerve-wracked trip into her stomach and unpacked its bags in its rightful home. She had escaped suspicion. Tiny-Ginny must have assumed her too cowardly or weak to make a move on

Mister E. Normally, this assumption would have been true, but Regular-Ginny had bottled up the rage in her life for far too long, and the pink inside her had taken the initiative to finally burst the bottle for her. She suppressed a smile.

Regular-Ginny looked down at Tiny-Ginny. "What's the plan?"

Tiny-Ginny glanced up at Regular-Ginny, murder gleaming in her eyes. The dwarf grinned. Her yellow teeth flashed into view from beneath her layers of pink membrane and grime. She dropped her voice to a whisper. "Follow me," she ordered.

Tiny-Ginny launched a tentacle from her hand, and its tip stuck to the dusty stone wall above the entrance to the chamber. She sucked the tentacle back into her pores, using this reabsorption to reel herself up. She slapped against the wall above the entrance and used her pink armor to stick to the wall like a pink spider. A tiny cloud of dust drifted down below her.

Regular-Ginny mimicked exactly what her counterpart had just done, and as she clung to the wall next to the dwarf, she whispered, "What're we doing up here?"

"Shut up, you fool," Tiny-Ginny whispered back. "The clay beasts cannot harm us, so they are of no concern. My Art, however, can. And he will be bursting through that doorway any second now. There's no way he will wait for us to finish these clay soldiers like I requested. Knowing him as I do, he'll want to take us by surprise while we're pinned from behind by the horde. So, we shall surprise him instead."

Regular-Ginny did not respond, noting the absurdity in the fact that her twin had ordered her to stay quiet, and then had monologued for what felt like minutes. She watched a monsoon of terra cotta falling in front of her as the seemingly endless army of clay kamikazes continued their bombardment. She smiled at the odd beauty of it. Mister E's gravesite disappeared underneath the dusty flood. A sad violin played sarcastically in her head as hateful giddiness bubbled up in her stomach. She burped, and a little bit of pink acid reflux rushed into her throat. It tasted a little like rainbows—or at least what she imagined rainbows must taste like.

In an odd moment of pre-fight clarity, she wondered if the Pink One's gift of power had caused her to go slightly insane. She shrugged. She realized she had been shrugging a lot recently, and according to her mother, it would cause bad posture. She noted to herself that she should probably stop shrugging, and then she went ahead and got one last shrug in for old time's sake.

CHAPTER 22

SWEET, SWEET SQUIRRELLY RELEASE

CHIRP-CHIRP-CHIROO DASHED LEFT and right, killing the *Holy Guardians of the Ancient Squirrel-Temple of Eternal Life and Destruction*. He knew that no matter how hard he tried, he could not control his limbs, so he did not even try. His evil master had willed his body to fight, so fight he did.

He wished he could sigh, because in addition to fighting against his will, he was also committing sacrilege. This tomb was sacred to his people. Every squirrel on this reality knew of this place and revered it. Every squirrel knelt in its direction when saying nightly prayers, though Chirp-Chirp-Chiroo had not been able to do so since the hag took control of his life. He hoped he would not be damned to some terrible hell as punishment for the sacrilege he was committing now and for the sacrilege he had committed outside the temple walls when he had been part of that blasphemous squirrel monster. He hoped the gods would understand that his will was not his own. Even if they did not, he reassured himself by noting that damnation would surely be better than the hell that his life had become.

He watched the pink spear in his hand shore its way through the terra cotta head of one of the clay warriors. Its angry eyes cursed him as it crumbled. Damn, he wished this pink suit of armor had not made him so invincible. He silently begged the gods for death because he could not say the prayers aloud. He knew his petitions were in vain, for the gods could not hear him. After all, he was not following the proper sacraments for praying that had been passed down through the generations, devout squirrel to devout squirrel. He wished he could cry.

When he was a runt, Chirp-Chirp-Chiroo's father had taught him that these pyramids had been erected to honor the ancient gods. Chirp-Chirp-Chiroo had known since he laid eyes on the markings outside of this particular pyramid that this one was the receptacle built to house the *Twin Gods of Life and Destruction*. His father told him that an ancient ancestor from his grandmother's lineage had helped build it, back when squirrels were much larger creatures than they were today. Chirp-Chirp-Chiroo had often sung of the glory of this ancestor to his own children, back before they had been killed and his will had been stolen from him.

These terra cotta warriors—the *Holy Guardians of the Ancient Squirrel-Temple of Eternal Squirrel Life and Destruction*—had been fashioned during that ancient time, carved from clay by the ancient squirrels and fire-hardened by the new bipedal creatures that had arrived on their planet—the ones who had feigned a neighborly attitude when they arrived long enough to gain the squirrels' trust, and then became harsh slave drivers, demanding slaves from the squirrels for each of their new arrivals. Chirp-Chirp-Chiroo recalled a memory from his childhood, a deep, dark one that involved his favorite uncle being pulled from his family's nest for a lifetime of slavery. When it happened, Chirp-Chirp-Chiroo had cried squirrelly tears for months.

In ancient times, the terra cotta warriors had been placed within this great pyramid and sealed away, an uncountable horde to ward off any fool power-hungry enough to seek harnessing the power of the gods. According to the myths, the dragon outside—the *Guardian of Death*—had breathed evil life into them. The legends were so old that Chirp-Chirp-Chiroo had spent his entire life not *really* believing them, though he had always prayed to the gods anyway and had memorized scriptures about them and had taught his children to do the same.

But his furry children had long been dead, and here he was, fighting and smashing amongst these ancient legends. His doubts about the myths lay smashed along with them. He stabbed another clay warrior, this time through the knee. The joint crumbled. The warrior continued to charge, even though it now lacked a leg. It toppled over and cracked to pieces. He silently cursed it, because the noise of the cracking warrior drowned out the yapping voices of his master and her tall twin, who were talking to each other not far away from him. They might be saying something that would be important for him to hear, but he could not understand any of it thanks to the background noise of the breaking clay.

He watched his master out of the corner of his eye while his body continued its marauding. She had already succumbed to her battle fury, as she had done countless times in the past when engaging in the unholy frenzy of war. Thus, she was in no mood to talk, so the conversation with her tall twin did not last long. She stalked away from her counterpart, running to fight the next approaching holy army. As Chirp-Chirp-Chiroo felt himself being forced to follow, a sensation of dread ran down his spine. It was that instinctual feeling in the wild parts of him that told him danger lurked nearby. If he could control his muscles, he would have smiled. His heart throbbed with anticipation.

A shadow fell over him, skinnier than those made by the clay warriors He thrilled at it. But he cleared from his mind the excitement and the happiness he felt. His master had never shown any inclination that she could read his thoughts before—if she had, she would have ground him to dust long ago on account of the insolent notions constantly running through his mind about her. But if he was *truly* on the precipice of sweet death, he did not want to risk it being botched because of a stupid little thing like joyous thoughts.

He went even further than clearing his mind, and as a little bit of insurance, he filled it as best he could with lies about how much he loved warring and killing his enemies. Out of his peripheral, he noticed his pink armor growing thicker, expanding to the point that his body was attempting to dash about inside a pink blob. His assailant, the taller Ginny, solidified the pink ooze around him so that he could not breathe. He began to choke, and his body thrashed.

But before he could suffocate, before he could even consider suffocation, the pink blob surrounding him jerked itself in a jagged pattern, snapping his spine in three places. Chirp-Chirp-Chiroo began to think about how smart it was of the taller Ginny to kill him instantly, because his master would be less likely to notice him being murdered until it was too late. But he did not get a chance to complete the thought.

His vision faded to black, and his brain stopped functioning.

*

Total whiteness. Total, utter whiteness everywhere.

Chirp-Chirp-Chiroo sighed. He had hoped to meet his family here on the other side, but instead he floated in infinite whiteness. The whiteness swirled into the angry visages of infamous squirrels who had died long ago, and then it continued swirling into the visages of long dead mustachioed dwarves, many of whom his master had backstabbed and murdered.

Chirp-Chirp-Chiroo realized that he was floating inside the *Guardian of Death*, where tradition held that sinful and evil squirrel-souls found themselves after dying. This was most definitely not the heaven for which he had hoped, but rather the damnation that he had expected.

On the bright side, he *could* float where he pleased, which meant that he was no longer under the hag's control. This meant that when her soul eventually showed up here, however long in the future that might be, he could give it a right thrashing. He beamed with happiness at the thought.

He lay on his back and tried to ignore the nipping of the ghoulish ghosts that floated around him. He found that he could not ignore the nipping, but he smiled anyway. The afterlife was grand.

CHAPTER 23

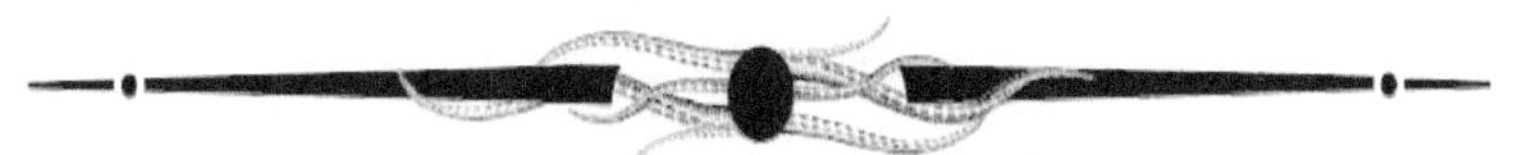

MORTAL (AND IMMORTAL) COMBAT

REGULAR-GINNY WATCHED AS the Arts dashed into the chamber.

Her boyfriend—positioned below her and to her right—screamed out some gibberish, and crimson light erupted from something in his hand. The light blazed in a wide arc, enveloping the entire room in front of him and dissolving every clay solder in its wide path. Ginny stared in amazement, glad that she was not down there in the path of that dreadful light.

The hordes that she and her counterpart had been methodically smashing to pieces, the hordes that had been swarming with inhuman gusto, the hordes that promised to take hours and hours longer to annihilate were completely vaporized by this fool in a matter of seconds.

But unfortunately for Art, while the light disintegrated the entirety of the clay hordes in *front* of him, it failed to dissolve the few soldiers clinging to the ceiling directly *above* him. They dove, and one crashed squarely atop him. He collapsed unconscious to the ground, and his right leg twitched. The object in his hand stopped blasting its crimson light.

Meanwhile, an Art with hair made from flames swept through the door and immediately flipped into the air in the direction of Tiny-Ginny. In one swift motion, he kicked her in the face and drew a dagger from his rope belt. The hilt of the dagger was fashioned from the paw of some green-furred catlike creature. The hooked blade of the dagger formed a crescent shape and a serrated edge ran along its underside. Thin runes had been carved into the sides of the blade, and they glowed blue in the dark chamber.

Fiery-Art muttered something, and green flames enveloped the blade. He stabbed it into Tiny-Ginny's torso. It pierced her armor, slicing through the pinkness and charring it black. The blade dove deep into the pale skin of her abdomen.

Tiny-Ginny's eyes popped wide open in surprise. She tried to scream, but dark blood poured from her throat, squelching the scream into an evil gurgle. Green flames surged from the dagger and tore through her body, erupting from her open mouth. Her eyes rolled back in her head. She attempted lamely to slap Fiery-Art off her with her pink membrane, but she only managed to whack him a few times with what amounted to a limp wet noodle.

"Did you *really* think I wouldn't anticipate exactly where you'd be hiding?" asked Fiery-Art, scorn dripping from his lips. He twisted the blade.

Regular-Ginny crawled along the wall, backing away from this terrifying visage of her boyfriend and hoping against hope that she would not draw his attention. Luckily, he seemed to enjoy listening to the sound of his own voice, so he did not seem to notice when she dropped to the ground near the unconscious Art, who now had a gigantic red knot rising from the back of his head and blood crusting amongst his thinning hair.

Every instinct she possessed began screaming in terror and begging her to flee as fast as she could from the flaming beast that resembled her boyfriend. She stepped over her boyfriend, and she obeyed her instincts.

She glanced back over her shoulder to ensure that Fiery-Art was not chasing behind her. He was not. But he did look up at her. He never removed his gaze from her as he ripped the blade from Tiny-Ginny's torso. Gore spurted from the ragged wound like lava from an angry volcano. He licked the dagger until it was clean of blood, and then he returned it to his belt. He grinned a mirthless grin, and the terrifying scene caused Regular-Ginny to soil herself. He mouthed, "*I will be with you soon,*" and then he dropped his baleful gaze away from her and focused it on the dwarf cradled in his arms. Regular-Ginny continued running, shivering in terror.

Fiery-Art spoke to Tiny-Ginny, and his voice boomed, "Your death came too easy, my lover. I would gladly resurrect you so that I might kill you again. I would gladly do it over and over, as many times as you deserve to pay penance for the crimes that you committed against me. But alas, time is short, and I have not enough of it to give you as many deaths as you have earned. So, you shall remain dead, and I shall chant your vigil *now*, for it is your mate's duty to do so."

Fiery-Art cleared his throat. His voice dropped two octaves and echoed across the cavernous chamber as he chanted in a cadence that reminded Ginny of a Catholic monk:

You were mortal, but you captured my heart.
Your beauteous prayers gripped me by the ears,
And drew me from my mountain citadel.
I came down to gaze in your graceful eyes.
I carried you back with me. I loved you.
I taught you secrets to divinity.
Oh, how we loved, and we loved, and we loved,
For ages and ages. Or so I thought.

You took the oaths we swore and twisted them.
You warped the secrets bestowed upon you.
You forced our Earth under your evil heel.
You were naught but a conqu'ring, whorish bitch.
You murdered my immortal family,
And stole their divine power for yourself.
To a rock you bound me with magic words,
And dripped venom on me for years and years.

You nourished yourself on our mortals' fear,
Glutting yourself like a pig on their prayers.
But like a fool, you killed without stopping.
Heeding not my warning: don't kill them all,
Because gods cannot live without subjects.
You dubbed me 'fool,' claiming fear strengthens prayers.
You genocided all, left none alive.
And when all were dead, you starved for worship.

While you wallowed in godly hunger pangs,
While you slowly weakened from starvation,
You found you were trapped in our dimension,
Because leaving would have cancelled the spells
That you wove through the fabric of our Earth.

You'd lose divinity. So, *while you starved,*
I escaped your prison. And now, after
Many ages have passed, I have revenge.

So, gorge yourself on the blade of Cringer,
My father's enchanted, feline dagger.
I'd prefer you to suffer forever
But your time in the Death Dragon shall last
Until I cause you and this Earth to end,
As mine ended ages and ages past
At the behest of your wicked treach'ry.
Farewell, my evil, misguided lover.

Fiery-Art's voice fell silent. Regular-Ginny, by now over halfway across the chamber, tried to resist glancing back again to see what was happening back there. She soon gave in, and she turned to see Fiery-Art close Tiny-Ginny's limp eyelids with his fingertips. He dropped to the ground and set her gently upon the floor. Regular-Ginny silently prayed that he had forgotten about her, and then she winced when her prayer seemed to grab his attention. He grinned at her and licked his lips. His tongue looked like a deadly viper as it flicked out of his mouth and rolled around his pale lips.

Ginny stopped fleeing, deciding that a better defense would be a good, *long* range offense. Fiery-Art's snakelike tongue gave her an idea. She launched her own vipers at him, one giant pink serpent from each of her fingertips. They slithered through the hundreds of feet of dusty air that separated them, gnashing their sharp, pink teeth at him. When they neared him, they wound around him from the feet up like a squadron of snakes wrapping themselves around Asclepius's staff, snagging and constricting him so he could not move. She willed one of the snakes to thrust its fangs into his long neck.

It immediately pulled away upon drawing blood. Then it melted as green fire burst to life around it, beginning at the fangs that had dug into Fiery-Art's skin. The fire burned down the length of the pink snake like it had become a lit fuse. Smoke filled the air as the green flame crisped the pink snake. Ginny gasped in surprise, and Fiery-Art winked at her.

The other snakes stupidly followed the first's lead before she had time to overcome her shock and will them not to. They each bit Fiery-Art's neck, and then they also erupted into flames. The fire streaked down the length of every single one of them, slamming into Ginny's fingertips with blistering fury. The green flames filled her vision, and she realized that her armor had caught fire.

Ginny instinctively sucked her pink ooze back inside her skin, and with it the green flames that had engulfed her. She fell to her knees in pain. Her blood boiled for a moment, but she found that the blazing flames had been extinguished. She looked at her fingertips and bit her lower lip when she saw that they had been charred into a crusty, black hide. She lifted her head, hoping to ensure that Fiery-Art remained far enough away to allow her the chance to heal herself before she launched another attack.

Fiery-Art's eyes stared into hers, a mere inch away. Ginny gasped and collapsed onto her backside. "Impossible," she muttered, and realized after she said it how stupid the expression was. If she had learned anything thus far on this stupid adventure, it was that nothing is impossible, let alone a fiery-haired version of her boyfriend traversing several hundred feet in the matter of a few seconds.

Ginny stared at her reflection in the blacks of his eyes. The image shimmered and shifted, and she found a skull now gazing back at her. It had eyes identical to hers, and these eyes were surrounded by white bone. She shuddered. The skull in her reflection opened its mouth, and black wings poked out of its cavernous maw. The wings gripped the edges of the skull's jaws, and a raven pulled itself free from the depths of the skull's throat. The raven perched upon the bony top of the skull. The bird wore a three-pointed jeweled crown, and each of the points glowed with yellow flame. The raven cawed, and then it ripped one of the fleshy eyeballs from the skull's face. It held the eye in the tip of its jagged beak, squeezing it until it burst like a grape. White pus dribbled down the creature's beak. It flipped the eyeball up into the air and caught the grisly flesh in its gullet. It swallowed.

Pain exploded inside Ginny's right eye. The pain brought her back to her senses, and she was finally able to wrench herself away from Fiery-Art's hypnotizing stare. She rubbed her throbbing eye with the heel of her palm, and when she pulled her hand away, she saw blood spattered and smeared across it.

"Oh, God!" cried Ginny. The vision in her right eye had gone black like a television screen that had winked out. She groped her face again with her hand,

and she found that she had no right eyeball in her skull, only an empty socket ringed with gore.

She looked at Fiery-Art. Tears streamed from her remaining eye. She squealed, "What did you do to me?"

Fiery-Art returned her petrified look with a grin that literally stretched from ear to ear. Sharp teeth poked out of his lips like rows of shark fangs, and Ginny found that she was unable to catch her breath.

"I've merely taken your eye," responded Fiery-Art. "I don't know you, so I needed to see the things that you have seen during your lifetime, so that after I kill you I shall be able to chant your vigil as I did for my mate. I may not be your mate, but because of the acquaintance I have established with *your* version of me, I shall take this sacred duty upon myself. I think we both know that if we left it to him, he would botch it.

Fiery-Art continued, "You can rest assured that your memory will carry on through me after you are dead, and that is more than most can say. On a side note, your vigil should be quite easy to chant and should last a much shorter amount of time than my mate's, because your memory involves little more than hours upon hours of reruns from some television show called *The Golden Girls*. What a waste of life."

The promise did not assure her rest very much. She had no desire to die, but she seemed to have little say in the matter, for he now gripped her by the throat, and she could not squirm free no matter how hard she tried. He tightened his fingers, and she found that she could no longer breathe. She thrashed, but he simply drove his knee into her soft belly as though he had performed this ritual thousands of times. His grip was so tight that she could not even whimper in fright.

"Hold still," he said, "and I shall make this transition painless for you. Look into my eyes and allow your spirit to drift away. If you keep squirming, then I shall take pleasure in hurting you."

Ginny yielded. She knew that she could not escape and that she could not beat him, especially if her war-mongering counterpart had been unable to do so. She was outclassed to an exponential degree. She began to bring her remaining eye up to rest on his, so that she could end this farce without pain. On its journey up, though, her eye stopped short.

Cords of thick pink goo had looped around his throat, creeping around his neck in arcs wide enough to not touch his skin, and thus not draw his notice.

Despite having turned blue from lack of oxygen and despite the pain that continued to flare from her empty eye socket, Ginny had to suppress a smile.

Suddenly, the pink cords yanked tight around Fiery-Art's throat, crunching his windpipe. The pink cords snatched him up and away from Ginny. His fingers lost their grip on her as the surprise attack overtook him. Ginny gasped and allowed precious oxygen to flood into her lungs.

Fiery-Art hung by his neck above her, high in the air and dangling upon a pink noose. He jerked his knees and hands, thrashing and trying his damnedest to escape. Ginny followed the pink rope with her eye and witnessed Tiny-Ginny, whom she had believed dead, standing precariously on her feet with a thin tentacle stretching from her back up to the hanging Art. The tiny hag rested a hand on her torso where Fiery-Art's blade had punctured her flesh. When she pulled her hand away from her wound, Regular-Ginny gasped at the lack of gore. Pinkness had filled the gaping hole and remained there, a cork in the bottle that was Tiny-Ginny's body, holding her life intact within.

High up in the air, Fiery-Art gagged and lashed violently at the end of the pink tentacle. The tentacle merely squeezed tighter. Fiery-Art's hair flashed brightly, and he changed forms into a great bear, and he attempted to use its strength to rip the noose from his throat, but the tentacle simply squeezed tighter. Regular-Ginny shrugged. *Never seen anything quite like this,* she thought.

Fiery-Art transformed again, this time into a phoenix, and he attempted to fly away from the tentacle, but the tentacle squeezed tighter. He transformed into a slimy fish, and he attempted to slip away, but the tentacle squeezed ever tighter. Like Proteus, he transformed into animal after animal, but with every conversion, Tiny-Ginny simply squeezed tighter. She reminded Regular-Ginny of a haggish, ugly, tentacled rendition of Menelaus.

After this routine dragged on way too long for Regular-Ginny's tastes, Tiny-Ginny must have finally squeezed tightly enough, for Fiery-Art's head popped off his body. He had just transformed into a tortoise when it happened. Tiny-Ginny morphed the end of the tentacle into a small pink birdcage and caught Fiery-Art's falling head inside it. The head turned back into its natural humanoid state, though the flaming hair atop the head had disappeared. The scalp shined with a newly waxed fineness. Fiery-Art's tongue swelled and poked out of the side of his mouth, and his eyelids slowly descended. The head was dead, and it reminded Regular-Ginny of a silly bald tweety-bird corpse inside the pink cage.

As Fiery-Art's beheaded turtle body THWONKed loudly onto the ground, it transformed back into its natural humanoid form. It decomposed within seconds, with the flesh drying into dust and only an empty white skeleton remaining. Hundreds of fluorescent green ants climbed from Fiery-Art's ribcage, disassembled the skeleton, and scurried away to the four corners of the chamber, each clutching a different bone. The tiny creatures all wore clothes that reminded Regular-Ginny of Vikings—horned helmets, battle axes, and round shields—and she giggled at the absurdity. As some crawled past her, the pink ooze in her heart loosed a fresh volley of hatred throughout her body, and she used her pink ooze to squish the ants and the bones that they carried.

Before the Ginnys had a chance to revel in their victory, they heard a shuffling sound behind them, and they turned together to face it. The second Art—Regular-Ginny's boyfriend, the normal one—limped toward them, dragging his right leg behind him. Clay shards and dust covered his head and matted hair, and the way he limped reminded Regular-Ginny of a zombie. He aimed the red orb at them, the device that he had used to disintegrate the clay army when he had earlier dashed into the chamber.

Regular-Ginny hoped she would get a moment soon to concentrate, so she could heal her eye and burnt fingers and other assorted injuries. She sighed, instead projecting a new set of large pink tentacles from her fingertips. She willed their ends to sharpen into points. She suspended these points in the air near Art, threatening him with the possibility of a good skewering.

"Let him out of your damned cage, or I'll blow y'all away!" yelled Art, pointing with his unoccupied hand at the head in the cage.

Tiny-Ginny made no move to acquiesce.

"I mean it! I'll do it!" he screamed.

Regular-Ginny smiled an impish grin and wiggled the sharp tentacles hovering near him, ready to pierce his soft flesh. Tiny-Ginny re-grew her pink battleaxes to fill her child-sized hands. She held them above her head, poised to crash down upon him.

"Looks like we've got a bit of a Mexican standoff here," replied Regular-Ginny.

Art stood silent for a moment, scratched his chin with his free hand, and then shrugged. "I'm not Mexican, and you two sure as hell aren't Mexicans," he said. "We can't have a Mexican standoff without any Mexicans."

"You are too a Mexican," responded Regular-Ginny. "You always told me you were half-Mexican."

"Well, I'm not. I just said that so I could make jokes about Mexicans without getting into trouble. According to my mama, I'm half-German, half-Irish, half-French, half-Portuguese, half-English, and a tiny bit Italian."

Regular-Ginny frowned. "So, what else did you lie to me about?"

"Silence!" squealed Tiny-Ginny. "You fools are annoying enough to make a warlord want to fall on her own sword!"

"Don't yell at *me*," said Art to the dwarven dictator. "Your twin started it. I'm just trying to do the right thing and set some stupid cosmic teddy bear free before you two can use it to destroy the Multiverse."

"You're an idiot," said Tiny-Ginny.

"That *may* be true, but I'd appreciate it if you would release my buddy's head from its cage, nevertheless. I don't really *want* to hurt you two, but you're about to force my hand."

When the pair of Ginnys did not respond, he winked at Regular-Ginny. He continued, "Especially you, babe. I totally dig the one-eyed thing you've got going on. We'll get you a patch, and you'll look like a pirate. I always wanted to nail a pirate. So ditch this bitch, help me free my buddy, and come with me to save the Multiverse."

"No, seriously," responded Tiny-Ginny. "You're being used, and you lap it up like a stupid puppy. You have no idea who you're tagging along with, do you?"

"I'd say I have a pretty good idea. He's me, only he's a god from another reality. Pretty sweet to know that I'm a god somewhere. Mama always told me I's special. I guess she just never knew *how* special."

"Fool, he is manipulating you. You don't know him *at all.* He's a god of mischief, and he's been swindling you the entire time you've known him."

Art shrugged. "He's saved my life about a dozen times so far. I'd say that makes him pretty reliable."

Tiny-Ginny rolled her eyes. "He's saved you because he knows you're the only way he can get his hands on the bear. It won't leave with him, you idiot."

Art smirked. "I'd rather be on his side than yours, because even if he *is* manipulating me, at least he's nicer about it."

Tiny-Ginny's eyes cut left and right, yielding her the look of a scheming cat. They stopped on Art's gloves and squinted. "Where'd you get those gloves?" she asked.

Art puffed up his chest with haughty self-satisfaction. "Before he met me, God-Me borrowed them from a reality where we're the king of the jungle. Pretty cool, huh?"

Tiny-Ginny laughed. "*Borrowed*, huh? I was with him when he attained those gloves. 'Twas ages ago, back when he was still courting me and before I'd murdered his family. He used that horrid Beverly to jump us to Earth 3,333, where Art-of-the-Jungle welcomed us into his home. We ate dinner at his table and drank his skunky beer. We were bound to goodwill under his hospitality. But Art got it in his head that he might be able to use the strength from those apish hands to slay one of his older brothers, a war god who entertained the rest of the pantheon by constantly humiliating Art.

"Art left our bed late that night," continued Tiny-Ginny. "He snuck into Art-of-the-Jungle's quarters. This version of you was a beast, a gigantic gorilla with a barrel chest and a huge gut. The gorilla looked like a hairy powder keg when he swung from tree to tree. I watched him earlier that day rip off an elephant's head without even really trying, and then do the same to its children, and then eat them all raw. Anyway, I wasn't in the room when Art snuck into the gorilla's quarters. I was asleep in the guest chamber. I don't know how Art managed it, but he murdered the beast in his sleep. He flayed Art-of-the-Jungle and kept his hide. He woke me, and we fled back to our home reality before any alert could be sounded. I don't know what he did with the rest of the hide, but I'm sure it's stashed away in caches he's set up all over the Multiverse."

"God, you're long-winded, maybe even more long-winded than *him*," Art replied, pointing with his free hand at God-Art's head. "What's your point?"

Tiny-Ginny growled and rolled her eyes. She glanced over at Regular-Ginny, and then back at Art. "You two really deserve each other, you know that? You're the biggest fools I've ever met. I was telling you that he's not afraid to use, maim, or kill anyone to get what he wants, even if it means sacrificing himself from another reality. You mean *nothing* to him. You are merely a necessary steppingstone to keep alive for now, but that will no longer be the case when he reaches his goal."

Fiery-Art's head laughed and opened its eyes. Its scalp ignited once more in flame. "OK, I can't pretend to be dead any longer," he said. "This is getting too ridiculous. Ginny, you're just as guilty of using people as I am. You used me, tricked me into loving you, and then you bound me to a rock for a millennium. Poisonous venom dripped in my eyes for a thousand years, for My sakes!"

Fiery-Art looked at Regular-Ginny. He continued, "She's going to murder you, you know. She killed everyone on our reality, from the tiniest child to the strongest warrior to her most loyal servants. You've no chance. She only kept *me* alive because she knew I would resurrect myself. If I remained alive, she could keep an eye on me."

Tiny-Ginny glared at Regular-Ginny. Regular-Ginny met her gaze for a moment, and then looked down at her feet.

"Don't listen to the bastard," said Tiny-Ginny. "He's a *god of trickery*. He's manipulating you, too."

"She was reborn on this reality for a reason," said Fiery-Art to Regular-Ginny. "She's a ruthless dictator. You stick with her, and you're dead."

"Come with us," Art interrupted, staring at Regular-Ginny with his best doe-eyed look, the one he had used to drunkenly pick her up in the first place. "I'll take care of you. I'll make sure the bitch doesn't touch you. And the bastard-head will have to go through me to get to you, too."

"I don't know," replied Regular-Ginny, staring at her feet. "I just don't know."

"Art, we need to move," said the head. "Remember, this world's going to end in a fiery ball of explosion soon."

Art shrugged. "Last chance, babe," he said to Regular-Ginny.

Regular-Ginny's eye never moved from her shoes. She blushed.

Art nodded. "OK, if that's the way you want to play it. Sorry, babe."

Fiery-Art opened his mouth, and flames glowed from within his gullet. His tongue danced behind his lips, splitting down the middle and forking in two directions. The tips of the two tongues bubbled and hardened in the flames, transforming themselves into pointed steel. They flicked from his mouth and stretched to epic proportions. They hung high in the air for a moment, and then they fell in opposite directions like primitive, salivating arrows. The speared tongues stabbed into the left foot of each Ginny, ignoring the pink armor surrounding them and piercing them clean through. The Ginnys squealed identical, high-pitched squeals.

Fiery-Art yelled to Art around his forked tongue, "Thoot them! Thow!"

Art shouted, "*Socky-Go-Go-Eyeball!* Go kapow! Go kapow now!"

CHAPTER 24

A PIXIE FEAST

NORMAL-ART'S FACE PALED as the *Socky-Go-Go-Eyeball* drew energy from within him and focused that energy into a deep red beam. The beam blasted across the Ginnys and enveloped them. They managed to stand their ground within the beam for a moment, thanks to their oozy pink armors. But within seconds, the beam tore vicious chinks in the armors, and seconds after that, the pinkness surrounding them was ripped completely from their bodies. The pink goo displaced from them evaporated in the energy beam before ever coming close to hitting the floor.

As the blast continued, it launched the Ginnys into the air. They hung suspended in place by the steely tips of God-Art's tongue, which the god had used to pin each of them to the ground by a foot. The fleshy portions of his tongue disintegrated in the crimson light. The women shrieked as the sharp steel shredded through their flesh and sinew and bone, ripping their bound feet in half. Once painfully free from their bonds, they were hurtled backward across the expanse of the chamber and smacked into the side wall. Their skulls absorbed most of the impact. They slid down the dirty stone wall and lay unconscious on the ground.

Normal-Art willed the *Socky-Go-Go-Eyeball* to stop its barrage. The crimson energy beam sputtered and fizzled out, and Normal-Art collapsed to one knee in exhaustion. He felt drained, like a battery tapped of its juice. He gasped for breath.

The pink cage that floated high in the air—the one that held God-Art's flaming head as its prisoner—was no longer connected to Tiny-Ginny, and it began to lose shape and melt. God-Art's head squeezed to freedom between a couple of the newly loosened bars, and then the head began a freefall toward the ground.

"Hurry! Catch me!" ordered the god.

Unfortunately, after the latest attack with the *Socky-Go-Go-Eyeball*, Normal-Art lacked the energy to do anything but watch the falling arc of God-Art's head. It crashed on the ground with a sickening crunch.

The flaming hair atop the god's head snuffed out. Blood poured from his ears and nose. Dozens of jagged pieces of bone pierced the skin where his skull had shattered, revealing the gray brain matter within.

As the god's brain encountered the air, it transformed turquoise in color before evaporating and morphing into a horde of pixies. The pixies glowed and danced through the air upon tiny butterfly wings. Each carried a knapsack tied to a stick, causing them all to resemble pixie-hobos, and as they fluttered through the air, they reached into their sacks. They retrieved hacksaws twice as tall as themselves, and then they flew directly over to the unconscious Tiny-Ginny.

As they stared at her, sharp fangs poked down below their upper lips and saliva trailed down their faces. They dropped their sacks to the ground and began sawing off her legs. All the way over here on the other side of the room, Normal-Art could hear the ghastly cracking of the saws carving through bone and the squelchy gurgle of the tools ripping through muscle and sinew. The blood that pooled beneath Tiny-Ginny shimmered in the glitter that sprinkled from the wings of the creatures.

When they finished severing Tiny-Ginny's legs, they tossed aside their hacksaws. As the tools tumbled across the stone floor, they sounded like jingling bells. The pixies and butterflies returned to their discarded sacks and removed from them tiny little bibs, and once they had these tied about their necks, they began gorging themselves upon the nearest leg, which happened to have formerly been attached to Tiny-Ginny's right hip.

Within moments, the little pixies had reduced the limb to nothing, devouring it like a horde of piranhas. They even gobbled down the bones. They hungrily eyeballed the second limb, but instead of bolting this one down their throats, they worked together to pick it up and carry it over to God-Art's cracked skull. They forced open his mouth, and then they shoved the bloody limb down his gullet.

Instead of poking out the bottom of his neck as reality and Physics and sanity should have demanded, the leg disappeared once it passed through his mouth. Normal-Art shrugged. He snatched one of the pixies from its work. He held the creature in his palm. It crossed its arms over its chest and tapped its feet, staring at him like an impatient spouse waiting for a good explanation from a cheating man.

"What are you doing?" he asked the pixie.

"What does it look like?" responded the pixie in a high-pitched squeal that he had to strain to hear.

"It looks like you've eaten one of that woman's legs, and now you're feeding her other leg to my twin's decapitated head."

"That is correct."

"But *why*?"

"Because she did the same to him ages ago. She cut off his legs and ate them. He *thought* orders to us as he was falling to the floor. He knew that you weren't coordinated enough to catch him as he was falling, and he did not want you running off without taking revenge for his legs. He had no time as he was falling to instruct you on what to do, so he told us."

"OK," responded Normal-Art with a smirk. "That makes *perfect* sense. He instructed his brain-pixies to amputate his ex-dwarf-lover's legs. I must be the stupidest guy on Earth to not have figured that one out from the beginning."

Normal-Art sighed. He released the pixie, and it fluttered back over to its comrades. They finished shoving the leg down God-Art's throat, and then they all flew back into God-Art's skull, where they melted back into turquoise brain matter. The brain faded back to a dull gray.

Normal-Art stood over his counterpart's head. He shoved his fingers into the dead head's nostrils, put his thumb in the god's mouth, and picked the head up as though it were a misshapen bowling ball. He placed the god's head in the crook of his elbow and turned toward the exit at the back of the chamber.

His entire body ached. His head and arm hurt where the clay soldier had fallen on him earlier, and his leg hurt where he had twisted it when he had crashed to the ground beneath that same soldier. Despite these setbacks, he compelled his left leg to step forward. His foot touched the ground, his head swam with pain, and then he dragged his right foot behind him.

The blue teddy bear beckoned him like a cosmic searchlight, and he knew it lay *that* way, ripe for the rescuing. Normal-Art could feel that he was close to the goal, so close that he could almost taste its pastel goodness. He tried to ignore the pain in his body, but he could not. He smiled anyway because his journey was almost over. He would get to go home soon. He yearned for his television and that dull ache he would get at the back of his eyes after he watched hours and hours and hours of it.

He trudged on. The Ginnys lay behind him, and he stupidly supposed them out of the race. But their pink god was calling, too. It screamed for Regular-Ginny's attention behind her remaining eyelid.

CHAPTER 25

A COSMIC JUNKIE

NORMAL-ART CONTINUED LUGGING God-Art's head in the crook of his left elbow. He used the wall on his right as a crutch, leaning heavily against it each time he dragged his useless right leg behind him. Pain overwhelmed his senses with each epic step. Thus, he allowed the wall to be his guide, so he would not have to pay attention to where he was going and could free up all remaining brainpower to focus on how sorry he felt for himself. He whimpered.

He felt cramped and claustrophobic in this narrow hallway. It ran on for far too long, and with each step that he took away from the grand chamber from which he had come, he felt a little more entombed and enclosed. He grunted and forced his legs to continue trudging—*left, shuffle-right, grunt, left, shuffle-right, grunt.* Without God-Art's flaming hair to light the way, Normal-Art could barely see more than a few feet in front of him, and after those few feet, the hallway disappeared into pitch blackness. He relied on the itch in his brain to tickle directions to him, though there were few of options in this narrow hallway, so the directions were rather simple: go straight. His fingertips began to rub raw where he dragged them along the rough stone wall, and his lungs seemed coated with the ancient dust that constantly trickled down from the ceiling.

With no warning, the wall upon which he was leaning for support ended, and he crashed to the ground. He cursed at the tickle in his brain for not giving him at least a *little* warning that the wall was about to end. It did not respond. He groaned, had a look around, and discovered that he *could see* in this room. He realized the reason that he could see in here was because the walls glowed an ethereal yellow beneath their coat of sand.

This room was open and significantly airier than the hallway, so Normal-Art breathed a sigh of relief at the reduction in claustrophobia. The walls curved up and away, so high that he could not see the ceiling. He spotted a door on the wall to the right from which a draft blew. He would have described the draft's average temperature as exactly lukewarm, but that was only because both frigid and sweltering breezes mingled together in perfectly balanced proportions to create the draft. The tickle in his brain told him to walk through the door, so he slowly stood up and stepped in its direction. But on a hunch, he stopped and turned around.

He set God-Art's head on the ground and wiped with both hands at the sandy wall nearest him, the one to the right of the door through which he had entered the room. He swept away the ancient dust and grit that coated the wall. The debris collected on the floor in a heap, piling up to God-Art's nose. With the sand cleared, this section of the wall beamed like a flashlight. Normal-Art limped back a few steps and nodded. Just as he remembered from his time as a gaseous ball.

Hieroglyphics covered the glowing wall. Squirrels toasted each other with giant goblets. Art knew that if he kept wiping away the years of dust covering the walls, he would witness the entire ancient story of this pyramid. But he did not need to. He had already seen it when he had died.

Behind him, Art heard a skittering on the floor, and then he felt insectoid legs crawling up his leg. He squealed and jumped backward. He lost his balance and fell onto his already ragingly sore pelvis. His skin crawled, and he wiped at his upper thigh where he had felt the crawling.

He felt the insectoid legs again. This time they moved up his back and rested on his left shoulder. He stifled a whimper and slowly turned his head to look. He expected to see yet another frightening obstacle he would need to overcome on his quest to rescue the blue bear, probably in the form of some disgusting bug. Instead, his reflection stared back at him, balanced on eight spidery legs that stretched from the base of a decapitated head. The face smiled, and then the scalp of the head ignited in flame.

"You just don't stay dead, do you?" asked Normal-Art.

"Takes a bit more than losing my body and falling a few dozen feet to keep me dead. You ought to know that by now."

"Well, for what it's worth, I'm glad you're not toast."

"Awww, stop. Or all these kind words shall go to my head," replied God-Art, giggling.

"Well, don't let 'em. I'm mainly glad because I was scared that I'd be stuck on this doomed planet without you here to get me off it."

"Whatever you say, tough guy. But either way, we must move. The supernatural power our lady-partners possess is not one that I've encountered before. I'd bet that any second now it's going to wake them up, and then they'll come riding down this hallway atop all kinds of pink hellfire and brimstone. We must reach our goal before them if we want to have any chance of survival."

"But how is that *possible*?" Normal-Art asked. "I thought we took them out of the picture."

"Really?" asked God-Art. "The guy who's jumped between realities, been attacked by dwarves possessed by the souls of dictators, created a magical sentient robot from a mystic anvil, fallen into an amoeba wall, and died only to be resurrected a few minutes later finds it hard to believe that his lady-partner could possibly return to consciousness after a hard knock against a wall?"

"Well, when you put it that way, I guess it *doesn't* sound so impossible."

Normal-Art sighed, decided to end the conversation and move. He tried to stand, pushing himself up by his left arm and his good leg. He slipped on the dirt and crashed back to the ground. He landed on his face and felt his lip bleed. The sand soaked up his blood, and he squinted at it like a petulant kid who just dropped his milk.

"You go ahead," whined Normal-Art. "I ain't gonna make it one more step. I'll hold 'em off when they get here."

God-Art's arachnid legs scritched across the ground, moving into position inches in front of his counterpart's face. Normal-Art had not noticed before, but the pores on God-Art's nose were exceptionally large, like deep black craters. Or maybe that was just the poor lighting from the god's fire-hair playing tricks on his mortal senses.

"You're kidding, right?" demanded God-Art. "I'm not sure if you could see how hard I rolled my eyes when those words escaped your lips, so I moved here to show you."

God-Art's eyelids popped apart, whipping open like a roller shade in the window of an old lady's living room. His pupils darted up behind his eyelids, and then they kept rolling up until they made a complete circuit and reappeared from below the bottom eyelids. The pupils gained speed, spinning round and round in this manner like they had become a pair of cherries in a slot machine.

I'll grant the bastard one thing, thought Normal-Art. *I've never seen anybody roll his eyes quite that hard.*

"Look at me," said God-Art, allowing his pupils to stop in the center of his sockets. "I've got these little spider-legs. I can't physically pick up our quarry without you, and even if I *could* pick it up, it won't leave with me, no matter how hard I try to force it. It has called to *you* from across the Multiverse, not *me*. So, you need to get up right now, or so help me *Me*, I'll make the last few minutes of your life utterly miserable."

Normal-Art sighed once more. He pushed as hard as he could upon the ground with both arms. He screamed in pain, but he managed to get his legs underneath him. He stumbled backward. He twisted and fell into the wall, barely managing to stay upright. His cheek smacked into the dirty stone, and he tasted the coppery flavor of blood in his mouth.

He used the wall for balance, leaning against it as he turned toward the exit—the door through which the draft blew. He trudged toward it as fast as he could trudge, the open door seeming *just* within reach if he simply continued trudging. God-Art skittered along the floor at his feet like some surrealist painter's drug-induced vision of a happy little puppy.

Normal-Art reached out with his right hand and grabbed the threshold of the doorway with his fingers. He pulled himself through it and entered a long hallway. It was narrow enough that he could touch both walls at once without too much effort, but tall enough that he could not see the ceiling. The only light source in this hallway came from God-Art's head, and Normal-Art could see from the flames that the hallway curved out of sight ahead. He pressed on, leaving his bloodied and raw fingerprints in the thick grime on the doorway behind him.

The ground quaked, and a wave of sand fell from the ceiling, coating Normal-Art's hair. God-Art muttered something about running out of time, and then he scrambled ahead, sprinting as fast as his tiny spider-legs would take him. He disappeared around the bend. All light in the hallway disappeared with him. Normal-Art shook the sand out of his hair and felt nervousness fester in his belly. He was surrounded once more by darkness, and he hated it.

He leaned his weight on the wall to his right raced ahead as fast as he could. He reached out his left hand and touched the opposite wall. He dragged his hands along both walls, distracting himself from his anxiety by cutting a pair of squiggly lines in the ancient dust. He prayed that he would not be stuck in the darkness for too much longer.

Just as he prepared to round the bend around which God-Art had disappeared, his prayer was granted. Dancing light appeared on the far wall, and the silhouette of a head walking on spider-legs within the light grew smaller and smaller.

The head peeped one eyeball around the bend, squinted slightly at Normal-Art, and then the head moved all the way into the open. God-Art's spindly legs curled underneath him like a spring. The arachnid legs were oddly flexible, though they twisted in such a jerky motion that Normal-Art wondered how their exoskeletons did not crack. God-Art's head turned slightly, and he cut his eyes to the side to look up at Normal-Art, as if calculating something.

"What're you doi-AAAH!" cried Normal-Art.

God-Art leapt from the floor and almost flew past Normal-Art's left shoulder. But the god stretched out his arachnid legs, snatching Normal-Art's shoulder and stopping his momentum by digging into Normal-Art's soft tissue. The god swiveled himself around to face Normal-Art.

"So what, you're a creepy flame-headed-spider-parrot now?" asked Normal-Art, frowning as he felt blood trickling from the holes God-Art's legs had poked into his shoulder. "That's just dumb. Also, I know the average head is supposed to weigh eight-and-a-half pounds or whatever, but you are much, much heavier."

"That added weight is the Earth Stone in my cerebellum, from which the Earth on my reality was formed when Monsieur Heaven inserted it into Madame Sky. I stole it during the Age of Heroes and swallowed the evidence before I could be captured. It all started when I groped Madame Sk—"

"That'll be *quite* enough!" shouted Normal-Art. "I need to concentrate here, and I can't concentrate when your damned blabbering is drowning out all my thoughts. So, if you don't have something *important* to tell me, then shut up!"

"Oh, look at me," replied God-Art with a smirk, "getting distracted telling a story 'bout myself again when I meant to be relaying *important* information to you. Apologies. Anyway, I scouted ahead of us, and we're getting really close now. But we must hurry. Our quarry apparently has a twin, and it is calling out to your lady-partner. If she is not awake by now, she *will* be very, very soon."

Normal-Art cursed. Instead of asking questions or letting the revelation about the blue bear having a twin sink in, he trudged on and rounded the bend in the hallway. Pink and blue lights swirled together from an open doorway about a hundred feet away at the end of the corridor. The draft blew more intensely from the open door. Normal-Art quickened his pace—*leftshuffle-rightgrunt, leftshuffle-rightgrunt*—nearly forgetting about the pain in his leg in the effort.

The swirling lights grew brighter the closer he moved to the end of the corridor. Pastel blue light rolled along the floor, reminding Normal-Art of the sea, and when the pink light intermingled with it, coral seemed to dance beneath the waves. Maybe it was all the blunt force trauma clouding his judgment, but when Normal-Art looked at the light, he really wanted to go swimming.

Normal-Art soon reached the brink of the lights, bit his lower lip, and stepped into them. He tingled all over, and he stopped walking forward. He felt the pores on his skin open and begin sucking in the light. It was a rather uncomfortable sensation, and it caused him to squirm. Millions of horrid slurping sounds squealed from his pores. His skin became cool to the touch where it consumed the blue light, and warm where it drank the pink. The world seemed to spin around him. God-Art yelled something into his ear, but he did not hear it, and he did not care. All he cared about was drinking more of the light with his skin.

Normal-Art felt drunk, but not drunk like he had ever been drunk before. This was intoxication on a cosmic level. Stars erupted into existence across his mind's eye, nebulas danced in creation, gods were born, black holes formed and drank gluttonously, and then death eventually consumed them all. He watched existence engage in a constant war with void, and both knew all along that the war would never end.

Whether two seconds later or two million years later Art could not say, but he eventually noticed in his peripheral that something funny was happening to his skin, so he glanced down at it. Where the blue light drifted over his skin, it glowed pale blue and felt as though it had been dipped in a salve of goodness. Where the pink light trailed, boils and blisters followed. Normal-Art panicked when he saw the wounds, but he could force himself neither to move out of the light nor to continue walking forward. He floated helplessly in place, and not even his hardest mental doggie-paddling moved him. He tried to whimper, but no sound escaped his lips.

"Save Me," a voice squeaked from the whirling blue. As the pastel blue light ebbed and flowed across his skin, it danced across the wounds that the pink light had given him. It mended and healed the boiled flesh, whilst the pink light moved on and burned new patches of death.

Normal-Art allowed the all-encompassing lights to drown him. He closed his eyes and stopped breathing. He accepted the hopelessness, the unrelenting destruction of the pink. He accepted the hopefulness, too, the unrelenting creation of the blue. He began to find a sort of peace in the constant war between existence and void, and he decided that he would stay here in this spot forever. The voice called from the blue once again, "Art must awake. Art must save m—"

CHOMP! God-Art's teeth bit the top of Normal-Art's left ear clean off. Blood gushed from the wound, turning the sea of blue light into purple where it spattered. Normal-Art turned toward his counterpart, his eyes distant and wrathful. He felt himself coming down from his cosmic high, and the killing of his buzz infuriated him.

"What the hell!" screamed Normal-Art, or maybe he didn't. The light confused him. His body quaked, expunging itself of the infinite tide that moments ago had overflowed his entire being. He felt hung over on a celestial level. Every synapse that flared was a new experience in pain. He had never realized a head could ache in so many places.

But his feet were on the ground, and he did not feel as though he were floating any more. He tried to recall the last few minutes, or eternity, or whatever it had been, but the harder he tried to concentrate, the quicker it slipped from his memory, tumbling from his head faster than the sand caked in his hair.

"Move!" shouted God-Art. "This planet is a couple dozen minutes away from exploding, and those hags we call lady-partners are likely awake by now. We've got no time for you to get high!"

"Huh?"

"If you remain motionless in cosmic light for more than a couple seconds, then you get high. And the longer you stay still, the higher you get! That's how these kinds of cosmic lights work—and we don't have time for you to stop for a fix! Now move!"

Normal-Art's body moved before he had time to think of a scathing quip. He used both hands to pull himself through the doorway at the end of the corridor—the one from which the lights and the draft originated. The room looked identical to the chamber that had housed the terra cotta warriors, only a third as large and lacking the terra cotta warriors. The walls were dusty and ancient, and the ceiling was so high that Normal-Art could not see it. What this room lacked in clay warriors, it made up for with the oddest thing Normal-Art had ever seen—and he had seen a *lot* of odd things since meeting God-Art.

This oddity was located against the back wall of the room. Inside the glass of a massive, old-fashioned kerosene lantern that stood just over six-feet tall, there mingled a pair of glowing, stuffed bears. The blue bear did not come as a shock because Normal-Art had been expecting it, but the pink bear and the manner in which the two bears presented themselves were both quite unexpected.

The teddy bears floated head-to-crotch and vice versa like a pastel yin and yang stuck in an exceptionally compromising position. They spun clockwise on an axis that stretched through their backs and between their belly buttons. This axis took physical form in the manner of a solid onyx saber, piercing them straight through their torsos and spinning them like they had been spitted and were roasting alive above a hot flame. The waving pink and blue lights, the intermingling ebb and flow, rose and fell and danced as they turned upon this spit. The draft also seemed to originate from the lantern, somehow gusting from its top despite the top of the lantern being closed by a copper latch.

The bears never looked up from one another. Normal-Art expected the blue one to beg for a rescue or something, but it remained silent. Normal-Art squinted and bit his lower lip. He looked down at the greenish copper base of the giant lantern.

The device was set up exactly like every kerosene lantern he had seen in the past. He had quite a bit of experience with them from his childhood, earned on long camping trips with his dad that he had never wanted to attend but had been forced to attend anyway. On those trips, Art had spent a large portion of the time out in the woods, playing with his dad's lantern. And the memory gave him an idea.

Normal-Art found the knob that adjusts the length of the wick on traditional lanterns. Turn it one way, the light becomes brighter. Turn it the other, it gets dimmer. Normal-Art grabbed the knob with his right hand and pulled down, the direction that snuffs the flame. The handle did not budge. He grunted and let go. He spit in his hands, rubbed them together, and gripped the knob with both hands.

Normal-Art pulled again, harder this time. His deltoids and biceps flared as he attempted to twist the metal knob. The metal creaked, squeaked, and gave a little. The onyx spit lowered a few inches toward the base of the lantern, and the lights emanating from the bears dimmed ever so slightly.

The bears did not look up from their pastel tryst, but their screams filled the room like an explosion of personified pain, physically knocking Art to the ground. Reality warped and twisted around him. His hands turned to liquid and floated inside pale bubbly spheres in front of his face. When he turned to look at God-Art for direction, his eyes literally popped out of their sockets and bounced across the room. God-Art's disembodied head had transformed into a massive hairy spider, which then inflated itself like a balloon overfilled with helium. God-Art's tiny arachnid legs flittered pathetically about underneath his round body.

The god turned so that his back faced the lantern and blew a mighty breath. The breath propelled him through the air and toward the lantern. He gripped the knob with his tiny spider-legs and twisted it back into its original position. The onyx saber raised. The lights brightened. The teddy bears stopped screaming.

As quickly as it had begun, the warping of reality disappeared, returning everything to its rightful place. Normal-Art touched his face with his hands, and he smiled to find his eyes back in their sockets. He did not even think to be relieved that his hands were back to normal. He turned his head to look at God-Art, who was now hanging by his spider-legs from the knob. Normal-Art noted the absurdity in his relief that the god was once again a disembodied head mounted atop spider-legs rather than a balloon-spider. He hated spiders.

"I don't think playing with that knob is such a great idea," said God-Art. "I think this lantern may be a *Reality Light*. You snuff it out and you'll probably snuff out this whole reality. Us included."

Normal-Art smirked in confusion. "A *Reality Light*? What's that?"

"Every reality has one. It's what powers the reality and keeps it in existence. Its energy is usually siphoned from the most powerful lifeform in that dimension, whether said lifeform wills it or not. And if the Reality Light is not continuously powered by the life force of some cosmic being, then that reality winks out of existence and everything and everyone in it are reduced to nothingness."

"But I've seen the hieroglyphics in this pyramid, and if there's one thing I learned from them, it's that these creatures are not *from* this reality," said Normal-Art, pointing at the bears. "Only the squirrels are native. The dwarves, the dragon, and the bears all came here from somewhere else. How can the bears be powering this reality if they haven't been here since the beginning? How did it exist before them if it would have winked out of existence without them? It makes no sense."

"Realities constantly evolve," replied God-Art with a shrug. "A reality may have an ancient power source, but when a more powerful energy signature appears within its boundaries, primitive and unenlightened realities snatch that new power up and use it as a battery, either setting the old mode of power free or simply ridding itself of it. Usually the latter, as realities are harsh bitches.

"More mature and cultured realities have a better sense of custom and manners," continued God-Art. "They provide their own source of energy and refrain from kidnapping any newer, more powerful visitors, no matter how tempting the power of these visitors may be. For kidnapping visitors would be bad etiquette."

"How do you know all this?" asked Normal-Art.

"Well, because I was once kidnapped and used in one of these Reality Lights," said God-Art. "I have lived a long time, and I have traveled far. We don't have time to go into the whole story, but here are the bare bones: eons ago, when I was merely passing through Earth 6, the forces at play there sensed my presence. It was a primitive reality, consisting of only two dimensions and barely any sentient light. I'd have never been there if I didn't need to pass through it to get to somewhere else.

"I was forced into a *Reality Candle*," continued God-Art. "It was similar to this *Reality Lantern* contraption in front of us, only more primitive. I was buried in hardened wax and had my power sapped from me. After a couple millennia of complete boredom, I managed to get word out to my father back on my home reality. I told him that I needed help, and I said that the only person who could save me was my youngest brother.

"At that point in my existence, the pantheon was still rather trusting of me. So, Papa sent my youngest brother, the big bad god of thunder, a real force to be reckoned with. He shows up with his Jump Bug in hand, and that reality *instantly* senses it. His bug's exterminated and he's wrapped in some bizarre energy tornado. Earth 6 pulls me out of the candle and forces him inside it.

"As soon as I'm out, Earth 6 has no more use for me. I'm disintegrated outright—a rather odd and painful sensation, I might add—and my atoms are scattered to the winds. Little brother's stuck powering the place for eternity or until something better comes along. Earth 6 obviously didn't know that I'm a god of death and rebirth, so after a few ages, I managed to pull my atoms back together through sheer willpower. With my body reformed, I re-birthed Beverly from my forehead, and I left."

"*After* you rescued your brother, right?" asked Normal-Art.

"Are you kidding? Rescue the bastard who tormented me day and night throughout my childhood? The kid who every holiday season skinned me and turned my hide into a winter scarf to impress Papa? Hell no!

"That *was* about when my family stopped trusting me, though," continued the god. "I returned home, and without my youngest brother there to thwart me, I rose to the top of my pantheon. I stayed atop it until Ginny came along and sent my life tumbling down into ruin."

At that exact moment, as if some unseen orchestra took God-Art's words as a cue to unleash a fierce staccato note, the planet rocked more violently than it had yet rocked since Normal-Art slapped it with his gorilla-gloves. Had Normal-Art not already been collapsed on the ground, he would have tumbled there now.

"I'd love to keep telling you tales about myself," said God-Art, "but I think *that* was our sign that it's time to grab that blue ball of powerful cuteness and get the hell out of here."

"But you said that this reality will cease to exist if the bears are removed, didn't you?"

"No, I said that if you *snuffed* them out, this reality would cease to exist. So, don't twist that knob again."

"OK, that was *my* brilliant plan. What's your suggestion?"

"We pull the bears out of the Reality Lantern," answered the god.

"I feel like I'm simply repeating myself here, but won't that make this reality cease to exist?"

"The reality must remove the power source periodically so the device can be cleaned. There is a five-minute window in which the device can be empty before total destruction occurs."

"That's comforting."

"Found that out during my time in Earth 6's *Reality Candle*," said God-Art. "I hated being pulled out for those cleanings more than anything else. Just when you think you're getting used to the pain of being a battery, a reality pulls you out, runs the equivalent of cosmic soda over you to clean off your crusty acid, and then plugs you back in. Hurts terribly, and you're tender to even the slightest gust of wind for years."

"That's a riveting story, really, it is," said Normal-Art with a smirk, "but what do we do? How do we get the puffball out?"

"Well, one of us is going to have to pop off the top of the Reality Lantern and pull it out," said God-Art, grinning at Normal-Art. "And I sure as hell am in no condition to do it."

"I hate you so much."

"I—as you may have guessed—do not care. Get moving before another tremor hits. I'd guess we've got less than eighteen minutes before this planet goes kaboom."

Normal-Art grimaced, and then he put his left foot on the knob he had used to control the wick. He boosted himself up with it and grabbed the top of the lantern with his left hand. His deltoids and biceps flexed, and he attempted with all his might to pull himself up. But then he flopped back down, barely hanging on to the top of the lantern by his fingernails. He cursed. He felt rather silly when he realized that he could touch his feet to the ground.

"We've got mere minutes to go before this planet explodes," squealed God-Art, "and that's the best you can do? You can't lift your own weight, even with the threat of death nipping at your heels? We may as well give up and acclimate ourselves to nothingness right now."

"I'm tired, and I've been through more craziness today than I ever planned to go through in my entire life. So please, just shut up and use your fancy god-powers to help a little. Can't you skitter on over here and give me a boost or something?"

"I'm a god, not a bloody stepstool!"

The Earth trembled again, and from the hallway behind the Arts a pair of feminine screeches echoed into the room.

"Oh, forget it," exclaimed God-Art. His spider-legs skittered faster than Normal-Art could see, and before Normal-Art's senses caught up to what had happened, he was standing atop God-Art's head, looking down at the top of the Reality Lantern. The head quivered below his feet as it strained its skinny little legs to raise him as high as possible.

Normal-Art unscrewed the latch on top of the lantern. He pulled it off and tossed it to the ground, where it crashed with a CLANG and stirred up a cloud of dust. He looked down into the hole at the bears. They continued to spin, never pausing in their disturbingly cute cosmic tryst.

More female screams echoed down the corridor and into the room. The walls shook. Waves of sand fell from the ceiling and dusted the room.

"You'll have to jump in to retrieve the blue bear," instructed God-Art. "Easiest way to do so will be to simply grab the saber by the hilt and bring both bears up here to the surface. Once we're safely away from this Earth, we can separate them and dispose of the pink one and be off with the blue one. But be warned! The Reality Lantern is going to be bigger on the inside than the outside. Everything in there operates on a different playing field than out here. Time, Physics, everything. But you've got to go in, nonetheless, because we'll never reach those bears any other way."

Normal-Art grunted, too tired of the god's voice to bother responding. He braced himself on the lip of the thick glass, preparing to hop into the lantern. But before he took the leap, a troubling thought crashed across his brain.

"Hey," he called down to the god, "once I get these little guys out of there, we've got five minutes before this dimension ceases to exist. That's how you said these *Reality Lights* work, right? And barring that, we've got about fifteen minutes before the world explodes. What's the point? Without Beverly, we're stuck here."

"Stop asking so many questions and go! Are you stupid? The Ginnys are awake, and they're coming! I can't hold them off while I'm boosting you up!"

Normal-Art shrugged. He pulled his legs over the edge and hopped inside the lantern, careful of his feet to make sure he wasn't aimed where he would stomp on the bears.

Normal-Art's senses reeled. The Reality Lantern *was* bigger on the inside than the outside, just as God-Art had claimed. Much bigger, like it housed an entirely new world. Normal-Art found himself swimming, paddling deep inside what felt like an ocean of fire. He burned all over, and in every direction that he looked, he saw an endless sea of burning liquid. He tried to breathe, but only succeeded in sucking the burning liquid into his lungs. He began to panic, but a tickling in the base of his brain sent reassurance through his body. He squinted, looking down deep into the sea. The tickle in his brain told him to go that way.

He did not understand why, but he did not die from the lack of oxygen or the burning liquid that enveloped him. Instead of questioning this outcome, he focused on paddling. He forced one hand in front of the other, and he choked down bile every time his hands passed in front of his face. His gloves melted and dissolved into nothingness, and with each stroke, a layer of his flesh burned away until only his empty white bones propelled him forward. Burning liquid consumed his eyeballs. He felt them ooze down his bony cheeks, but he found that he could still see. He ignored the impossibility and continued to paddle.

He stroked for eternity, always stroking in the same direction, always following the tickle in his brain. He stroked, and he stroked, and he stroked, deeper into the interminable, burning sea.

CHAPTER 26

SANDSTORMS AND GLASSTORMS AND GODS

GOD-ART WATCHED NORMAL-ART fall over the lip of the glass and into the Reality Lantern. The mortal disappeared. *Hope that didn't kill him,* he thought.

God-Art had not exactly told Normal-Art the *whole* truth about the Reality Lantern. The god *could* have gone in after the treasure, and he could have done it without disappearing into whatever hellish plane of existence awaited the mortal inside the cosmic artifact. But God-Art was afraid. Afraid to be kidnapped again. Afraid to be drained of his energy for a thousand lifetimes. Afraid to be reduced to an existence that consisted only of tedious boredom and all-consuming pain. More afraid than he was of the angry women coming down the hallway behind him, that was for sure.

God-Art turned to face the entrance to this room, preparing himself for a final showdown. He took a deep breath and then exhaled through the side of his mouth. The sand stirred from the ground near him. He blew harder, again and again, and it began to whirl. He kept this up like he was a godly bellows, and soon a torrent of blinding, stinging sand twirled around the room, a Category Five dust devil. Layers upon layers of ancient sand from the walls and floor and ceiling joined the sandy tornado. God-Art could feel the coarse sand peeling layers of skin from his face. He blew harder. The tornado continued to grow.

He listened as the Ginnys rampaged down the corridor toward him and noted how close their furious shrieks had come to this room. These furious shrieks danced into the room to surround God-Art like frolicking one-legged go-go dancers. And when the dance abruptly ceased, God-Art nodded. He knew his ex-lover well, and if she had gone quiet, then it meant that she would be standing just outside the entry to this room, finalizing her plan of attack. The time for this showdown had arrived. God-Art steeled himself.

A thin, pink tentacle crept into the room from the corridor like a periscope poking just above the surface of some stagnant cesspool to peer at its surroundings. God-Art subtly changed the direction of his blowing, aiming at the pink tentacle. The dirty cyclone unleashed its fury against the pink tentacle, severing it in half. The little appendage fell to the ground and writhed in place like a dying snake. Then a second tentacle snaked in and snatched the detached piece, disappearing back through the door from whence it had appeared.

God-Art blew harder than ever. His flaming hair flared brighter and brighter as the wind continued to pick up speed. More blinding dust joined the cyclone, and the sandy tornado spun with such rage that had God-Art not been a god with divine senses, he would have been unable to see more than a couple feet in front of his face.

Wearing a thick membrane of pink armor, Tiny-Ginny burst into the chamber, murder in her Dictator Scout eyes. She rode toward God-Art on a tidal wave of the pink goo, sitting upon its crest and using it like it was a gelatinous wheelchair. The tiny stumps that remained of her legs pointed at God-Art like bloody, accusing fingers.

God-Art blew more fiercely, whipping the sand faster around the room. Blood trailed from his raw skin where the sand slapped against it. But the sandstorm did not slow Tiny-Ginny, and as she blasted through it, she used her pink tidal wave to raise herself high above the god-head. She spread her arms wide, and chunks of the ooze followed her motion, extending to her sides like oversized pink wings. She leaned forward, screaming with fury, and slapped these gigantic pink wings down upon the spot where God-Art stood.

Just when Tiny-Ginny's attack was about to crash down upon God-Art, he ceased blowing. He skittered backward on his skinny spider-legs, and he dove out of the way. He rolled—his head sufficiently round enough to not slow his momentum much—and he managed to barely dodge the massive pink wings. They crashed to the ground just behind him with a sickening THUD. He knew if he had not managed to dodge out of the way, he would have been stuck resurrecting himself for a *while*, which would have been lost time that he could *not* afford to lose right now.

God-Art yelled, "You bumbled right in here where I wanted you, you fool!"

Then God-Art executed his *true* counterattack, for the sandy tornado was only part of his stratagem. He screamed, more fiercely than he had screamed in a millennium. His flaming hair flared into an all-consuming inferno. Fire engulfed the room, burning and crisping everything in the chamber except the Reality Lantern. When he finally stopped screaming, the fire died down to its normal heat atop his head.

Tiny-Ginny remained exactly where she had been before the attack, raised high upon her pink ooze and staring at him with furious eyes. But now her pink armor and pink tidal wave burned, God-Art's magical flames having caught them on fire. She squealed in anger. Then she fell to her stomach and wallowed on the ground in pain as she retracted the pink ooze into her pores. She did so at blinding speed, and it was fast enough to snuff the flames. However, because her pores were teaming up with the pink ooze to snuff the fire, a layer of black, crusted skin was left covering her body where the flames burned her as they died.

Less than a second later, she had already regained her composure, though one could argue whether she had regained her dignity—for all the hair on her body and all her clothes had been burned away into a pile of ash. She balled her fists and yelled, "I'm basically fireproof, you fool. All I have to do is pull my pink stuff back inside me and replace it with mor—"

God-Art grinned, for his firestorm had also flash-fried the whirling sand grains so that they had become splinters of razor-sharp glass. The sandy cyclone had transformed into a tornado of glass particles, and just as he planned, Tiny-Ginny had not noticed. She had assumed the firestorm was the entirety of his attack when it was but a precursor to his true attack. He began blowing again before the glass shards could crash to the ground, and they resumed their places in the tornado, spinning at an insane velocity.

Millions of glass splinters crashed into the now-armorless Tiny-Ginny, moving at such high speed that the tiny shards pricked her everywhere and drew blood from all over her body.

God-Art blew harder, and the thrashing glass slivers picked up even more momentum. Blood flowed from thousands of wounds on his face, but he continued grinning anyway, for Tiny-Ginny had become bloodier by many orders of magnitude. She squirmed and tried to wipe the shards of glass from her body, but she only managed to press the tiny particles deeper into her pores.

And for every second that she attempted to free her skin of the glass, the cyclone dumped more of it into her hide.

Just when God-Art was preparing to give one last forceful blow to *really* hammer home this attack, he found himself overcome with a bout of dizziness. He realized that he must have spent all his remaining energy stores on that supernatural scream, the one that he had used to create the magical firestorm from his hair. Before he could blow another breath, his spindly legs wobbled and then collapsed out from under him. He crashed to the ground in exhaustion. The glass shards on the floor crunched beneath the weight of his overlarge head.

As he stopped blowing, the storm of glass lost its momentum. The particles rained down across the chamber and created an eerily beautiful symphony of tinkles. He stared at the shimmering glass covering the floor. It was mesmerizing. It reminded him of the sea in the morning, just when the sun hits it and gives it the appearance of a painting.

Meanwhile, Tiny-Ginny lay on the ground, struggling for breath and shimmering like a diamond in the pink and blue light of the Reality Lantern. She rolled onto her side and lifted herself up onto her palms. She turned her head toward God-Art. She met God-Art's mirthful grin with a pitiful expression. God-Art remembered the girl he had once loved, and he almost felt sorry for her.

Then, Tiny-Ginny's expression seemed to implode and transform, shifting into the grin of an insane Cheshire cat. Tiny-Ginny's pink ooze began secreting from the few remaining pores on her body that were unclogged by glass shards. The pink soon enveloped her, and then it wiggled between and beneath the shards of glass stuck in her skin. Whirlpools danced across her pink membrane as the pinkness that had forced itself beneath the glass disappeared inside her. The glass shards got sucked into the whirlpools along with the pink goo, vanishing inside her skin. She bled more than ever, but the shiny epidermis of glass no longer covered her. She laughed.

Then she opened her mouth and hacked up what looked like a furball the size of her head. It consisted entirely of glass. She caught it in her palm, held it up to show God-Art, and then dropped it to the ground.

"Tell me you can do better than *that*," she said. "You're the last obstacle for us to overcome on our quest to obtain our pink god—the power that will fuel *my* conquest of the Multiverse—an*d this* was all you could do to stop us? I am most disappointed."

God-Art heard a splat behind him. He turned to see Regular-Ginny landing on the ground. She must have climbed along the ceiling, sticking to it with her pink ooze and avoiding the brunt of the storm as she sneaked behind him to flank him. A thin layer of glass lay embedded in her pink armor, yielding it a sheen like it had been dropped into a gigantic bowl of glitter.

The Ginnys rose above him on matching pink tentacles, fury in their eyes. They screamed in identical shrieking voices, "Die!"

"Well, bugger the both of you," replied God-Art. He had failed in holding them off. He stood as best he could upon his spindly legs and prepared to die. He had died many times, and this would not even compare to the most painful.

But as he closed his eyes, waiting, the deathblow did not come. Instead, the ground rumbled and cracked. A fissure opened, and a crack spread across the floor. The Ginnys leapt backward in opposite directions to keep from falling in.

"What's happening?" called Regular-Ginny to her counterpart.

"I don't know," answered Tiny-Ginny, peering over at Regular-Ginny through a new pink membrane of armor that she had grown. "But it can't be good. Let's just squash my bug-of-an-ex, grab the Pink One, and get out of here."

Both Ginnys looked back down, only to find no sign of God-Art. All that remained down there was an inanimate fissure in the floor, which was growing wider with each passing second.

"I think he may have fallen in," said Regular-Ginny, raising an eyebrow.

"Impossible, you dimwit," replied Tiny-Ginny. "We took our eyes off him, so he ran. He's here somewhere. He can't have gotten far on his tiny legs."

Tiny-Ginny was right. God-Art *had* scampered away, using his spidery legs to flitter up the wall. He did not stop until he had reached the corner where the back wall met the ceiling, high, high, high overhead. He willed the flames atop his head to extinguish. He crouched in the darkness, hiding to allow himself time to formulate a plan. He wished Normal-Art would hurry it up with the stupid bears.

Tiny-Ginny's expression grew furious. The membrane surrounding her swelled, expanding to become a colossal blob and forming dozens of tentacles that she whipped all about the chamber.

But God-Art would not be bested so easily. He remained in his hiding spot, assuming that she was merely lashing out blindly in her fury. He narrowly dodged a tendril and crouched again, waiting to dodge another when the time came.

Below, a geyser of lava erupted from within the fissure in the ground, smacking into Tiny-Ginny's pink blob. It glowed white hot in a thick layer on her pink membrane, and then it cooled almost instantly into a rocky, hard blackness. Her tentacles slowed almost to a halt under the weight of the rock.

God-Art breathed a sigh of relief. But then Tiny-Ginny raised herself high into the air and smacked herself onto the ground, cracking the rock off like it was the shell of a nut. She began lashing again, so God-Art breathed a sigh of despair.

He looked back down at the fissure. It had by now spread across the entire expanse of the floor and widened to the point that God-Art might consider calling it a gorge. Molten lava overflowed from the crack and began pooling on the floor, its orange and red light intruding upon the pastel illumination from the Reality Lantern.

Tiny-Ginny momentarily stopped lashing her tendrils like she was a furious, blind drunk, just long enough to look over at Regular-Ginny and bark, "Get the Pink One. I'll find the head. Stay off the lava—it won't harm you, but it shall slow you."

Regular-Ginny nodded. She used her pink ooze to sling herself across the room. She stretched pink tentacles from her pink membrane and used them to snag herself onto the side of the Reality Lantern. She pulled herself to the lip at the top and looked inside. She leaned over it, inserted her left hand, and then screamed. She removed her hand from the lantern, only to reveal a bloody mass of melted skin and muscle and boils. The skin fell off her hand in a sloshing heap. It smacked into the glass on the side of the Reality Lantern and slid down, leaving angry red streaks. It dropped into the pooling lava and burned away into nothingness.

"Oh, god, whadoo I do?" cried Regular-Ginny.

Tiny-Ginny was climbing the wall, rolling along it inside of her pink blob. The blob made slight popping sounds when it rolled, like thousands of tiny suction cups were gripping the stone and then popping off as it moved. She circled around the walls of the room, checking every crevice for God-Art. When she finally acknowledged Regular-Ginny's question, she stopped and looked back at her counterpart, saying, "It's of no matter. It's an enchantment. You'll still be able to use the arm. Now cease your whining and grab the Pink One!"

And with that, she ignored Regular-Ginny and continued her frantic search for God-Art.

Regular-Ginny nervously turned back to her task. The Reality Lantern now floated atop the growing sea of lava like an awkward version of Noah's Ark, whose only goal was to save the oddest creatures in existence. Regular-Ginny again peered down inside the Reality Lantern. She sucked in a deep breath. The bears seemed just out of her reach. She sighed and leaned forward. She balanced herself on the lip of the opening and stuck her left hand back into the lantern. She bit her lip, hard, and a thin trickle of blood rolled down her chin. She pushed her entire arm into the lantern.

Meanwhile, God-Art had tucked himself as far into the corner as he could. His respite up here had allowed him time to recover enough that he felt capable of expending a *little* more divine magic. He just needed to figure out on what he should spend this new store of energy. And then he grew overjoyed, for he felt a humongous CLACK inside his brain as it birthed a new scheme. He would shrink his head until he was so small that Tiny-Ginny could never find him. Then he would grow himself back to normal in time to escape with Normal-Art when the mortal returned from his sojourn inside the Reality Lantern—if he ever did so.

In a single fluid motion, God-Art stuck out his tongue, stretching it far enough that he could give his entire head a single good lick. When he was nice and lubed with his enchanted saliva, he quietly mumbled some magic words. He felt his head begin to tingle, and then it contracted. The world around him grew larger, and Tiny-Ginny took on the proportions of a pink Kaiju. She continued to grow larger as he grew smaller. The experience was most disorienting.

Tiny-Ginny's pink blob catapulted her like a legless human cannonball, up over the geysers of lava launching from the cracked ground. She hurtled straight toward God-Art. He gasped in surprise.

But God-Art was now small enough to duck inside a crack in the wall, which he did barely a second before Tiny-Ginny crashed into the stone upon which he had just been crouched.

"You really are the stupidest god ever invented," said Tiny-Ginny, sticking her eyeball up to the crack to peer in at the god. Her giant voice boomed deep and echoed all around him. "I've known you for what feels like an eternity, and this exact same tactic has gotten you caught dozens of times. Your fire-hair glows from your scalp whenever you do anything magical, even if you try to will it not to. Even now, tiny as you are, you radiate like a searchlight."

God-Art gulped. He had forgotten about this habit of his flaming hair. But instead of showing fear, he fixed a smirk to his face. "I thought your breath was bad before," he replied. "But its terribleness must be directly proportional to your size. Because bloody hells, you stink."

A tiny pink tentacle slithered and smashed its way inside God-Art's cubby hole. He tried dodging it, but the crack was already a tight squeeze for him. The tentacle snatched him by the legs, and he found that he could not escape. The pink was both hard and gooey all at the same time. It was liquid enough that he sank into it, but hard enough that once his legs were submerged, he could not move them. The harder he jerked, the more solid the gel became around his limbs. It reminded him a bit of fast-drying pastel cement.

God-Art sighed and stopped struggling, resigning himself to another death. He felt his conscience tingle a little, angry that he would be leaving Normal-Art to his fate amongst these hags. Then he remembered that he was a god of mischief, and that ruining his counterpart's life did not really bother him, so the tingle vanished.

Nonetheless, he tried to think of a way to kill Tiny-Ginny, to bring her with him to ring Death's doorbell. Nothing came. He had already exhausted all his power, and none of it had stopped her. He needed to rest.

He waited for Ginny to kill him. He wished he had a pipe to smoke.

CHAPTER 27

SWIMMING FOR ETERNITY

STROKE, KICK, STROKE.

Normal-Art had been swimming for thousands of years, but still he could see no end to the burning sea. He only knew deep down in his gut that he could not stop swimming.

So, he stroked and stroked through the liquid flames. When he grew bored of swimming freestyle, he paddled like a little doggie. When he grew tired of dogpaddling, he rolled upside down and backstroked. Eventually, after exhausting himself of every imaginable stroke, he returned to freestyle to start the cycle over again—as he had done so many times since entering this burning sea that he had long ago lost count.

He wondered whether Earth 1,000,000 had already come to an end, if his slap to the ground had already come full circle and he simply did not know it, if he was dead and this was, in fact, Hell. If this place was Hell, it was not as bad as they made it seem in Sunday school. He had grown used to the burning a couple thousand years ago, and he *was* getting plenty of exercise. He had not heard a single sinner's wail, either, so it was at least peaceful and quiet.

Normal-Art pushed the thought from his head, again. He'd had it more times than he could count. Without really understanding how, he knew it rang false. He knew in his gut that he was still alive. So, he simply continued swimming, the doubts disappearing for a while.

After swimming for a few more millennia, he caught sight of something up ahead, a glowing blue that swirled with pink. He grinned as well as a skeleton can grin. He could not tell how far away the lights lay, but he thanked every god of whom he had ever heard mention—including his alternate-self—that his destination was in sight and that his journey was *finally* almost over.

He swam faster. But despite a thousand more years of paddling, the lights barely moved closer. So, in turn he cursed the gods, every god of whom he had ever heard mention—including his alternate-self.

But he continued paddling. He had done it *this* long. He could not stop now. He paddled for tens of thousands more years. He paddled for so long that he could not even remember his own name. All he could remember was swimming. Stroke, kick, stroke. He knew nothing else, and he did not think he had ever known anything but swimming. Stroke, kick, stroke.

Finally, after ages more had passed, the pastel lights grew close enough to fill his vision. He could not remember *why* he cared about the lights. He simply knew that they were important. He stroked into them, watching his skeletal white hands glow blue and pink. He laughed at the colors, knowing not why they made him happy. He simply delighted in the fact that they were new and different, that they were not the same flaming liquid at which he had stared for an eternity.

He stroked again, winding his left arm over his head and cupping it, pushing himself forward through the endless sea of flames. And for the first time in forever, the stroke was different. On *this* stroke, his fingertips crashed against fluffy fur. It felt soft and cool and reassuring, and he knew—without knowing why he knew—that he could finally stop swimming.

He stared at a pelt of bright blue fur. He realized that it formed the back of a stuffed animal. Beams of pink light flared from behind the blue doll, haloing it in rich shades of pink.

The head of the blue doll turned completely around to stare at him with its bright blue button-eyes. "Save Me, Art," said the blue teddy bear.

"My name's Art," whispered Art, reverence filling his voice. *Of course, my name is Art,* he thought. *How could I forget?*

Art felt a tickle in his brain. And then he remembered why he was down here in this nearly endless sea: to rescue the cosmic blue teddy bear.

"Save Me, Art," the blue teddy bear repeated.

Art gripped with his right hand the hilt of the onyx saber that stood erect from the blue bear's back. "I shall save you," he answered.

He felt another tickle in his brain. It told him to begin the swim back the way he had come. He obeyed. All the while, he lugged behind him the saber as though he had become a skeletal tugboat.

Art glanced over his shoulder. The blue teddy bear stroked its tiny paws through the fiery liquid. So did a nearly identical pink teddy bear. They churned the burning sea, and Art could sense that he was swimming much faster now than he had on the way down here, like he had hitched himself to a supersonic motorboat.

It took the trio a mere thousand years to reach the top of the Reality Lantern. As they approached the top, Art watched a hand poke itself into the magical flaming liquid—a hand that was enveloped in a pink membrane. Both the pink membrane and the skin covering the hand melted, and the hand disappeared back out of the flaming liquid. Art could not tell to whom the hand belonged, for the surface of the burning liquid obscured the view outside the lantern, but he *knew* that whoever was reaching in here desired what he had worked so hard to obtain.

So, he grunted and decided that he would handle this mystery hand—this potential thief—with extreme prejudice. He glanced down at the sharp tip at the end of the saber, the end that poked out of the pink bear's back. This saber had been strong enough to impale both of these cosmic teddy bears. Surely it could handle whoever waited outside.

Art stared up at the surface of the burning liquid, focusing on the fuzzy pink-encrusted person lingering just outside the Reality Lantern. The person shoved the now-bloody hand back into the liquid, and then the rest of the arm to which the hand belonged. The arm flittered about in the water above him. It dangled there for a few minutes as it stretched and searched. Art watched it as its flesh disintegrated. And then it disappeared back out of the lantern.

Art shrugged. He jabbed the saber up. It emerged from the surface of the flaming sea. He felt the shock of the blow run down his arm as the tip of the saber ripped through flesh. He shoved the sword into the person with such ferocity that the momentum knocked his victim off their perch on the lantern and lifted Art out of the surface of the burning liquid. Stale air washed over him, a relief from the burning innards of the Reality Lantern. He caught himself on the lip of the giant lantern before he could tumble over its edge.

He stared at the back of a woman's head, his eye sockets wide in surprise. He had expected to impale someone much shorter, though after all his time in the Reality Lantern, he could not quite remember whom. Blood gushed from her wound, and her head lolled weakly to one side.

She attempted to speak, but she only managed to choke on blood. She fell forward, losing control of her body and beginning to slide off the end of the onyx saber.

A peal of thunder and bright light exploded in front of him. The light blinded him even though he no longer possessed eyes. He looked away and buried his face in the crook of his bony arm. The light disappeared, and he looked back up to where it had been. When his vision returned, he saw that the woman and the pink teddy bear had disappeared.

"Well, *that* can't be good," he muttered. He glanced around the room, and memory flashed back into his mind, despite an eternity away from this place.

Before he had a chance to revel in the return from his nigh-eternal detour, evil dove straight at him, hoping to swallow him whole.

CHAPTER 28

DEUS EX MACHINA

GOD-ART'S SKULL CRACKED like the shell of a walnut. The headache that followed was blinding, and he grunted in pain.

Tiny-Ginny held him before her eyes, suspended between two thin pink tentacles. She had begun repeatedly squeezing them together like a vice, squishing his miniature head and then relinquishing every time she felt the crack of a fractured skull. Before commencing this torture, she had ripped each of his spider-legs from his head. She had giggled like a sociopathic child as she yanked them off one by one and dropped them, watching them flitter and tumble lightly down to disappear into the rising sea of lava.

She squeezed again and squealed with glee, exulting when this round of crushing not only resulted in another crack, but also caused his left eyeball to pop from its socket and dangle against his cheek. God-Art wished that she would just end it already and kill him, for he could not heal himself if she continuously broke him.

Just as she began squeezing once more, a screeching bellow filled the chamber, vibrating everything within it. God-Art grew confused. He had been crushed to death *many* times, but he could not recall ever hearing a screeching bellow and feeling the world vibrate just before such a death.

When the bellow and the vibration were followed by a loud clicking and whirring, God-Art realized the odd noises were not some byproduct of this imminent death. His left eye, hanging out of its socket, snaked around his face so that he could see below him to where the noise had originated. In the middle of the growing sea of lava, a whirlpool had formed. The liquid rock sucked into it for a few seconds, counterclockwise.

Then the whirlpool exploded outward, and lava rocketed up to crash harmlessly against Tiny-Ginny's pink blob. Molten rock also splattered across God-Art's face, managing to sear through his skin and make him even more miserable. The Reality Lantern, still floating on the rising tide of lava, tossed but stayed afloat in the resulting waves.

The translucent dragon burst forth from within the whirlpool. Drillbot was still inside the dragon, stabbing it over and over with his single drill. The dragon crashed into the wall opposite the feuding Tiny-Ginny and God-Art. The dragon completely ignored the laws of gravity and perched itself on the wall, crouching upon it sideways as if it were on the ground. The dragon opened its mouth and roared. Cloudy spirits flared out of its mouth, dancing in the air like pale fire before being sucked back inside the beast.

Drillbot continued stabbing, ripping the beast apart from the inside like a bad piece of sushi with an incredibly high pointy steel count. The dragon screeched in pain as the drill pierced its skin. The souls of dwarven dictators burst forth from the punctures and were sucked back into the monster's nose.

But this time, instead of instantly healing the wounds, the dragon thrust its mighty paw into one of the holes and grabbed Drillbot. The beast encircled the robot about the torso with its pale claw and yanked Drillbot out through the hole, ripping the wound open wider in the effort. The dragon's skin sealed itself within seconds in a bright flash of light, leaving no evidence at all that Drillbot had ever been inside the beast.

The dragon smashed Drillbot's head into the wall, smacking the stone with the robot like a slobbering monkey cracking a tiny rodent's skull on a log. The wall cracked upon impact. The beast smashed the robot's head into the wall again. And again. And again. And again. Gears and cogs fluttered down into the molten lava like they were steel raindrops from a thunderstorm sent by some robotic version of Valhalla. They floated for a few seconds atop the lava, and then they sank.

By the time the dragon stopped smashing, the robot had become embedded into the wall up to its torso. The robot clicked and clacked a few times, spun its wheels, and whirred. The whirring stopped after a couple seconds. Drillbot yelled something from within the wall, but the stone muffled the sound, and God-Art could not understand what the robot had said. Drillbot's voice abruptly cut off with an odd, squelchy gurgle.

With Drillbot no longer a threat, the dragon turned its attention to God-Art and Tiny-Ginny, who had stopped their feuding to gawk at the battle between the beast and the robot. The dragon screeched at them. God-Art and Tiny-Ginny stared dumbly at the behemoth, their mouths agape.

The dragon launched itself from its perch on the wall. It flapped its peculiarly thin, bat-like wings, flying directly toward them. But when the dragon was partway across the chamber, Regular-Ginny grunted as she dug her arm inside the Reality Lantern, and the grunt was enough to grab the dragon's attention. It whipped its bristling head down to peer at the Reality Lantern. It snarled at Regular-Ginny.

God-Art and Tiny-Ginny breathed a simultaneous sigh of relief when they realized that the beast had turned its fury elsewhere. But then they uttered a simultaneous curse when it dawned on them that the beast focusing its attention on their mundane counterparts meant that the chances of obtaining their quarry had just become much bleaker.

The dragon shifted its flightpath and soared toward Regular-Ginny. Regular-Ginny heard the furious, snarling creature behind her. She removed her arm from the Reality Lantern—pausing her attempt to grab the cosmic teddy bears—and swiveled to face the dragon. Its screechy breath blew through her matted hair, tossing it heavily to-and-fro in a breeze of stinking death and decay.

To Regular-Ginny's credit, she did not balk in the face of oncoming Death. She reached into her pocket with one hand. With her other hand, she balled her fist and prepared to fight. She screamed something in Tiny-Ginny's direction, but it could not be heard over the dragon's screeches. But then a look of confusion appeared on her face. She glanced from the approaching dragon down to her chest. The skin below her sternum stretched outward, and then it split open.

Black onyx poked out from the broken skin, and blood gushed around it like it was a dangerous rock in the center of a bloody stretch of rapids. Her face paled in bewildered terror. Behind her, Normal-Art's skull and right hand emerged from the top of the Reality Lantern, his right hand gripping the handle of the saber upon which the cosmic bears—and now Regular-Ginny—had been skewered.

Regular-Ginny's body slumped forward. She began to tumble from the lip of the lantern, her pink tentacles going limp and ceasing to grip it. The useless weight of Regular-Ginny's limp body on the end of the saber yanked Normal-Art up and out of the cosmic artifact. He grabbed the lip of the lantern with his left hand and shifted his weight so that he landed straddling the lip of the lantern, holding himself steady with his thigh bones so that he and Regular-Ginny did not tumble down into the lava below.

Regular-Ginny opened her mouth and tried to say something, but she choked on her own blood instead. The dragon, less than a hundred feet away, continued to soar toward the Reality Lantern. It opened its lips, exposing a mouthful of sharp teeth and sinister dwarven spirits. Normal-Art's pure white bones looked gray in the shadow of the dragon.

Though the bears had emerged from the Reality Lantern continuing to cuddle each other in their head-to-crotch grip, the pink bear ended the embrace when it turned its head 180° to look at the impaled Regular-Ginny. Its lips curled into a snarl and it bore its fangs, which were pastel blue darts the exact same color as its counterpart's fur. It bellowed a deep growl, lifted its paw, and formed a fist.

Two thin tentacles of pink ooze whipped out from the back of Regular-Ginny's head. They grabbed the pink bear and yanked it up the onyx saber toward Regular-Ginny, a trail of pastel blue blood remaining on the blade to mark its passing. The pink bear grabbed Regular-Ginny's impaled body from behind. For a moment, they hung there together on the end of the saber looking like the oddest, most unappetizing shish kabob in the universe.

The dragon loomed a mere few-dozen feet away. Regular-Ginny's tentacles pulled her and the pink bear off the saber, and as they started to fall toward the lava below, a blinding light exploded from them, accompanied by a deafening peal of thunder.

Tiny-Ginny covered her ears and closed her eyes in response to the deafening thunder and blinding light. In the process of doing so, she apparently forgot about God-Art, because she dropped him. Unfortunately for God-Art, this freedom did not signal the easy victory that it might have otherwise signaled, for the explosion of light had blinded him. Because he could not see, he flicked out his tongue wildly through the air, stretching it like a long length of sticky rope and hoping to snag it on *something* before he could land in the lava and burn to death—a death from which resurrection would likely take too long to ensure he could escape this doomed Earth.

After a moment of panic, he felt his tongue touch the sandy wall. The wall tasted like arid dirt. But he ignored the hideous flavor and instead concentrated on making the end of his tongue stickier. He soon slowed to a halt. He could tell from the blistering air wafting around his face that he was dreadfully close to the rising sea of lava, and milliseconds later when his vision healed and returned to focus, he found that he that he did indeed hang mere inches above the inferno. He used his tongue to pull himself higher onto the wall, swallowing it an inch at a time like some mystical, lifesaving licorice rope.

Meanwhile, the dragon swooped across the top of the Reality Lantern, snapping its teeth at Normal-Art. Normal-Art leapt off the side of the lantern, narrowly dodging the dragon maw. He snagged his left hand on the lip of the lantern and hung precariously there over the sea of lava. He gripped the saber in his free right hand, clinging to it so tightly that his knuckles would have turned white had they been covered in skin. He gritted his teeth and stabbed upward with the point of the blade.

The dragon yelped and careened past without swallowing him, which surprised God-Art. He thought his counterpart had been a goner for sure.

The creature lurched wildly and crashed against the opposite wall. The saber had torn a long gash deep into the creature's translucent skin, stretching from the middle of its torso down to its right hind leg. Tiny souls escaped in droves, cycling back in through the creature's nostrils.

To God-Art's surprise, this wound did not heal itself as the others had done. The souls simply continued to exile themselves out of the wound and immigrate back in by the nose as though they were playing in some grotesque revolving door with no ability to ever leave.

Tiny-Ginny screamed from her perch up near the ceiling. God-Art glanced up at her and saw that her face was twisted in rage. She cried, "That bitch! She left me! She stole the Pink One!"

God-Art followed Tiny-Ginny's wrathful gaze. He must have been too distracted by the blinding light and the swooping dragon, because he had not noticed that Regular-Ginny had disappeared, along with the pink half of the pastel teddy bears—the pink bear having apparently been Tiny-Ginny's quarry throughout this whole ridiculous ordeal.

Tiny-Ginny leapt from her roost. As she fell through the air, she formed dozens of thin tentacles from her pink ooze. She pumped these appendages back and forth like a dog does its legs when it is being held over water. She smacked atop the sea of lava, but by the time she hit, her tentacles were pumping so fast that she did not even sink. She raced forward across molten rock, aimed straight at the Reality Lantern. Lava splashed behind her like the wake of a motorboat, launching into the air and smacking into the stone walls of the room.

On the opposite wall, the dragon thrashed, the translucent skin around its wound turning an opaque black. The blackness continued to spread across the beast's skin, veining across it like some hyperactive strand of gangrene. The dragon beat its head against the wall and screeched a pained screech so loudly that its breath smacked into God-Art, way over on the complete other end of the chamber. God-Art, still dangling by his tongue, whipped to-and-fro like a kite being flown during a hurricane.

Then the dragon dashed toward Normal-Art like a starving, rabid wolf on the verge of death. It ran along the wall as though the wall had become the ground, again ignoring the laws of gravity.

The Reality Lantern, still floating aimlessly along on the currents of rising lava, made a tinking noise as it smacked against the back corner of the chamber. Normal-Art pulled himself up on top of the lantern and stood there straddling it, positioning the balls of his feet on opposite sides of the open lid like a skeletal version of the Colossus of Rhodes. He shifted his position so that his back rested against the corner of the chamber, and so that he faced outward toward both Tiny-Ginny and the dragon.

Normal-Art gripped the hilt of the saber in both hands and held the blade pointed out in front of him. The blue bear remained spitted near the hilt of the saber, but now it smiled. It sang a song like a happy, delirious drunk, with a voice both melodious and hypnotic. Pink fangs flashed from behind its lips as it sang, and a pale blue gas drifted from its mouth. The gas twirled through the air and down to Art's feet. The gas began mending Normal-Art, rebuilding the muscle, tissue, and skin over his bare bones.

The viciously thrashing dragon and the furious Tiny-Ginny bore down on him from opposite directions. They were both seconds away from ending him in a crash of broken bones and pink goo and dictator-ghost-clouds. He tried to back away, but his back was already pressed up against the back corner of the chamber.

God-Art cursed, for he had no more spare power to help Normal-Art. He felt drained and needed rest, so he simply watched and prepared himself for a death possibly more permanent now that the Reality Lantern had been robbed of its power source.

Normal-Art crouched. The dragon opened its maw and gnashed its teeth, now only two-dozen feet away from Normal-Art. The cancerous black infection continued spreading rapidly across its body, and in response, the dragon roared louder. Tiny-Ginny scrambled across the lava, a caricature of rage, a mere dozen feet away from Normal-Art and closing fast. She raised her fists and razor-sharp pink spikes formed from them, extending in front of her like bristly battering rams.

"The Blue One is mine!" she screamed. "And then you're *all* dead!"

God-Art screamed for Normal-Art to move, but the god's voice was drowned out beneath the dragon's beastly roaring and Tiny-Ginny's maniacal screeching. Normal-Art crouched even lower, his legs coiling beneath him like a pair of bony springs. He was an odd sight to behold, a skeleton with flesh now regrown up to his calves, crouching atop a giant lantern and wielding an onyx saber that had skewered a cosmic teddy bear. God-Art had been around nearly forever, and he did not think that even *he* had witnessed anything quite so bizarre.

Tiny-Ginny leapt, diving spikes-first at Normal-Art. The dragon, scrambling sideways across the wall, also dove at Normal-Art. It stretched its mouth open wide enough to swallow both Art and the entire Reality Lantern in one fell gulp.

Normal-Art's legs sprang into action, launching him high into the air, higher than he had ever jumped before. Later in life, when telling of his adventures in failed attempts to pick up loose women in bars, he would attribute the height of this leap to his light weight—a direct result of his lacking skin, organs, and muscles. But he would also never quite be able to explain why he was still able function at all, considering that he *was*, after all, missing these selfsame skin, organs, and muscles.

Normal-Art stabbed the saber high into the dusty wall, sinking the blade into it like a knife through a grimy block of butter. He used his momentum to swing himself up atop the blade, using it like a miniature onyx ledge on which to perch. He grabbed a crack in the wall with his bony fingertips and steadied himself. The blue bear hung upside down near the hilt, a bastion of singing teddiness.

As soon as Normal-Art leapt into the air, Tiny-Ginny sailed across the top of the lantern where he had just been crouched. The dragon swallowed Tiny-Ginny and the Reality Lantern, and then it smacked headfirst into the wall beneath Normal-Art. The entire wall rumbled and shook. Normal-Art's feet slipped. He jabbed his fingertips deeper into the crack, so deep that a sharp pain flared inside his bones. But he managed to keep himself steady.

The Reality Lantern dropped out of the bottom of the dragon's skin, returning to its floating trek across the lava. But Tiny-Ginny thrashed within the beast. The pale dictator spirits nipped at her like a school of vicious piranha-vampire-ghosts, draining the life from her body. She fought and punched and bit and slapped her tentacles at them, but her efforts were in vain. Her pink ooze simply dissolved more quickly than she could regrow it. She cried a wailing death rattle, and her lifeless body shriveled like a prune and fell from the wound in the creature's torso. It crashed atop the lava and sank, as if the whole scene were some callous burial at sea.

"And I thought *I* was the *deus ex machina*," remarked God-Art, staring at the dragon.

The black infection raged and festered across the dragon's hide, spreading faster than prospectors pillaging land during a gold rush. In the span of a few seconds, the thrashing dragon's hide no longer appeared translucent at all, but rather a hazy opaque. The dragon attempted to shift shapes, and it dove in and out of the lava, but nothing slowed the festering magical wound. Finally, the black malady ascended across the dragon's eyes, its last inches of translucence, and the creature ceased its violent thrashing. It belly-flopped onto the sea of lava and burst into flames.

God-Art could hear the souls within the dragon crying out and squealing as they roasted and crackled. The god grinned. And then he scowled because the air smelled vaguely like flaming ghostly dwarf hair. He spotted Tiny-Ginny's spirit, furiously writhing and squirming amid the sinking ship of the dragon, her spirit being pecked at as it burned by what looked like a howling, angry squirrel's ghost. Witnessing her torment, his scowl shifted back into a grin. As a matter of fact, he positively beamed until he realized that he had less than a minute to traverse the entire room, make it to his counterpart's side, and jump out of this doomed reality before this entire dimension winked out of existence. God-Art doubted even *he* could come back from such finality.

Still hanging from the wall by his tongue, God-Art inhaled some deep puffs of air, and with each breath his head expanded and filled like a party balloon. His facial features stretched across the swelling sphere of his cranium, and soon his pursed lips and oblong eyes gave him the appearance of a fiery-haired toad.

His head floated higher each time he gulped air, and his sticky tongue acted as an anchor that held him fast to the wall.

Within seconds, God-Art's head had grown to the size of a metropolitan bus. His left eye still hung out of its socket, but it had become inflated, too. It stretched up even higher than the rest of the head, like a bloodshot-red balloon tied by a string to the wrist of a child. God-Art used the eye like a periscope, shifting its position to focus on Normal-Art, who was now only half-skeleton and was becoming a little less skeletal with each passing second. When the mortal caught sight of the expanding god-head-balloon, he waved and yelled for God-Art to hurry. He pointed impatiently at his wrist where he would have worn a watch if he cared one iota about being anywhere on time.

God-Art stopped inhaling. He wiggled his tongue, detaching it from the wall. He began to float up toward the ceiling. He puckered his distended lips into a tiny hole, swiveled them ever-so-subtly to take better aim, and exhaled.

He shot across the open expanse of the chamber like a popped balloon, zigging and zagging as the air escaped from his head through the tiny hole he made with his mouth. He kept his left eye trained on Normal-Art, and each time he began to zoom off target, he rotated his lips to compensate.

When God-Art's head had flown almost completely across the room, a bubble popped in the lava beneath him and fiery rock splashed across his face. The sudden pain made him whelp and threw him off course. He smacked into the wall just below Normal-Art, rather than into his counterpart's chest as planned. His unfortunate tongue once again held him in place, sticking to the dirty stone and preventing him from falling into the lava below. With all the hoarded air drained from his head, God-Art looked like a raisin hanging by a bright red stem.

"Melb! Bobeabe be!" cried the deflated God-Art around his tongue.

Normal-Art craned his neck and looked down at the dangling god-head. If Normal-Art still had a face, he would have smirked. He crouched and grabbed God-Art by the bottom of the head. He lifted the head and shifted it to the crook of his arm, where he held it like it was a pruny, flaming baby. Normal-Art yanked God-Art's tongue from the wall. It sounded like Velcro as it peeled away.

"What did you say?" asked Normal-Art.

God-Art retracted his tongue back inside his mouth. "I said, '*Help! Don't leave me!*'"

"Oh. Well, I wouldn't know how to leave you, even if I wanted to."

"Seriously?" asked God-Art. He gestured with his eyes toward the blue bear. "You simply needed remove your cosmic buddy from the saber, and he could jump you out of here. You didn't figure that out when your lady-partner disappeared with the pink bear?"

"I don't need to click my heels together or anything? That's good, I guess. I think they'd be a little too sore to click, anyway."

"No, you don't. But you *do* need to hurry. We've got about twenty seconds until this reality implodes into nothingness—and takes us with it!"

Normal-Art stared down at the bear. Seeing no other options, he grabbed the upside-down bear and yanked upward. This ripped the bear off the saber, slicing it nearly in twain as the blade passed through its torso and exited where its neck met its shoulder. Pink blood gushed from the wound, and the blood transformed into beautiful forest creatures that fell immediately into the lava. As they collided with the lava and burned to a crisp, a badger thrashed, a deer squealed, and a unicorn neighed rainbows from its nostrils. The cosmic blue bear's wound healed itself almost immediately.

"Hey, blue bear," said Normal-Art. "Get us out of here."

The bear stopped singing. It grinned. It seemed not to have noticed that it had just been ripped in half, nor did it seem to notice that it had just been healed. "Moo," it said, and then it giggled.

"Huh?" asked God-Art.

"I believe that it *moo*ed at us," responded Normal-Art.

"What an odd creature," replied God-Art.

Three large, white spots popped and zapped and bamped around the blue bear like an insane Jack Kirby drawing. The spots of energy grew into large bubbles, and one encompassed each of the trio. Normal-Art was swallowed by the largest of the white bubbles, saber and all. He floated in pure white light, and he felt as though he was drifting in a numbing, healing sea.

Before the pure whiteness could overwhelm his senses, Normal-Art yelled out, "Oh! And don't forget to bring Drillbot!"

"Oh. I forgot about the robot," remarked God-Art from his own white bubble. "I hope slowing down to save the robot is worth the risk of being caught in eternal nothingness."

"Well, he *did* save our lives," replied Normal-Art.

Normal-Art poked his head out of his white bubble and watched a fourth bubble break off from the one circling the bear. It darted across the room and grew large enough to envelop Drillbot. Drillbot was still embedded in the wall, so the bubble simply surrounded the robot, along with the section of wall that had gobbled him up.

Normal-Art pulled his head back into his white cocoon and watched the air outside it waver and wiggle and shudder like a heat mirage. Normal-Art's stomach turned.

"Here it comes!" cried God-Art from his nearby bubble, tears lingering behind his words. "We're too late. That feeling in the pit of your stomach is this reality preparing to disintegrate into nothingness. We're all dead! For good this time! And we would've been safe, but *you insisted* that we stall to save Drillbot, you dim-witted, compassionate fool!"

The bear mooed again. Normal-Art managed a tiny shrug. At this point, he was too exhausted to care whether he disintegrated into nothingness or he lived, so long as he finally got the chance to relax.

Then the whiteness that surrounded him flashed even brighter. It seemed like he had been suddenly surrounded by a blinding womb. He closed his eyes, yielding himself to whatever Fate had in store for him.

*

The fissure that Normal-Art had created in the ground of this planet came full circle. The planet cracked in half and exploded.

At nearly the exact same moment, the lack of a power source in the Reality Lantern caused Earth 1,000,000 to lose power. It winked out of existence.

Nothing remained of the entire tiny reality except total, bleak emptiness.

CHAPTER 29

COSMIC CHOICES

NORMAL-ART DID NOT realize that he had lost consciousness until he awoke. A familiar pair of bright blue button-eyes hung less than an inch away from his face.

"Art be safe. Where to now?" asked the owner of the button-eyes, the blue teddy bear. Its voice rang with a savage undertone, but it somehow sang with a cultured accent at the same time.

Normal-Art floated backward through the infinite whiteness, attempting to distance himself from the blue button-eyes. Being under their gaze felt like being pinned beneath some sort of celestial drill press, for they bored right through him and glimpsed down into the depths of his soul. He closed his eyes and rubbed his head, ignoring the piercing gaze as best he could. He ran his hands through his hair. Something felt a bit different, but he could not explain exactly what.

"Me healed Art," said the bear, answering Art's query about what felt different before he even had the chance to ask. "Art no longer be skeleton-man. All done, all healed. Where to now?"

Normal-Art opened his eyes. The stuffed bear sat cross-legged before him, looking like a two-foot tall, glowing pastel icon of a Buddha. Behind the radiant bear floated God-Art's unconscious head. Beside God-Art, four massive stone blocks drifted together in a clump. Drillbot's lower torso and wheels dangled out from them. And near the blocks, the onyx saber tumbled end over end.

"I dunno," answered Normal-Art. "Maybe we should ask the other Art."

"No, no, no siree. That one be afraided too much. He be so scared of permanent death that he goed comatose with fear when that other reality started going bye-bye."

"Hmmm. OK. Well, you used some sort of magic powers to heal me. Use them to heal him from his coma, too."

The bear shook its head and said, "He be an entity entirely made from hoodoo. And he be operating under a different nature of hoodoo than Me hoodoo. Me hoodoo be no good for him. So, Me no be willing to use Me hoodoo on other Art."

"Hoodoo? What's that?"

"What Art calls magic."

"OK, hoodoo equals magic. Got it. Seems like it would've been just as easy for you to say *'magic,'* since you apparently knew that I would understand that term. But OK. Hoodoo it is."

"Where to now?" asked the bear again, ignoring Normal-Art's sarcasm.

After a moment of awkward silence, Normal-Art suggested, "Hmmm. If you can't wake god-me with your…your hoodoo, then maybe we should just wait for him to wake himself. That usually doesn't take long for him to do—even when he's supposed to be dead. While we wait, you can tell me who you are and what you *truly* are—because there's no way you're simply a magical teddy bear, and I wouldn't believe you even if you tried to tell me it's that simple—and why it was so important for us to find you."

The bear frowned. It said, "No can do. No siree. Me tell all that stuff to Art later. We in limbo-life dimension. It be cut off from all dimension-jumpy travel, except to Me. Art be the first other being besides Me to ever be visiting here. But if we be staying much here longer, we all will be dissolving into the white light."

"That doesn't sound very pleasant," replied Normal-Art.

"No, siree. So, Art must decide. What reality? Where to now?"

"Well, I guess we can go back to my place. I don't remember what the exact Earth number is."

"No worrying," said the blue bear. "Me find it."

Art felt a tickle inside his skull. He stared down at his feet and waited for the bear to complete its search through his brain. He realized that he was naked—the bear had healed his body, but it had not restored his clothes. He shrugged. Then a rectangular shape beneath the skin of his chest caught his attention. The *Bureau of Interdimensional Travel* identification card! It had lain embedded beneath his skin since his first meeting with the god-version of himself. The bear must have thought it was a part of him, for it had apparently restored the card when healing him after his trip into the Reality Lantern. The card revealed Art's Earth number, 6,076. He opened his mouth, intending to divulge this information to the bear. But he did not get the chance.

The tickle in his brain intensified, and his mouth stopped working. All that came out of it was a thick strand of drool. This tickle grew even more tickly than *all* the previous tickles he had felt in his brain since this adventure began combined. This tickle felt like an entire family of worms had burrowed inside his skull and had begun writhing through his gray matter. But somehow worse. He scratched his scalp until it bled, trying to rid himself of the tickling sensation. It did not help.

Then, as suddenly as the tickle had begun, it vanished. Art's raw scalp stung.

"Me got it," said the blue bear. "We go now."

The blue bear closed its button-eyes, a process which consisted of them bending themselves in half to look like small semicircles. It bit its lower lip. More large, white spots popped and zapped and bamped into existence around the creature. Normal-Art did not question *how* he was able to distinguish them against the background of sheer whiteness. He simply accepted it.

The bear hummed and made a rhythmic clicking sound with its larynx. It danced along to the beat, rocking at its hips and waving its shoulders. With each click of its larynx, more spots appeared. When dozens of them hung in the whiteness, they smacked together and formed one gargantuan, white bubble.

"I've got a headache," said Normal-Art, unable to stop staring. "Feels a lot like brain freeze. Only it burns behind my eyes, too."

"Close eyes and plug ears. Me forget to warn Art. Me hoodoo will hurt Art's brain if Art watches and listens. It maybe be turning Art's brain into a vegetable."

Normal-Art did as ordered, closing his eyes and jabbing the tips of his index fingers into his ears. He had no desire to become a vegetable.

He sensed his surroundings shift, and the shift felt as if a whirlpool had formed around him. And then without warning, his surroundings shifted again, and he felt himself being lurched in every direction at once—a sensation that felt like he was falling in an infinite number of directions.

Normal-Art grew anxious and cracked open his eyes a wee bit. He saw colors that he had never before experienced mingling in an odd, interdimensional rainbow cocktail. His stomach heaved. He panicked. He stopped plugging his ears and began flailing his arms, trying to find something onto which he might grab for safety. Loud, booming cracks thundered in his now-unplugged ears. His ears bled like a pair of stuck pigs with hemophilia. His body began whirling around and around from the feet up, as though he had become a flesh-colored ribbon in the wind. Nausea overwhelmed his stomach, and he began vomiting.

"Keep eyes closed and ears plugged!" yelled the bear in a booming voice that transcended all the surrounding noise.

Normal-Art clenched his eyes shut. He jabbed the tips of his thumbs deep into his ears and felt blood damming behind his fingers. He felt better at once. His stomach stopped turning inside out, and it stopped purging itself of every meal he had ever eaten. After what seemed to take years, he felt himself land with a thump on a familiar, cheap rug.

A pair of soft, tiny paws pulled Normal-Art's thumbs from his ears. The paws caressed his ears. Normal-Art felt them heal.

"Open eyes now," ordered the bear's sing-song voice.

Normal-Art opened his eyes. His home looked much more mundane than he remembered it looking. Well, it looked mundane if he ignored the utter surrealism of his new houseguests.

The stone blocks with the Drillbot stuffing took up much of his dining room. The robot had appeared in this reality atop Art's dining room table, completely crushing it. Broken table legs extended from beneath the colossal blocks like the legs of a collapsed racehorse poking out from underneath a morbidly obese jockey. Art shrugged.

God-Art's unconscious head lay on the coffee table, having knocked over the expired cup of milk that Normal-Art had poured the day before God-Art had appeared on his doorstep. The milk had curdled while Art was away. God-Art's head lay on its side, and his flaming hair burned and caramelized the curdled milk, releasing a putrid, milk-scented incense into the air. When Normal-Art smelled the sour odor, he pinched his nose and gagged. He decided he could do without the smell, so he kicked the god's head away from the spilled milk. The head fell from the coffee table and rolled to a stop next to the onyx saber, which was lying on the floor near edge of the rug.

Normal-Art walked to the kitchen—circumventing Drillbot on the way—and turned on the kitchen sink. He splashed water on his face and rubbed his eyes. He grabbed his cow-themed kitchen towel and dried himself. He sighed. Then he turned to face the blue bear.

"Alright, time to answer some questions," groaned Art, his patience with this entire ordeal completely exhausted. "And then you can get out of here and leave me the hell alone so that I can catch up on my shows."

"Yes. Me answer questions now," replied the bear with a nod of its head.

"What are you? Why were you *so* important that I had to leave my couch to run off and rescue you?"

"Haven't figured out yet? Me be creature of immense power. And that make Me important."

Normal-Art sighed, stroking a hand through his newly re-grown hair. "Is it going to be like this with every interdimensional entity I ever meet? I ask a question, and then they answer me as literally as possible, all the while giving me absolutely no clear information?"

"Art asked questions, so Me answered questions Art asked."

"Well, what *type* of immensely powerful being are you?" asked Normal-Art.

"For this age, Me be a stuffed bear."

"Get bent," replied Normal-Art. "I saved you, just like you asked. Now *stop* being an ass and *start* giving me some solid answers that will actually help me to understand what's going on, or I will beat you to death with the head of that unconscious god over there."

"Art should ask better questions," said the bear.

Normal-Art squealed in exasperation. "Fine! When we were in the pyramid, God-me said you wouldn't leave with him. Why would you want to leave with *me*? Why did *I* need to help you? It doesn't make sense. That other Art over there has a zillion god-powers. He didn't need *me* to help him on a rescue mission, and neither did you. You could have just glommed yourself onto him and left me out of it!"

"The answer to be found with him. Ask him when he be back to the land of awake."

"Screw that," replied Normal-Art. "I'm too tired for this bullshit. You're going to explain yourself right now! He told me from the beginning that he didn't know the exact details of our quest. But he knew that *I* was the key to it, so he decided to come get me and then work the rest out along the way. If *you* can't fill in the blanks for me, then I don't think *anybody* can."

"Art's god-self be a mischief deity. He be borned from chaos. *He* telled Art he not be knowing details of Art's quest. Should Art really trust the things a mischief deity tells him?"

"I trust him right now a helluva lot more than I trust *you*," said Normal-Art, glaring into the bear's ancient button-eyes. "*He* could have left me to die half-a-hundred times, but he didn't."

"Wrong. God-Art *needed* Art to get his hands on *Me*. Me am power. He be wanting power. He be using Art this whole time, and then he will dispose of Art like toilet paper. Heh-heh-heh. You be Toilet-Paper-Art. He still plans this killing, too."

Normal-Art frowned. "But why?"

"Toilet-Paper-Art be just a means to an end to God-Art," replied the blue bear. "Way, way long time ago when the mischief god learned of Me existence, he called to Me with his hoodoo and telled Me that he be seeking Me. He demanded for Me to tell him where Me be so that he could come to get Me. Me say no way, no siree, for me knowed that he be wanting Me just to siphon Me powerful hoodoo into himself. Me keeped refusing the leaving with him every time he contacted Me, and Me much more powerful than him, so he knowed that he could not force Me to go with him. But after much time passed, he learned where Me be, anyhow—the Earth number and the general map coordinates, but Me hoodoo blocked him from learning much beyond those things. All the while, Me be searching for the *right* person to free Me. Me wanted one who didn't want to harness Me power when Me be free, one who didn't desire *Me* for selfish reasons or for unselfish reasons, one who simply wanted to live own life. Me been seeking for long time for such a one to be born, one whose soul be truly neutral, one who be equal parts void and life. Me found Art and called to Art most of Art's life. God-Art was spying on Me communications and heared Me. Then he goed and finded Art.

"And sometime along the way," continued the bear, "God-Art's lady-partner learned of his quest to obtain Me and Me hoodoo. She began her own quest for Me, a quest that the stupid Multiverse be making so much easier with its foolish edict to resurrect dictators *on the exact same prison-Earth* where Me be stuck. Neither of the fools knowed that the prison that holded Me also holded Me own partner, too. They never thought to focus their hoodoo to check more into Me immediate surroundings. The fools.

"But Me partner not as foolish as they. Me partner learned that Me was calling to Art, so Me partner thought it would be funny and symmetrical to call to Art's lady-partner. Me partner used her hoodoo to subconsciously implant the idea into God-Art's lady-partner that she should gather Art's lady-partner and bring her to the prison-Earth."

Art sighed. Then he said, "Let me get this straight: Art-Head over there manipulated me into helping him because he knew that *you* were already calling out to me to save you, which you were doing because I wouldn't care about gaining your magical powers once you were free. He was using me to get to you, so he could somehow obtain the power inside you. All the while, his Ginny has also been seeking you to gain your power, too, without knowing that the pink bear existed—but really the pink teddy bear was using *her* to get to my girlfriend, who the pink bear chose as her rescuer solely because she's my girlfriend?"

"Positive," replied the bear. "Though not solely because of being Art's girlfriend, Me did not completely finish telling Art about that part. It be because of the symmetry. Because you and she be linked as a cosmic pair."

Normal-Art shrugged. "I dunno about being a cosmic pair. We'll have to see if the relationship lasts. I'm not big on commitment."

"Celestial powers be at play. You two be linked for a lifetime. Me be foreseeing it."

Normal-Art sighed. "Whatever. That's future-me's problem. What I really wanna know is whether I understood this part correctly: you've been calling to me most of my life?"

"Also positive."

"That doesn't make any sense," said Normal-Art. He pointed to God-Art's head. "If you've called to me most of my life, how come I never heard from you or saw you before I met *him*?"

"Art must not remember is all," said the bear. "Art must have blocked memories. Me make Art remember."

Normal-Art felt another tickling itch in his brain. This time the itch was so powerful that it felt like chicken pox had sprouted inside his skull and had spread across the nooks and crannies of every single lobe in his brain. He slapped the back and the sides and the front of his head, attempting to rid himself of the uncomfortable sensation.

He squealed. Something clicked into place inside his skull, like a bridge that had fallen into disrepair and had just been fixed. Memories flooded over the newly connected synapses, desperately scrambling over each other to be reunited with the working parts of Normal-Art's brain that they hadn't glimpsed in ages. Normal-Art's legs turned to jelly, and he collapsed onto the dirty rug in a sprawled mess. His cheek splashed in the curdled milk where some of it had dripped off the coffee table, but he did not notice.

Art remembered dreams, childish visions of button-eyes in the sky and voices talking to him. He remembered his dad's death. He had been eleven, and lonely, and scared. He lay alone in his room after the funeral. His dad's corpse appeared, crawling into his room through the window. The blue teddy bear was translucent like a ghost and perching on the decaying shoulder of Art's father like a pirate's parrot, digging its paws into the pinstripe suit in which his father had been buried. The bear whispered something into the corpse's ear, and Art's father looked Art in the eyes and said, "Save Me."

This kind of thing had happened frequently when Art was alone—not necessarily the schtick with his dad's corpse, but rather the appearance of the blue bear floating somewhere nearby and begging to be saved. And to make matters worse, nobody other than himself could see the bear. He remembered psychiatrist visits, and the doctors telling him these visions were only dreams or the product of an overactive imagination or hallucinations brought on by stress. And he remembered scaring his mom so badly with descriptions of his visions that she convinced the doctors to put him on some pills to stop the visions. Whether the pills actually did anything, or whether he simply convinced himself they worked because he wanted them to work *so* badly, the visions stopped. And faded. And he had forgotten them, somehow managing to shove them away into some unused sock drawer in the back of his mind, where they stayed right up until the sock drawer was overturned by the bear's meddling in his brain.

"Why *me*?" asked Normal-Art again. His voice cracked as more forgotten memories continued flooding through his mind.

"Me telled Art already. God-Art even told Art, but Art would no listen. Art be life outside but void inside. Balanced. Numb. No lust for power. Me choose only to leave Me prison for Art because of this."

"I don't understand. I'm not a void inside. I feel things, I love, I hate. I'm definitely not evil."

"Void no evil. Me no say Art evil. Void give balance to Multiverse. Void have perpetual gluttony for eating life, but that not mean it's evil. Every time life be brought into existence, life kills part of void. Void then eventually kills life, returning equilibrium to Multiverse. Art born part of both. Art's soul be equally intertwined with both life and void. Void deep in gooey center, but life-giver in equal layers surrounding Art's void. Only Art in all Multiverse with *equal* layers of both. All others more one than the other, either a destroyer or a creator. Art does neither because neither side can win over the other in Art's soul."

"So, I'm the only person in all of existence with a soul perfectly balanced between life and void?" asked Normal-Art. "Am I supposed to be the mythical next stage of evolution or something?"

"No, no, no siree. Art simply unlucky," responded the bear.

"Unlucky? But I thought you said that I'm one of a kind."

"Just because Art be unique doesn't mean Art be better. Art be alive, but Art be cursed. Art may *believe* he feels emotions, but it just be mimicry what he be seeing around him. He never be understanding true love, nor true hate. Art never be caring about anything. Art no feel awake. Always numb."

"Well, when you put it that way, it sounds like my life rather sucks. But it seems to me that everyone on my Earth is cursed with this same feeling of discontinuity with the world. This same numbness. How am I any different?"

"No. Not true," said the bear. "Not like Art. Not in exactly equal measures between the two parts."

Normal-Art suppressed a giggle, his mouth foaming with rabid sarcasm. "I guess that settles it. The alien teddy says I'm wrong, so I'm supposed to drop all the empirical evidence I've experienced and trust its word as truth. My life is shit and everyone else's is fine because *you* say so."

"Art no believe Me, but that's because Art only sees what Art wants to see. Millions sacrifice on this and every other reality for life and goodness, and many more for their own gain and to destroy others for power. Art does neither. Art drifts."

"Whatever," replied Normal-Art. "I don't need a sermon, and I don't feel like preaching one to you, either. Let's agree to disagree and move on."

The bear blinked.

"The hieroglyphs on the wall of the pyramid we rescued you from made it seem like you weren't from that reality. Is that true?"

"Positive."

"Where *are* you from?" asked Normal-Art.

"Me from center," responded the bear. "Middle of everything. Number one reality."

"OK. And *who* are you?"

"Me is you. Me is Art."

"Huh?"

"You're so dense," called a voice from behind Normal-Art. A flaming ball of cranium rolled into view and then halted between Normal-Art and the bear. God-Art sat on his severed neck, and Normal-Art twitched his nose at the smell of the burned, curdled milk drifting up from the head's scalp.

"That thing is *us*, from the center of the Multiverse," said God-Art.

"Hey, you're awake," whispered Normal-Art, and then he felt stupid for stating the obvious.

God-Art smiled. "Glad you noticed. Been listening for a little while. Hope this stuffed fool hasn't turned you against me too badly."

"That depends," responded Normal-Art, his eyes boring into the god's. "I'm apparently numb because I'm equal parts void and life, but that doesn't mean that I don't care if I die. Do you plan on killing me?"

God-Art pursed his lips. Then he dropped his eyes and gazed at the floor. "Did originally. Even considered doing it while your back was turned, while you were distracted and talking with our quarry. But I think I've decided against going through with it."

"Not that I'm complaining, but why?" asked Normal-Art.

"Well, mainly because I don't really feel like it, but also because there's really no point. I don't think that you would try *that* hard to stop me from harnessing the power of this blue cosmic entity. You simply wouldn't be too inclined to put forth the effort. The components of void and life that are the building blocks of your soul perfectly balance one another out to make you the numbest, laziest individual in the Multiverse. As the bear implied, you're a piece of driftwood in the scheme of things."

"Well, the name calling hurts," responded Normal-Art.

"No, it doesn't. Not when you *really* think about it. You pretend to have feelings simply because you've seen them in everyone around you. You think that if you act like a mummer and put on a routine, then that means you truly feel feelings, too. But you don't. You're *too* balanced. Neither attribute—neither void nor life—wins over the other."

Normal-Art pursed his lips and furrowed his brows. He stared down at the floor. "I do *too* feel feelings."

"Stop it," shouted God-Art. "You're acting like a blubbering child. Be as happy as your numb soul will allow you to be that I'm not going to kill you. Besides, I've found that I enjoy your company. Maybe it's because you're me, or maybe it's because your unique nature makes you a bit unpredictable. But I *like* you."

"Gee, thanks," said Normal-Art. "That's like getting a pat on the back from Satan."

"The fat-cat prosecuting lawyer of your Earth's Christian pantheon? Puh-lease. I've been around much longer than *that* windbag, and I've supped on celestials bigger and badder than him. He's nothing."

God-Art nodded toward the grinning bear across the room, and then he continued speaking. "Your buddy there, though, he means *a lot* to me. He's the most powerful being from any charted reality. I plan to eat his heart."

Normal-Art glanced back over at the blue bear. The bear did not appear overly concerned.

"This plan not be a good idea for a mischief god," said the bear. "Not good for one borned from chaos."

"Shut up," said God-Art, rolling his eyes. "Hand it over. I know it won't kill you. At least not for long. You'll simply grow another. We can all go home happy, and nobody has to get hurt."

"No good idea. No good."

God-Art sprang from the floor, somehow launching up to the bear's torso despite his lack of legs or a body. As he flew, his teeth sharpened into rows of spears that pierced the blue flesh of the bear. Pastel pink blood poured from the wound, dripping down the god-head's chin. A widening pool of the pink blood gathered on Art's rug. Little forest creatures formed from the blood and scattered to all corners of Normal-Art's apartment. He was particularly annoyed to see a doe, a wolf cub, and a tiny unicorn disappear into his bedroom.

Normal-Art defied his exhaustion and stood back up onto his feet. "Stop!" he screamed. "I'm not done asking it questions!"

Normal-Art ran to God-Art's head and reared back with his fist, preparing to knock the god loose from his attack.

A thin bolt of lightning zipped from God-Art's eyes, zapping Normal-Art in the gut. He lost feeling in his entire body, and he fell backward. He crashed into the coffee table and knocked it onto its side. He lay on the ground, his eyes open but his body unable to move. He stared at the ravenous god-head in horror.

The flames on the god's scalp grew higher and brighter. A dancing strand leapt from the scalp and landed on the rug. It slithered across the ground like a snake, stopping in front of Normal-Art. It rolled in place back and forth, giving birth to other snakes of fire. As each was born, it stood on one end. The flaming snakes crisscrossed each other, forming a cage around Normal-Art. He did not really understand the purpose of the fire-cage, though. He could not move a single muscle.

God-Art pulled his mouth away from the bear's torso for a moment to say to Normal-Art, "Don't worry, you'll be able to move again soon. There's a tiny, sentient bolt of lightning living in your spine right now, severing it. It has an exceptionally short lifespan, and without other lightnings in there, it won't be able to procreate. It shall die momentarily, the nerve endings in your spine will mend themselves, and you'll be able to move once more."

God-Art returned to his furry, cosmic meal. Normal-Art stomach might have turned, but nothing in his body was cooperating right now.

The bear had more blood inside it than Normal-Art would have expected. It mouthed, "Save Me," to Normal-Art. But Normal-Art could do no more than what he had already tried.

Normal-Art gazed at the bear's eyes, which were fading in color. God-Art gulped at an extraordinarily large object, and over the next few moments, he worked the oversized rounded lump down his gullet. Normal-Art grew a little confused, because the object that God-Art ripped out of the bear's innards and swallowed had been bigger than the bear itself. It dissolved by the time it reached the bottom of God-Art's neck. God-Art released his vampiric grasp on the bear. The bear collapsed and lay still on the rug, further staining the rug as its pink blood continued to pool beneath it. More woodland creatures sprang forth from the pinkness to make themselves at home in Normal-Art's apartment.

Normal-Art discovered that he could move once more. It felt as though his foot were asleep, except the feeling enveloped his entire body. He managed to sit up, but he singed his newly regrown hair on the roof of his tiny, fiery cage. He lay back down, curled on his side in a fetal position, and watched God-Art with dread. And annoyance. Why couldn't the god have waited for the bear to answer just a few more questions? At least God-Art no longer planned to kill him. Or did that plan change when Normal-Art had tried to stop his attack on the bear? Normal-Art shrugged, relishing in the return of his motor skills.

God-Art rolled his disembodied head back around to face Normal-Art. "This is amazing. I feel so pure, so powerful," said the god. He opened his mouth, and blue mist drifted out. It swirled beneath him, lifting him into the air. He closed his eyes, and his disembodied head began to spin around and around. The mist grew denser, to the point of being opaque. And then it shattered. Shards crashed to the ground, where they busted into tinier particles, which reverted into blue gas and floated away.

The disembodied god-head was no longer disembodied. God-Art's body stood below his head, back to the same divine form it had taken when Normal-Art had first seen it following the god's resurrection on Earth 1,000,000. It even had the necklace of severed ears back in place.

However, there was a difference between God-Art's appearance before and now. The difference was apparent in his face. It seemed swelled, and it did not match his muscular body. It looked like the face of a morbidly obese man who has been carbo-loading nonstop for his entire life. Blue gas leaked from his nostrils and ears, and his eyes now glowed pastel blue. The head steadily continued growing larger and getting puffier.

"That's better," said God-Art. The blue mist leaking from his mouth formed his words in the air as he spoke, like word balloons from a comic strip. This development seemed totally unnecessary to Normal-Art. God-Art stared at the wall, seemingly lost in a trance.

"So, you got what you sought from the very beginning," said Normal-Art. "What now?"

God-Art glanced down and pursed his lips. He said, "Oh. *You.* Behold, I am now an entity of cosmic power, and I see things on a much grander scale! I must admit, I had completely forgotten about *you.*" His voice seemed to originate from all around Normal-Art, vibrating every atom in Normal-Art's body.

"I'm going to do what I've always wanted," continued God-Art. "I'm going to create a reality in my own image. I'll finally get to be the all-powerful creator, rather than the trickster whom everybody loathes."

"That doesn't sound too bad," replied Normal-Art. "At least you won't be hurting anyone. Well, I guess other than those you bring into existence. I don't think a reality based on mischief and chaos will be very pleasant."

"Well, yeah, I don't really plan to *hurt* anyone," said the god. "I plan to be different. But that'll start once I've got my reality up and running. And to do *that*, I'll have to destroy *this* one to make room. There's not infinite real estate in the Multiverse, you know."

"What?" asked Normal-Art.

"Don't worry. I'll keep you around. The only me in any reality I can stand—besides myself, obviously. Going to keep Drillbot around, too. I like the guy. Other than that, we're going to start over."

God-Art turned to the kitchen. He blew a quick breath in Drillbot's direction. The stone blocks surrounding the robot melted like ice cream basking in the sun. They transformed into sand that gathered on the floor of Normal-Art's dining room. The sand mingled with Normal-Art's other décor to bestow upon the room the vibe of a trashy beach.

Drillbot lay on the smooth sand, its head crushed into its torso, and its torso crunched together like a beer can on the lawn of a fraternity house after a raging party. God-Art snapped his fingers, and the robot floated into the air, drifting atop a bed of blue mist. Now airborne, Drillbot expanded. Its crushed crinkles flattened out, and an invisible hand pulled its head out of its torso. A new drill-arm grew to replace the one that the robot had lost, and its dead eyes glowed anew with crimson life. The mist set Drillbot gently atop the sand, and the robot stood in the kitchen, looking brand new.

"[whir] Drillbot lives – CLACK – lives – CLACK - lives again."

Normal-Art smiled. Then he remembered God-Art's plan, and the smile faded. "I don't think you should go through with your plan," he said.

"This is what I've wanted all my life, and you're in no position to stop me. Count yourself lucky that I've decided you're worthy to survive. I plan to make the transition quick, so nobody will know what hit them."

"Why do you need to demolish *this* reality to make yours?" asked Normal-Art. "Didn't we *just* destroy one? Why don't you use the space opened up by that one?"

"Because I plan on making mine twice as big as any other," replied God-Art. "I plan to use the space from that one *and* this one to make mine."

"Oh," said Normal-Art with a frown. He glanced at the card embedded in his chest and decided that asking about it was worth a shot. "But what about the *Bureau of Interdimensional Travel*? Is this within their jurisdiction? Will they get angry and come arrest you or something?"

"I don't really care how they feel or what they do," responded God-Art. "Let them try and stop me. I'm all-powerful now. I'll simply zonk them out of existence."

"*Zonk* them?" asked Normal-Art, unable to prevent sarcasm from lacing his reply. "*Zonk*? I guess you're already using your powers to create new words. Wonderful. I can't wait to see what other awesome abilities you have up your sleeve."

"With the heart of that little bear from the center of the Multiverse inside me, I can do anything I want. As a matter of fact, now that I think about it, I may even zonk *all* realities out of existence. And then I'll simply create one behemoth reality for myself. I'm a god, whose power has just been multiplied to the exponent of God, so why should I stop with something simple like a double-sized reality when I can go all out? Great idea, me! Hooray for being all-powerful!"

"Well, I'm all-confused," interjected Normal-Art. "Wasn't there another cosmic bear with cosmic powers packed inside that Reality Lantern with our little blue fella? Does that mean that you're *both* all-powerful? Creates a bit of a conundrum, doesn't it?"

"Bloody hells. I forgot about that other cosmic bear. *You* ask too many questions. I don't think I like you anymore."

"For being all-powerful, you're pretty forgetful," replied Normal-Art.

"And for being someone who wants to survive the transition to my new vision of the Multiverse, you're pretty stupid."

Normal-Art shrugged.

Then God-Art's eyes bugged out of his head, and a gag hurtled its way up his esophagus. He brought his hands up to his throat and clawed at it. He bent over at the waist and retched. His body rocked and quivered with each spasming gag. He looked at Normal-Art and mouthed, "Help me!"

Normal-Art shrugged again. He did not know how the god expected him to help. He was simply a human being, half-void and half-life, who was stuck inside a fiery cage. What could he do? He glanced over at Drillbot. The robot waved at him eagerly, and it reminded him of a puppy wagging its tail when happy to see its master.

God-Art's throat exploded in blue fireworks, disintegrating the hands clawing at his skin. His blue eyes melted and streaked down his face. The rest of the blood and tissue and organs in his head followed out of his eye sockets. The departure of this flesh left an empty shell where his head had been. The god's body collapsed to the ground and thrashed. Then it melted. His gore pooled on the floor, dammed into place between Normal-Art's cheap rug and the sand in his dining room. A thin blue film dried on the top of the bloody mess like skin atop pudding.

A soft wind blew through Normal-Art's apartment and sent a chill up his spine. The blue film lifted itself into the air above the gore, hovering in eerie stillness. It imploded into a tiny dot of blue, and then it expanded large enough to envelop the entire apartment. Two large button-eyes appeared, and they stared at Normal-Art from the pervasive blueness. The slit of a smile formed in the blue near Art's refrigerator, and when he stared past the lips of the smile, he gazed into an infinite abyss of stars and galaxies.

"What in the hell just happened?" asked Art to the face on his wall.

"Me warned God-Art: no eat Me. A chaos-god's hoodoo be void-hoodoo. It no mix good with life-hoodoo, and Me formed completely from life-hoodoo. He should have eated Me partner, pink destruction-bear, for they both fall into realm of void-hoodoo."

"*What?*"

"Me be ultimate incarnation of life. Pink bear be ultimate incarnation of destruction. Me be similar to Art's world's *yang.* She be like *yin.* God-Art be a mischief god, borned from chaos. He should no eat life-hoodoo. Life-hoodoo be his opposite. He be a destroyer. He no can handle life-hoodoo. He can no handle being a creator. He be completely and utterly *void.* Every atom of his rejects Me."

"Oh. So, his plan would've worked if he'd have eaten the pink bear's heart instead of yours?" asked Art. "Seems a little convenient for the Multiverse that he didn't do his research very well."

"But that be the story of life everywhere. Life thrives because of death's careless mistakes. And opposite true in other places, too. Balance. Balance holds Multiverse together. And Art be balance personified. Life without, destruction within."

"Guess I'll take your word for it," replied Normal-Art with a shrug. "I don't feel so balanced most of the time. But at least Drillbot's back, and that crazy god-version of me is out of the picture, so we can sleep easy at night."

"Negative. Never sleep again. Balance gone from Multiverse. Pink One gone from Me side. Life and Destruction now be separated from each other. Each out in Multiverse alone. Each other no there to balance each other out. She will no rest until all existence be void. Me will no stop until all void be life. We both apart now and free, and we will do as pleases we. Many will die and live in our wake. Many others will live and die."

"Sounds grand. Good luck with all that."

"Not grand. Should be terrifying for Art. Art should see that the only way to save all of existence be to find the Pink One and send we both home. Art should *try* to end the Life-Void War before it begins, even if Art has no desire to get involved. If Art sends both bears home to center of Multiverse, to prime reality, and locks us away there, then no one will have to die or be forced to live. If Art does nothing, then there will be no balance, and there will be infinite war across the Multiverse. Me no willing to stop this war. Me be the leader of the life-side. It be in Me nature to lead this side. But Art could stop Me and Me partner if he decided to try, for Art's unique balanced nature would help him on this quest."

Art sighed. "I'll go ahead and pass," he said. "I think I speak for Drillbot, too, when I say that he passes. I'm tired of dealing with gods and dictators and monsters and cosmic bears. If it's time to die, then it's time to die. If I'm supposed to live, then that's fine, too. Not playing around with friggin' cosmic entities is one thing I *can* control, though."

"[whir] N-N-N-N-No. Drillbot – CLACK – Drillbot speaks for himself. Drillbot needs purpose. Drillbot will s-s-s-s – CLACK – Drillbot will serve the blue bear."

"Then life thanks Drillbot." said the encompassing blue.

The enveloping blue transformed into gas. Then it shrank, growing denser and denser. It turned into a liquid that floated in the air. The liquid shaped itself into the outline of a bear, and then the outline filled with a solid blue substance. Finally, a white light flashed, and the blue bear floated before Art once more. It looked to be fully healed and back to normal.

"Me will no force Art to do anything Art no want to do. Me will leave with Drillbot."

Art strummed his fingers against his chin. Then he asked, "Don't I get a reward or something for saving you?"

"Reward? Reward is knowing self. What Art is. Other reward is meeting self from first reality."

"So, this whole adventure amounted to a journey of self-discovery? That's dumb. And might I add that meeting other versions of myself isn't nearly as rewarding as you make it out to be."

"But me be the ultimate Art. First Art. Me name Art, too."

"Yeah, I got it," said Art. "You're me from the center of the Multiverse. I'm not really one to be star struck, sorry. You mind if I keep the saber? At least that way I won't leave this whole shindig completely empty handed."

The bear nodded. "Me insist Art keep it. Art be needing it when chaos-god-us resurrects self. He will be angry. May try to take anger out on Art, but he cannot harm Art if Art holds saber. Its hoodoo be extra strong. Its hoodoo be so strong that it holded Me and Me partner in place together. Art should be keeping it on Art forever."

"Wait, if I keep the saber on me at all times, then my god-self won't be able to harm me? That's kind of annoying. I'd planned to hang it over my mantle."

"Then Art should break off piece, hang around neck. Long as Art be touching it, then chaos-borned god cannot hurt Art. But be careful. God-Art will forever feel incomplete after he be experiencing infinite power and then be losing it. His hate grows. He shall try to take revenge on Art and all of us who he blames his loss, however wrong that blame be."

"Alright," said Art. "Got it. Now, clean up the sand in my dining room and the dead god on my floor. And then get the hell out of here. I've got a television to watch.

"Oh, and get me out of this fire-prison," added Art.

As the bear dispersed the fire-prison and zapped the sand in the kitchen to some other reality and zipped the dead god into nothingness, Art hugged Drillbot goodbye. It made him feel a little awkward. He had never been a hugger, but he felt it was the least he could do after the big lug had sacrificed itself to save him.

Drillbot hugged back. Then the robot rolled over to the bear's side. Drillbot waved his drill again, making Art think of an innocent, excitable child.

Large white dots zipped, zapped, and bamped into existence around the bear. They smashed together to form a white bubble.

"Art should close eyes and plug ears," said the bear. "Or will turn Art blind or deaf or into vegetable."

Art closed his eyes and plugged his ears. A loud pop echoed through his apartment, and vengeful winds stormed through the place, knocking items off shelves and pictures off walls. A few seconds later, the wind abruptly ceased, so Art opened his eyes and unstopped his ears. Drillbot and the bear were gone.

Art walked over and picked up the onyx saber from where it lay on the rug. He stared at his reflection in the deep, hypnotizing blackness of the hilt. He smiled, and his reflection smiled back. The contours of the hilt stretched the reflection of his mouth, giving it a cartoonish quality that reminded him of God-Art. He spit on the reflection and polished it with a pillow from the couch.

He sat down on the couch, laid the saber across his lap, and grabbed the remote. He flipped on the television. He smelled the putrid milk.

"Damn," he said. "Should've gotten the stupid bear to clean that up, too."

He shrugged. He would clean it up later. Or maybe not. Actually, probably not.

CHAPTER 30

THE RIGHT HAND OF DESTRUCTION

REGULAR-GINNY SLOUCHED HER shoulders. She sat on a hard, wooden park bench and could not shake the feeling of being impaled. No matter on what else she attempted to focus, every time she moved, she felt the hole in her torso. The Pink One had stopped the wound from killing her and had stopped the bleeding, but the bear had not healed the actual hole. If Regular-Ginny wanted, she could poke one finger through the hole in her front and one finger through the entry wound in her back, and she could touch the tips of her fingers together inside her body. But she did not want to. Even the thought of it made her shudder. She shuddered.

The scene that had created the hole played out in her head, as it had over and over since it happened. After the skin on her hand had melted off when she first attempted to reach the Pink One inside the giant lantern, she obeyed Tiny-Ginny and tried to reach inside the giant lantern for a second time. She discovered that the bears were inside the damned thing much deeper than they looked from the outside. Her pink ooze did not work inside the lantern, so it did not protect her flesh from being burned off and it was unable to simply form into a tentacle to snag the Pink One. Even now, her left arm remained skinless and meatless from its jaunt into the burning depths of the lantern. And the unhealed pearly white bones stared back at her every time she glanced down.

During her attempt to reach the Pink One, she heard the dragon thrashing toward her from behind. She removed herself from the lantern and turned to face it. She thrust her remaining flesh-covered hand into her pocket and gripped Tiny-Ginny's petrified heart. It warmed to her touch and began beating, and she knew she had nothing to fear from the dragon. She balled the fist of her opposite hand, the one that was naught but bone.

"I still can't reach," she had screamed past the roaring beast, toward the far wall where Tiny-Ginny perched toying with the fiery Art. She was unsure if she could be heard over the dragon, but she continued screaming, undeterred. "And my pink stuff doesn't work in… in…what the fuuurckgg?"

Regular-Ginny glanced down at her chest. She furrowed her brows. A third breast had formed between her two natural ones, an immense triangular lump in the middle of her chest. The skin at the arc of the lump between her cleavage broke to reveal the tip of a jet-black nipple. This lump then bulged and ripped outward. Not until the moment when her organs seized did she realize that she had been impaled by the cursed saber around which the pastel bears hung.

She cursed her luck as she felt her heart stop. Her body went limp, and she could not hold herself up anymore. Her entire weight hung on the end of the sharp saber like a sagging knapsack on the end of a tramp's stick. She remembered how painful it felt, and she winced.

Her pink ooze had gone straight to work on its own, so blindingly fast that it moved almost too quickly for the eye to see. It grabbed hold of the Pink One and snatched it away from the Blue One's grip, and then it unceremoniously ripped her own lifeless body from the end of the saber. The Pink One and Ginny began falling toward the lava, and as they did, Ginny's pink membrane cradled the Pink One under one tentacle and wrapped Ginny's body warmly within its folds.

Free at last, the Pink One had jumped them away, but Ginny did not remember the jump. All she could recall from the moments after her impaling was darkness and the panicked sensation of life fleeing from her body.

Later, she had awoken feeling stiff, surrounded by opaque blackness that stretched unto eternity in every direction. The only object that cut through the blackness was the glowing pinkness from the bear that floated in front of her.

Ginny panicked at the darkness and tried desperately to flee. But there was nowhere to run, and no matter where she twisted, the Pink One moved to float in front of her. Finally, she exhausted herself with her panicking, and she fainted. She awoke in a place that she had never been before.

She sat slumped on a wooden park bench in a bustling city where thousands of humans in business suits rushed past her. Men, women, and children all moved about at work and play. They wore black suits, navy suits, brown suits, beige suits, and plaid suits, and they paired these suits with ties of every color in the visible spectrum. Ginny felt out of place in her tattered Dictator Scout uniform, sensing the confused stares of the passersby. She looked down at her chest and grimaced at the gaping hole. She recalled and relived the experiences that had caused the hole a few more times, wincing at the memories each time they played out in her head.

"Ginny be dead," said the Pink One, interrupting Ginny from once more cycling through the nightmare of the past few hours. She sighed, realizing she might have sat there forever reliving her pain if the bear had not spoken to her and distracted her from the memories. "Me couldn't save Ginny's body. Too far beyond repair. That be Blue One's domain. But Me be keeping Ginny's soul from escaping."

"Huh?" asked Ginny. Her chest throbbed.

"Ginny be dead. But Ginny still be alive. Me no let Ginny's soul go. In there so long as Me grant pink gift to her to flow through her veins. Ginny shall be Me *Right Hand of Destruction.* We destroy realities together. That be Me purpose."

"What?"

"Ginny shall travel with Me. But Ginny's body be dead. Ginny's soul will live eternally inside Ginny's body, like Ginny's body be a flesh-jar. Ginny shall use Me pink gift to move normally, as an alive person would. But Ginny's body be dead. Stiff, but can still move."

Ginny sighed. "I do not understand you," she mumbled. She rubbed her temples, and then she continued, "You are speaking English, but it makes no sense. Your grammar is off, and you are terrible with tense and pronouns. You sound like someone reading English phrases out of a translating dictionary. I heard something about destruction, and a flesh-jar, but pretty much it was all just *blah, blah, blah* to me."

The Pink One then hopped onto Ginny's torso. A thick, putrid puss oozed from the black hole in her chest. It both hurt and stank. The Pink One crawled forward, so that their eyes were only inches apart. "Quiet," it ordered. "Look in Me eyes."

Ginny stared into the Pink One's button-eyes. The pink within crackled, and Ginny saw flames behind those eyes. Ginny felt something moving inside her skull. She began to shrink back, and she opened her mouth to scream, but the Pink One gripped her hard. It pinched her cheeks with each of its cute, burly paws. Ginny felt blood rushing to her cheeks, and she squealed.

"No speak," reiterated the bear. "Look in Me eyes."

Ginny kept her mouth shut and stared where she was told to stare. The sensation inside her skull grew stronger, until it felt as though her brain had been put into a cocktail shaker and was being jumbled into oblivion. She felt dizzy, but something inside her shifted. The odd pedestrians on the surrounding streets seemed to fall away, stretching into the distance, and images flashed before her eye.

She saw what looked like a Claymation image of herself standing next to a dark mahogany coffin. The image of herself blinked and swayed with stop-motion jerkiness. Blood spurted from the wound in her image's chest and black rot began to spread from the wound and into the rest of its body. Its eye sockets turned into cartoonish *X*s, and it collapsed to the ground. Some sort of giant invisible spatula scooped it up and plopped it into the open casket. Its mouth opened, and its cloudy soul began to float out into the ether. The Pink One materialized in the air nearby. The bear shook an oversized finger in a disapproving manner, rebuking the disembodied spirit, and the soul returned to the corpse. The body's single remaining eye opened, but the body still looked dead, like a reanimated corpse. The Pink One then zapped the body's festering wound with lightning from its eyes, and the black rot surrounding the wound stopped spreading.

The scene changed, and the image of Ginny whirled and spun, finally coming to a stop atop the park bench. The Pink One sat on Claymation-Ginny's shoulder, and a ball of pink gelatin grew from the bear to surround them. The image of Ginny floated in the middle of the ball. Gigantic, sinewy legs formed from the bottoms of the pink ball, and as the image of Ginny walked in circles inside the blob, the blob mimicked her by walking itself in its own wide circles. Arms sprouted from the sides of the pink blob, and as the Claymation image of Ginny wiggled its arms, the blob's arms did the same.

The Pink One barked, and a word balloon formed above its head that read, "Attack!" Inside the membrane, the image of Ginny punched and flailed and kicked, and tentacles and pink arms and pink legs smashed the surrounding city. The pink blob grew to titanic proportions, rising tall enough to make the tallest skyscraper look like a child's toy model next to it. The image of Ginny squashed people and demolished office buildings, and with each person it killed, the Pink One grew larger.

Soon, the image blurred, and the blackness of space filled Ginny's vision. The Earth floated into view. The Pink One, half as large as the planet, drifted into view beside it. The Pink One grinned and bared its blue fangs. The bear opened wide, biting deep into the planet. Liquid magma trailed down the messy eater's face. The Pink One sucked deep, draining the planet like it was a juice box. With every swallow, the Pink One grew larger, and the planet grew smaller. Finally, the celestial bear discarded the planet and wiped its face with the back of its arm. It floated happily in the infinite blackness, and then a word balloon appeared above it that declared, "Again!"

The Pink One launched black bubbles from its hands, and it used them to teleport itself and Ginny. The scene morphed once again to a new Earth, and the process repeated itself. The Pink One sucked the life from this new Earth. This time, however, it looked at Ginny after it was finished, breaking the vision's fourth wall. It held up its right paw and pointed at Ginny.

Ginny looked closer, and she saw that the Claymation image of herself was now growing from the bear's right shoulder. She stared at herself, and the Ginny growing from the thing's right arm said, "You're going to be the Pink One's right hand in the time to come. You will destroy when she orders you to destroy, and you will obey without question. She has kept you alive for this purpose."

Ginny thought, *What if I don't want to destroy things?*

"Then the Pink One will take back the gift of power that she bestowed upon you," replied Right-Hand-Ginny, "and your soul will leave your body, and you will die. And then the Pink One shall immediately destroy your Earth.

"Become the Pink One's right hand," continued Right-Hand-Ginny, "and enjoy immortality while you travel amongst the nigh infinite universes, destroying and devouring everything in your path. Sleep easy knowing that by the time the two of you return to your home reality—which will be last in line for destruction if you commit to the cause—enough time will have passed that your Earth will have died off anyhow."

But why me?

"Simply because you were there, and you were available, and using you was symmetrical to what the Blue One was doing with your mate. But ultimately, it comes down to bad luck. Fate. Whatever. Oh, and also because the Pink One is you, from the first reality, the one at the center of everything. And on that reality, you are the ultimate incarnation of destruction."

As quickly as the images had appeared, they faded from Ginny's eye. Ginny found herself back on the park bench, her cheeks still being pinched by the oversized pink bear. Ginny sat up straight and pain shot through her dead chest. She grunted and watched the people in business suits continue about their business.

"Ginny help?" asked the bear, pinching Ginny's cheeks harder.

"Doesn't look like I have much of a choice, do I?" asked Ginny. "Either I kill for you, or you kill my Earth and everyone I've ever cared for."

"There always be a choice."

"Yeah, yeah, yeah. Sometimes every choice is wrong, though. But fine. You got me. I'm yours. But you've got to answer a few questions first."

The pink bear's button-eyes glowed. It looked proud. "Fine. Glad other Ginny join. Me named Ginny, too. Me from Earth 1."

"We're going to stay away from my home reality, right? Until long after my Earth is dead?"

"Yes. This already be expressed to Ginny inside Ginny's mind."

"Fine. Where are we now? Why are we starting here?"

"This be Earth 770,000,971. Bankers and economists, everyone, since birthed. We be starting here because there be no resistance. No military. No hurty things. We destroy, we take time, we gain power. Move on after Me become more stronger."

"So, we are starting here because these people don't have the ability to defend themselves?"

"Affirmative."

Ginny sighed. "And if we don't start here, you'll eat my Earth first?"

"Affirmative."

"God, I hate you."

"As long as Ginny works and follows orders, hate Me be OK to do."

"Screw it," replied Ginny. "Fine. We'll put these peaceful people out of their misery. Where do we start?"

"Here. Now. Concentrate. Hold paws and grow pink gift extra-large."

Ginny grabbed the bear's paws and concentrated. She felt the pink membrane surrounding her dead body begin to grow. It grew first into a large pink blob. Then it continued growing larger and larger. Soon, it grew so large that the passing pedestrians no longer passed. They fled.

Ginny slapped the pedestrians left and right with monstrous tentacles of pink, leaving red smears of snappily dressed gore on the ground. After a while, she stopped herself from growing larger, and she stopped swatting people. Their screams faded as they escaped down the streets. She looked over at the pink bear.

"Something's bothering me, though," said Ginny. "You're supposed to be the ultimate incarnation of destruction, right? That's what you said when you were inside my head? Then how come you're a pink teddy bear? That doesn't really seem like it would fit the job description."

The Pink One turned its head and looked into Ginny's eye. It smiled, and its fangs glowed blue. "Me be no bear. Me have no shape. Me shape be determined by Me home world's age. Now be *The Age of the Stuffed Bear.* Come after *The Age of the Cute Puppy* and before *The Age of the Dish Sponge.*"

"Your reality is stupid," replied Ginny. "I can't wait until we destroy it."

"Ginny need to shut mouth. Ginny need to concentrate. Ginny need to kill for Me. Me power need to grow."

Ginny shut her mouth and returned to destroying civilization. She sighed. She could already tell that it was going to be a *long* eternity.

EPILOGUE

FOR NEARLY A month, Art sat in his underwear and left the couch for nothing more substantial than going to the bathroom or answering the door for the pizza delivery man. The pizza boxes that he had tossed into a pile near his couch stacked almost to the ceiling. Even had he mustered the energy to throw them out, most of the little forest creatures that had formed from the blue bear's blood had taken up residence in them. So, he could not throw them out. The unicorn in particular had grown vicious from its weeks of hoarding stray pepperonis.

The phone rang. It was without a doubt his boss, Mr. Reynolds, as it had been every day. Mr. Reynolds was almost certainly calling to belittle him, order him to return to work, and threaten that this was the last chance he was going to get. Art did not feel like listening to the ringer any longer, so he pressed the button to answer the phone and then he immediately hung up. After all he had experienced, he was never leaving this couch again.

When the deep, sad thrum of a foghorn blared through the apartment, he grew confused. It was the doorbell, but he was not expecting anyone. He had ordered a pizza for lunch, but he had yet to order his pie for dinner. He stood and shrugged. Maybe the shop had simply cut out the annoying necessity of him dialing the phone and had preemptively brought him one. He salivated in excitement.

Wearing no other clothing on which to wipe the grease from his previous pizza, he wiped his hands on his underwear. He realized that it was probably time to change them when his hands came away greasier than before he had rubbed them. He shrugged again, wiping them on the back of his couch.

He tiptoed past the stack of pizza boxes, ignoring the growling creatures within, and stepped to where the door would have been if he still had one. But he did not have one, because it had been destroyed and he had forgotten to get the stupid blue bear to replace it, just as he had forgotten to get the damned woodland creatures removed from his apartment.

When Art realized that it was not the pizza delivery man who had rung his doorbell, he cursed. When he realized *who* was standing in the entrance to his place, he cursed even louder.

A mirror image of himself stood in his doorway, attired in what appeared to be a British police officer's uniform. The hat was checkered and upon the badge was the symbol for *B.I.T.* that stood out so prominently on the identification card embedded beneath the skin on Normal-Art's chest. Behind his twin stood a woman decked out in an identical uniform. She looked exactly like Ginny. A gigantic eagle with a pair of dangling antennae perched on each of their shoulders.

Art's twin said, "*Bureau of Interdimensional Travel* Agents 27142 and 29333, at your service. You mind if we come inside?"

Normal-Art stepped out of the way and waved them in. Officer-Ginny looked him up and down. She shook her head and frowned, apparently not liking what she saw. Once the pair entered the apartment, Officer-Art retrieved a device from his holster and used it to scan the identification card embedded beneath the skin of Normal-Art's chest.

"It has recently come to our attention that you have been involved in an illegal and unauthorized interdimensional caper in which you were personally responsible for the demise of an entire dimension," claimed Officer-Art. "Is there any truth to this report?"

Normal-Art giggled. "Who says *caper*?" he asked. "I've never met anyone who's actually used that word in earnest."

"He thinks we're a joke," called Officer-Ginny. "I think we should show him we're serious."

Officer-Art grinned and nodded. He retrieved another device from his holster. This one looked like a tiny brass pill. He pressed a button on its side and three petite spikes appeared from its bottom. He grabbed Normal-Art's left hand and stabbed the spikes into his pinky finger. Normal-Art screamed as the finger melted off his body, dripping to the floor to form a small puddle of gore.

"I do that to your genitals next if you don't answer the question."

Normal-Art gulped. "Y-Y-Y-Y-Y-Yes. Another me sh-sh-showed up on my doorstep, and he made me go with him. He told me I was helping him s-s-save the Multiverse."

Officer-Art scowled at him. "That's all we need to know. I hope it was worth it. Unregulated capering and unsanctioned mass genocide merit a life sentence on one of our prison realities. 29333, please be so kind as to radio Earth 8,733 and find out if they have an opening. That's an especially bad one."

"At once," she responded.

"Wait!" screamed Normal-Art, nervously stroking the piece of onyx that he had broken from the saber and hung on a thin gold chain around his neck. "I know this is going to sound like the stupidest thing you have ever heard, but on our…our caper, we rescued a pair of stuffed bears that claimed they were from the center of the Multiverse. The pink one made off with my girlfriend. According to the blue one, the pink bear is going to destroy every reality in existence. The blue claims it is going to heal them all. You might want to deal with them instead of wasting your time on me. I don't mean anybody any harm. Or good, either. I just want to relax."

Officer-Ginny slapped Normal-Art across the face. "Why didn't you mention this earlier?"

Officer-Art also slapped Normal-Art across the face. "Did you not think there was a reason those bears were stuck on that backwater reality? You've unwittingly unleashed the greatest threat the Multiverse has ever known."

"Sorry," Normal-Art muttered, barely in a range that was audible.

Officer-Art grabbed Normal-Art by the arm. "You're coming with us to help us stop those beasts, whether you like it or not."

Officer-Ginny grinned, spite flooding from her mouth. "And *then* it's off to a prison dimension with you," she said.

Normal-Art squealed, "I just want to sit on my couch and watch television. Why won't anybody just let me relax?"

Officer-Art's eagle stood to its full height and flapped its wings. It screeched loudly enough that Normal-Art had to cover his ears. Lightning flashed from its antennae, enveloping the trio.

Art cursed his luck. He turned to take one last longing look at his couch, and then he was swallowed by the lightning.

***

THANK YOU FOR PURCHASING THIS BOOK.

To receive special offers, a free short story, and info on new releases, sign up for the Christopher Brimmage mailing list at cbrimmage.com

ABOUT THE AUTHOR

Christopher Brimmage is a writer, teacher, marketer, brand manager, and former boy band front man. He has a wife named Geraldine to whom he loves to sing Meatloaf, a son named Augustus with whom he has formed the *Steam Roller Boyz*, and a pair of brothers that he loves to annoy.

By Christopher Brimmage

THE MULTIVERSE ASKEW TRILOGY

The Multiverse Askew (Book 1)

The Endless War That Never Ends (Book 2)

And Now, Time Travel (Book 3)

NOVELLAS:

Mandrill, P.I.: *Dial M for Murdered Coyote*
(A Cartoon Noir Detective Tale)

Plug 'em Good
(A Space Western)

Bridge Troll
(A Suburban Fantasy-Horror)

NEW SERIES COMING IN 2021:

THE MANDRILL, P.I. TRILOGY

Manny Mandrill is an old-school, hard-boiled private dick, the last in the sprawling cartoon metropolis of Toonsville. When this anthropomorphic cartoon mandrill is hired to solve a string of horrific murders, he uncovers a deadly criminal conspiracy that threatens to engulf the entire city.

Read this series for: Cartoon Noir! Humor! Detectives! Werewolves! Vampires! Mad Scientists! Mummies! Assassins! Dog Mobsters! Dinosaur Gangsters! Otter Archaeologists! Alien Invasions! Horse Cowboys! 80s Movie & Cartoon Nostalgia! And so much more, there are not enough exclamation marks to contain the excitement!